SIEGEL

May you rise with the power of the dawning day, and let the shackles of the past fade away.

With Love,
Cara

SIEGE

CARA AMY GOLDTHORPE

BIG MOOSE
PUBLISHING

© 2022 Cara Amy Goldthorpe
Cover Design: @Antonio Cesar
Published by: Big Moose Publishing
PO Box 127 Site 601 RR#6 Saskatoon, SK
CANADA S7K 3J9
www.bigmoosepublishing.com

ISBN: 978-1-989840-41-2 (soft cover)
ISBN: 978-1-989840-42-9 (e-book)

Big Moose Publishing 12/2022

for mum and dad
you set the sparks of the Universe
alight within my soul
to dance beyond time
so wild and free
in their quest for home

and for my husband
you've been guiding me
to fill the expanse of eternity
with the winds of your spirit
since before I was born
infinitely, alive

PREFACE

At the time of writing this, as I prepare for publication, Siege has been with me for nearly two decades. I was 11 years old and I had just returned from a visit to my grandparents in Poland. That was my first trip to Europe, and indeed my first time out of Australia. I came back feeling inspired by old palaces, ancient alleyways and mystical forests. My child's imagination was running wild, conjuring fantasy tales of princes and princesses, of medieval battles, and sacred rituals. That was how the story of Siege began...

There is so much of me that is in this book: so much of my heart and soul, as I've reworked these pages over and over, putting more of my essence into the story and drawing inspiration from my travels through life. At the same time, the longer I've carried this book with me, the more I see it as something beyond me. I am merely a vessel, a conduit, for its birth.

Part of an earlier version of this book, under the title of The Awakening: Dawn of Destruction, was publicly available in 2012 on the writer's community Authonomy (by HarperCollins). It was during that year that the story really came to life and went through a thorough editing process: maturing, just like I had.

Then, for nearly 10 years, the manuscript lay untouched in a rarely-opened folder on my computer. I had become very absorbed in my legal studies, then was focussed on recovering from illness, and later my career took priority. Life took its course, and the work lay forgotten, just an echo in the back of my mind. It wasn't until I was locked down in Costa Rica during the pandemic that something in my heart prompted me to take another look at the manuscript.

As I read, voices from my subconscious jumped out at me. It was like the story was simultaneously activating old memories and awakening new perspectives, illuminating the world around me with more clarity. By this stage in my life, I'd emerged from a challenging personal journey into the abyss of physical and mental illness. I'd found peace in the void, which had given me the spark needed to see in the dark, and begin a new chapter of my life – more connected to myself and the world around me, and feeling a greater sense of purpose and meaning.

I realised then, more than ever before, the power in stories. And my child self had been onto something, before I became boxed into linear thinking and lost my sense of magic and wonder. The time had come for reactivating that childish essence, and infusing it with the teachings of all I had learned over the years. There'd been things my child self had been unable to quite comprehend or express: now I could breathe new life into that voice. I reviewed the manuscript, bringing out the ethereal whisper of the wind, and writing a thread into the story that blended the world of the physical with the world of spirit.

I hope you enjoy this book, and may the voices within it serve as a companion for you on your own journey through life: as you remember the interconnected nature of all things, and the beautiful web of existence that we are all a part of.

I also want to say this: that no matter what you are going through, remember, always, that you have a choice. A choice over how you perceive hardship and struggle. A choice to look inside, to take lessons from every situation, and use them as fuel for the growth of your inner fire.

A choice to alchemise every emotion, and rise above every fear. A choice to wake each day and see the world with fresh eyes, to forgive those you feel have wronged you, and give others and yourself another chance.

And in the end, the ability to choose unity over separation. Unity within your own heart, and unity with others and the world around. Remember that the inner realms ripple out: world change always begins inside.

With Love,

Cara

Those fortress walls
you built to defend
your gold, your riches
from your neighbour's clutches;
sturdy stone, would stand
many egos, over aeons,
and yet, could never
protect you from
that darkness lurking
within your own heart
that sickness, breeding
from the depths of that
very earth you spoilt
when you made her a slave
to the whims of your greed
and your toxic human desires

* * *

We think we're safe behind locked doors. We think we can shut the demons out. But in the end, the truth is the demons are there inside our own souls. It's time to look them in the eye, awaken to our light, and chase them out with the brightness of our love.

Map of Meleka: Northern Meridisia

Kenalas Empire

Shevad Karaoded

Narda

Majeara

Omarn

Great Lakes

Blorak

Lake Ine

Alevedh Nemash

Lamina

Ladaris

Iruina

Brekvid Rand

Kayoame River Wood

Renala of Rena

Hanigan

Kingana

Alevedh Suhiij

Jabis

Regofalya

Ilarn

Keptna

Volesa

Soonada Kingdom

Alek Karadid

Tarvesi

Herranekn Sea

Minaut

Eceraf

1

SHADOW ON THE RAINBOW

A streak of red.

Red.

The vividness of the tulip field gleamed through the thin arrow slit of the keep's walls.

She moved on, past the next tower.

Pink.

And the next.

Yellow, yellow like the glorious sun when it shone in the springtime. When it shone over the colourful paddocks, and there was no…

Black.

She paused, exhaling sharply as she saw them. The army stretched out to the horizon, covering the fields as they surged forth. Trampled beneath the feet of enemy soldiers, the beautiful flower petals no longer shimmered in the morning light.

"Taali!"

Taalin turned at the sound of her younger brother's urgent voice, hammering in the reality. There were no more flowers. No more colours.

"Taali!"

Christophe appeared, running around the curved wall with an oversized velvet coat swishing at his heels. It gave the boy no grand appearance, his blond hair lacklustre against the royal purple fabric. Dwarfing his young body, the battle garb made him look small and weak.

Inadequate.

"I know, Chris," Taalin whispered, lips stretched in a grimace. She saw her brother tremble, his hazel eyes darting from side to side, betraying his fear.

Taalin pulled him into her arms. But clad as they were in their rigid armour, the embrace offered little comfort. She could not feel the warmth of their flesh.

"We'll defeat them, like always. We're survivors," she stated with all the courage she could muster.

Christophe pressed his adolescent body closer, nodding his head senselessly. Shaking fingers entwined in hers, but Taalin pulled away.

The touch of her brother's clammy hands did nothing but sap her spirit's strength. She fought to hold on to the resilient voice inside her mind, and convince herself it was only another siege.

Yet…

Taalin looked out through the arrow slit, at the shadowy expanse encroaching upon the outer city. Limestone houses huddled together, long-abandoned by residents who had left to seek shelter in the fortress.

"Taali, father wants to talk to you."

Taalin pulled her eyes away from the ominous sight. Something within her knew that this was going to be different. The other forts along the river had already fallen, and the hope of the nation resided with them.

"Chris?"

"Yes," came his soft reply.

"If they penetrate the walls, go to the temple."

And if it came to that, she prayed the Gods would protect him.

* * *

Taalin ran up the stone stairs, making for the highest point of the fortress. Screams echoed in her wake, from all those witnessing the death of the King of Regofala.

Her father.

Mighty warrior, reduced to nothing but a moaning heap.

Taalin squinted through her tears, pressing on. One, two, then three at a time, she took the steps of the winding staircase.

There was no time to think.

No time to feel.

She had to execute her father's instructions.

"Filpai," she called when she reached the top. At once, a dove flew to her outstretched hand.

Taalin paused for a second to stroke his white plumage, but the silky feathers only brought tears to her eyes. Swallowing, struggling to suppress emotion, she thrust the roll of parchment into her dove's clawed foot.

"Fly! Fly southwest to Soonada, where the air is clean. Warn them of our plight. Then go east, to Linuina. Go, Filpai, my hope."

The dove gave a soothing coo and nibbled her finger. Taalin bit her own lip, fiercely. The self-induced pain helped, for it reminded her that she still had some power over her body.

* * *

Voices of chanting priests reverberated up to the arched marble ceiling. The sound bounced back and forth between the walls, entangling Christophe in a web of vibrating frequencies.

He huddled against a nearby column as the deafening, desperate prayers filled his ears. It all felt useless. Like the Gods had abandoned their people.

Christophe cast a despairing glance up to the four petals of the cloverleaf carved in the dome. There would be no more beauty. No more Justice, Faith or Love. Nothing…

Then different cries pierced the humming of the priests, as soldiers appeared at the front entrance to the temple.

Christophe gulped and slipped out the side door. He simply fled, away from the slaughter and the crying and the screams of the dying civilians. He ran, down and down, into the bowels of the fort. Light faded as he made for the underground passageway, the only escape not blocked by the enemy.

And he knew he would be the last to bear the message of their downfall.

* * *

Misty rain dampened Taalin as she turned to meet the soldiers. They were tumbling atop the tower in a continuous stream, armour clanking against the stone archway. Evil had arrived to touch the highest point of her fortress.

Behind her, Filpai stretched his glistening white wings and took off in proud flight. She looked up and saw him cross a rainbow that had formed from the blurry drizzle, and a faint ray of sunlight illuminated his body.

Then she saw *it*.

The strange arc of *black* in the sky, as if the rainbow had a shadow. It reached up to greet Filpai.

That was the last thing Taalin saw before the soldiers descended upon her.

2
VOICE LIKE NO OTHER

One step
I take, and another
towards this light
pulling me on

One step
through a tunnel of shadow
pain and burden
I feel before I rise

For there is no escaping
no shortcut for mortality's weeping
that we must live,
each moment appreciating

the lessons come
to prepare us for
the stairway up to
Heaven

* * *

His heart thudded in time to the rolling syllables of the storyteller's words. Louder and faster it thumped, fuelling his body with the zeal of a religious madman.

Magical sounds twisted through the air to join with the throbbing energy of life itself. Like musical notes, their harmony tugged at his soul, beckoning softly and drawing him into a hypnotic trance.

"… And on this Midsummer Eve, we look within ourselves and we honour that place where the Universe resides: the Love and the Light and the Truth and the Peace."

A sigh escaped his lips, a soft moan of pleasure as the words made his body tremble and ache with awe.

"In times of difficulty, too often we run from Truth. Failing to be Just, we are no better than grovelling cowards, who betray their families to save their own pitiful lives. Starved spirits are those beggars who turn from Faith, traitors to the Gods themselves!"

He shuddered, the words striking him as physically as an anvil on a lump of hot metal.

A pause came. He leant forward in his seat, tunic sticking to his body in the heat of the crowded tavern. The air hung thick with fiery silence, which yearned to be filled once again by the storyteller's words.

Motionless, he waited. Dozens of other bodies around him were likewise held captivated.

A word sounded.

Then another.

"Go to the girl. Stay by her side as she walks the beach, bare feet treading the pale sand. Smile at her, and illuminate the bleak coast. Be the sun that is missing from the dismal sky, covered with clouds to protect a wounded heart of blue."

The sounds were softer now. He shivered as he felt a cold touch on his neck, a ghostly finger trickling across his skin that left him quivering with anticipation.

"Shelter her from the bellowing wind. Lick the salt stains from her cheeks, white rivers formed by the union of sea spray and ancient tears. Blow life into her hollow, sunken features, and wipe away the sooty smudges on the flesh beneath her eyes."

Body tense, he gasped. His heart pulsed like a glowing star, and warmth radiated from his body to interweave with the tobacco smoke coiling through the room.

"Tormented, the waves roar high as the wind drives them against the jagged cliffs of the shore, and trails of foam from the whitecaps linger like the remnants of a binding memory."

He gripped the table, fingers clutching at the wood as the words reduced him to shakes.

"But remember happiness in its pure, glimmering form, and swallow the sea, her grief incarnate. Drink the salty waters, and once and for all, banish the pain from mind, the fear from spirit, and the darkness from heart. You can relieve her burden."

Tranquillity settled over the hushed audience, before the murmurs came sifting through the stillness. Contented sighs blended with the sound of the breeze tapping the window panes, while he sat there transfixed. Wanting nothing but to remain forever, listening to the words that sustained him in more ways than food ever could.

But soon enough rowdy cheers erupted, in harsh contrast to the storyteller's voice, and a tinkling chime of coins showered through the air. Cain exhaled slowly, stirring. His mind crept tentatively back to the present, as around him the tavern buzz returned. Serving-girls rushed to fill the jugs of thirsty men, and a group of dancers prepared to take the stage.

Through the smoke and the crowd, Cain eyed the storyteller gathering his earnings into a leather pouch. A low hood masked the boy's features, revealing nothing but a smooth chin cast in shadow. With such narrow shoulders and slim body, he must be young. Yet he held such a powerful gift. He could even remind the men, rough from poverty, of their faith.

Cain had to thank this teller of fables for the calm brought to his own life. The words made him feel purposeful, like more to life existed than the fight to get food on the table. More existed than forging blades, day after day, hammering at the molten metal as though that action could beat out the creases of pain etched in his heart.

Cain dug into his pocket, pulling out what remained of his week's earnings. He tossed the chips of metal without hesitation, for the storyteller deserved it all. He had reached a new level tonight. Midsummer Eve.

At that moment the reedy sound of fiddles piped up, and the dancers began twirling to the claps of excited men. All eyes left the storyteller to gaze lustily at the girls.

But Cain remained focussed on the storyteller, who was sidling along the wall, making for the exit. He would catch him tonight before he slipped away so stealthily. Cain's children would be spending Midsummer Day at the farm with their grandmother, but perhaps he need not celebrate alone.

Maybe the storyteller could use some company too.

Cain drained his mug of ale, moistening his mouth that was parched from the smoky atmosphere of the room. Then he rose, hurrying for the door, before it was too late.

"Adrian?"

The storyteller stopped, the hood turned. "Yes, Cain?"

He breathed deeply. So the mysterious boy had remembered him, despite their only encounter being a brief one, long ago.

"'Ave ye got someone to spend Midsummer Day with?"

The excited strumming of fiddle strings resonated in his ears, and colours flickered on the periphery of his vision. Whirling dresses, tapping feet.

And still, no response came.

"It's fine, don't worry."

The head dipped lower, the storyteller's face just a hood.

"Cain." The voice sounded gentle, but laced with needy undercurrents, like a hurt child reaching for the comfort of a mother's embrace. "I will come to the smithy in the morning." The voice cracked and the storyteller's words came out forced, unnatural for one with such mastery. "Be waiting."

A command. Almost.

Before Cain could respond with anything more, the storyteller slipped out the door, into the summer night. Mysteries eluded him though he searched to understand, a quest as fruitless as a journey to the end of a rainbow.

But perhaps tomorrow he would make a new friend.

3

ANOTHER GIRL

With the first rays of sun illuminating Linuina valley, a lively city came into focus against the hazy dawn sky. Fortress towers soared mightier than ever, while the adjacent fields glowed a verdant green, as though assuring prosperity for the coming year.

Many had already risen to prepare for Midsummer Day, and now more people streamed out onto the decorated streets. Everyone was buzzing with excitement, the festival promising to be the greatest since the Henalas invasion.

For generations, war and famine had crippled the world of Meridisia. But it had been three years since the last siege, and Linuina was recovering. The progress was especially visible today. Minstrels lit up the streets with their melodies, where beggars had once lurked. Children squealed in delight as they watched clowns and magicians perform, their mothers making no effort to calm them.

And today, another young woman would stroll proudly through her city.

* * *

Fingers fumbling nervously on the knob, she closed the door of the little terrace house belonging to her grandparents, and began the descent to the bakery below. One hand trailed along the wall for support as she negotiated the steep, uneven steps. The other held up the hem of her dress so she wouldn't trip over it.

As she descended, the familiar, comforting scent of bread wafted up the staircase to greet her. There seemed to be a touch more spice in it. Or maybe that was simply an illusion, which came from the thrill of dressing as a woman again.

"Adrian 'ad 'imself a gurlie last night 'ey?" the stout, middle-aged baker called to her.

Her cheeks flushed to match the red of her dress, but words rolled quickly off her tongue. Years of disguise had forced her to be alert and ready, lest someone discover her identity.

"I'm a visitor from the west, his grandparents are family friends," she responded.

The baker raised one of his scraggly eyebrows, and gave her a wink that made her shudder. Suppressing her disgust, she simply nodded in polite greeting.

As she left the bakery, her worries eased away in the fresh summer air, which tantalised skin that rarely saw daylight. But she was not pale, for a childhood on the coast had dyed her complexion the tint of rich, golden honey, which had retained its colour despite confinement.

Smiling, she walked towards the smithy. Today, unmasked. Truthfully, she could honour the Gods, who had filled her empty heart with dreams and hope.

But upon reaching her destination, she hesitated. *Was this foolish?*

No. She tossed the negative thought and summoned her courage to knock on the wooden door. Before long a bolt slid out of place, and a burly blacksmith emerged on the threshold.

"By the Gods!" he exclaimed. Making no further move to speak, he simply stared while the breeze caressed her bronze ringlets, glinting with flecks of gold in the midsummer sun.

She cleared her throat to break the barricade of silence between them. "May the Elements bless you," came her greeting.

He just kept staring, while she silently begged for him to say something.

"Well, happy Midsummer Day!" he replied at last. "Er…" The huge man glanced over his shoulder, before turning back to her with a frown. "What brings ye 'ere, young miss?"

She lowered her head timidly, feeling like a young girl about to ask her father an embarrassing question. "I'm here to see Cain, although he won't recognise me. Please, he has not already left for the markets has he?"

"Nah, but…"

"Father!" a voice sounded from behind. Cain's voice.

The blacksmith turned, blocking the entrance. She waited, as whispers of their hushed conversation teased her ears. It seemed like they were making a fuss over something. Perhaps she should leave now, while their discussion occupied them. She still had a chance, before the truth erupted out of her.

But to spend a life in disguise is to spend a life alone, and in conflict with one's own identity. Voices hissed through her mind, reminding her of the reasons for her decision. She needed this for her sanity.

And then the opportunity to flee disappeared as the blacksmith stepped back from the doorway.

She inhaled as Cain took his father's place, and his gaze fell upon her. Warm brown eyes shone in alarm, along with a hint of some other emotion she could not define.

"So tell me, ye said ye were 'ere for me?" His lip twitched in what appeared to be a grimace more than a smile, and unruly eyebrows curved downwards. "Young miss, I can't say I know ye. But er… if ye ain't got company on this fine day, well I won't leave ye to celebrate the Gods on yer own." Something flashed across his eyes. He seemed to be slightly distressed about something.

Foolish idea. The negative voice in her mind sounded again. But the words came gushing out instead. "Cain, I have to tell you something. The storyteller Adrian… I am him."

Cain froze as astonishment replaced all else, and she used the opportunity to hurry on with her rehearsed explanation. At least storytelling in rowdy taverns had developed her confidence.

"Please, I did it for safety! If people knew I was a woman they would think less of me, not to mention give fewer coins, steal my earnings, or follow me on my way home. But last night, when you stopped me at the door, I just knew I needed this today. Please, let it be our little secret. For once in my life maybe I can have a true friend." The voice of a storyteller hovered in the air, commanding attention with its mesmerising quality.

She swallowed as the doubts rose within her again. *Foolish girl.* She clenched her hands into fists, searching for her strength.

A life in disguise, a life of falsity, has no meaning. For no one knows who you truly are, not even you. Your identity gets hidden away beneath so many masked layers, until you forget yourself.

And the Gods: she preached to others to be truthful, to themselves and to others. Her own hypocrisy beat her conscience like a whip. She would pray for forgiveness today.

She cleared her throat, prepared now, ready to face Cain…

"Ma lady. What's yer name then?" he managed to utter before she spoke again.

She twitched, then prayed he had not noticed, that he would not be suspicious of another betrayal.

"I'm Adrianna. Only for today, you promise?" Her heart jumped with an unnatural beat as she twisted her true name slightly. But it was still necessary to be cautious, and she was sure the Gods would understand.

Cain nodded, although his eyes appeared misty and she wondered if he had even registered her words.

"It's nice to see who ye are," came his response finally, though his forehead remained creased as though some doubts about her remained.

She supposed she could expect nothing else, given her revelation. So she just waited, and finally his expression softened. Although, worries of another kind made her tremble now. She hoped he would not simply see her as a pretty girl and nothing more.

Part of her wished she had never experienced better living. Then maybe she could settle for the current situation, and the way most men treated women around here. Maybe that was the real reason she had shed her guise today, as an act of defiance against reality.

No, it was more than that.

She also craved human interaction, and Cain hadn't seemed all that bad. He certainly never behaved like the men who lustily grabbed the buttocks of serving-girls and dancers in the tavern.

"Cain..." she murmured, her voice quavering with all the emotions storming inside her.

As though he sensed her discomfort and wanted to lighten the mood, Cain bowed like a gentleman. Scruffy chestnut curls bounced around his ears as he bent, giving him a comical look.

"I always thought ye a smart young man tellin' tales, but even though ye're a woman, ye'll still be me damn brilliant storyteller."

The muscles in her jaw relaxed, and Adrianna silently thanked the Gods that her judgement of Cain had been correct.

"Thank you," she said softly.

"Well, ma lady, let's celebrate."

With that, Cain took her arm in his. Her skin tingled from the energy of that simple physical contact. After so long without, her heart leapt forth in her chest like a bird taking flight.

This was freedom.

This was truth.

4
CAPTIVE

Stumbling across ashen fields, jerked along by the ruthless chain around her wrists, Taalin walked on.

It was dusk. A thick veil of mist from the nearby mountains hung in the sky, choking the air like the fear and despair that bubbled up from her stomach and into her throat.

She squeezed her eyes shut to stop the tears oozing out. She had to hold on. Be strong.

Remember who you are.

Her entire life she had trained as a warrior, like all the northern women. But no training had prepared her for this.

Why did they spare me?

She wanted to scream, to wail, to let a gurgling howl rip from her throat and make the Gods aware of her anguish. Maybe then they would notice her. Maybe they would send a bolt of lightning to strike her, and end her life before the hell began.

But nothing happened. She remained alive, and alone. A captive.

Her insides shook as fear tore through her body, eating away what glimpses remained of her courage. She was nothing but a girl. A weak… little… child.

"Faster!"

One of the soldiers barked, pulling the rope attached to her chained hands. The metal scraped against her chafed wrists, opening up the cracked skin. She watched as ruby gems of blood seeped out and trickled down her flesh.

The soldier's face leered in front of her and she flung a ball of spit at that smirking, pasty excuse for a human.

But humans had hearts. He didn't.

She felt the hand whipping across her cheek before she saw it coming. Spots appeared in her vision, strands of gossamer white globules forming a web in the darkness. Trapping her.

She blinked. Licking her lips, she tasted something salty and metallic.

Blood. Her blood.

Legs trembling, Taalin sank to the ground. Her knee struck a rock and daggers of pain fractured through her being. A whimper escaped from her lips into the cruel night, as the heavy weight of her loneliness descended down upon her.

"Move."

She did not lift her head. She just stared down at the earth that had failed her.

No more flowers. No more colours.

"Please." The word slipped past her lips, and immediately a pang of self-loathing coursed through her. She had been so much more than this, yet now allowed herself to be reduced to a weak and helpless girl. Her warrior spirit had deserted her, and she was begging the enemy for mercy.

"Move."

The next thing she knew was the impact of a boot in her belly. She tensed, struggling to stop another cry erupting from her throat.

Be dignified. Be strong.

Blinking back tears, Taalin staggered upright. She kept her gaze averted from the soldier, staring meekly at the ground, unable to look the essence of repulsion in the eye.

One step.

And another.

She clenched her teeth to fight the agony, as the cracked lining of her boots allowed the metallic outer shell to scrape her heels. Scratching the skin, peeling back the layers of flesh, engraving hideous marks and reminding her of her weakness.

She winced, but no one noticed. The soldier holding the rope had returned to his position some metres ahead, and she was the only captive.

Time was marked by her wincing, broken footsteps.

She focussed on those steps and succumbed to the feeling of her feet being torn apart. It dulled the other pain – the agony of loss and failure, the torture of being a captive.

Nothing more than a weak little girl, who pleaded for the Gods to kill her.

Life had nothing left to give. She was done with it, finished.

Time now, to close off to the world.

5

MIDSUMMER FESTIVITIES

The atmosphere on Linuina's streets throbbed with increased excitement, while the sun dwindled to make way for twilight. Soon the festive rituals would begin, hosted by none other than King Melchior himself.

Adrianna looked up to the sky to find magenta and gold streaks saluting her eyes. The colours decorated the sky like pigments on pale cloth.

Like blood, blotching the bandages of wounded warriors…

Before the memory seized her into its midst, she was brought back to the present by Cain tugging on her arm, drawing her closer in the thickening crowd. The pair made for the barbican gates, while above them the passionate sunset hues faded to inky black. The stars were yet to twinkle alight but guards held flaming torches to illuminate the surroundings, and also to form a divide between the citizens and the coming parade.

Adrianna drew closer to Cain as a cool wind stirred her hair and teased her flesh. He took her hand and she felt his fingers sweaty with anticipation. They could already hear the parade in the distance: the tinkling of saddle bells, shouts of jubilant citizens, and trumpets announcing the royals.

The drum of hooves on cobbles grew louder, and she strained her neck above the bobbing heads of the throng. She spotted the royal guards clothed in regal navy blue, riding atop stallions white as frosted fields.

Then King Melchior and his son appeared. Adrianna flung the bouquet she had bought at the market, and it joined a storm of other flowers pouncing through the air. Petals swirled in a vivid shower, and through the colourful curtain she watched Prince Fredrik turn her way.

Despite the mayhem, serenity settled upon her. She stared into the mystical depths of the prince's eyes, which reflected back her own crystalline blue. Within her distant spirit, a spark of emotion ignited. But she could not put her finger on its source.

Her vision blurred and she became oblivious to everything, save those chips of azure so clear and certain, penetrating a sensitive place deep inside. Then the parade carried him away, abruptly cutting their gaze.

Closing her eyes, Adrianna concentrated and tried to bring the feeling back. But however hard she tried, no clarity emerged. There was nothing except a faint prickling on the edges of her consciousness.

She thought of the prince, like a hero from one of her stories. But a hint of envy stained her thoughts. Despite the pressures on his shoulders, at least he didn't have to worry about shelter or sustenance. At least he could sleep at night, without fear of robbery or whether he would even eat the next morning.

Once again, it was Cain who startled Adrianna from her reverie, pulling her in the direction of the valley. She realised that other nobles had already passed by, along with earth-scientists and robed priests who would conduct the sacred rituals. The commoners were flooding after the parade, and she grasped Cain's hand tighter so as not to lose him in the sea of bodies.

They proceeded through the gates, and a momentary thinning in the crowd gave her a chance to admire the view. On her right flowed the River of Rena, sweeping in a graceful ark down from the northeast. Extending into the south, it embraced the western wall of the fortress in glistening arms. Then it branched into the east, leaving a small grassy region between the southern side of the main city and the waters.

Three bridges radiated over the river as it curled, constructed of precious white marble transported from the north. The central one led straight through to a private palace entrance, protected by a wooden drawbridge that was lifted during times of siege. The peripheral two were for the commoners, wide highways connecting the trade routes of east and west, north and south. On the outer bend of the river and opposite from the main city lay a small haven, harbouring the boats of wealthy merchants.

Cain flashed her a smile as they descended into the valley. They walked down the gentle slope, until the terrain levelled at the riverbank where the ceremonies would occur. Near the southern bridge, nobles and priests assembled behind a ring of guards, and beside a massive pile of wood and discarded items.

The Linuinans had spent their week bringing old, broken items out to this pile, which would soon become a bonfire. At the end of the night, the ashes would be cast into the river to signify the old year ending, and a release of energy from the past.

Adrianna gazed at the pile, meaningless in any other place. Yet here it symbolised rebirth, and perhaps the coming year would indeed be a joyous one. Maybe the Gods would aid them to heal further, after so much war.

She watched the priests prepare the bonfire, and then King Melchior came forward to address the people. Though he was just one man in a huge valley, somehow his voice boomed out to reach the ears of the farthest person, as though amplified by the Gods.

"Fellow people of Linuina! I call you here, on this Midsummer Night, to celebrate the Gods of Earth, Sea and Sky. In their name, we unite to face whatever future awaits us. In our hearts, we remember Truth, Justice, Faith, and Love. And never shall we steer from these guiding values!

"As the New Year arrives, we call to the Gods to give us strength and to keep the light of Faith aflame in our hearts. May you all be blessed with the powers of Nature, and the Elements aid us in our cause. And may everyone heed my words tonight, and the words of the Gods. They speak to us every day, and they alone will guide us!"

A cheer sprang up through the crowd, a deafening chorus that grew in volume and soon became a chant praising the king. In the heat and passion of that cheering, Prince Fredrik took the burning branch of a tree from the hands of a priest, and flung it atop the pile. It caught alight in an instant, flames spreading across the heap. Within minutes it was burning ferociously, and fire leapt up like a signal to the heavens. It symbolised unity of the elemental gods, and the energy it carried cried out just as loud as the chanting people.

Close as she was standing, heat tickled Adrianna's eyes and sparkling drops of moisture appeared on her cheeks. The glow of orange beckoned her spirit, fuelling that inner desire to restore the glory of her world. It sparked the true radiance within her, too long subdued by disguise.

Suddenly, looking into the inferno, she saw licking fire tendrils writhe and twist into the shape of a human form. It was a woman wrapped in white robes, her figure slender and graceful as a young birch, her silver hair streaming in the scorching breeze.

The woman called to Adrianna, arousing something within her that started to pulse and glow like a second heart. But instead of pumping blood, it pumped hope and courage and strength to every extremity of her body.

The fire overwhelmed the starlight sprinkling the heavens, and the rubbish continued burning as if it would do so forever. She did not know how long everyone stood captivated for in that moment, time seemed to lose all meaning. Perhaps they all sensed a divine presence.

The minutes drew on, then gradually the multitude broke from its trance. Shouts of joy and musical notes swallowed the silence, as men and women of all ranks began to dance.

Adrianna smiled and squeezed Cain's hand, and he drew her close before twirling her around. Their feet beat against the ground to the rhythm of drumming minstrels, her skirts swishing about. Oh! It was worth it, to dress as a girl again.

If her revelation to Cain caused any problems, she would deal with them later. She just needed this tonight, to refresh her. Odours of sweaty bodies mingled with wafts of stale perfume, but caught in her blissful mood, Adrianna smelt only the fresh river breeze.

Sounds of revelry clashed, in a hideous but vibrant cacophony. People with revived spirits cheered, and rowdy ruptures of drunken song entwined with the pure voices of bards.

As she was among the dancers closer to the bonfire, occasionally Adrianna caught glimpses of King Melchior and Prince Fredrik. Like everyone else they were forgetting their fears, though they were still separated from the commoners by a ring of guards.

Hours passed, but all that measured time for Adrianna was the dimming bonfire and subsiding heat. Her world wheeled, excitement and endless dancing disorienting her in a wild spin.

Flashes of light and bursts of sound existed like a new dimension above reality. It was all a blur that came as an assault to the senses, as if humans were incapable of experiencing such depth to life.

And then, from out of a chaos that rivalled the universe's creation, she met his pure eyes before her.

6

BLACK PEARL TEARS

Rope jerked the chain, pulling her forward again. Harder. Taalin stifled another cry as the open wounds on her wrists dripped blood upon the earth.

But they were stopping.

The soldier in charge of her approached, and she fought the fear gnawing in her gut. *Strong. Be strong.*

His hot breath blew into her face. Stinking, vile, putrid. She swallowed, keeping down the bile that surged up her throat. Water. She needed water. And air, fresh air.

But there was only a diseased, suffocating earth, its soil choking her lungs.

* * *

Blue calm: fill my hollow, empty soul.

There is a crater in my heart, a void in my memory, and a cavity in my spirit.

Fill me up, so that I know how to feel, how to think, how to be…

But please don't use me.

I just want to find myself.

* * *

Like a spirit, she glided fluidly over the lush valley grass. In a white silk robe, she looked like an angel of peace, moving with such ease and grace.

Then she came to an abrupt halt at the sight of a girl, hunched on the edge of a tranquil pond.

A girl. No older than her.

She approached slowly now, lacking the freedom of before. Her feet sank heavily into the grass, as though the sight of the child was weighing her down. It hurt to move, because every muscle in her body shuddered as if ropes restrained her.

But she kept pushing herself forward. She needed to get closer, so that she could see the child's reflection in the smooth water of the pond.

And she saw tears, glistening on the child's cheeks with the paradoxical dark brightness of black pearls. Tears brought by a grief that no child should ever experience: the tears of an ancient sorrow, belonging to a wounded land.

But as those tears streamed down the child's face and landed in the pond, no distortion appeared on the water. Not a ripple, not a mark, as though they were insignificant, unseen, to the forces of nature. The Gods didn't seem to care.

She had to take their place. She had to hold this child.

With a touch, she could share the burden of grief.

Torment surged through her and she cried out for this other soul. A squeezing sensation overcame her heart, and it beat rapidly, frantically, filled with compulsion to save the child.

The feeling coursed through her blood, and her heart throbbed with a passionate rhythm. Desire erupted in her veins: to save the world from all its evils so that no child would ever cry again.

But though she called out, though her voice echoed down the valley, the girl did not move. In desperation, she tried to touch her.

And fingers clawed to no avail, through thick, polluted air.

7

STORY FOR THE KING

Prince Fredrik gave a smile capable of seducing the most chaste and stubborn of virgins, and took her hands in his.

Panicking, Adrianna looked around. Somehow the prince had slipped out from the ring of guards, and for all her storytelling skills, words struggled to escape her throat.

"Your Highness, I am sorry… I forget my place," she said and managed to bend in an awkward curtsy. An uncanny mix of thrill and anxiety rippled through her.

"Your place is here," he replied. A grin revealed perfect white teeth, shining in the firelight. "And mine with you. Nothing separates us tonight."

Adrianna knew his reference was to the rich and the poor, and the nature of the Midsummer celebrations where all were supposed to stand equal beneath the Gods. But still, that never really happened in practice. Her lip trembled as she searched for a response, her mind giddy with unspoken thoughts.

"Don't be shy," he murmured. "It is not often that I meet a commoner, and the ladies at the palace do get rather boring."

Though his voice was kind, Adrianna recoiled. Luxurious living should not be dismissed so… *flippantly*.

A cynical laugh erupted from between her lips. But Prince Fredrik didn't seem to notice, as instead he trapped her in a dance. Then music overcame her body once more, loosening the nervous tension in her muscles. Harmonies hid all hints of bitterness, and melodies washed her worries away.

As Adrianna twirled, her lively spinning also softened the prince's formal, upright posture. Several times she took the lead, and erratic sparkles of confidence made her heart thud faster, daring to break down those barriers further. Tantalizing thrills rode her blood, and she tasted those moments of control like addictive nectar. At once satisfying, yet making her crave more power.

Then the music faded as the bonfire diminished further, the burning mound now a crumple of glowing embers and steaming piles of ash.

Adrianna slowly returned to the present. Avoiding the prince's eyes, she looked desperately into the crowd. Convention told her that she should leave his company, even if it was Midsummer.

"There ye are! Why don't ye come and tell us a story 'ey?"

Adrianna jumped at the sound of Cain's eager voice. Standing on the border between nobles and commoners, she hesitated. Caught between worlds.

"Your Highness…" Cain stammered, beholding his very own prince over her shoulder.

She turned back to Prince Fredrik, forcing her legs to fold in curtsy again. "Thank you, Highness."

Common sense instructed her to walk away, but a reckless urge to join the world of the powerful grounded her. Firmly.

"What is your name, my lady?" the prince said.

She took a breath, and the lie rushed out of her mouth. "Adrianna, Your Highness."

"Well, wouldn't you oblige us with a story? If that is what you do?"

Engulfed by feverish eagerness, Adrianna nodded. Then she noticed Cain hovering behind, gazing at her with uncertainty. A pang of regret tainted her excitement, but she brushed it aside, thinking of this opportunity.

She sent Cain an apologetic glance and followed the prince to where his father sat on several cushions at the river edge. The quieter celebrations of the night had begun, with the crowd breaking up into smaller groups to converse and share stories.

As the pair approached, men and women of the court eyed them, more than a few frowning at Adrianna. She tried to ignore them – she would prove herself.

"Father, may this young lady tell a story for us?"

King Melchior studied her, but not unkindly. His eyes seemed to go misty, as though lost in memory. Then the distant stare vanished and his gaze became attentive, inquisitive. "What is your name?"

"Adrianna, Your Majesty," she whispered, curtseying. She had to maintain her lie, but it was getting easier to say the fake name. Besides, after tonight it wouldn't matter, for they would not meet again.

The king looked pensive for a second, but simply cleared his throat and nodded. "Very well, the stage is yours." He smiled so warmly that her spirits lit up. How lucky Renala was, to have such a gracious leader! And to give her this chance…

Her blood pumped as the prince gestured for her to begin, and she searched her memory for a story fit to tell on this wondrous night. She recalled the figure in the flames, the white-robed woman who had filled her with hope and strength.

Yes, this was the night to tell the story of that magnificent, godly woman. She would weave her words to bring legend to life. Summon the White Woman, to restore the glory of the Gods' land.

Adrianna couldn't help but smile, and she thought of her father and mother up in the Sky Kingdom. She would make them proud.

That thought banished her nerves, giving her courage to look King Melchior in the eye. Her voice rose to occupy the silence as her confidence grew into full bloom, her words creating wonders for all who listened.

"When our earth was nothing but a barren lump of rock, when the breath of the universe was sterile and cold, the Gods looked down from their heavenly abode. They yearned to create, to pass on their legacy."

Writhing words crept through the air, like whispering spirits from an ancient realm.

"They travailed for aeons, striving for perfection. Rock crinkled to form majestic mountains, and wide oceans surged without restraint. Rivers snaked across sweeping plains, cascading into waterfalls beneath an unblemished sky. In the tropics, jungles teemed with life, and desert heat swelled in reminder of Nature's force."

Murmuring echoes hovered on the edge of awareness, like the hidden mysteries floating beneath the sea depths, and engraved in solid rock.

"… She was named Meridisia, jewel of the cosmos, heart of Love fused from Rock, Sea and Sky…"

Tantalising chorus of sounds, they morphed into existence like the four children of the Gods.

"Two souls went to the sea realms, two remained on land, and thus was born the great Races of Sea and Earth!"

A harmonious melody, her voice arced through the night. It curled in the air, brushing over the river like a gentle breeze, nudging the soil with a tender touch, and then rising up to the stars. Balancing the elemental powers of air, water and rock.

"With time the races separated, and all communication between them faded. It was a natural divergence, a peaceful parting."

But her tone sharpened to slice into the minds of her listeners, reminding all of the prophecy of reunion. When Meridisia would restore balance to a crippled universe.

"Daughter of a Sea woman and an Earth man, the White Woman was the first of her kind. For blood did not mix between empires, and cursed with strange talents, she wandered into the wilderness. Alone…"

A pause. Sound hovered in a bitter vibration, like the cry of an abandoned girl, the birds and the fish her only friends.

"It was she who uncovered the secrets of the Gods, the Lore of the land, blessed but cursed knowledge!"

Piercing, stabbing words, urgent and angry, for the Gods had not planned this. The planet flourished, fruit adorned the trees, and the heart of Meridisia had no need for awakening.

"So the Gods put her to sleep, restraining her until the time came for her to rise and join Sea and Rock empires. Her blood will seal our union."

As one, the audience gasped in awe, hearts fuelled by newfound hope. For these days, angry dreams plague the White Woman. She knows of the cruel Henalas who invaded from across the icy Northern Sea. She feels the pain of the conquered northern lands, scarred by the enemy empire.

"We are yet to defeat the Henalas: their attacks have merely abated. But when war returns, never fear. For as long as we stay faithful, the Gods will send help. As long as we are truthful, we will have justice. And as long as we love purely and cherish our world, we will emerge victorious."

8

BLUE STAR

Powerful words.

I tell stories, because the words fill me up.
They give me meaning, and it seems they help other people too.

I listen to stories, because the words carry me away.
They distract me from reality, and make me feel an important man.

Or perhaps the words create reality.

* * *

As the sound of Adrianna's voice faded, for a moment the magic of her words hovered in the balmy night air. Then, first hesitant but soon enthusiastic, the nobles clapped in delight.

Adrianna could not help but grin as the applause hailed her ears. She had somehow managed to tell a story to noble men and women, and they were congratulating her.

"Beautifully told, Adrianna," said the king.

Her cheeks flushed and she lowered her eyes. Deep within she knew that it was time to go, to leave before she was consumed with greedy longing to cross that bridge into another world…

She curtsied, and then hurried away from her royal audience. Still transfixed by her potent tale, it was as though they did not even notice her departure.

Had it even happened? Like a wraith she flitted away, like the shadow she had always been.

She slipped by the guards and they closed back into position after her, shutting off that alternative reality. Tomorrow her routine would begin again, of masking as a boy, hiding beneath her hood.

Sighing, Adrianna looked up to the heavens, speckled by stars. She could see some of her favourite constellations that her father had shown her as a little girl. And her wandering eyes stumbled upon a new stellar jewel, different from the others, shrouded by teal mist. Although bright, it seemed frail, as if it could be blown away.

She turned back toward the great bonfire. A few hours ago it had been blazing as ferociously as the underworld, but now the flames had devoured nearly all of the fuel and only a dim glow remained. Soon it would be time to cast the ashes into the River of Rena, and with it, any bad luck from the previous year.

As though following her thoughts, King Melchior went to speak with the robed men who would conduct the ceremony. After a few words the head priest nodded and called out to the people in the valley. His voice was amplified like the king's had been earlier, and despite all the revelry, everyone fell silent and turned to watch the last feeble flames of the bonfire die out near the ground.

All firelight vanished, and shouts of celebration reverberated along the valley while the night plunged deeper into darkness. With the death of the fire, the past was released, and all souls freed from lingering fears and pain.

She watched as priests in white and navy robes congregated around a barrel of sacred water, which would protect their skin from burning. They dipped their hands into the holy liquid and then went to grasp a handful of ash from the bonfire, which they flung ceremonially out into the glassy river waters. While they moved back and forth between the water and the fire remnants, the people prayed.

In those drawn-out moments, Adrianna thought of the White Woman again. *Oh!* How she hoped her vision was an omen, and the restoration of Meridisia was near. Surely, such a display of faith as shown by the people of Linuina could not be ignored.

After they'd uttered their prayers, groups of families and friends began dispersing back to the city. The celebrations were over, and the time had come to rest and refresh their bodies for tomorrow and the year ahead.

Adrianna watched as the guards assembled protectively around the king and prince, and the royal entourage prepared to return to the palace. Her heart ached with a bitter longing to join them. Perhaps the palace library would give her answers.

"Well, ye sure did well tonight, didn't ye?"

She snapped out of her thoughts and turned to find Cain approaching, his features crinkled by a huge smile. Laughing lightly, she let him take her hand and lead her away from the bonfire remains.

They wandered down the valley in search of a soft patch of grass where they could sit and relax. Both silent, they thought about the wishes they had made during the casting of the ash. Their memories spiralled within, like light bouncing around in a prism.

By now, most Linuinans had already returned to their homes, leaving the valley near-deserted. Those still celebrating lounged closer to the main city gates, their noise a faint mystical hum that accompanied the whistling wind and rustling water.

Adrianna lay back against the springy turf and looked to the glittering heavens. Powerful and unfaltering, those stars lived on for aeons, burning like beacons over mortal life below. Did they lament the invasion of Meridisia? Were they personifications of the Gods, strong and omnipresent in the cosmos?

She imagined being a star or a god. An immortal being, untouchable and with nothing to fear, existing above and beyond earthly troubles. She could do without the grief and fear.

But then, what about happiness and love?

Sighing, she let her guard down and allowed some emotion to wash over her. That emotion was what made humans special. The blissful depth of a feeling, that came with savouring the precious eternity of a mortal moment.

Her eyelids drooped while the breeze lilting off the river caressed her face. Her senses adjusted, tuning in to the tiniest movements and sounds around her.

In that tranquil moment, images from her childhood began rising to mind: visions of a life in far-off Soonada, in the beautiful port city of Tarvesi. She could still remember the lime-green plains dotted with buttercups in the springtime, rolling to the edge of granite cliffs that overlooked a glimmering turquoise ocean.

Colour.

Everything had been so vibrant and colourful, even her clothes. She had owned dresses of violet, rose and emerald, of saffron, lilac, and celestial blue.

Soonada was known for its beautiful silk fabrics, and the dyes made from the volcanic minerals produced by the Fhea Karadid: a fiery mountain range that divided the kingdom, acting as both a blessing and a curse. Its extreme altitude drew moisture away from the east, leaving desert, while the west thrived from the fertility brought by rain and volcanic soil.

A land of conflicting opposites, just like the human soul. You couldn't have one half without the other.

Her head spun and her body soared, reminiscent of times playing with her father. He would twirl her in the air, making her fly like a bird. Gliding up near the Kingdoms of the Sky, were those birds closer to the Gods? Should they be watched, their signs followed?

She thought of her father's face, but the whole image eluded her these days. She could only grasp individual features, and wondered when those blurry fragments of memory would vanish altogether.

His skin had been weathered, his cheekbones rough and chiselled. Though he had never spoken of his past, a creased brow told of many hardships endured before her birth.

But beneath evident layers of sorrow and pain, he had been free like a minstrel. Mischievous and well-travelled, knowing the soil of the earth. With his beautiful tenor voice, he had sung to her in the evenings, and together they had escaped to worlds of peace, love and joy… or sadness, when the time called. For those feelings were also parts of life.

Sighing, she let the memories fade away. They were strange memories, for it was as if she was an external observer on her life. She was somehow detached, empty… And she had no one to talk things through with.

She barely had a connection to her grandparents here in Linuina. Although she cared for them and they survived off her earnings, they had been strangers to her for so long. Not to mention she had arrived from Soonada with a resolve to remain distant. It was her defence to pre-emptively reduce the pain she would feel when she eventually and inevitably lost them too. She could take no more pain.

Yet in some ways, emptiness dealt a heavier blow.

Adrianna slowly opened her eyes and turned to face Cain. Faint starlight spilled across his features, making his mellow brown irises glint warmly.

"I've been thinking about who ye are," he said hesitantly, as he shyly brushed a few strands of his chestnut hair.

"What exactly… have you been thinking?"

Cain shrugged. "I dunno, just 'bout how ye've lived yer life for so long. I still can't believe ye managed to deceive me."

"I'm sorry." She smiled crookedly. "When I came here, life was so unsafe. And now… Well, I needed this tonight. Otherwise I'm just a caged bird, trapped by disguise."

"But perhaps better days ain't far off." He winked, his hand reaching up to cup her cheek. "I never knew ye were a woman, and I never saw much of ye. Ye always wore that hood… ye had to, otherwise I would've seen how beautiful yer features were, and would've guessed yer secret."

She lay there, heart thudding in her chest, unable to respond. He drew closer, and she could smell the strong but not unpleasant odour of a man who spent his days forging metal by the hot furnaces in a smithy.

"Cain?" she questioned, eyes widening as she noticed his gaze wander up and down her body, like a warrior assessing a fine sword to buy. Thoughts scurried through her mind as she tried to classify his intentions. They didn't seem to be lustful. *That* look did not glow on his face.

9

ECHOES OF MEMORY

Cain noticed her hesitation, but thought and reason had deserted him. The sight of her engulfed his attention, more captivating than those stories she told.

The magnificent dress only enhanced her ethereal beauty. Despite the fabric's coarse weave and poor quality, its crimson hue added a regal touch to her presence. Flaunting her slim body and feminine curves, it gathered sharply at the waist then flowed out in all directions, to make her body look like the centre of a scarlet flower.

And she reminded him of Lily, on their wedding night.

He grimaced as he remembered the young woman he had sworn his life to half a dozen years ago, and lost to the spirit realms.

Tenderness spread out from his heart. Suppressed grief mingled with attraction for Adrianna in a bizarre melange of soothing warmth and stabbing pain. Helpless to the surge of memories, he recalled Lily with a gracious smile blooming upon her lips, an adoring glint in her eyes. The radiance of her love had shone so bright despite her suffering, that no one had even realised the extent of her affliction.

He would have to keep Adrianna away from the house when the children came with Lily's mother to visit. He couldn't expose them to more emotions, which the sight of Adrianna might trigger.

But gazing across at her now, some force wrenched his own doubtful thoughts away. He had not been with a woman for so long.

"Everyone kisses someone on Midsummer Night," he said softly. "If ye were still the Adrian I knew, we could've gone into town and found two young lasses. But now ye're Adrianna."

The words slipped past his lips without him even realising, as he hungered to draw her into an embrace. Perhaps if he squeezed hard enough, Lily would reappear. Perhaps the Gods had sent this girl to him for that very reason.

Lily deserved to return.

* * *

"Cain, stop it," Adrianna retorted, more harshly than she intended. Cain drew back with a wounded expression dancing across his features.

Alone with Cain at this end of the valley, only then did she realise he had not gone off with his friends. He had stayed after she had abandoned him for the nobles, waited until she had finished her story, to accompany her on this special night.

An overwhelming urge to cry overtook her, and she almost reached for his arms. "I'm sorry, I don't mean… but men just scare me. Well, I'm used to seeing the violent ones in taverns, who abuse women. And I know you're not like that."

"I didn't mean to hurt ye," he muttered awkwardly. "I wasn't going to force you into anything."

Then he rose, first brushing the grass off his clothes, then aiding her to her feet. Despite the ale she had seen him consume, he still seemed sober.

Adrianna looked at him long and thoughtfully, before a shiver passed down her spine and a sense of wrongness assailed her. It had nothing to do with their conversation.

Suddenly, a sound of hoof-beats penetrated the still night. Her eyes darted nervously over Cain's shoulder.

Spotting *it*.

10

THE LAST MESSENGER

Every particle inside him clenched, his body threatening to seize up.

But he forced himself onwards.

Every leap across the earth jarred his bones. Every movement brought bloody tears streaming from his eyes, to flow like lava down his cheeks.

He could not remember the last time he had stopped to rest. His mouth was devoid of moisture, dried out by burning flames.

Ammonia. The stench produced from decaying muscles swamped him, piercing his nostrils. He sensed the acid building up, corroding the tissue away.

He was dissolving, his body ceasing to exist as the cells of his flesh converted into energy required for the motion.

He had to give them the warning.

That one thought propelled him forward, for the last chance resided with him. There were no more men to spare in this gauntlet run. No one had the strength to do it, anyway.

So he would survive and deliver the message.

Before it arrived.

A tide caused by something more powerful than a supernatural moon: when it came, it would bring the waves of destruction surging forth. Fast and deadly, smothering everything…

But no matter how fast he ran, the shadows still pursued him.

And they were getting closer.

Then from out of the night's darkness, a new sensation overcame him.

He tumbled to the ground, falling as a horse galloped past. The rider swerved back to face him for a moment, mount rearing in the phantom moonlight.

The scene was grey monochrome, a world of black and white.

* * *

They say that in those moments before death, your life flashes before your eyes.

But now I know that is not true.

As you die, you see the light of life.

You *see* the world, in all its colours.

You realised you lived your life as a blind man.

You see that death is an escape, from the constraints of sleeping mortality.

But then there are those who are left behind.

And they are the ones who must heal our future.

If only I could give them a message…

11

MIDNIGHT STRANGER

Her breath quickened as the figure drew closer. Any travellers ought to have arrived in time for the festival, not after the merriment.

Something was wrong and she could feel it, deep within her. Her instincts never lied – sometimes she could really *feel* things. And now, the chambers of her heart were clenching frantically, in spasmodic beats. She had the urge to scream, though why, she could not say. It was as though she felt a pain that did not belong to her.

Sensing her distress, Cain placed a hand on her shoulder. "What is it, Adrianna? What troubles ye?"

She did not know. That was the worst thing.

With the life she led, of course she was prone to caution. But she was certainly not the paranoid type.

"Please, tell me what troubles ye?"

When she still didn't reply, Cain simply turned to follow the direction of her gaze. "What, it's just a…" But his voice trailed off, as if he too sensed something was amiss.

Suddenly the night seemed so much colder, petrifying Adrianna with its chill. Without Cain to jerk her into motion, she may well have remained frozen in her place.

"I believe that ain't no traveller," he whispered as they ducked down in the valley.

The horsed figure continued his approach, but was still too far away for them to make out any features. Even illuminated by the stars, he was blacker than a moonless night. Cloaked man and midnight stallion appeared to be one entity, a shroud come to smother them.

"I think it be best if we stay low," Cain murmured.

They crept through the undergrowth, angling towards the right and their homes in the outer town. They could hear the horseman cantering along, the ground resonating with disturbing hoof-beats.

They were at the end of the scrub now. The buildings of the town loomed close by, but they'd have to run across a short open stretch first, where they risked being seen. Behind them they heard the rider slow, and they paused, hiding while he swept his gaze around the valley.

For a moment it seemed as though he had spotted them, but instead he directed his mount towards some citizens still drinking around a fire. Although they cast him suspicious glances, none showed any signs of the fear crippling Adrianna.

Words wafted ominously down the valley, and fragments of a dream resurfaced.

* * *

A sensation of cold night air tearing through her lungs besieged her. She was running, faster and faster. She was running from the shadows that followed her like men in black cloaks, like stealthy and silent villains with their minds set on achieving one deadly aim.

She ran with all the speed she could. The past was chasing her, new truths were chasing her. Half of her tried to shut out this reality, and insisted it was all just a mistake. But mistake or no, she was in danger.

Before she could cry out for help, a hand materialised out from behind and clamped her mouth shut. She twisted and turned, her arms flailing wildly, as she tried to resist the force. But all strength deserted her and she sank like a melting wax statue into one of the bushes lining the valley.

Cain!

In her mind, she frantically called the name of the only person who could save her, who knew her current face. And with all honesty, he probably knew her better than she knew herself...

* * *

"Do you know a young woman by the name of Arian?"

She reeled, her heart thumping so loud she thought the rider would hear it. Something stirred in the depths of her mind, like a puff of smoke unfurling to tease her memory. Spectres danced in her vision, as she felt her awareness merge into the night air until there was no distance between her and the group down the valley.

Her true name: a name long ago concealed. A feeling of power rippled through her, as the word echoed over and over in her being.

Arian.

It had been so long since anyone, herself included, had said that word aloud.

She heard one of the more sober people reply after a brief pause. "Perhaps ye mean Adrian?"

"Perhaps…" the horsed figure murmured in a slow, slippery voice. Like it was not quite real, not quite present. "Describe this Adrian to me."

"Well he lives with his grandparents, but no one knows much 'bout him, sir. He tells stories 'round the outer village."

A pause.

"And what does this Adrian look like?"

The Linuinan took a swig from his mug, obviously bored with the interrogation. "No one knows really, though he is rather slight. Secretive too, he always wears a hood and keeps to himself. Strange really, if he travelled 'round I reckon he'd gain quite a following. Lovely stories, and such a beautiful voice…"

"Where does this Adrian live?" interrupted the horseman.

"In the outer village, sir, but why don't ye come have a drink and ye can settle yer business later. 'Tis for celebrating, tonight."

The rider shook his head. "It's urgent. Do you know the directions?"

"Whoever ye after, he lives in the third street off the main one leading into the barbican. Turn right, number five I think, 'tis above a bakery."

With the information he needed, the horseman dug his heels into the flanks of his mount. Galloping up the slope, he soon disappeared into the streets of the outer town not much further along from where she and Cain were perched.

A distant clop of hooves on cobbles was all that remained of the abnormality.

* * *

"Adrianna?" Cain whispered.

She avoided his eyes. It didn't seem as though he had heard the horseman asking after Arian.

Her true name.

Part of her wondered if she had simply imagined the entire exchange. It seemed impossible that anyone could know her *real* name.

She gathered up her dress in her hands, preparing to make a run for it. Though she had no idea where to go or what to do, there was no use remaining in the open valley.

"Adrianna, wait." Cain placed his hand momentarily on her arm, and she allowed herself to meet his gaze. His warm touch softened her, made her want to melt into his arms and allow herself to be taken care of. Made her desire an ally, someone to walk the lonely road of her existence with. Perhaps she didn't have to do it all by herself.

But in the light of the moon, she saw his troubled gaze. She wondered if his unease was targeted not at the horseman, but at her. And she knew that she couldn't stay with him. She would bring nothing but danger, so she ought to take her own path. Alone.

"Is there more to yer story, that ye haven't told me?"

"No!" She realised she had nearly shouted, and dropped her voice as she continued. "Cain, I swear, I know nothing more than you do, it doesn't make sense to me." Despite all that she did know, she still could not comprehend this. "Well, it's only that my whole life I've been living in secrecy without really knowing why…"

He didn't respond.

"I must get inside the city walls, where there are more places to hide."

Cain just stared at her. With his eyes, she could see him asking the question: *Who are you?*

And that was a question she could not answer, much as she wanted to know the answer for herself.

Suddenly she felt a force plunge into her chest, nearly making her yelp. Her hand flung to her father's pendant where it hung between her breasts, realising that the chill striking her like an icy cold finger, was emanating from it.

Then she heard a distant shift in the sound of hooves on stone. The direction had changed.

"Goodbye Cain," she whispered, staring into his eyes. There was no time to say more, and she turned to make the last dash across the grass to the first row of clustered houses.

She didn't look back.

It was her body that made the decision to run, for her mind had abandoned her and was not with her in this reality. Instead, it was playing through horror scenes of a dream where she was lost in dark alleyways, despair overtaking her soul, until she forgot where she was even running.

But her legs moved, and like a skittish foal she bolted along the alleys of the outer town, making for the city gates. They were wide open for the festival, and there weren't even any guards on patrol. The city was oblivious to her need for protection.

A snickering voice filled her ears.

Coward.

All she could do was run from the danger.

Weak little girl.

Part of her wanted to turn around and find Cain. Find someone who could protect her.

Cain!

She had lost all sense of direction and had no idea where he was. But it didn't matter. She had to get away from him, just as she had to get away from the horseman. She couldn't put him in danger too.

An absurd idea came to her. But it was the safest option, the only option she really had, if she wanted to find some kind of safety. The ominous sound of hooves pounded in the background, spurring her on.

She wasn't sure if it was her imagination, or if they really were getting louder. Either way, fear fuelled her, and she let go of everything except the one aim to reach the palace.

She fled the shadows that followed like men in black cloaks, silent and stealthy villains, minds set on achieving their deadly aims.

No, they were not shadows.

They were footmen, robed in the same garments as...

Realisation hit her, panic flooding her body like a river raging after snowmelt. They were spreading out in an attempt to surround her and block her path.

Stifling a scream, she continued with all the speed she could muster.

Then it was over.

All strength deserted her and she sank like a melting wax statue... onto the ground before the palace guards.

"Please, help me. There are intruders in Linuina. These men, they are everywhere, and..."

"Are you mad?" One of the guards laughed, pointing his spear at her. No doubt she looked dishevelled, with her tangled hair and dirty gown.

"Help me, I am not mad!" In the corner of her eye she noticed the black-robed figures waiting in the shadows like feral felines. They could pounce any moment and snatch her away, and these two guards wouldn't do anything to save a peasant girl.

"Please, I know Prince Fredrik! I am Adrianna, he will recognise me."

"A girl like you?" The guard snorted. His breath wafted before her face, smelling of tobacco and ale. Fury rose inside her, vexation at their bias and inability to see her, and her need for protection. The figures were looming, waiting for her.

"But she is a pretty one," said the other guard. "Perhaps we could have some fun."

Another insane idea sparked in her mind and she curled her fist into a ball.

She punched the man who had spoken to her so insultingly. It was only a soft blow to his chest, but she had nevertheless committed an offence against a royal guard.

Outraged, the first guard seized her arm and pulled her towards the palace courtyard. She neither resisted nor worried, for she had reached safety.

But she stumbled on an uneven cobblestone, and tripped on the hem of her dress. The last thing she remembered was her cheek hitting the ground, then blank cold. An observer would have witnessed a thin streak of blood oozing out to stain ghostly white flesh, but she did not feel the wound.

Unconscious, she rested safe in her oblivion.

12
LOST CHILD

I watch you play
in the shadows of my night
when my body is weak
from my heart's fading beat
you strengthen, and you fight
with your desperate, angry claws
vying for attention
to sate that hunger deep

But I see right through your pain
I see the child there
crying out for love
beneath the daggers and the blame
for I am that child
yearning to be held
and I take that child sweet
in my open, loving arms

I breathe deep and slow
to invoke a wisdom beyond
this mortal body, weak
from my mind's uncertain beat
I remember that I am
connected to a light
that with love we can outshine
even the darkest night

* * *

She was at the pond again, and she bent over the hunched body of the child at her feet, struggling to catch a glimpse of her reflection.

Only then did the ghastly truth become apparent.

A cry tore from her mouth and a shudder rippled throughout her body. She tried to turn away and rip her eyes from the sight, but an invisible force bound her there, stronger than iron chains.

Her teeth gritted together, but at that same moment she evaporated out of the physical world. Suddenly she had no teeth. Her body was just a phantom, with no grounding in reality.

She had no teeth to grind. No grass beneath her feet.

But still, somehow, incredible pain pummelled her.

In the same moment she was nothing but she was everything. Her existence was impossible, but she was real. She had to be, because she had *awareness…* of her location, of this pain, and of the need to do *something*.

From the depths of the pond the innocent eyes of a child looked up at her. They were *her* eyes. But also the vermillion pupils of a tyrant, and devilish horns protruded from the place where ears should have been, a wild distortion of her angelic features.

Mist shrouded the entire image. Like her mind was foggy, clouded with confusion.

The grieving child was her body, a malnourished frame that the wounded earth could not provide for.

The force lifted abruptly and she broke away from the nightmare. But although she turned and tried to run, she could only glide slowly down the valley path. She wandered like a spirit, between the realms of the living and the dead.

She kept gliding away, slipping further from the truth and the lost child who needed her.

But that girl was part of her fragmented self. Mind, flesh and spirit, that somehow was unable to coexist.

She closed her eyes to this truth, wailing a scream of agony. And the world shuddered, the earth groaned. The people cried for help, because they could not save themselves.

No one had the answer. The balance had been disturbed, the universe in turmoil.

She had to find herself. Bring the lost child home.

She opened her eyes.
Bright cyan irises bled with rippling crimson.

13
PURSUIT

Cain watched as the strange girl, the storyteller he barely knew, turned and ran. His brain still registered the delicate tingling of her skin beneath his hand, from when he had reached out to touch her. For that single precious moment, calm had cascaded over him like the gentle glow of a golden sun. All thoughts faded, all memories dissolved, the summer air soothing his flesh.

But soon enough jittery thudding pierced the night, and the noise of hooves on cobbles brought him back to reality. Cain shivered as the cold air snaked toward him from the direction of the rider.

Echoes thumped in his ears, like the pounding of metal as he forged blades, and the air seemed to hiss.

He punched a fist into his palm, jerking himself into action. He must distract the rider. Save the girl. *For Lily!*

Cain took a deep breath and made for the town. He could hear the *clip clop* grow steadily louder, reverberating down the alleys, clicking in his mind like a clock signalling the time he had left to live.

Then, in the moonlight, he spotted the figure at the corner of the very same street he was headed down.

The rider had no shadow.

Cain tried to swallow, only to find that his throat was raspy, deprived of moisture, more parched than after a day's work in the smithy. Hot flames seemed to burn in his mouth.

He snatched his eyes from the sight of the rider and inhaled deeply to calm his nerves. But when he did, a pungent odour permeated his nostrils, stinging the tender skin inside and crawling through his face. His eyes began to water.

Something salty dripped into his arid mouth. Then something bitter…

Metallic.

Move Cain, remember Lily. Save her.

He had been unable to aid Lily when she choked to death giving birth to Karl. Pleading prayers to the Gods had all remained unanswered.

Lily.

She had been volunteering in the previous siege, serving rations to the soldiers in the valley during their offensive march. She should never have left the city walls – he should have prevented her.

Run.

An arrow had pierced her chest and collapsed a lung, an injury she had been lucky to survive. Ever since then, she had suffered from constant cramps and shortness of breath. But she had never complained, and they had all nearly forgotten her affliction.

Until the difficult birth of Karl last year completed the ruin of her fragile body.

Don't go.

Cain remained frozen. He stared into a vision of her shining eyes, that had never been dimmed by suffering. They held him there, unfaltering sparkles.

But he needed to flee. *Now.*

The rider was close, too close.

He ripped away from the wall and in a stumbling run, slipped around the next corner. Good. The rider had seen him, meaning he'd successfully diverted attention away from Adrianna.

Lily.

The whinnying neigh of the horse followed him as the rider jerked on the reins. Hooves beat in a vicious rhythm, underpinned by the screeching of metal horseshoes skidding across the stone.

The street seemed to tilt in Cain's vision, rebelling against him. He swayed over to the right, ducking into another, smaller alley.

Louder and louder came the thudding, and his ears screamed for release. He smelled the wet foam from the horse's mouth, hot breath nibbling his neck. There was no time.

And the pounding was there, in his mind, hammering away, over and over.

Again.

You failed Lily. You can't fail me.

A hand descended to clutch his shoulder, yanking him into the air. His body smashed against the smooth flank of the horse, and tears streamed uncontrollably from his eyes, down the weathered lines of his face.

"The girl," came a sibilant voice. "Where is the girl?"

Cain didn't respond. Thoughts ricocheted within his brain, and he closed his eyes, as metal bars seemed to grow up from the ground. Trapping him.

Wispy slithers of darkness wrapped around his body, squeezing tightly. He began to gasp for breath as a strange compression assaulted him.

Was this how she had felt?

The air spluttered out of his lungs.

The world bucked beneath his body.

14

IMPRISONED BELIEVER

I am Alexander. My name means defender, protector of the people.

And yet, in the name of my father the Emperor, I bring terror to foreign lands.

I am prisoner to his whims. I blame it on *them* for forcing me, but in the end I am responsible for my own actions.

And so, I am a prisoner of myself.

The storm clouds rage around inside my head. There is only ever this confusion. I rock back and forth between different emotions, as I struggle to cope with what I have done.

Oh, yes I have done so much. And none of it am I proud of.

I send men into battle and I watch them trample cities beneath their feet. I hear the screams of crushed civilians echoing constantly in my mind.

Failure! I have failed my mother's people.

I am trying to break free from this spell. I heal the wounded, tend to the dying, attempt to atone for my crimes. Yet what does it mean to save a few lives? What does it mean, compared to all this destruction?

I must do more.

I need to escape.

I want to escape, just as I want it all to end.

But I am a prisoner of myself.

* * *

Sweating, the prince surfaced from his thoughts. He sat alone in his tent, where he always sought refuge after they pitched camp. He would go there, and he would grapple with the demons conjured by his mind. Sometimes he wept, other times he raged. It all depended on what phase of the madness he was in.

His mother. Her people.

Alexander remembered what tonight meant. She had taught him when he was a young boy, when her protective arms had still sheltered him from his father's tyranny. She had sacrificed everything to try to raise him as a good person. Now, every day, he ached with the knowledge that he was failing her.

At least if he had turned out cruel like his father, he would be able to simply forget her. But he was not cruel. *Just weak.*

He could not understand how he had inherited such weakness. His father had strength, however much of a monster he was, and his mother had shown great courage in raising him. Even in her dying moments she had been brave, withstanding without a scream the torture she had endured.

Tonight was Midsummer, celebrating the Gods of her people. He prayed to those deities instead of the ones his father worshipped – that commanded human sacrifice.

But he wondered if his prayers would ever be answered.

He rose to his feet and moved across the tent, searching for a candle.

He lit the candle. He lit it for her.

He lit it for the Gods.

And he watched as the little flame grew brighter.

15

UNEXPECTED VISITOR

Fredrik sat mindlessly turning the pages of the book in his hands. He wasn't looking at it. He wasn't reading. He was just breathing in deeply and recalling the words of the young storyteller.

Still mesmerised, ears still aching for the sound of her voice, he stared blankly ahead at nothing in particular.

"Someone's pensive tonight."

Fredrik glanced up at his cousin who had walked over from the cluster of ladies on the other side of the room. She giggled and sat down beside him, swishing the skirts of her dress as she did so.

"What are you thinking about?" Thera persisted, when he made no reply.

"Nothing."

She pouted and began to twirl a strand of her long blonde hair. "You're not thinking about the storyteller, are you?"

Fredrik didn't answer. He didn't want tedious, superficial chatter to spoil the memory of the girl's enthralling words.

"Well I'll just go then." Thera stood, her lips curved downward with noticeable disappointment.

"Sorry, I'm just..." Fredrik fell silent, his voice trailing away. He returned instantly to his brooding, thoughts focussed on the girl. Recalling how she had stood there by the river, face shining from the bonfire flames and her own inner, fiery zeal.

Then a distant shout from outside startled him, followed by footsteps hurrying along the hall. No one else seemed to have noticed, too occupied with their drinks and whatever they were gossiping about.

But something compelled Fredrik to rise, and he tossed his book down on the couch. He rushed from the candlelit room with the image of the storyteller imprinted in his mind, the magnetic blue eyes of the girl staring into his soul.

Outside in the hall only a few torches provided light. The flickering flames made shadows wriggle across the floor. They appeared alive, like spirits.

He looked toward the staircase that wound down to ground level and the main palace entrance. Sounds whispered up the steps, faint shuffling echoes that grew louder in volume, until he caught his father's voice.

Fredrik hurried in the direction of the noises, a little unsteady on his feet after the liquor he had been drinking. The polished wooden floor reflected the light of the torches, to create a piercing orange glow that stabbed at his head.

Then silhouettes appeared before him.

"Father?"

He spotted Melchior at the top of the steps. Despite his reeling mind and the dim lighting, Fredrik could see the deep, creased knots in his father's brow.

"Father, what is going on?"

There were guards on the steps behind. Holding something. A body.

He gasped as he saw it was the girl.

"Father?"

Melchior grabbed hold of his shoulder, nudging him aside. "Go to your chambers."

"Father?" he repeated again.

The guards were hurrying past him now, the heels of their boots clicking on the wood. The sharp, staccato sounds spiked his thoughts, preventing them from properly forming.

"What happened?" Fredrik insisted.

She was right before him: limp in the arms of the guards, a ruby slash on her cheek and a bead of sweat on her brow. A torch directly above them shone light upon her face, and her graceful neck cast a long shadow that speared the pendant between her breasts.

His father held him back and the guards moved on, while shockwaves of emotion struck Fredrik. He felt like a little boy again, crippled by grief. The sight of the lifeless girl triggered bitter memories within his heart – of his mother's death.

"Mother."

The word slipped out of his mouth and he saw his father's expression darken. A strong arm wrapped around him, holding him tightly.

"Get some rest my son. She is only unconscious."

Fredrik swallowed, nodding senselessly. The guards disappeared, taking the body into one of the guest rooms, while his father helped him to his own chambers.

"Rest my son."

Fredrik collapsed down onto his bed, the sight of the girl and her limp body embedded in his mind like a thorny splinter.

Mother.

Stricken with fever, dripping with sweat, he remembered the day that life had been sucked out from her once and for all. He felt it as though he was her. Confusion pummelled him as so many images and memories started turning through his mind.

The minutes stretched on. He just lay there.

Then footsteps sounded again outside. A solid, real sound, they distinguished themselves from the murky swirling of his thoughts, like a clear dewdrop in turbid water.

"My son?"

A hand touched his forehead. His father was here again.

"She looks like... like mother," he murmured.

"Yes."

"Is she alright?"

"Yes."

Fredrik swallowed. His father's blunt responses gave him no calm, instead only fuelling a deep longing within him to know more.

He remembered being a little boy. He had forgotten, but now it came back. They had said it was illness. They had said she was contagious, and for months she had remained alone in her room.

He remembered a few whispers. His uncle. *Pederos.* The uncle he had never known.

"My son, rest now. We will speak in the morning."

The hand left his brow.

Silence. Then came the sound of the door closing, shutting him in, away from the world.

But he heard his father's footsteps, echoing down the hallway like the voice of fate, reminding him of a time and place far, far away.

Reminding him of a memory that was not his.

16
SECRET ADVISOR

Allow the ink to run, in this age
of mystical spell
as I bleed through
day into night
the shadows long
with ancestral spirits
roaming into
the opening crevices
of a heart
that's ready to be
reborn

* * *

Melchior stood at the window, looking out over the moonlit courtyard and playing the scene over in his mind: the sight of the girl who had appeared, stumbling after the guards. Then the touch of *their presence*, along with the tug on his heart that had told him he must see her. Take care of her.

Instinctually, he knew who she was.

Sighing, Melchior turned from the window. She was safe now, tucked inside the palace walls. He resisted the urge to go and check up on her yet again, and instead made for the stables. He knew he wouldn't sleep, and though he hoped his suspicions were true, though for years he had yearned for reunion, the reality of it made him shake inside.

There was no safe solution. But he knew of one person who could help.

* * *

Melchior spurred his horse onwards, pressing his knees harder against the beast's muscular flanks. Through the trees of the Kayamara Wood he rode, cantering blindly in the night, his body slapped by recoiling branches.

He was deeper in the forest now and could feel the energy of the ancient trees. A thick veil of tension hung between the foliage, but the spirits did not resist him. They knew he had permission to enter this land.

He gulped for breath, his lungs expanding and contracting with sharp ferocity. Air rushed by him in gusty eddies, and the dull thudding of the stallion's hooves hammered in his ears. He could feel the desperation rising in him, an almost violent desire to have the truth confirmed.

Bolting blindly forward, guided only by intuition, he finally arrived at the clearing and jerked at the reins to bring them to a halt. He tossed his hood back, pausing for a moment to savour the fresh night breeze before he dismounted with a leap.

He tethered his steed to a nearby tree, then made for the rundown hut at the far side of the clearing. Overgrown with vines, it looked like a malignant growth on the forest floor. A dim yellow glow shone through the windows, its light almost sickly in comparison to that of the blazing moon that peeped through the canopy above.

As Melchior approached, he saw a man standing before the door. So he was expected.

"Your daughter has returned."

He had had no time to gather his wits before those verifying words came to jar his ears, and simultaneously confirmed both his hopes and his fears.

"So it is true?"

Erik nodded, tangled silver hair bobbing around his face. Eyes the colour of midnight black, like giant pupils, stared deep into Melchior's own.

"Come good king." The old man smiled, a wide grin revealing crooked teeth that caught the gleam of the moon. "Fear not. You will have your answers."

Melchior took a deep breath and stepped inside the hut. Smoky incense assaulted his nose, the strong fumes making his own eyes water.

"Forgive me," Erik muttered, apologising for the effect of the smoke.

"Not at all." Melchior knew the sage needed these vapours for his arts. But they caught the king off guard and he had to pause while his senses adjusted to the new atmosphere.

"Come." Erik motioned to the little oak table, and Melchior took a seat on one of its rustic wooden chairs. He scrunched his nose, the source of the smoke right before him now. Steam the colour of volcanic ash spewed up from a bowl of thick, bubbling liquid.

"My daughter…" his voice trailed away.

Erik passed him a cup of water and he drank greedily, as if to quench not only his thirst, but also his concerns that history might repeat: only this time, so much worse.

"Not yet," the sage said. He moved away from the table, disappearing into the opposite corner of the hut behind a curtain of haze.

Melchior waited, his muscles tense as the questions spiralled around in his mind. He needed answers. Not so much for him, but for her.

Then Erik returned with a bird perched on his hand. The creature hopped onto the table and began to drink from the bowl, and Melchior peered at it with curiosity. As he followed its movements, his head inched closer to the fumes and he felt their strange, mind-numbing sensation. They seemed to wash thought and feeling away, making space for the maddening thrill of emptiness. For the void.

"He needs it to recover, poor dove," the sage murmured lovingly. He caressed the bird's plumage with one long, gnarled finger. It stopped drinking, cocked its head, and turned around to face Melchior: a gesture which exposed its grotesque deformity.

Half the bird was white. Pristine dove feathers, snowy and unruffled.

The other half was burnt, making it look like a demonic creature. Its one beady red eye stared at Melchior with a vicious intelligence that made him flinch.

Then came Erik's voice: "Regofala has fallen."

Melchior sprang upright in surprise, accidentally striking the cup with his hand. It rolled off the table, the glass splintering into pieces that crawled like spider webs across the floor.

"A new front?" he asked, taking a deep breath of the soothing, emptiness-inducing smoke. He was getting used to it again.

"You will know soon. Trust in Jerim when he arrives."

"Jerim?"

"He commands the forces of Narda and Lamina. Recently they united to improve the coordination of the northern defensives," the sage explained.

Melchior committed the detail to memory, calmer now that he was focusing on reliable facts that he could understand. Unlike…

"My daughter."

Erik smiled, a chilling grin. "You want to know whether you should make it public."

Melchior suppressed the unease he felt at having his intentions and feelings already known to the elder. "Yes. Will she be in more danger if we reveal her?"

The creases in Erik's face deepened as he frowned. "The Henalas are not the only threat, you know."

"What do you mean?"

The old man simply waved his hand in dismissal and muttered some indecipherable words. Melchior struggled to fight back his irritation. He knew the sage would only say what he wanted to, and never a word more.

Yet he trusted him. He had to.

"I must tell you first, that you cannot visit me again," Erik warned. "It is no longer safe." His eye shifted colour, an inky spark amidst the black.

As though vying for attention, the dove opened its beak to release an angry squawk. Two distinct noises twisted together, one coming from the mangled, ruined half of its beak, and the other from the side smooth as a polished pebble. It was like conflicting sounds lunged at each other, wrestling for control.

"Son of Peace," Erik whispered, calming the bird. Melchior waited, and finally the answer he needed came. "Your daughter must have her coronation as soon as possible. Times have changed, you cannot deny her birthright any longer."

Melchior closed his eyes and once more inhaled the misty air, this ethereal fog with no grounding in reality, timeless, free, and uncertain. A reminder for him to let go of trying to control the future. To let go of any attachment to a belief in how things *ought* to be.

"But what about the danger? And what if…" His voice trailed away, unable to bear the thought that had sprung into his mind. He'd already mourned her once, thinking her dead. What if it happened a second time? For real?

"My friend," Erik said, placing a hand on the king's arm. That was unusual, for the old man normally never touched people, or animals for that matter. Birds were the only exception. "You must not make choices on her behalf. It is up to her now, and we cannot interfere, not in any way. Besides, the ceremony will strengthen her. The drink will enhance her spirit."

"And what if she is not ready? What if it enhances the wrong qualities?" Melchior asked, staring long and hard into Erik's dark eyes.

"Then she will never be."

17
SCENT OF REMEMBRANCE

Arian woke in the most comfortable bed she had ever slept in. Her body rested atop a springy mattress, and a soft blanket caressed her flesh. Looking around, she saw a richly decorated chamber.

But the unexpected surroundings made her body shudder with unease and a rising storm of questions. Searching for a clue, she tried to remember the events of the previous night. All that she recalled was the sight of the horseman upon his stallion, rearing in the moonlight.

Arian sat up, suppressing those sinister memories as the palace splendour consumed her attention. She lay in the middle of a magnificent bedchamber, with a bathing room and sitting room adjoining it. The floor was formed of tessellating patterns of different coloured wood, while a painting of fruit trees and birds covered the ceiling.

Across from the bedchamber was an archway, with the sitting room visible beyond . She spotted a small cedar table surrounded by chairs, piled high with pastel blue cushions.

Arian slipped out of bed and walked over to a window, framed by gauzy drapes matching the colour of the cushions. She opened the hatch of the window to let in some fresh air, and the bustling sounds of the city's markets drifted up to her ears. Gazing out, she took in the comforting sight of the palace towers and imagined herself as a noblewoman, watching over her realm…

Then a noise came from behind and Arian turned to see a girl in a little white frock. The young maid performed a low curtsey, her plaited blonde hair dangling on either side of her oval face as she bent.

"I hope you slept well, miss," the girl said. "Now, King Melchior will see you soon. I will prepare hot water if you want to bathe, and bring clothes. Breakfast is in the sitting room, quite a feast His Majesty ordered! And when you are finished, you may go to the gardens until called for."

Arian frowned, opening her mouth hesitantly. "What is happening?"

The maid shrugged. "I don't understand. Last night all of a sudden His Majesty was here, ordering me to patch you up and get you ready for bed. You were in a sorry shape, arms bruised, a cut on your face. Cannot say I know what everything means..."

"Please," Arian interrupted. But she didn't speak further, and simply looked out of the window again. Despite the sanctuary of the palace, anxiety began to sprout its ugly black flowers in her mind. So now the king had interest in her, and although that was preferable to the men last night, she had only ever received attention when telling stories. It was as though she didn't know how to interact, unmasked in the real world.

"I'm sorry miss, please excuse me. Would you like a bath?"

Arian nearly jumped at the mention of bathing, which was such a luxury for the poor. It had been so long since she had had a bath that the prospect of doing so actually made her feel uncomfortable. "Ah…" But she should accept the offer. She had to meet with the king after all. "Yes, thank you."

The maid nodded, her hazel eyes glinting. "Well then, if you would like to go and eat now, I will prepare your bath and bring clean clothes."

"Thank you," Arian repeated, managing a smile. "What is your name?"

"Well… it's Sarah. But really…" The girl dropped her eyes to the floor.

"Thank you, Sarah," she whispered, the power of the word pulsing in the air. Names shouldn't be hidden.

There was an awkward pause, but then Sarah beamed and darted off, leaving Arian to wander to the sitting room for breakfast.

Indeed a king's feast, there were pastries filled with cream and berries, little jam and custard pies, a platter of fruits, and a jug of yellow juice. She took a seat on one of the cushioned chairs, like none she had ever sat in before, and tentatively began to eat. Buttery pastry flaked effortlessly and dissolved in her mouth, and fresh cream melted upon her tongue.

She sighed, having forgotten that food could bring such a sensual experience. Then she shivered, chilled by the realisation of how fortunate she was to enjoy even just this simple moment here. Irrespective of what was going to happen next.

When she had eaten all that she could manage, she made for the bathing room where a huge tub of hot water was releasing scented steam. For a moment she just stood there, watching the vapour rise in lazy rings. Delicate, fragile, unable to hold its own form, the individual rings merged into a cloud of white fog.

Her lungs filled with the moist warm air and then she exhaled slowly, feeling the embrace of the steam curl around her. Seductive. Almost. It lured her in, telling her there was nothing to fear. The water would not hurt her.

Arian eased into the bath and felt the silky fluid envelop her body, the water thick from the perfumed oils. She closed her eyes, and the smell of frangipani aroused memories from so long ago.

Tarvesi.

She saw Mathieu bringing water from the well, and Jasmine picking the flowers for her bath. The beautiful young couple had been more like parents to her than her real ones.

Frangipani flowers.

She squeezed her eyes shut, clenching her fists. Her nails dug in hard as the cold winter ground beneath her feet, when she had fled with Jasmine for the capital. When Jasmine had laid her head upon the frozen earth, unable to continue. Her body ruined, destroyed by the journey, lustrous hair now a scraggly clump of grey. Eyes, once sparkling emerald like the Herramekan Sea, had faded to a hollow and dim echo.

She gritted her teeth.

No teeth to grind.

She gulped, and snapped her eyes open to escape from the vision.

No!

Arian gasped, noticing coils of blood in the hot water, blossoming in serpentine forms. She saw her nails had carved deep crescent slits into her hands.

"I have a dress for you on the bed!" Sarah's cheerful voice filtered into the misty room. "I have others to attend to now, but if you want to see the gardens, take the stairs at the end of this hall."

Caught in the aftermath of her vision, Arian was unable to reply. But it was over. Her muscles loosened, the trance broken.

She kept herself present by moving. She towelled herself dry and returned to the bedchamber, to find the dress that Sarah had promised. It was made of lilac silk, beautiful like her Soonadan clothes had been. She put it on and approached the ebony-framed mirror.

Tight around her slender waist, the gown flared out on either side in a similar fashion to the one she had worn for midsummer. Short sleeves hung off the edges of her shoulders, and silver thread lined the neck. It was a perfect fit, as if made especially for her overnight.

She observed herself, looking like a heroine from one of her stories. Although it seemed unnatural and unreal, she nevertheless savoured the momentary thrill of being in the palace. Her quest for truth had failed in Soonada, but perhaps the answers lay here. For too long locked away, secrets in stories, perhaps she could at last unravel the threads and solve the riddles.

A mark on her left cheek added something more to her image. A dull red line ran from below her eye to her jaw, probably from the fall last night. Proud, defiant eyes stared back at her, blue eyes that seemed almost not quite hers.

Arian coaxed her gaze away as fanciful ideas began creeping in again, and turned her back to the mirror. Dreaming could be good, when it filled you with motivation. But it could also be dangerous. Make you greedy, pull you into fantasising about a future that did not exist, until you lost touch and failed to appreciate the present.

She needed a distraction, and so decided to explore the gardens to pass the time. At the door, she found a pair of slippers matching the dress. Then she cautiously turned the handle and peeked out into the corridor, to be hit by the full grandeur of the palace.

Tall marble columns stretched up to the ceiling, decorated by frescoes and embellished with gold leaf. Portraits of Renala's rulers lined the walls, and the floor was polished timber from the Kayamara Wood.

Warily, Arian walked along the hall in the direction of the staircase. She descended it to the lower level, and pushed at a heavy oak door. As it opened into the gardens, vibrant colours inundated her pupils, bringing the memories of Soonada back into her mind.

She clenched her hands again to control her emotions, wincing as her nails traced over the recent scars. But the sensation reminded her to let go, and she inhaled deeply, focussing on the courtyard. She spent a few moments just watching the water splash from the hands of a sculpted woman, and tumble down into the marble basin. Roses circled the fountain, pearly petals bright against the stone.

Then Arian followed a pebble path leading to a bench, where she sat down to try and relax her thudding heart. Her eyes traced the contour of a nearby archway, covered by a vine that had huge violet and cream flowers. A sugary aroma with undertones of lemon seemed to be coming from that direction.

On the other side of the garden, the ruby fruit of apple trees shone between leafy foliage. Slithers of sunlight peeked through the branches, dappling the grass and tinting it a thousand shades of green. Luscious and alive with colour, it glinted like the Herramekan Sea.

Calmer now, Arian allowed herself to return gently to the past. She had to look at it sometime, or else it would keep trying to force its way up and she'd remain forever in internal conflict.

She remembered sitting on the balcony of her Tarvesi house, peaceful and untouched, with its whitewashed walls and a position on the cliff top. It was like she was right back there with Mathieu, who was picking grapes for her, popping them into her mouth. She could almost taste their refreshing juice sparkling all over her tongue, while she watched the sun set over the water and tinge the wave-tops with fuchsia and gold.

Oh, the sea!

A beautiful gem, how it had radiated with vibrant hues. One day turquoise and other times emerald, or a rich lapis during a storm.

Until that night, so black, to gaze down into an endless abyss would have been brighter.

It was all so vivid again, the images playing over in her mind with such sharp clarity.

Why now?

Answers. She needed to know why the Gods had punished them, what crime had been committed.

Why?

She thought she had passed that stage. That she'd found acceptance and turned to the future, forgetting the pain and moving on. Never to look back, only forward. Advancing with trust and faith.

Recall.

The voice sounded in her mind and there was no way of stopping the flood. When things have been suppressed for too long, it gets to a point that they come bubbling up in an explosion. Now, something forced the memories upon her.

18
BLACK WATERS

Urgent hands shook her awake as screams sounded outside. Burning, she smelled burning, but a different type of scent to the sweet aromas of their fire in the wintertime. This was different: the chaos of fighting, as men bled and houses blazed. These were the flames of evil men, razing a beautiful trading city to the ground.

Jasmine pulled her out of bed and hurriedly wrapped her in layers of warm clothing. Then she dragged her from the room, not pausing to gather any possessions.

Arian had nothing but her father's pendant, which was supposed to be special and bring aid in times of darkness.

Not that she would ever know its mystery. Not now.

* * *

Airy voices joined the tinkling chorus of birds, bringing Arian back to the present. She turned to spot several ladies on another seat nearby, and a man reclining on the grass with his back against a tree. He looked so casual, in simple brown leggings and a loose cream shirt.

Then he stood up, nodded to his companions, and began walking toward her. Arian simply froze. She didn't even know how she'd missed the group before.

She should have jumped to attention and curtseyed, but it was too late.

"Adrianna?" The prince smiled kindly as he sat down beside her.

Arian's response gushed out of her in a rambling tumble, lacking her usual eloquence. "Please, Your Highness. Last night... strange people pursued me.

I just wanted to find safety. Hitting a royal guard seemed the only way to get entrance to the only safe place in the city, and…" She paused, in need of breath, only to notice the strange look in the prince's eyes. They seemed grey, his expression sorrowful.

"Please, don't worry."

But thoughts of her grandparents were sharpening her attitude abruptly. She had to make sure they were alright.

And Cain, too.

Remembering him made tears sting her eyes, and she jumped to her feet. "I need to go," she said roughly, heedless of whom she was addressing, swept up in the whirlwind of her confusion.

The prince had risen as well, his eyes glued to hers. "Please," he said again.

Breathing deeply, Arian controlled herself and fought the impulsive behaviour that was making her act rudely. "I'm sorry, my lord. I just don't understand anything. I don't… I don't know how to behave, or even why I'm here. And my friends and family…"

Her lip quivered as she spoke those last words.

Glimmering sea, swallowed by black.

* * *

She rushed out of the house with Jasmine, terrifying sights and noises assaulting her senses even more. She stumbled with fatigue and fear, unable to carry her own weight. Then Jasmine picked her up, somehow finding strength despite her own petite form.

"Father, where is father? And Mathieu?" she called amidst the chaos. Jasmine didn't reply, and deep down she knew the answer. They had gone.

The pair sought refuge in one of the cliff's many caves, where they watched merchant vessels and fishing boats burning in the port below. Foreign ships were unleashing the terror, their black sails invisible against the night sky.

She screamed despite the safety of their perch, and Jasmine pulled her close to mask the child's eyes from the horrors. Jasmine had been the mother she had never had. The mother who had rocked her gently all night long on that fateful night, to the rhythm of hopeful lullabies.

Then, dawn.

The sun had dawned over the sea. But though the waters were lovely once more, Arian only saw the blood and the carnage. The daylight revealed the full extent of the massacre in the destroyed city. The evil men had already fled, their senseless pillage and slaughter complete.

Throughout the day she waited with Jasmine, refusing food and water. Crushed as her spirit was, neither hunger nor thirst afflicted her. Her body was an empty vessel, like her soul was missing.

They waited for the sun to set, and by then Jasmine's anxiety showed plainly upon her youthful features. She was merely a girl herself, marrying Mathieu at fourteen, just several years earlier.

They left the cave and cautiously returned to the city, picking through ruins. Holes from fire arrows speckled crumbled walls, ash staining once pure-white paint. The dead and dying littered the streets, bodies ruptured and torn.

As she passed, pleading empty stares and ghostly moans followed her, echoes that would forever haunt her. Imprinted in her mind, she would remember the faces of all those suffering a slow, agonising death.

When they reached their house, they found nothing but wreckage. From its position on the cliff edge it had borne the full brunt of the attack, and only burnt debris remained. Never would they see that beautiful home again.

And never would that young girl return, after all that death.

19

SHIPS OF DARKNESS

"Adrianna, are you alright?"

Arian opened her eyes and sunlight flooded her vision again. She tottered back down to the seat, her legs shaking.

"Adrianna, I know you must be worried for them. Father is away as we speak, investigating what happened last night. If you give us directions we will send guards to check on your parents."

"My parents are dead," she responded bluntly, surprised at the harshness of her voice.

The prince lapsed into silence, his expression glum. "I am very sorry to hear that," he responded finally.

"It's alright," she said, her voice a sad whisper. Blinking back a few tears, she forced a smile. "Anyway, I never knew my real mother. She died in childbirth."

Sitting beside her, the prince laid a sympathetic hand on her arm, though his eyes avoided hers. "I know how you feel. I don't have a mother either. When I was twelve she died from a high fever, although we suspect she was poisoned by a traitor."

Arian looked over at him. It was her turn to feel unsure. How to console a prince?

He met her gaze now and changed the subject for both of their sakes. "Why don't you tell me about yourself? The story you told last night was marvellous, do you tell many like that?"

She nodded, following his lead to shift the direction of their conversation away from painful topics. "It is what I do to make a living."

"Well, we should definitely employ you as a royal entertainer here at the palace. You spoke beautifully, the best I've heard in years, which is saying something considering where I live and what I've heard."

"Thank you," she stammered. Then, before she could control herself, a harsh laugh at the absurdity of the whole situation burst from her mouth.

The noise attracted the attention of the ladies nearby, who curiously glanced her way. A pronounced smell of jealousy tainted the air, no doubt because she had captured Prince Fredrik's undivided attention.

"Oh don't mind them," he said, noticing her unease. He hurried on with another question. It was almost as if he was trying to distract himself from something. "You have an interesting voice, a slight accent, though your Renalan is perfect?"

"I spent many years in the west," she replied carefully, refraining from using names so as to avoid the memories. There was so much potency in those names.

Smiling, the prince continued. "Well then, since you have such a gift with words, tell me about Soonada. I've never been beyond Renala's borders. Father doesn't like me travelling much, because he cannot risk losing his only child. He refuses to take another queen, and of course there must be an heir to the throne."

Arian nodded in understanding, but didn't respond.

"So," the prince said, his tone slightly insistent. "Did you like Soonada?"

Her eyes widened. "I was there," she murmured hoarsely.

The prince frowned. "Where?"

"I was there!" she repeated. "You would know it from the history books, but I *remember.*"

"Adrianna... what...?" His perfect brows creased into a puzzled frown, as he stammered out those broken words.

Her head began to spin again with surfacing snapshots of a childhood infused by colour, sound and joy. Followed by such pungent pain and bitterness that she could taste it upon her tongue.

She closed her eyes, realising more than ever that detachment didn't work. It made you cold, emotionless, and not quite human.

Words: fill that hole.

She so desperately needed to voice her story.

"I was there," Arian repeated, her voice raspy. The prince just kept looking at her. She wondered if she should calm down, but the pain had pulled all reason away and somehow the prince seemed so caring. He was drawing the one story out of her that she had never uttered to anyone before.

"Oh, you cannot imagine how it was," she whispered. "The way the wind howled and the thunder roared like the booming of cannons. There was something unnatural about that storm, because not a drop of rain fell upon Tarvesi."

She watched the prince shift uncomfortably in his seat.

"You…" he stopped. "The Henalas took them from you?"

A few tears broke from her eyes and Arian nodded vigorously, as if that movement could somehow shake away the trauma.

Here was the prince gazing deeply at her, his eyes shining. Heavy sorrow lay engrained in their depths along with something that looked like pity. Perhaps pity for her, and what she had endured.

"I'm so sorry. I can't imagine how it must be, to have lost so many," he said gently.

Arian swallowed, managing to regain some composure. Her mind returned to practical matters, as it always did. A defence mechanism, snapping up like a lifting drawbridge,

"My lord, please excuse this assumption, but things don't add up. I think someone wants me. Last night, strange men chased me, and that is why I came to the palace. I'm not mad, I swear!"

"Yes, I was there when you arrived," the prince replied. "I don't really understand. Father didn't tell me much either. It's just…" His voice trailed away and he stared off into the distance. "You look like my mother," he said softly.

Arian hesitated, but at the same time failed to really register his words. "I don't understand anything. Last night reminded me of the battle of Tarvesi. Those men were like the men that came in from the sea, on those black-sailed ships that night. I never came close to finding any answer, you know… about that random attack."

"The Henalas are never random," the prince responded. Of course he would know of that battle, widely discussed, with the debate continuing even today.

It seemed the Henalas had influenced the weather on that night, for weather so strange had never been documented before. It had been stormy to conceal the ships, the thunder drowning out the noise of their arrival. But it had not rained a drop, for rain would have prevented them from using the very flames that had secured their victory.

"I know that," Arian replied. "But the purpose of the attack has eluded everyone. I myself spent so many years searching for answers, with no luck. The Henalas no doubt want their secrets kept."

"Of course."

"But I think they are looking for someone," she hurried on. "Perhaps they've mixed me up with someone important."

The prince lowered his voice. "Or maybe they aren't mixing anything up."

Silence descended over the two and Arian shifted her eyes to the fountain and the water pouring from the woman's hands. She watched the ripples fanning out in the pond, and the way the creased water reflected the trees above. A marriage of green and blue, water and earth.

"Adrianna?" His voice was quiet, as if he didn't want to disturb the birds nesting in the trees.

She looked back at the prince, twining her fingers together to steady their shaking. The disturbing feeling that squirmed within her was a blotch upon the dreamlike quality of the morning.

Then the prince reached forward and cupped her chin in his palm, raising it gently. She felt some of her tension soften. She couldn't help but feel so comfortable with him, like she could say anything and it would all be alright. Yet at the same time, the idea of trusting in another human was so alien to her. Her upbringing and experiences had always kept her on guard. She had had to be, to survive.

His eyes penetrated hers, a gaze she could not break.

"Son!"

The voice of the Renalan monarch sounded from behind them, forcing Arian to gather her wits. She hurriedly jumped to her feet to curtsy, nearly tripping over as she did, startled by the sight of the king. He wore a simple tunic and breeches and a tattered travelling coat around his shoulders. Garbed like a poor man.

"A...drianna." He looked as though caught in a trance, but recovered quickly. "Both of you please come."

He gave no further explanation or instruction, and simply turned to walk back to the palace. Arian hurried after him, her eyes fixed firmly ahead, focusing intently to help deaden her inner turbulence.

* * *

For a moment Prince Fredrik just stood there. The curved frown of two handsome eyebrows sat above the inquisitive depths of deep blue eyes, staring after his father and Adrianna.

He was thinking about last night. About Adrianna's body, limp in the arms of the guards, and his sleepless night of thoughts and foreign memories twisting through his mind.

She appeared before him like an enchanting illusion, in a wild and unsettling image. He pictured her hair stirring in the breeze, flame, auburn, and gold in the afternoon light. Her face was lowered timidly to the ground, but then she raised her head, and he found himself looking into those ever-blue eyes. They led him on a journey deep into her soul, and into his own soul too.

In his vision, he watched as the coy girl transformed into a powerful woman standing proudly atop the castle she ruled, a white cloak rippling about her in the gusty wind. She raised a sword to the unblemished sky, and the metal glinted in the sunlight. Around her, the wind picked up speed until it whirled in frenzy, pummelling the pennants raised in her name.

Almost instantly, a force snatched the image from Fredrik.

But one thought remained. And as he willed himself into motion, following his father and the strange girl, he prayed his instincts were right.

20
COLOURS OF THE FLAMES

When the shadows strike
oh I fall
and this kingdom burns
from insanity's grip

When the hunger storms
and my senses leap
through the night fire
I scream, I cry

But oh we are
perfect just as is
and life, she tumbles
around full circle

* * *

Prayer.

It gave Alexander some strength, some confidence. Made him feel less alone, because in those moments he became immersed in the belief that there was a greater power. And that power had the ability to stop his father, to prevent total carnage on earth.

It made him feel better, as a sense of peace and relief would wash over him. In those moments, he could stop blaming and hating himself. Because after all, he had been born this way.

Still, it was up to him to take action.

He had to begin by overcoming his fear of fire, so every night he lit a candle and stared into the flames. He consciously put himself through the torture of looking his fears and weaknesses in the eye, watching as they illuminated before him. The ritual helped him to feel more in control, and more of a man rather than a slave and puppet to his father.

The flame always appeared slightly different. He supposed that the way he perceived it depended upon his mood and his feelings that day.

But on the other hand, the flame was always the same.

Because in it, he would always, always, see his mother.

* * *

The Henalas prince found some comfort in the Meridisian legends. They sang of renewal and a grand circle of life, where everything was reborn in one guise or another. For the universe consisted simply of swirling manifestations of energy that could be neither created nor destroyed, only transmuted.

The stories told of three races: the people of the Earth, the Sea, and the Sky. It was said that every soul was split into three, with a being in every race. Upon death, the split soul would unite and ascend to divinity in the Starry Kingdoms, where the elements of rock, water and air would unify to create a complete being

Ascension was conditional upon living by the Trident Laws – to be Just, have Faith, and show Unconditional Love for all. Failure to abide by these principles resulted in a descent to a fiery underworld, where the soul would atone for its crimes and be cleansed by the burning flames, before being sent above.

There were myths of the Sea People, a race that had fallen into legend. But nothing in history told of a Sky People. So the stories just said that those of the Sky were the Gods themselves, and when you ascended you found your heavenly side.

It gave Alexander some comfort to know that his mother was up there, free from the painful constraints of mortality.

But it also hurt him, because he knew she was watching down from those heavens and could see him.

She could see how much he was failing her.

21
BARREN WOMB

In the clutch
of this dis-ease
I shiver, and I burn
with malignant
unease —

All I knew
all I wanted
washed away
by the rancid river
of your penetrating
unconscious
flaming
touch

* * *

Taalin shivered, her thin blanket offering little protection against the river breeze. The cold pervaded every inch of her skin, sinking deep into her bones. It wouldn't allow her body to rest.

It felt like even the ground beneath her was rejecting her with its hard touch. So close to the river, it should have been a soft and moist, comfortable bed.

Maybe if the earth had felt more inviting, she could cope. But as it was, it just served as a painful reminder of all that she had lost, and how cold and cruel the world could be.

No home.

The snores of her captors echoed mockingly in her ears. The Gods wouldn't even grant her the calm peace of silence.

Peace!

She looked up to the stars as pangs of grief and hatred stabbed once again through her heart, urging her to scream. But there was no use in that. If she cried, her captors would wake. Beat her, spit on her. Shower her with reeking piss.

Taalin pressed her face against the ground to muffle her sobs. If only her mother could glide down on a moonbeam, take her hand, and lead her up and away into the sky. To the Starry Kingdoms, where she could find tranquillity through death.

* * *

She burned. Fire was consuming her heart, and her blood bubbled as a molten liquid, making even her flesh shine furious red.

The body of the child lay before her, spoiled remnant of youth, crippled by injustice.

A corpse.

Too late, she had arrived too late. The wakening call had come from the lips of a ghost, the command an echo in time.

She opened her mouth, howling a tribute to the destruction of purity. The pores of her ethereal skin widened, rifts spewing forth the haunting noise.

But no one heard. No one else mourned.

And she remained trapped, unable to save the others.

22
REUNION

Arian hurried after King Melchior: neither speaking, nor daring to ask why he wanted to talk to her. Instead, she distracted herself by focussing on the wonders of the grandly decorated halls, her eyes darting around to drink in the sight of the many tapestries and paintings. She knew she could get lost for days staring into their intricate detail.

Then the king stopped and opened a door, gesturing for them to enter. "Please, take a seat."

She followed, so nervous that she almost tripped as she entered the room. She didn't see the friendly smile the prince cast her way, and simply sank down into a chair to wait for some sort of explanation.

"Please," Melchior began. "Tell me about the men last night. The guards said you claimed to have been followed."

Arian nodded. "But I don't understand," she stammered, after describing what had happened. "The horseman knew my true name, though I disguised myself for so long." She paused, realising she had revealed too much.

"Your true name?" the prince asked. She could feel his inquisitive stare, while the king's cobalt eyes trapped her own. It felt as if he was reading all her secrets.

She lowered her gaze to her fingers, noticing that they were shaking uncontrollably. She tried to steady them by grabbing at the hem of her dress and continued her story. "I... I lived in Vulesa after Tarvesi was attacked. I don't know why, but there I was instructed to assume the name Adrianna, and have done so ever since."

King Melchior was leaning forward now, gripping the table that separated them.

"In Tarvesi, you lived with Pederos?"

Arian opened her mouth, shocked. He knew, oh he *knew*.

How?

"Yes," she murmured. "We had a cosy home by the sea, four of us living there. Father had a nephew, Mathieu, who had been orphaned at fifteen. He was married to a young woman named Jasmine, and since she couldn't have children of her own, she treated me like her daughter." The words were springing out of her now, yearning for their story, *her story*, to unravel in the light of day.

Arian paused, feeling the rush of her emotions. The prince's hand brushed her arm, as though giving her permission to continue.

"You see, my real mother died in childbirth… I have nothing left of her. My grandparents in Linuina, her parents, never spoke of her. But… but the horseman… Your Majesty, they may be in danger."

The king's shoulders sagged as he looked down into his hands. "I will have men check on them," came the uncharacteristically muffled voice of Renala's leader.

Arian took a deep breath before she dared to ask: "and what about me?"

"Your true name is Arian."

The king had looked up again to meet her eyes, and she stared across at him, her mouth slowly widening.

She couldn't bring herself to ask him how he knew. Strange, black-cloaked men knew a name she'd disguised for years, and now the King of Renala himself. There was no explanation for it.

Her heart thudded faster as the king passed her a piece of parchment.

"Read this."

She took the document with trembling fingers. Part of her hoped it would finally reveal to her the truth. Another part wondered if she even wanted to know it.

She sat there frozen in silence. Her lips mouthed the words on the page but her brain refused to comprehend.

Then the prince ripped it from her, and read two words aloud for them all to hear.

Princess Arian.

The sound vibrated around the room and its three motionless occupants, the syllables hanging in the air.

"There must be some mistake," she murmured, avoiding eye contact. But on the edge of her vision, she spotted a tear leaking out from one of the king's eyes.

She waited for him to speak, and when he did, she recognised the detached tone. It was the very same emotional detachment she had resorted to, to protect herself and close off from the pain of losing loved ones.

"Kristina and I had a daughter, three years after you, Fredrik, were born. You'll remember the months she stayed in her room, ill." The king paused, and she could tell he was struggling. He had seen his people die in battle, but this was another matter.

"We smuggled her to Tarvesi in the Soonada Kingdom, with the lie that her mother had died in childbirth. Pederos, Kristina's brother, was looking after her. He was a spy, and one of our best – no one should have been able to trace the connection."

The prince had been sitting just as still as Arian, but as the stories aligned and realisation dawned on him, he leaned forward to grab the edge of the table. His cheeks turned an aggressive red hue. "Why hide her?" His tone was bitter, but then it became sorrowful. "Oh father, why did you deny her birthright?"

The blood drained from Melchior's face, leaving it pale as the whitewashed terrace houses of Tarvesi. His blue eyes, though not as lustrous as those of his children, lost their shine.

"Why?" Arian whispered. "Was that why I was never allowed to play with the common children, because of my noble blood?"

Her voice echoed around the room, lost and forlorn, as she found herself ripped from the security of knowing her identity and place in the world. Oh…

But now she had power.

Yes.

Remember the men who burnt your home.

Now she could lead the war against them.

Justice.

And yet…

Who was she?

Her spirit faltered, stumbling lost in a foreign land without any knowledge of its language or culture.

"My daughter!" the king whispered. "We did it all for the best. Why do you think Tarvesi was attacked? Because the Henalas have been after you since before you were born!"

"Why?" the prince insisted.

"We had our reasons," Melchior continued, "reasons that I shall never speak of, for the truth is too deadly." His voice rose, thick with passion and assurance. "But Arian, I watched over you through my spy network. Pederos spent all that time in Vulesa because he was meeting others, to pass on news of you to me. I know of your talents and achievements, I know you can ride and wield a sword, and that you have excelled in everything you have ever studied."

A glimmer, perhaps pride, appeared in the king's eyes. But it quickly faded with the next words he uttered. "Then... everyone disappeared when Tarvesi fell."

She stared at the King of Renala.

"Believe me, Arian," he pleaded. "Kristina and I would never have abandoned you. And I don't understand. We took so many precautions. Your identity had been completely disguised. Only a handful of us knew, and no one who could have betrayed you!

"Arian, all those years I thought you had been taken by the Henalas, and that my spies had been murdered. I resigned myself to that truth, and I mourned you to this day, far more than my dear wife." Shuddering breaths reduced the king, as he choked back heavy sobs. Arian just sat motionless, unknowing of what to do or say.

"Oh, the long nights I sat, begging that the Gods had given you a quick death and spared you from abuse at the hands of the Henalas. My daughter, I love you."

With both his arms, the king heaved the table separating them sideways. The next moment, Arian found herself in his embrace, being squeezed tightly as if he could sense all the empty spaces within her and was trying to fill them with his affection.

She relaxed in his hold. Ancient grief merged with unfamiliar joy, a delayed reaction to the unveiled truth, and to so many years alone. She let the tears run freely from her eyes, crying her past away.

None of it mattered anymore, for she had found her real family at last. Once again, the image of the White Woman she had seen in the flames returned like a sign from the Gods.

"Forgive me. I am so sorry, Arian, that you have been living as you have, for seventeen years." Her father sobbed, his distress making her weep more.

"Father," Arian stated, savouring the sound, the word rolling naturally off her tongue. She felt a strength rise within her. She would be strong for him. "There is nothing to forgive."

Melchior pulled away, giving Fredrik a chance to take her into his clutch.

She felt the sweet sensation of warmth radiating from him. It had been so long since she had been held this way. Perhaps the last time was before Pederos, Mathieu and Jasmine had left the realms of earth.

But though her father had relaxed somewhat, his features still showed evident concern.

"Why so grave?" Fredrik begged.

Melchior didn't respond, and she sensed his fears. "Those men last night…" Her words trailed away.

"I sent guards out to search the city," the king began. "But they have no news, yet."

She focussed on her breathing, in and then out. "What will happen to me?" He had hidden her for so long, for a reason he would not reveal. With that same logic, she wondered if this new life she had only just stepped into was about to disappear. "Don't send me away," she begged. "Please, don't send me away again."

Her father shook his head and pulled her close once more.

"I won't." His tone was firm, a deep promise. Yet Arian cringed nervously. She waited, along with Fredrik, both looking expectantly at their father.

"Now," Melchior spoke again. "Fredrik, I want you to stay with your sister. But do not speak about the truth for the moment. You must keep this secret until the ceremony in two days' time."

23
SOUL DEBTS

All I would ask
is for you to hold me
pure and lovingly
erasing your ego
that I feel clawing
for my soul
as though you want
to trap my wild
luminous
Spirit

* * *

Impurity comes with a price.

Blood oozes from open wounds, dripping into the earth. Over and over, down and down.

Numbing, ceaseless hammering, soft but persistent, growing louder in the mind.

Echoing repeatedly, over and over, again and again.

The cycle of suffering repeats.

Weeds splutter up from lifeless soil. Prickly stems, thorns like daggers, growing and blooming maliciously.

Choking, squeezing, tighter and harder.

Razor flowers cut through flesh. Salty, warm metallic blood bursts through ruptured veins.

Cain.

She kept gazing into his eyes as she slept. She saw them flecked with an unexplainable, heavy sorrow.

And now, pain.

Flaming pain, erupting after action so noble but…

Senseless.

Sacrifice comes with a price.

* * *

When sacrifice is impure, it fuels a field of distortions. It's like if we make a gift, but aren't truly giving, instead acting out of an expectation to get something in return. We may not even realise it, so entrenched the unconscious habits of our existence have become.

When sacrifice is impure, we create a debt. A kind of contract between souls, sealed with an entrapping chain, extending into the ether in a helical vortex of contempt.

It doesn't just affect those souls.

It catches others in the sticky web of bondage.

It persists through generations.

And it never allows us to simply *be*. So we find ourselves, unable to truly love from the depths of a pure, free, and unconditional heart.

24
STOLEN IDENTITY

Arian followed her maid down the corridor, which was crowded with people today. She was led past the main doors of the great hall, to one of the small anterooms reserved for royalty and special guests.

Sarah curtseyed. "This is where I leave you, my lady."

Arian nodded her thanks, but her mind was elsewhere. She had just glimpsed her reflection in the golden panel of the anteroom door. It was taking some time to get familiar with her new appearance.

A guard opened the door, and she entered to find her brother. He was dressed smartly in white pantaloons and a brocade jacket of the royal Renalan blue, with golden tassels hanging from each shoulder.

They refrained from embracing, until the door closed and left them alone in the room.

"Sister dear, every noble man will want you, you look that beautiful," he said with an encouraging smile. The dress was another perfect fit, as all her mother's clothes had been. This one was sleeveless, with a low, curved neckline. Pastel pink fabric contrasted subtly with her eyes that radiated light like jewels in the sun.

Sarah had made up her hair in an extravagant arrangement. Half of her long, wavy curls were pulled into a bun at the nape of her neck, entwined with roses and cream flowers, while the rest wisped over her shoulder to frame her face.

"Not more attention!" Arian joked, but with an element of seriousness. Although she felt confident now, perhaps it would be different with a hundred faces turned towards her. She wasn't particularly comfortable with male attention either, or at least certainly not the kind that only wanted her for her appearance.

Her brother kissed her cheek, and she looked up into those eyes, resembling hers. Family: a reason to live for, to stay strong no matter who was after her or what *they* wanted.

She sighed.

Truth.

This was who she was.

"Arian, are you alright?"

She blinked. "Yes." Her voice was hoarse, her words forced. "Yes," she repeated, stronger now.

"Good." He smiled, though she knew concern lurked in his mind too, betrayed by the slight frown.

"Don't worry," she murmured. "We're together now. And father made the choice. It must be the right one."

A trumpet sounded in the hall, cutting further conversation. She peered tentatively through a crack in the door to find King Melchior processing down a red carpet, between the rows of nobles.

He ascended the steps to the stage where Arian could see him more clearly. She watched in admiration as he turned to face the gathering with a sweep of his violet coat. A brilliant gold crown glowed atop his head.

The trumpeter ceased his song, leaving the king standing in silence at the head of the assembly. He gestured for the people to sit, and they did so with a flurry of their bright clothing.

"I call us together on this fine morning, for another day of festivities. After so many disasters, the Gods have provided reason to celebrate further. I believe that a new age is dawning. Because today we welcome an inspiring young leader, bringing hope to face the future and whatever it holds."

Despite the multitude of people, not a whisper interrupted the king's speech, everyone waiting with anticipation for his announcement.

"A new leader, a new chance against our enemies: I am proud to announce my daughter into this world!"

Now the crowd did break from their trance, and uneasy murmurs rippled around the room along with more than a few surprised cries.

But when King Melchior raised his hand, a respectful silence fell once again.

"I have hidden her for many years to protect her from the Henalas. But today, my loyal subjects of Renala, she claims her birthright. I present to you my daughter, Princess Arian. Please welcome her, and join me in celebrating her coronation!"

Arian exhaled as a guard opened the door to the anteroom, indicating for her to proceed. She began to walk down the aisle with Fredrik beside her, and a troop of guards who had swarmed in from behind.

Fredrik cast her a reassuring smile, and she swallowed in an attempt to banish her nerves. From the anteroom, the group had not looked so big. But now it was different. She could feel the mixed energy of the immense crowd, people staring at her in awe, or disbelief, or uncertainty.

Then it was time to mount the steps to the throne where her father sat. Fredrik led the way, first kneeling before the king, then taking his place at a smaller throne on the right.

Her turn now, and Arian curtseyed low and gracefully. She bent her lips to kiss the great ring on her father's index finger, before he gestured for her to rise.

At that moment, another side door opened and a priest entered, followed by a young boy who held a navy silk cushion. A glimmering silver coronet perched atop it, inlaid with diamonds and sapphires.

The priest approached, white cloak swishing against the stairs, and turned to address the nobles. "On this joyous summer day, let us unite, celebrating the coronation of Princess Arian. May we bless her, guide her, and follow her lead. Beneath the Gods we stand, as Princess Arian is crowned!"

When he finished, the young boy accompanying him descended to his knees. The priest took the coronet and lifted it slowly and regally to Arian's head. Then he passed her a crystal goblet, filled with inky blue fluid.

"Do you accept your role, pledging to the Gods to be Faithful, uphold Justice, and show Unconditional Love?"

Arian nodded. "I do."

"Then drink, and embrace the powers of water, rock and air."

She took the cup from his hands. Fredrik had explained the ceremony. She would drink the distillation, prepared from the root of a sacred tree in the centre of the Kayamara Wood. Legend told that it had been planted at the birth of Meridisia, on the edge of the great inland sea occupying most of the region. It was a symbol of the union of earth, sea and sky, and was supposed to awaken the elemental power that dwelled dormant in every soul. The part of every soul that was already one with the wild forces of nature and the spirit of the land.

She pressed the goblet to her lips. Its cold crystal soothed them, before she started to drink and an intense heat flowed into her mouth. The liquid coated her tongue with a bitter film, and a pungent smell of rotten wood coiled into her nose before it softened into a sweeter, nutty aroma.

The fluid coursed its fiery trail down her throat, then into her stomach to warm her insides.

And in one unified sweep, the nobles filling the hall rose to their feet and cheered.

From that moment on, Arian lost all sense of clarity and connection to the scene around her. She didn't realise she had moved to sit beside Fredrik, or that her father had begun another speech. There was only a blur of colour around her, as her senses became distorted by new feelings that surged within.

Once her eyes regained their focus, they were focussed through a different lens. She saw with the eyes of an heiress, the long history and blood of the Renalan Kings running down her veins.

* * *

A lone figure hurried stealthily along the royal corridor, though his precautions were unnecessary. The coronation ceremony occupied all members of the court, while the servants were in the kitchens preparing the coming feast.

There was no one to stop him.

He reached the private quarters of King Melchior before long. The study was locked, but he had been taught how to open it.

Sneaking inside, he began to rummage through the papers in the drawers. When he found the desired item, he left as easily as he had arrived, the document hidden in the folds of his cloak.

He continued in a new direction now, and descended to the ground level where he quickly made for the main palace entrance. This area was guarded, so he weaved through the maze of smaller rooms beside the hall. It wasn't hard. He melted into the shadows, like his people always had.

He found the room with ease. It was a simple one, with a sofa and some chairs, where visitors would wait before an audience with the king. But the parquetry of the floor made it special.

He had been trained well, and despite the distractions of the patterning, he found the edges of the trapdoor and rotated the floor. Then he began down the ladder, until his feet met the stone surface of the passage.

He groped for the lantern, and struck it to illuminate the tunnel. Now he could see his partner, waiting a short distance from the entrance.

"Ahead of time," the other grunted, and waited for his accomplice to hand over the parchment.

The man nodded, silently giving up the document. Then he carefully retraced his tracks, thinking all the while about what awaited him later in the week. It would all be over soon, and the girl would be a pawn for him to command.

Smiling for the first time since he had been given his risky task, the traitor returned to his rooms where he should have been all along.

25
IMPENDING TORTURE

It was coming. The night was approaching.
Soon the destruction would begin again, with his hand commanding it.

Alexander had left his tent to take a walk in the fresh night air. The countryside was beautiful here, as was all of Meridisia.

Until *they* had come along, bringing evil with them.

The north was a spectacular place, with its great mountains and lakes. It was a land of power, of mighty stretches of rock and water, resonating with natural forces.

But he couldn't see that beauty now. To him, it was just the location of his father's seat of power: the land where the Emperor issued tyrannical commands for the conquest of the world.

The prince liked it that his tent was always on the outskirts of the camp, where he was freer. Although in a sense, it proved just how much he was constrained by his own weakness.

But running away was not the answer. If he tried to run, he would be hunted across the land. And if he were not in the lead, then another pawn would be. Either way, it did not matter for the Meridisians.

This was his torture, and he would bear it.

His father didn't need whips anymore. His father knew of his true mental weakness, and so he punished him with it.

* * *

Alexander had heard talking amongst the priests, and he knew that this was going to be a special siege. They were going to fight a new kind of battle.

He shuddered. Not because he knew what sort of conjuring the priests were capable of, but because he had heard rumours about a girl. It made him tremble to think what they wanted with her.

But then, what had they wanted from his mother?

26
RESCUE

The litmus test
for your awakening
measured by
the lotus prayer
in your mind's eye
unravelling a vision
of life beyond
as coming into
new clarity
you rise and shine
as the soaring star
you are

* * *

Someone was shaking her. But his touch was soft, gentle, kind.

His breath did not reek.

Taalin swallowed. Inhaled, then exhaled slowly. She kept her eyes closed, uncertain, and focussed on her breathing.

"I'm not going to hurt you."

His voice was smooth, unlike those of the other Henalas soldiers who could barely speak her language, and whose crude imitation of it grated her spirit just as physically as the chains that rubbed her skin.

Quivering, Taalin opened her lashes a fraction and peered out from beneath the protection of her half-closed lids.

It was night, but a lantern rested on the ground by their side, illuminating the man's weathered face. It was criss-crossed by deep crinkled lines, as if someone had carved his features up with a knife.

He smiled, a warm smile.

Father!

She could not control it any longer. One strangled sob escaped her lips, then another, until she was gasping for breath as hot tears burnt her cheeks. She hadn't properly grieved her father's death, and it was all coming up now.

The man gently pressed a hand over her mouth, silencing her choked cries. She did not resist, for his touch filled her with calm. He began to stroke her hair, fingers untangling her curls, and going deeper still. It was like he was brushing out the contorted knots of painful memory.

Father.

The tears flowed more smoothly now, lacking the disjointed, desperate struggling of before. The grief tenderly unfurled from her heart, as the scene of his death played over in her mind.

Her father.

"It will all be okay."

The voice of the nice man sounded again, like a cool mountain breeze blowing against her face, like a gentle river current washing her body.

"Who are you?"

Her voice was that of a child, the voice of a little girl. Needy. Lost. Weak.

No longer a warrior.

No strength.

Her father was dead. Slaughtered. His head had been sliced roughly from his neck. A few clinging shreds of skin had desperately tried but failed to hold him together.

Broken.

Her father was gone. Her rock. Her earth.

"I have come to help you."

Her eyes widened as she looked into the stranger's murky irises. Brown, warm brown. Kind brown. The colour of the furry squirrels that scurried around in the autumn, gathering nuts to last the winter.

When it was cold. Bleak.

Winter.

"Why?" The concept of help seemed so foreign to her. Both the idea that someone was offering her assistance, and that she could even accept it.

He held a silencing hand to her lips and rose to his feet to peer around the camp. She followed the direction of his gaze, and saw her captors snoring around the remains of a campfire.

Up above, the crescent moon cut a slash through the bitter night sky, a ghostly finger curved like an accusing claw. It shed enough light to reveal her immediate surroundings. They were in a small clearing, surrounded by woods. Tall aspen trees caged her in, the silver bark glinting like a knife's blade.

Her father.

She pulled her knees close, hugging them tightly, suppressing her shivers. Then the man returned to her side. Kneeling down, he took something out of the folds of his cloak.

A key.

Freedom.

She hungrily drank in breaths of the crisp night air.

"Are you saving me?"

His eyes shone in the light of the lantern flame. Warm brown, with a hint of gold.

He nodded. "You must flee west, to Soonada. We are nearing the Great Lakes, and if you do not go now, the Emperor will take you."

The Emperor. He was the one who did this, who commanded the destruction. Destroyed her world.

She opened her mouth to speak. But her lips shook with ugly fear.

Be strong. A voice whispered inside her. Reminding her that she was a warrior, a brave girl.

She was being given a chance to survive. She must live on.

"Are you coming with me?"

Why did she ask that? She was strong and independent. She didn't need to rely on anyone. She was a survivor.

She already knew the answer before the man shook his head. He reached for the chains around her wrists and inserted the key into the lock. With a click, he gave her the gift of freedom.

"I cannot come with you. You need to do this alone. Can you do that for me?"

She stared at him with wide, frozen eyes. But the chains were gone. The weight was lifted. She was free. She could fly like a bird, like Filpai.

Black.

Black arc in the sky, rainbow shadow piercing his white dove wing.

No!

Be strong.

Taalin staggered to her feet, moaning as the wounds on her heels cracked open again. She clung to the pain. Breathed into the pain. Pain was real, and as long as she felt pain, she was living. Alive.

She could survive.

Survive.

"Good girl."

The man smiled at her again, his friendly warm smile. She stared into the cavity of his mouth.

Empty space.

He picked a leather pack off the ground, which she had not noticed before, and handed it to her along with his coat.

"Go now," he urged. "See the star up there?" He waited until she found the bright blotch in the sky that was shrouded by a kind of teal mist. "Follow that star. It will take you to the Fhea Karadid. Can you find your way from there?"

She nodded again, looking up to the guiding light. There was hope.

"Go, young princess. Before it is too late."

She took a small step. Felt the pain rush up through her legs.

But it was okay. Duller now.

Another step.

She glanced back at his face. His weathered face, creased features, engraved frown. He was a kind man, not evil.

"Why me? Why did they spare me?"

She had been the only one to survive. *The only one.* Her people butchered, her home smothered by flames.

The man's expression was sombre. She could sense that he too felt pain.

"If you do not make the choice to go now, the corruption will take us. Find the strength within you. I can do no more."

For some reason, the sound of his voice was different now. It was a low hiss that rasped her ears. Not so friendly anymore.

Her muscles tensed. Then they uncoiled, and launched her forward in a frantic run. She sprinted across the ground with such speed that she could have been an arrow flying through the air.

Escape.

She was free. *She was strong.*

* * *

Pain doesn't have to translate to suffering. Pain is just a physical sensation that the body experiences sometimes, comprehended by the mind.

Suffering stems from pain and attachment. We suffer when we allow our soul to become entrapped by the physical, absorbed in the details of the perpetual cycles of death and rebirth. When we cling to mental meaning in a desperate attempt to make sense of that which the logical mind cannot know.

Suffering comes when we forget that above and beyond all we feel and perceive, there simply is existence. And all souls exist within a fluid, dynamic web, an ecosystem in constant ebb and flow, interdependent but non-attached.

The nature of true existence is that we are already whole.

We are already free.

But we will continue suffering, until we truly *remember*.

And it is in remembrance that we find our true strength.

27

DARK KNIGHT

A whistle blow pierced the arena, and Fredrik leant forwards in his seat. The tournament for the title of his sister's champion had begun, where knights and warriors of the realm would battle for the role of protecting the princess.

First was a knockout round, with the aim being to fight for oneself but work in a team to remove those in the other groups. The competitors only used wooden sparring swords, and elimination occurred immediately if you were touched.

He eyed the action below, only half aware of what was going on, as he thought about his sister. In many ways she was just a stranger. Even though he could feel that strong connection to her, even though his heart swelled with love and joy at their reunion, it was like she existed in an entirely different dimension to him. Like she was separate. How could he even hope to cross that bridge, of all those years and diverging experiences that distanced them?

The line of Arian's jaw, the shallow crease between her brows, all warned of something lurking beneath her young, pretty face. How he wished he could jump into her mind. Perhaps understand a little better.

He probably had many things to learn from her. She had not been sheltered from poverty and hardship, unlike him.

Deep down he cringed, realising that part of him did not want to know about those things. Did not want to contemplate a reality that was outside the protection of his city walls. Did that make him weak?

As the question came into his mind, he realised just how much he was afraid of looking into that weakness.

Then, as if reflecting back at him his own fears, he noticed Arian's face pale – turning white as marble from the northern mountains.

* * *

Arian's eyes were fixed on the black-garbed warrior, his features obscured by a helm and a mask covering his eyes. Darting back and forth, his sparring rod whipped about in a blur, too fast for her to follow.

She tilted her head sideways and squinted at the figure. Opponents scattered in the winds of his swordsmanship, as he moved with the power and ferocity of a storm.

Slicing, stabbing…

"Arian?"

She exhaled as Fredrik spoke her name, realising she had been holding her breath.

"Are you alright?"

"That man?" she asked.

Fredrik smiled. "Brilliant, isn't he?"

"You know him?"

The flicker in her brother's eyes told her that he did. She breathed in deeply again, her heartbeat slowing down.

"Who is he?"

Fredrik laughed. "My dear sister, you will find out soon enough – if he wins that is!"

Calmer, but a little annoyed about the secret, Arian returned her attention to the arena. The more experienced knights had defeated all the hopeful beginners, and the commander regrouped the competitors into pairs for the next round.

"Where's the black knight?" she asked, eyes searching but unable to spot him.

"Fast-tracked to the final," Fredrik responded. "His reward, for eliminating the most opponents."

Another whistle blew, and the men began fighting alongside their partners to defeat the other pairs. Arian's attention bounced from one competitor to the next, as she wondered who would make the final. All bar one were older knights, and none of them moved with the grace of the black figure who had been fast-tracked.

There were four remaining now, all fighting as individuals to secure the single remaining place. Arian noticed the youngest knight drop back, waiting for the others to weary each other. The minutes passed, before he darted in confidently, his sparring rod slicing through the air to knock out his opponents.

Cheers erupted around the amphitheatre at the selection of the second competitor for the final. The youth punched a fist into the air, and looked up at her.

Reminding her of Cain.

Arian closed her eyes, shutting away the sight of the young knight, who was grinning with pride at his victory. Darkness settled in, mottled with red from the arena light that tried to break past her sealed eyelids.

Cain.

She must have whispered his name aloud, for Fredrik wrapped an arm around her. "Sister, dearest."

"Do you know the name of that competitor?" she asked, her voice soft.

"Richard Bettinglam, you speak of," Fredrik replied. "Aye, I've trained with him. He is good. Had a common upbringing, then was invited to join the royal forces after an outstanding display of bravery during the last siege. He's yet to really show his best – probably saving himself."

Arian nodded, trying to prevent her feelings from showing on her face. At least the competition occupied the nobles. The last thing she wanted was anyone thinking of her as weak and emotional.

"Do you want a drink?" Fredrik asked, and didn't wait for her reply to call a servant. "Is everything alright?"

Arian nodded again. "Just… he reminds me of my friend. The one who…"

She didn't finish. Fredrik knew whom she was talking about. The old couple she had known as her grandparents were fine, but Cain hadn't been located, and they all feared the worst.

Arian mouthed a prayer to the Gods that Cain lived on. Or else, that he had been granted a swift passage to the heavens. Then she prayed this young man would not win the title of champion. She couldn't bear the thought that if he did, one day he might also die to save her. The resemblance was uncanny – she wondered if Cain had a brother, realising in that moment how little she even knew about the man who had most probably borne the consequences of the twisted story of her life.

Fredrik handed her a glass, and she sniffed some liquor. She frowned, wishing that it was water instead, but knowing that this would at least help to numb her feelings.

"Just have a little sip." He squeezed her hand reassuringly. "Listen Arian, your friend was a good man. He did the right thing, and the Gods will reward him for it – if that be the case."

She knew he was right. The karmic cycle would rebalance in the end. And one day, perhaps she would make the Henalas pay for what they had done.

She looked back down, just as a stable boy brought two horses through a gate. One was a stocky charger such as those used in cavalry brigades, and the other an elegant black stallion, which the dark knight mounted.

The competitors took their positions on opposite sides of the arena, and squires produced lances for them. Then a whistle pierced the noisy crowd for the final time.

The men charged, meeting at the centre. With a skilful aim, the masked knight knocked Richard easily to the ground, and she winced at the impact. Though she did not want him to win, nor did she want him injured.

But it was not over yet. The youth struggled to his feet while drawing the rapier from his belt. It was time for real weapons. Following suit, the masked man jumped to the floor of the arena, while the stable boy swiftly took their horses away.

"Now you just watch them. The real excitement begins," Fredrik told her, while she nervously clutched the railing.

Arian's eyes did not miss a thing. She watched intently as the two men struggled back and forward. At first it seemed like Richard would easily be defeated, but he gained confidence with every failed lunge of his opponent. Before long they were both parrying and thrusting with equal speed and precision. It was only a matter of timing now.

Then Richard took the upper hand, catching the masked man off balance with a skilful reprise. In his effort to dodge the blade, the black knight tripped over his feet and tumbled to the ground. His helm came off to reveal tufts of wavy chestnut hair, but Arian could still not see his features, because a strip of cloth covered the eyes.

How strange. It must be transparent to the wearer, but opaque to the observer.

She held her breath, begging the Gods that the masked man would regain his feet. To have this Cain look-alike as her champion would be too much for her to handle right now.

"Ha!" Richard laughed in victory, swaggering up to his fallen opponent. He paused momentarily to turn and look up at Arian, as if already swearing his vows.

But then the masked knight hauled Richard's feet out from under him, sending him sprawling face down on the ground. He quickly pressed a boot into the small of Richard's back, confirming his own victory.

The event master arrived in an instant, separating her new champion away from the furious youth. Arian sighed with a combination of relief, and then surprise, at how relieved she was in fact feeling.

She clearly had some inner pain to resolve and to release.

28
TWIN MINDS

Voices called, children wailing for a mother. They pulled her, commanded her, leaving her with no choice. She had to fight. She had a responsibility to the people, an obligation to the Empire, and above all a duty to her land.

Her head pulsed with the echoes of those calling voices. Pounding, hammering.

Release me!

In response to her call, the sounds dimmed. Silky fingers stroked her flesh. A warm, enticing caress drew her close, and a calming voice whispered in her ear. It coaxed her to dance amidst the swirling formations of energy that were starting to spin around her in a mass of vibrant colour.

Colour.

Perhaps different combinations of this colourful energy created life. Maybe pain was felt when colour was destroyed, creating holes in the rich fabric of living memory. When the storm clouds of evil came, and drowned all with their grim, imbalanced rains.

Evil.

Preventing humans seeing a full spectrum, and connecting with the spirit of the universe.

Her eyes stung with sensitivity, cringing from the light as it refracted into more colours than she had ever seen before.

It was too much

Get out of my head.

Maybe this was a sensation that came with suddenly obtaining such power and responsibility.

Perhaps it was just the feeling that accompanied the fact of becoming someone new, and having your identity remoulded.

Or, more precisely, remembering and becoming that soul that deep down, you always were.

Possibly.

*   *   *

Arian recalled the moment of her coronation. Gazing down the aisle to the entrance, to the massive oak doors standing tall and mighty and proud.

Then she looked back in the other direction, towards the throne. Marble pillars reached up to support a great domed ceiling that was covered with engravings and the sculpted faces of previous rulers. Beneath it stretched a wide, open space for people to gather, with a red carpet in the centre that rolled down the length of the hall and up to the dais with the golden throne.

But she didn't look at that. Her subconscious mind had no real interest in that seat symbolising power and status. Instead, she gazed upon the ancient tapestry of Meridisia that hung behind it, sprawling across the entirety of the back wall.

A weaving scene of animals and plants, people and landscapes, covered a navy background. The White Woman stood embroidered in the centre, framed by gold thread. She symbolised learning and knowledge, and held the perfect sphere of a blue-green gemstone raised above her head. The stone reminded Arian of that star shrouded in teal mist she'd seen on midsummer night.

It was the legendary stone of the Gods. It was supposed to guide the wielder, ensuring they made the right decisions for the benefit of the people.

No one knew if it really did exist, for all knowledge of it had been lost in the sands of time.

The tapestry didn't show the White Woman's face either. It was veiled to protect her secrets from those who would misuse them.

Veiled so that people would not understand.

Because one has to be ready to receive such knowledge, or else it can bring great inner pain. For it forces us to face truths and to confront our shadows, and not just ours, but those of the *collective*. At heart we are all one, and to witness collective pain can be an overwhelming experience.

The wielder who is not ready to see often becomes trapped by the flood of new insights, caught up in their own suffering and the cyclical suffering of generations. And then they project their pain further, onto the rest of the world.

Through time and space and dimensions.

29
DANCING WITH FIRE

Somehow I knew
deep in my blood
that we were connected,
beyond this world
that we'd danced before
to a spiralling song
that had carried us through
to a land beyond
where the wisdom of truth
shines bright and fierce
ever guiding us towards
the radiant star
guarding the gates
of our soul's sweet home
defended with light
protected by love

* * *

Taalin ran, darting between the slender aspen trees. Branches whipped her face, while leaves collected up in her tangled hair.

She had kicked off her broken boots, unable to bear them scraping her skin any longer, and now she fled barefoot like an animal. But the hard earth was cutting at her soles just as mercilessly.

She ran. Into the night and the unknown.

Alone.

Pain consumed her, but it kept her in the present, spurring her on. She felt a fire rushing up from her feet, and a burning sensation in her leg muscles.

And her heart raged with the flames of grief, anger and hate, that swirled in a devouring blaze, overtaking thought and reason.

Overtaking even fear itself.

* * *

Arian eyed her champion who stood before her, poised ready for the dance. It was the last one of the night, and she stood alone with him in the middle of the hall waiting for the music to begin.

His armour had been replaced by a forest-green doublet embroidered with gold, and a pair of breeches. He was still wearing a mask, but a different one, with open holes that revealed two soft and gentle blue eyes.

She was grateful he'd changed masks into this one, that made him look more normal and less threatening. Besides, they say that the eyes are the gateway to the soul. It unnerved her to feel blocked from truly seeing: there was something empty about such a blind interaction.

The song began with a crescendo of violins, and she concentrated on the beat. Steps forward and back, then a spin about his body, all very rehearsed and mechanical.

Her champion kept his eyes fixed upon her face, firm and judging like he would to an opponent fighter. Then the music lulled and in that moment of softening, Arian began to let go into its gentle current. She circled him like a tigress, absorbed in the billowing vortex of her skirts.

As the musicians increased the tempo again, she found herself wheeling around the floor in full surrender to the sound. Oblivious to everything but the rhythm, she allowed herself to be guided by something deeper and to move freely, without thinking. She was heedless of her curls escaping their hairpins, or the sweat trickling down her back.

Lost in the faraway place of the music, caught in another world…

Her feet whisked across the wooden floor, this time leading her champion in a furious game of cat and mouse. But he brought them together again with a flick of his wrist, and grasped her firmly against his body. Trapped together in a sensual hold, their legs glided across the floor in perfect unison.

Then the music stopped with a final bang, and rapturous applause erupted through the hall as her partner sank to one knee.

Their hands remained connected, and a ripple of energy flowed into Arian like an electrical charge. She reeled with the sensation, the atmosphere shifting before her.

Suddenly, an eye came into her vision. An opaque dark pupil, stained with vermillion around the edges.

She blinked, the image pulsating before her like a heartbeat.

She faded from the present, head spinning with colours and thoughts, and the music of the dance.

She saw bonfire flames, and felt the heat of Midsummer.

30
COMPLICATIONS

Autumn leaves spiral
through the winds of emotion
that tumble, from my heart
blowing round and round:
then through the cold and darkness
I emerge, to the calling
of a sweet little songbird
that ushers in the dawn —

Before backwards
into winter
I fall

* * *

A faint golden glow spilled through a gap in the curtains and Arian turned over with a gentle sigh, in the bed that had once belonged to her mother. She buried her face against the feathery pillow and smiled in delight at the fresh feeling washing over her. She breathed in the air of her new reality as the leader of an empire, with power to change the world.

Arian waited a few moments, her breathing slow and deliberate. Then she allowed her lashes to open, finding her gaze on the beam of sunlight streaming into the room. As she stared at it, she saw the white light split into the colours of the rainbow, and it seemed to beckon to her like a whispered message from the Gods. So she rose, and the silky covers of her bed rippled off her body like the stirring of forbidden water.

Approaching the windows, her legs trembled ever so slightly as if they had not yet grasped the full meaning of her position. She drew back the gauzy fabric of the curtain with one slender hand, and the morning beauty shimmered before her eyes.

Her back straightened as she beheld the private courtyard where a bubbling fountain glistened in the sun's radiant touch, and an occasional maroon leaf dotted the boughs of the trees.

Gripping the sill, Arian leant out to feel the breeze against her cheek. Then a piercing bird cry broke the enchanting stillness and she glimpsed its origin: a little brown creature with a spotted red belly flickered across the clear sky.

A smile inched across her face. Her dreams would fly soon, like the bird ready to make its journey to the warmer lands in the south, once summer drew to a close.

Arian savoured the thought as she drew back from the window and walked across to her dressing room, slippers brushing against the ornate floor. She covered her nightdress with a mauve silk gown, ran a brush quickly through her hair, then made for the door.

But the moment she stepped out into the hallway she knew instinctively that something was amiss. The air hung thick with the weight of an unnatural gloom, dulling the splendour of the palace.

The creak of another door sounded from down the hall, and in the next moment her brother appeared, exiting his room. Fatigue lined his features, and great black smudges smeared the skin beneath his puffy, bloodshot eyes.

"Uh, Arian," Fredrik said with a slur, rubbing his forehead.

"Drank too much last night, did you?"

"Aye, and…" He stumbled and caught himself, coming to lean against a marble statue for support while he woke himself up. "Father called me. He needed to see me, urgently."

Arian paused, her mouth opening and closing without a word. "Why?" she finally managed. "He didn't call me. What on earth could he want?"

"That's what I want to know too," Fredrik grumbled with a shrug. Then he sidestepped her and continued dragging his reluctant body down the hall.

"Fredrik?"

He motioned for her to go in the other direction. "I'll see you after, in the dining hall. Thera will probably be there."

"But…" Arian pursued him, having no interest in simply sitting around with her cousin, doing nothing.

He paused while she caught up to him, and pulled her into a loving embrace.

"You'll tell me what father says, won't you?" she whispered into his ear.

"Course I will." Fredrik groaned and rubbed his forehead. "Curse this, just leave me will you," he sighed grumpily and Arian could not resist a chuckle. Most men she observed were all the same with their drinking habits. Whether they were rich or poor, noble or common.

But her grin faded quickly, as her brother continued on his way.

* * *

Fredrik hammered at the door in irritation, though his lack of energy meant his fist made little noise. When a bolt eased out of place and the door creaked inward, he almost fell into the room.

"What..." Fredrik's voice trailed off as his mind finally cleared, and he realised his father was wearing armour. He was joined by his uncle and older cousin, Roman.

"Wake up boy."

His father's tone was more than enough to snap Fredrik out of his sleepy haze. He slumped into a chair, weary but alert, and hoped that his fears were wrong: praying that the peace was not over, and he could simply spend a leisurely day actually getting to know his sister.

"This morning a patrol found an army of several thousand to be approaching. Then a messenger arrived, a Laminan man. He said this army contains the remaining citizens of the northern provinces. You know what that means."

Fredrik's jaw moved up and down senselessly as Melchior relayed the news. Finally, the prince managed to utter a few words of his own. "What does the messenger want?"

"He says that King Farrow of Narda and King Oras of Lamina wish to see me, and that they bring news of a Henalas threat," Melchior answered. "I did not tell you before, but three days ago I also received word of Regofala's collapse."

Fredrik shook his head. "So now we are completely exposed to the Henalas from the north, and Soonada is threatened." He took a deep breath in. "What are we going to do? One of us must go and speak with the Northern Kings. Or is it a Henalas ploy?"

"No," Melchior said firmly. "It is not a ploy. You will go to see the commander of the united northern forces, Lord Jerim."

"Are you sure?" He didn't understand how his father could be so trusting when the Henalas were impossible to predict. The attack on Tarvesi, which had shattered Arian's former peaceful life, had proven that.

"You will go," his father repeated. "I have other issues to attend to."

"What?" Fredrik mumbled. "Does it get worse?" He looked at his uncle, Duke Nerilek.

"Arian's..." But his father stopped, his face pale.

A chill washed over Fredrik. "She can't have come to any harm! I saw her just then."

"No, she has not," Nerilek answered. "But the Henalas do have spies in the castle. Her birth certificate is missing."

Fredrik closed his eyes for a moment, the muscles in his forehead screwing into a frown. "Why would that matter? It doesn't change anything, she has already had her ceremony."

His father sighed, just as a knocking on the door halted further discussion. Roman opened it and Duke Numelov of Jalas, highest advisor to the king, entered with a military official.

"The army has halted on the western banks of the River of Rena, due north of our farmlands across from the widest fringes of the Kayamara Wood. We suspect they are setting up camp. Captain Ureves has sent men to monitor the situation and scouts to patrol the region."

Melchior thanked Numelov for the update. "And Ureves, please prepare the mission and inform the messenger we will depart soon."

The captain saluted, then left the room. Fredrik watched him go, admiring the man's composure that did not flinch at the prospect of war.

Melchior turned back to his advisor. "Nerilek and I will be leaving for Karama to lead the offensive there. Fredrik will reign in my absence, but I assign the charge of Linuina's battle preparations to you."

Fredrik swallowed. So this was it. The time had come for him to take the lead, after years of training. He had been younger in the last siege, and only a minor participant. It would be different now, and he would be alone while his father fought at Karama.

Frederik had visited the military base at Karama once before: it was a huge granite fortress built in the foothills of the Hevedh Suhil. Those lands were gorge territory, jagged and ruthless. It was said that long ago the earth had ruptured there and evaporated the great inland sea with the heat of the exposed molten lava.

"Fredrik," his father said simply, bringing him back to the present.

"Never fear my prince," Numelov told him. "You are not alone."

Fredrik straightened his shoulders, finding his own strength. Something in the tone of the duke's voice irritated him. It was almost patronising.

"Now my king," Numelov continued. "What about your daughter? Should she not be evacuated south, to Illarn? Or perhaps the east will be safer?"

"No," Melchior insisted with a strange forcefulness in his voice. "It is not safe for her to be travelling and anyway, by launching strong offensives from Karama, the attention of the Henalas will be diverted there."

"Of course, my king. I will commence the Linuinan procedures immediately," Numelov replied.

With a salute, the Duke of Jalas made his exit. Once the door closed behind him, a curtain of silence descended as those that remained plunged into their own brooding thoughts.

* * *

Arian held her breath and squeezed her hands to steady their shaking. "Please, no," she begged.

"I'm sorry to say it, sister dearest. But it's true."

Arian looked away as she shivered with fear. *The Henalas.* The moment she had found her family, the instant she had people to love again, they had returned to haunt her.

Remember the men who burnt your home.

Her terrified shakes subsided, morphing into something else now: an angry determination to fight back.

"Father has instructed that you remain here in the palace. I will take you to the armoury now, and then you will have a sparring lesson."

Her brother led her out of the room towards the staircase, and they headed down past rooms of learning, where scientists gathered to discuss their inventions and elders tutored young geniuses of the realm. The great library lay at the end of that corridor, filled with thousands of histories and tales.

For a moment the temptation to slip away into stories rose within Arian. It would be so easy to fill her head with words as a distraction from the truth of what was happening.

But the time for reading about heroic deeds was over. The time for taking action had come.

They were beneath ground level now, and the dimmer light reflected Arian's mood. Then Fredrik stopped, and she waited in silence for him to unlock the royal armoury. His fingers were fumbling with the keys.

"Fredrik?" she murmured, the sound of his name echoing off the stony faces of the walls.

He avoided her gaze, making no move to speak. She opened her mouth to try and fill that suffocating stillness that persisted between them, but no words came out.

She had no words…

Eventually, Fredrik broke the silence. "Sister, I'm scared for you." He met her eyes, his face gleaming faintly in the light from a far-off oil lamp, features blank with a weary emptiness.

"Everything will be…" But Arian could not even complete her sentence, because she herself didn't have faith in what she desperately wanted to say.

Instead, she sought the sanctuary of her brother's outstretched arms. That too brought little comfort: the embrace was stiff and uncertain.

History was preparing to repeat.

"None of this should ever have happened, Arian."

She closed her eyes, but that only meant that black night swelled in.

No more flowers. No more colours.

Arian's imagination ran free with visions of war, of dying warriors and slaughtered innocents. Those images filled her with rage and a bitter sense of purpose, chilling her blood.

Motivation should always stem from positivity, lest corruption consume the spirit.

"Come on," Arian urged. She pulled away from Fredrik and reached for the engraved handle of the armoury door. Entering, she drowned her eyes with the sight of mighty swords, banishing fear from mind.

31
A DULLED WORLD

Onward she walked.

West.

That was the only thing Taalin knew.

She travelled by night like a wraith flickering between the trees, her body thin and malnourished. Her flesh was drying and peeling off from her bones, like the sun-scorched bark of a tree that flaked off to leave a tender trunk behind.

She followed the star, a shining torch that guided her on the journey. But it was just a distant light. Distant like her heart, her spirit removed from her body. Her physical form was just an empty shell left behind, a vessel waiting to be filled with its purpose.

When the dawn came, Taalin would stop and lie down on the moss covering the forest floor. She would rest her weary head upon the ground, burying it in the loamy soil. With each day, the sensation of the earth had been moistening a little more. Like it was softening to hold her.

Above, the sun would shine. It was still summer, and the days gently tried to warm Taalin's spirit.

But today she shivered. The coat gave no comfort. The sun seemed nothing but a dim yellow orb, the lacklustre colour of bleached wheat.

The moss should be luscious, viridian green. The colour of fresh limes, tinted with little rainbows as the sun shone upon the dewdrops, refracting the light.

Instead it was dull, as if coated by a sprinkling of ash.

The sky should be a bright crisp blue, a marriage of water and air.

But today it was grey, smothered by the choking haze of enemy fires.

32

THE ENCROACHING THREAT

Fredrik headed for the western courtyard to find Roman and several guards already waiting. He felt alert despite the lack of sleep, his mood sharpened by the change into battle attire.

Guards lowered the small wooden drawbridge that connected the sweeping arches of the royal bridge to the fortress walls and the public bridge beyond. The envoy slowly crossed the oak planks, and once they reached the flecked cream marble of the sturdier outer bridge, they picked up speed to a brisk trot. Beneath them to either side, the River of Rena glistened. Sunlight tinted the waters, ripples forming patterned arcs of gold.

But that beauty was lost on the small company, focussed as they were on their mission.

They turned north after the crossing, and Fredrik spared a backwards glance over his shoulder. Barbican walls enclosed the city of Linuina, the towering stone creating a shadowy patchwork on the surrounding fields.

It hadn't always been like this. Before the Henalas invasion, cities had flourished without need for fortifications. These had only been constructed much later, hurriedly built from the nearest natural resources.

Cities closer to the northern mountains, the Hevedh Nemash, had pristine marble in abundance. Those forts were at least a beautiful white, the colour of purity.

Further south, and the forts were dark. The Renalans had made do with slate left behind from the huge inland sea that had covered the region millennia ago. They had also used granite from the nearby Hevedh Suhil, but that granite was similarly sombre in its tone.

Fredrik's gaze lingered one moment longer, thinking of Arian and hoping that fate would not seize the sister he had only just found. Then he ripped his eyes away, and sped the company on, heels digging into the flanks of his horse.

They rode across the verdant fields that stretched out along the river. But Fredrik only thought of how they looked after a siege. After the Henalas touched it, burn marks would scour the earth, bodies trampled into the soil.

He spotted the Renalan flag, fluttering in the breeze from a nearby tower. A white and green chequered background bordered a navy blue circle, with the golden tree of Linuina embroidered at its centre. The colours of white, green and blue symbolised the elements of air, earth, and water, and the tree had three branches to represent the universal guiding laws of Justice, Faith, and Unconditional Love.

He gulped, wondering what laws the enemy abided by.

None.

He tuned into the sound of thudding hoof-beats to distract himself from the thought of exactly *what* had spawned the Henalas, with their evil souls and inhumane hearts. And why the Gods allowed this situation to persist.

When they finally arrived at the camp, the sun was at its zenith. Tents and wagons clustered along the river, and soldiers were moving around. Yet despite the movement, a phantom feeling of desertion hovered in the air.

Men with pikes arrived to greet them, and Fredrik followed them to the main command tent with Roman at his side. He entered, almost recoiling when he saw the young warrior who sat at the foldout table. The man had a strange, foreign look about him, with cropped black hair framing a tanned, chiselled face. Two bright green eyes, almost poisonous-looking, stared out from sunken sockets.

The man motioned for them to be seated. "You may call me Jerim," he began abruptly. "I speak on behalf of King Oras of Lamina and King Farrow of Narda, who are resting after our intensive march."

Fredrik nodded, but remained silent. The warrior held him captivated by the sharp aura of authority that emanated from him.

Then Jerim sighed deeply. When he spoke again his voice was only a whisper, even though it still echoed around the tent with its commanding weight.

"I fear the end of Meridisia as we know is about to come. Several months ago, my scouts reported another fleet of ships crossing the Northern Ocean. The greatest number yet, we sent more men to investigate, whilst preparing our homes for war.

"Only one scout returned alive. Fatally wounded, he brought news that an army numbering several hundred thousand had invaded Regofala, destroying her cities in a matter of days.

"We knew the Henalas were not far off, and that we could not stand a chance against such a force. So our cities packed up, and we began the march for Linuina. We thought that in joining and centralising our forces, perhaps Meridisia would stand a chance."

Fredrik leant forward in his seat, hands at his temples, attempting to dilute the tidings into something less terrible. He realised he was gritting his teeth, and managed to loosen his jaw enough to voice a question. "But why are there so few of your citizens, if you brought all the peoples of both Narda and Lamina?"

A spasm of emotion rippled across Jerim's face, before he regained composure. "At least half of us went east, seeking shelter in Hajeara. Those remaining are our warriors and the women who insisted they help. But the Henalas have been at our heels all this time. Ambushes along the way have reduced our numbers… And I do not understand." He paused. "We sent so many messengers, calling for help."

"We never received any word," Fredrik responded softly.

Roman had been silent all this while, his face drawn. But now, as though sensing Fredrik's inability to respond, he mustered an assured voice on their behalf. "Lord Jerim, we grieve your losses and extend our deep sympathy. We also thank you for joining our forces and bringing this support. May I ask, how far are the Henalas?"

Jerim's jade eyes flashed like those of a predatory bird. "Our attacks have delayed them. Alas, I do not know far precisely, perhaps a week? I had to turn my efforts on simply reaching Linuina. My men are weak and wounded, and those remaining are lucky to have come this far. We had no more energy for scouting."

"Have… have Lamina and Narda been totally abandoned?" Roman asked.

Fredrik held his breath, dreading the reply that he knew was coming. When Jerim confirmed their worst fears with a nod, the prince groaned inwardly. No matter what happened in the coming siege of Linuina, the Henalas were now free to inhabit more of the northern lands. They were encroaching too far into the heart of Meridisia.

"It was our only option to abandon," Jerim hissed, hatred for the enemy evident all over his face.

Fredrik closed his eyes briefly, thinking of Arian and their meeting on Midsummer Night. *Her story.*

"I know it was," he murmured. His voice came out soft, but firm now. "And this battle does not concern any individual nation. United, we will fight for Meridisia." Fredrik extended a hand to the northern commander, who clasped it strongly.

In that moment of contact, energy rippled between them. It felt as though their minds had joined, and the strength of an experienced warrior flooded into Fredrik. But something else spoiled his thoughts. He could also *feel* it. The sour taste of pain, mingled with bitterness of loss: all that Jerim had witnessed.

Roman's voice brought him back to the present and the task at hand. "Join us at Linuina as soon as you can. Renala will fight proudly for Meridisia, and your suffering will not have been in vain."

Jerim nodded. "Indeed. And rest assured, we came prepared."

"Then we still have hope," Fredrik said with finality, desperate to return to Linuina, as though he could flee the future with the momentum of the ride. He saluted the commander, and left the tent with Roman close behind.

33

HEART OF A WARRIOR

She's whispering to me
from that hazy place
between night and day
that's filled with shadows
dancing out of time
in desperate search
for answers
for unity
and for Home

* * *

Arian emerged from the armoury looking like a war goddess. They had found her a small suit of chainmail that hugged her body tightly, and she wore it over a simple silk chemise. To complete her attire, Fredrik had given her his old battle coat of green velvet, and a belt of daggers.

Her brother now gone, a guard escorted her to the sparring chamber where she was told to wait for a lesson. She didn't protest. She was eager to prepare for whatever was coming: to keep moving forward, and not stagnate in the stifling clutch of all the emotions that were threatening to overtake her senses.

It had been a long time since Arian had picked up a sword. She remembered her first lessons in Tarvesi and then in Vulesa, and her love of sparring. It challenged her, commanding her to concentrate on the tiniest details. In those moments of focus her mind functioned with increased awareness, and forced her to be so very present in the here and the now.

The guard had left Arian to wait in a spacious chamber. Weapons and suits of armour lined the walls, and lanterns lit the hall, shedding a rich gold light like droplets of sunshine. She explored the room while she waited, her attention caught by a particular statue of a warrior that reached proudly to the ceiling. The marble of his great broadsword was polished to a gleam, and the skilful workmanship made his features seem real.

A man.

She noticed the feeling of disappointment that dwelled in her belly. If she had been born a man, surely she would be stronger. Maybe then her father would not have thought her so vulnerable that she needed to be hidden away. Maybe she could have done more for her people by now.

"Arian."

A hand descended on her shoulder, and she turned around to find the king himself. She quickly averted her eyes, returning to stare vacantly at the statue of the heroic figure.

"That's what I want to be like, father," she whispered. "When blood coats the plains of Renala, and death sings its ghostly song through the air, I want to fight like an ordinary soldier. We are all equals in this fight for freedom."

He touched her lightly on the back. "Arian, war is a horrendous burden that women were never supposed to bear. That is the task of men, of warriors."

"No!" She punched the sculpture, though she was the only one to suffer any damage. Pain shot up her arm from the impact, and she saw a mark spreading its blemish across her skin.

She traced one of her fingers over the edge of the bruise, staring at it pensively as she came to a more balanced perspective. "War is a disease that no man or woman should be cursed by."

He said nothing, and they stood there side by side. Then she finally met his eyes. "Why?" She needed to know why she had been hidden. He was going away, leaving to fight another battle. He might never return. She might never find out, never learn the truth.

Now it was her father's turn to avoid her eyes. Just for a moment.

"My daughter, do not be angry at the Henalas."

His voice was soft but it held her captivated, even though he had not answered her question.

"I must go now," he continued. "But please promise me that you shall remember who you are."

Who am I?

Still, his authority held her. Calmed her.

"I will, father," she promised. "I will."

He nodded, but when he next spoke his voice was a hollow echo. "You have full command alongside Fredrik in my absence. Please," he broke off, "be wise."

Then he strode from the room without looking back, without turning, without another word or a touch or an answer.

And Arian just stood there, unable to move. She should have called in farewell, should have gone to him, done something.

But she just stood there, all energy consumed as she struggled to fight through her confusion.

Be strong. A voice crept into her mind.

Caught in her inner battle, at first she did not notice the door open again and that another man had entered.

"My lady."

The voice was familiar, but only just.

"Last night at the ball, you ran away before I could introduce myself," he continued. "I am Marcus, youngest son of Duke Nerilek. But most importantly, your champion." He bowed low and kissed her fingertips.

She almost pulled back with irritation. She did not want a champion, a man who was supposed to protect her, who might die for her. The possibility of death felt too close now that the Henalas had returned.

They would always return.

"My lady, I have been sent to give you a lesson. Shall we begin?"

Gathering her wits, Arian raised her head. *Remembered who she was.*

"Yes." She would focus and devote all attention to sparring, to perfecting her skill. Being useful.

"We'll start with these," Marcus said, pointing to a cupboard of wooden practice swords.

She picked up one suitable for her size and weight, and walked into the centre of the hall. But though she tried to recall her lessons in Tarvesi, the rod felt unnatural in her hands.

Be strong.

She had to remember how to fight. She was no use if she couldn't wield a weapon.

"You ok?" Marcus asked gently.

She nodded despite her nerves. "It's… just been so long."

"Don't worry, we'll take it slow." But he nicked the rod from her hands before she could even react.

She bent to retrieve it, watching him warily. Then she sank into a crouch, poised and determined that he would not catch her so easily again.

He sprung, muscles unleashing, and she wheeled around to block the attack. Their rods locked in a parry, and she gritted her teeth as the pressure sent her arm throbbing. But he pushed down with all his strength and she was helpless to prevent her knees from giving way.

"Please," Arian pleaded, as she collapsed and they toppled to the floor, his body crushing hers. She let her rod go and pushed against his breastplate, trying to make him budge.

Marcus laughed as he climbed back to his feet. "Not bad, not bad for the first attempt." He leant back against one of the wooden wall panels, sword hanging loose in his hand.

The casual stance only fuelled her annoyance, and Arian lunged once more, her breath ragged from the exertion. He leapt out of the way, parrying her next thrust with ease, and catching her shoulder with a swift riposte.

"Very good," he drawled.

She tried again, her movements driven by a furious response to his demeanour. She jumped to the side, and aimed to bring her wooden stick down on his back. But he dodged, and playfully rapped her shins. Crying out in surprise, she tried to retaliate, only to find he had already circled around behind her.

"Calm. Focus," he instructed, resting the point of his rod under her chin.

She turned away, and made for the basin of water that sat on a nearby bench. She splashed her face, welcoming the cool liquid against her flushed cheeks, and dabbing at her eyes that were now teary with frustration.

Be strong.

More composed now, she returned to Marcus who was selecting swords from the wall.

"You're doing well." He ruffled her hair as he would to a fellow knight. But beneath the light-hearted gesture, his mood was reflective. "I hope you don't mind my method," Marcus added. "It was how I learnt quickest. I never appreciated people going easy on me."

"Thank you," she murmured, warming to his sincerity. "I... just want to be able to fight. Well enough."

He smiled. "I know, though that makes my role less important. But come now, shall we try with the blade?"

Arian responded eagerly, despite her fears that she would make a fool of herself. She accepted the heavy broadsword from him, clipping the protective leather pad onto the tip. Her hand was shaking so much with the combination of nerves and adrenaline that she pricked her finger on the blade, and a trickle of blood spilled onto the grey steel.

"Careful now," Marcus lectured, but with genuine concern. "You ready?"

Nodding, she sluggishly lifted her sword, tip forward as she circled him. Her eyes locked with his, watching and waiting.

He pounced, and she parried with a huge swing. Their blades locked, sending shockwaves rippling up her arm. Her shoulder whined from the pressure and once again, her knees threatened to bend under the weight pushing down.

As if sensing her discomfort, Marcus withdrew. He stepped back, pausing for her to regain her composure and think.

She was smaller, weaker. She had to win by strategy, not by force.

She focused again as Marcus feinted. This time she wasn't fooled, and sidestepped out of the way. He was unbalanced for a split second while the momentum of his swing carried his body forward, and she used the opportunity to make an attack on his side.

Marcus managed to recover and defend the blow, but Arian spotted a gleaming twinkle in his eyes.

"Amazing," he whistled as they circled each other again, and the comment made her smile.

34
CORRUPTED PEOPLE

Night was already falling when Fredrik's company returned within sight of Linuina. Watch lights burning atop the barbican towers greeted them, giving the ancient fort a menacing look and revealing battlements busy with silhouettes.

From down in the valley the walls looked impenetrable, massive granite brick towers standing tall against evil. But that was just a false illusion, conjured by the stone. Fredrik knew that the threat posed by the Henalas was much deeper than a physical one.

The group traversed the bridge at a gentle trot, the sound of their thoughts drowned out momentarily by the tapping of hooves on marble.

Then they slowed to cross the wooden drawbridge in single file. The planks rocked ever so slightly under the weight of the horses, as beneath them the river flowed swiftly and gracefully. The scattered reflections of stars illuminated the rippling water, while smoke from the lookout torches gave the air a mystical haze.

Pausing, Fredrik gazed into the river depths. Black, like the disease spreading throughout Meridisia, slowly choking her to death since the Henalas had arrived.

He stared at his own reflection. The patchwork formed by the flowing water and luminous contours made his image appear distorted, his features mottled by complex patterns of light and dark.

Two shades, wrestling for control.

* * *

Alexander had met some of the new soldiers, fresh from the journey. Of course, it was always in secret, without the Emperor's knowledge. The

Emperor would never have allowed it.

But sometimes Alexander found things out.

He didn't seek the knowledge. He was too afraid. But at times the knowledge came to him: whispers in his sleep, from the ghost of a tortured soul.

Many of the newcomers were young, naïve men. They didn't seem to know what they were doing in these foreign lands. They were confused, like saplings uprooted and planted in an unfamiliar environment.

These men seemed ordinary enough. Nothing wrong with them, they were just people.

But after they arrived, they were taken into the mountain caves. They would disappear for weeks, only to emerge different.

Evil people.

Something corrupted them. He thought he knew what it was, and strangely, he remained protected from it. That was why the Emperor hated him so much, and saw him as a failure.

Yet why had the Gods spared him, protected him? It wasn't like he did anything useful.

Sometimes he wondered about that other place. He wondered what it was like there.

Sometimes he imagined it. The vision of a diseased world always came to him, with corruption everywhere.

And now, the disease was spreading.

35
FADING AWAY

There's bliss in the stillness that weeps,
in the silence that yearns
and the aching emptiness, that tumbles
in the searching heart

There's always an answer
in the murky folds of time
in the wilderness of promised lands
forgotten and overgrown

And there's a love, in the shadows
that's waiting, watching, ready
to catch you when you fall
to hold you when you crumble —

You just need to let go

* * *

Pale silvery moonlight filtered down between the trees, casting a gentle glow on the glade where a young boy sheltered. He sat beside the remains of a campfire, staring into red coals that he poked half-heartedly with a stick. It was something to occupy himself when he couldn't sleep.

Wind rustled through the trees, a song that was both haunting and soothing at the same time. He shivered. Though it was still summer, he was in the foothills of the Hevedh Suhil, and after sundown the air had a frosty mountainous chill to it.

Chris… If they penetrate the walls, go to the temple.

A few lonely tears squeezed out of his eyes. But it was hard for him to cry now, like there was insufficient moisture left in him. It had evaporated, disappearing with each step along the journey, as though the earth itself had sucked his grief away.

He pulled the tattered remnants of his velvet coat around his body. It was all that remained, all that he had left, connecting him to home.

He lay down on the loamy ground and sniffed the smell of the soil. Let it penetrate his nostrils and seep into his mind, a calming balm, encasing his flesh.

Earth: embrace me.

His spirit faded. Soul blended with the air about him, while the ground opened beneath and Nature claimed his body in slumber.

36

UNEARTHLY TOUCH

Hours after her brother had returned with the sombre news, Arian was still awake. But as she lay in the darkness of her chamber, her awareness was floating in another plane. Visions drifted in and out of her mind, her spirit detached from her body. She had always been sensitive: feeling things and seeing things, as though from another dimension.

And now, over these past days, something had been accelerating. She was seeing more clearly, and more deeply.

* * *

Something broke Arian's trance. A cry. A wail. She snapped upright in bed, the covers falling away, leaving her exposed to the chill night breeze.

Rubbing a palm across her brow, Arian tried to brush aside the images and dispel the aching of memories that infiltrated her like weeds, invading her mind.

She slipped out of bed and found a gown. Then she quietly left her chambers, heading for the sanctuary of the palace temple to seek refuge. Perhaps a prayer to the Gods would soothe her soul and provide respite from the nightmares.

She arrived at the temple and pushed open the door. Her arm was tired from sparring, and throbbed as she struggled with the weight of the heavy wood. But as soon as she crossed the threshold and entered the sacred room, all feelings of weakness disappeared. Her mind detached from her physical aches, an invisible presence captivating her with its unearthly power.

As she beheld the interior of the temple for the first time, she trembled with both delight and apprehension. Its grandeur was unlike any other room in the palace, stemming from the simple beauty of its architecture as opposed to riches and luxury adornments.

A circular boulevard of arches formed the main chamber of the temple, their curvature varied slightly to create a rippling effect. It brought the marble ceiling to life, the cream stone sentient, beams angling towards each other in harmonious support.

The round temple signified the revolution of life, the continuous cycle of death and rebirth. And in the centre stood a granite statue of a tree, with the characteristic three branches. A fire blazed from a cavity carved into the trunk, providing eternal glow to the chamber. Every morning and every night new logs were brought to ensure an endless supply of light.

Arian approached slowly, making for the navy blue stretch of carpet that surrounded the statue. She kneeled, bowing before the flames with her eyes closed, feeling the waves of heat wash over her. Inhaling deeply, she smelled their crisp scent, laced by spices from the oils they had been soaked in.

Her lids opened slightly, halfway. Beneath the thin veil of her lashes she saw twitching saffron fire. The flames were like fingers and as she watched them, they prised her eyes wide open with their majestic gold hue.

The luminosity made her head twinge. The foreign memories were gone, but an echo of their emotion remained. She noticed a yearning within her. It was the yearning ache of another soul.

A hand.

Arian jumped, startled by the touch on her shoulder. But her unease faded nearly as soon as it appeared, for the contact of the hand brought a soothing warmth.

"Your mind is at war," came a whispered voice.

Arian nodded. For some strange reason she did not fear.

Could not.

She could not fear. Something was controlling her, altering her natural reaction.

Arian felt panic momentarily erupt in her, but just as before it dissipated quickly. The voice sounded, bringing peace.

"Hush."

Arian swallowed, and tilted her head to the left, away from the fire. "Who are you?"

A woman sat down beside her. In the dim lighting of the temple, her tanned face and dark hair merged into the shadows. Except for the eyes, illuminated by the flames and also lit within by an inner spark. Chrome green, washed with grey. Flecked by a metallic edge, yet softened by the faint tinge of a turquoise haze.

The woman shrugged, and looked straight ahead into the fire. "I study the mind," was her simple answer.

They sat there, both of them, for long moments. Arian started to tremble again, missing the reassuring touch of the woman's hand on her shoulder.

"Be strong," the woman said, and brushed an arm against hers as if noticing Arian's deep desire for that comforting human contact. "You have control. Remember: harness your emotion. Feel it, acknowledge it, but never let it rule you."

Arian breathed in deeply, holding on to the woman's words, and the memory of that touch.

It grounded her firmly in the real world, despite its hollow serenity.

37
BATTLE PREPARATIONS

Arian sat curled in an alcove on the upper battlements, just above where the wooden drawbridge connected to the fortress walls. Beyond, the white marble of the main bridge glowed in the sunlight, a gleaming pathway across the pristine waters of the river.

She gazed at the boat sheds on the riverbank opposite. The figures of merchants and soldiers flitted about the haven, which swarmed with people. Boats were arriving with citizens and supplies from the farmlands, while wealthy sellers prepared to sail downstream in the opposite direction, to safer lands in the south.

The haven itself had its own fortified wall, and served as a secondary point to launch attacks from during siege.

Arian watched as another convoy of boats slipped out from the docks, hungrily leaping into the current to be pulled down and away from the city, away from where the chaos would strike.

Some of the boats would follow the River of Rena where it split eastwards and curved around the Kayamara Wood. Then they would turn south down the Amani River to the southern kingdom of Minaut. Arian had not been there, but she knew it was a region of deep gorges and menacing cliffs, making it a difficult land to traverse. Being the southernmost kingdom, it had not suffered from the Henalas invasion, but fortresses had been built in anticipation of the worst. A last place to seek refuge, if Linuina was overcome and the Henalas occupied Renala.

The other route for the boats was a slight west and then down the river leading south to Illarn, a port city on the Herramekan Sea. It was the easternmost harbour on the sea, whereas Tarvesi had been in the west.

Tarvesi.

The place where she had grown up, and lived in sheltered peace until they had torn her sanctuary to shreds.

She remembered her father's recent confession. *We did it all for the best... because the Henalas have been after you since before you were born.*

Arian picked at the mortar of the stone wall where she was perched. The more she scratched at it, the more desperate her movements became.

Why me?

The tempo of her scratching increased again.

Then she stopped, noticing she'd split the skin of her fingertips open and blood was dripping down to gild her nails. She thrust her fingers into her mouth, sucking the crimson fluid away. Her pendant started to burn its icy chill into her chest.

She took one deep breath, then another, remembering the words of the woman last night. As she did so, the stone of the pendant returned to normality. She brought it close to her eye to examine its blue-green surface, a gem the hue of the sea.

Pederos had given it to her. It was the only possession of hers to have survived the pillage of Tarvesi that night. The only remaining connection to her other life, and to Pederos, the man she'd thought had been her father.

She had never said goodbye.

* * *

She tugged on Jasmine's arm, asking where Mathieu and Pederos were. And Jasmine looked gravely down into her eyes, explaining they had already left for Vulesa. Now it was time for Jasmine and her to leave the ruins and make for the city, where they would be reunited.

But the journey to Vulesa had claimed Jasmine's life.

"Hullav, remember Hullav?" Jasmine had asked Arian softly, as she took her last breaths. The words had barely escaped her dying lips.

The man Jasmine had spoken of was one of Pederos' friends. Arian had met him only once before. He lived beneath a tavern, underground. Following Jasmine's dying instructions, Arian had shown the pendant at the door as proof of her identity, and been admitted into a secret chamber

"Where are they?" she had cried. But the look in Hullav's eyes told her that Mathieu and Pederos had not arrived.

It was Hullav who had taken her in and arranged for everything, from her literary education to sparring training. He had also told her to assume the name Adrianna.

But it did not make sense.

Melchior had said that everyone associated to her, everyone who knew of her secret, had disappeared at the fall of Tarvesi.

Yet Hullav had lived.

"Arian!"

She jumped eagerly out of the alcove at the sound of Fredrik calling her name. He would have something for her to do, to distract her from the melancholic prison of her mind.

* * *

A pleasant breeze blew across the battlements as Arian strode alongside Fredrik, checking the progress they had made with their preparations. The freshness of the air offered some respite from the stale mood that hung thick over the city and its citizens.

It was hard to believe the change from a week ago at the Midsummer festivities, when Linuina had been alive with excitement, colour, and celebration. Now, women clothed in simple russet gowns made wearily for their homes, bundles of supplies in their arms. Wide-eyed children clutched rags about their frail forms, darting away from the paths of soldiers.

And beggars sat in the gutters, surrounded by their filth, the shadows of the buildings not enough to hide their heinous deformities. No one even cast a glance at them now, with the focus on preparing for war.

An endless rush of carts flowed through the main eastern gates, bringing people and supplies from the surrounding farmlands. Soldiers rounded up young men, equipping them with weapons. Everyone was needed in the fight.

"Arian, come," Fredrik said, taking her hand.

She turned her face into the wind, willing it to blow away her fears. At least they had made good progress with the preparations, although that was not surprising. After so many sieges, the commanders and soldiers knew the protocol. Weapons were always being forged, and supplies stockpiled, in case of an emergency.

Like this.

As they neared the end of their rounds, Arian recalled the siege notes she had studied the previous day. She could tell Fredrik was uneasy about her remaining, and her desire to prove her knowledge was as much to reassure him, as it was to satisfy her own ego.

"Have the oil-soaked logs been positioned on the bridges?" she suggested. Fredrik gave her an affectionate squeeze, and she smiled. "See, I know what I'm doing."

But he didn't respond, his expression solemn.

They walked on, past a group of youths who were supplying arrows to baskets at each slit in the fortress walls. The senior archers had already hinged tiered crossbows in the brackets, devices that enabled the simultaneous firing of arrows through a lever that connected multiple limbs.

Fredrik acknowledged the boys with a nod, and they immediately fell to their knees, joining in a chorus of praise to their rulers.

Arian knelt to their level, and lifted the chin of one youth to look him in the eye. "Rise," she commanded softly.

They followed her order, their grubby knees trembling beneath the frayed rims of their breeches.

"You have done well to assist in preparing our city for the upcoming battle."

"Thank ye, Highness."

Arian pressed a finger to the lips of the speaker. "Are you hungry?"

"Er…"

Another youth, the most daring of the three, managed to speak. "Yes, Highness. We come from the outer village, so we haven't eaten much."

"Ilos!" One of the other children hissed for his companion to be quiet, but Arian placed a comforting hand on his shoulder.

"You will eat, so that you can return to your task with renewed strength." She signalled to a passing soldier and gave him orders to bring food. It was the least she could do for these poor children.

"Thank ye, Highness," Ilos said with a warm smile. "We'll remember this."

Then the group returned to their work, and Arian continued with Fredrik.

"You were born to be a leader," he exclaimed, smiling truly for the first time since the threatening tidings had arrived.

38
RIFT

Sweet radiance of the dawn
oh she's kissing me
with the tenderness of
a fairy's touch
as the golden sky
erupts and brings
the eternal force
of Truth's calling

* * *

Taalin stopped, unable to carry on. Ebony shadows flickered between the silver trunks of aspen trees, and she looked up to see the star. Her guiding star.

She would rest now, realising that night, not day, was the time for sleeping. She had become a creature of the darkness, closing her eyes from dawn till dusk, never seeing the sun.

The only light a star: shining torch, hopeful beacon.

But it dimmed the further she walked.

Aching limbs, unsteady as those of a newborn foal, collapsed to the ground, and she lay down against the earth. Wrinkled moss rubbed gently on her cheek, like the withered touch of her dead mother's hand.

Her eyes closed. Her nostrils flared, opening to welcome the smell of soil, curling into her mind, murmuring a secret.

Dawn.

She saw a dawn from aeons ago, when a glassy sea covered the continent's heart, rock and water embracing as lovers. Light skipped sensually over the ripples, blue and gold mingling in exquisite layers. A tingling breeze lifted water droplets to flicker and dance in the air.

She shuddered. Quaking, the land shook. Cracks split in the earth's bowls and released bubbling lava, a carmine flow. The poisonous stench of sulphur fumes rose up to the heavens, hazy steam obscuring the sky. Heat evaporated moisture, hungry flames drinking.

Then the ash settled. Calm again.

But only a small lake remained, remnant of former glory.

And a legend was sung on a whispering wind, Nature's secret an echo in time.

39
Fall of Innocence

Christophe sighed with relief as he emerged from a thick tangle of pine trees to behold a fortress on the ridge top. He was standing in a great gorge, with jagged slate cliffs rising protectively on either side. The elements had weathered the granite rock to a mellow grey, which was speckled by lichen and hardy shrubs that clung desperately for a footing.

Hold on.

Like the prickly vegetation to the stone, he would be strong.

He had wandered in the wilderness for endless weeks, lost and abandoned, with no sense of direction or guiding star. No clue from the Gods, no hint, no answer. A child of the night, he had become an insignificant splinter, so tiny that the earth had not noticed him.

But now he heard noises, beyond just the forlorn echo of the wind.

"It's a boy!"

The voice was sharp and commanding, but smooth – as opposed to the harsh, guttural barking of the men who had ransacked his city.

He noticed the sound of hooves, a beat bouncing back and forth against the walls of the gorge. The rock seemed to twist the noise and distort it, turning it into a haunting harmony like the voices of chanting priests.

Deafening, desperate prayers that would never be answered, never be heard.

His instincts told him to crouch down and he bared his teeth defensively like an animal, waiting for the riders to arrive. There were about a dozen armoured knights, with two men in the lead upon great chestnut stallions. The sight of one of them in particular held him fast: tall, strong, a violet cloak billowing about his shoulders.

The man pulled at his reins, and came to a halt before Christophe.

"Young child, what are you doing alone in this territory?"

Swallowing, he summoned all his courage and rose to stand as tall as he could. He nearly faltered. But the endless weeks alone had toughened him, forced him to become more of a man than when he had left home.

"I am Christophe, Prince of Regofala."

"My young prince," the man said softly. He jumped from his horse, landing with a dull thud upon the hard soil. He bowed respectfully, humbling himself despite his own great appearance. "You survived?"

Christophe nodded, but didn't speak. He couldn't.

"I am Melchior, King of Renala. Will you join me as we prepare to fight the Henalas?"

Christophe gulped, sucking in as much air as his little lungs could hold. The heroic king stood before him: an image of the man he should become, a man like his father who had fought and died to defend his people.

He looked up to the fortress he had first sighted in the distance. Up on the ridge, it was a huge granite structure merging with the rock of the land. *Strong.*

"They slaughtered my father," he said, surprised at the sound of his voice that echoed with a bitter malice.

And Melchior's fierce blue eyes turned grey, as though sharing in his sorrow. "My dear boy, I am sorry for the darkness they have brought. But be brave, and fight for Justice. The Gods will reward your Faith."

Christophe tried to speak but his lip only quivered, and he bowed again before the mighty king. He did not dispute the wise man's words. The tone of voice assured him, though he had long given up on the Gods.

"Please join us, young prince." Melchior leapt brusquely atop his stallion, and held a hand down to Christophe. "Come."

Grabbing hold of the king's proffered arm, the young prince hauled himself up to take a seat on the horse.

"Thank you," he said. But they were already galloping down the gorge, and the drumming hoof-beats and whirring wind took his words away.

* * *

Melchior walked along the little track that wound its way to the Karama fortress. They had to go on foot now, their horses snorting anxiously at the sheer drop, hooves tentatively crossing the loose stones.

Nerilek, his brother, was behind him. This would be the first time they both fought together, side by side. Normally in times of war, Nerilek took charge in Karama while he remained in Linuina. But this time was different. They had to try and divert as much attention as possible away from the capital. Away from Arian.

Melchior focussed on the path ahead. In front of him, a knight carried the young prince, whose malnourished body had collapsed. The king thought of his daughter, making the journey to Vulesa all alone after Tarvesi had fallen. They were lucky to have found Christophe before the Henalas, not that they could promise him much comfort though. Karama was a crudely equipped fortress for soldiers, a structure designed for the sole purpose of launching attack after attack, in a cycle of endless struggle.

An inner chill made Melchior shiver, though he was sweating from the exertion of the climb. He knew that the young prince would either become a warrior in a matter of days, or die. Innocence was being cast from the world, the young transformed into brutal killers, driven by forceful vengeance and hatred for the enemy.

How far they'd all fallen, from the pure teachings of Love.

40

ADDICTION

It was twilight, and Fredrik was occupied by a meeting with Numelov. Arian had not asked to attend, for she had her own plans. Her heart had compelled her to the temple, where she had been sitting since before sundown, gazing into the weaving flames of the eternal fire.

An external observer would see her eyes glazed, like a phantom vessel, a creature not of this earth.

She began to move her torso in a slow, circular motion, a silent seated dance that stirred up the energy from her pelvis to fill her womb and rise up through her body. Through the ethereal mists of her swirling trance, in the fire she saw children.

They were crying and they were laughing.

She lifted her hands from where they rested on her knees, placing one on her belly and the other over her heart. She felt a deep craving in her body: a desire to be held, to be touched, to be loved. At the same time, she felt warmth radiate from her own hands, a tenderness that mellowed her aching spirit.

And then her arms wove across her breast, as though she was cradling a baby.

A boy's sweet face looked up at her, smiling.

* * *

Arian stirred from her trance and stretched out her limbs, stiff from sitting. It had been a week since midsummer. A week since she had told a story and let her conscious mind evaporate, while she became a channel for the wise words of something that was so much greater and beyond her mortal being.

A compulsive urge overtook her: a knowing that she had to go back, as if an important clue to her existence lay upon the stage of that tavern where she had once stood, day after day.

Arian climbed slowly to her feet, body bowed before the fire, and then turned from the temple. She went to find a simple travelling cloak, and began to ceremonially robe herself in familiar disguise. It was part of her identity.

Then she left the palace and made for the guardhouse. She knocked on the wooden door, and when it opened, just stood there for a moment in shock.

Please, not him.

"Who's there?" he said gruffly, hand jumping to the dagger at his belt.

Arian lifted her hood slightly.

"Your Highness!" Richard Bettinglam exclaimed, making a hurried bow.

"Please," she murmured breathlessly.

"Your Highness, what troubles you?"

Arian paused, as something compelled her to speak the truth. "I am sorry, you just remind me of someone who… I lost recently." Cain's body had not been found, but nothing else explained why he was missing.

Richard looked at her long and hard, and she noticed sadness in his eyes. "Cain," he said simply, his voice low and gruff, as though reading her mind. "He was my older brother."

"I am so sorry Richard," Arian murmured. She turned away, unsure of what to do now.

"You cannot blame yourself."

Frenzied neighing pierced her ears, and hooves pounded over and over.

Soft at first, caressing the cobbles, then harder and harsher, ferociously fast.

Louder, lurid, a putrid pulse it cascaded from the chambers of her heart and filled her blood.

"Your Highness," he interrupted. "Why are you here?"

She blinked, and straightened her shoulders to help her regain focus. There was a battle ahead and many more would die. "I want to go to the outer town, to a tavern where I used to tell stories."

Now his eyes lit up with worry and concern. "Your Highness… Now?"

"When else?

A vein pulsed at his temple. "But your safety!" he protested.

She impaled him with her determined stare. "I have survived for many years in the shadows of night... they conceal me, protect me."

He fell dutifully silent and made no further effort to dissuade her. After informing the other guard on duty that he was heading out, Richard led her across the courtyard and they departed the safety of the palace grounds. Arian walked with her arms wrapped tightly around her chest. Not because she was cold, but because it was comforting.

The sight of this young man, and the confirmation that he was indeed Cain's brother, brought the memories of that fateful Midsummer night back. Bringing with them so many questions, gnawing at her soul, that threatened to break down her mental defences.

The simple act of physically clutching her body helped her feel grounded and more in control of herself, as opposed to some insubstantial spirit. But still her head ached as her emotions surged, her body shuddering with the weight of the earth.

What weight?

Arian gulped.

Go away.

She begged the noise to stop hammering her ears, and the visions to cease pounding her eyes.

Take the colour away.

It was too bright.

Even the moon seemed to shine too vividly. A glinting crescent, it peeked out from behind thin, wispy clouds. A frigid light, its harsh luminosity seemed unearthly and detached from human suffering.

The wind whispered through cracks in the stonework of ancient houses, like a mother singing gently to calm a distraught child. It rose and fell, ebbing and flowing, lapping at her ears like waves against the pink granite cliffs of southern Soonada.

Arian shivered, and slapped a palm against her forehead to force her mind into the present. Richard turned, checking she was all right, before he continued on through the streets.

Occasionally, the yell of a drunken man punctured the hushed background sounds. But mostly the city was calm, with all noise a dim background blur that lacked meaning. Individual words eluded her, dancing beyond her hearing. It was like she was unable to piece together any bigger picture, however hard she tried to focus. And it made her panicky, reminding her that she barely knew who she was.

She was nothing without words.

She held onto stories, seeking hope in their depths. But shadows still pursued her, like the men in black cloaks on Midsummer night. She knew that she could never run away from this enemy, for it lurked inside the chaotic depths of her mind and memory.

They left the protection of the walled city, and finally arrived at the tavern. Arian stepped inside and for a moment relief filled her, the nightmares conjured by the gloomy streets fading.

Familiar. This had been her home for so long: the place where she had told stories to fill the emptiness within her. Despite the rough men lustily eying the dancers, their vulgar slaps and rowdy conversation, entering in this moment felt like she had arrived in a place of sanctuary and escape.

How ironic, that this thought was coming to her now. Before, putting on her cloak and living in disguise had felt entrapping. Now it was the opposite: safety in illusion.

That was until she smelled *it*.

Not the smell associated with dirty, unwashed bodies. But the smell associated with crushed hope as once again Linuina was threatened by siege. They had been betrayed. Midsummer prayers for another year free from invasion, for recovery and healing, had been ignored.

Swallowing, Arian motioned for Richard to find himself a seat, while she edged her way over to the tavern keeper.

"Got another story for ya," she said, roughening the edges of her voice for normal conversation. It was different when she told the stories themselves. Then, her listeners were so mystified by her words that she didn't need to disguise her true tone.

"Adrian, 'tis been a while, ey?"

She dipped her head lower in a mysterious nod.

He rubbed a stubby finger over the balding patch on his head. "Well er, 'tis good ye came. With war 'ere again, men could use a bit of cheerin'."

She nodded once again, and waited while he bustled over to the musicians. Their song was just finishing, the notes of the fiddles dying in the hot, smoky air.

Her turn. Time to tell another story.

41

LOVE AND PASSION

Possessive passion
is merely the expression
of a physical body
disconnected from spirit

For my soul already
has all it needs
knowing, deep down
that you and I are one

And so it doesn't matter
what you are to me
in this lifetime
this physical world

For together we stand
forever, beyond
in perfect harmony
in freedom and love

* * *

After taking a seat on one of the crude wooden stools, Richard called for a serving girl. When she arrived with a mug of ale, he sloshed it down quickly, his hands shaking with nerves as he watched the princess move into the middle of the stage.

A ridiculous idea, he should never have agreed. He started to worry that something would happen, like it had with Lily. He had been so foolish that time, and now he felt a surge of guilt along with concern that history was about to repeat.

He called for another mug and downed it just as fast. His vision blurred slightly, the world more distorted, the princess but a spectral figure veiled by the tavern haze.

Men puffed at their pipes, blowing smoke into the stale air. Torches in brackets along the walls cast their flickering flames in an orange glow upon the tables. Shadowy contours shifted and danced like caged spirits trapped in the wood.

But suddenly, words captured him in spiralling arms that wound fiercely through the air to captivate all. They pulled Richard out from his melancholic mood.

"They command you to love. Yet you ask: how? How to feel anything but hatred and spite toward those who would murder innocents? How to stay true to the Gods' call, when those slayers have no values of their own?"

Richard shuddered as the sharp edge of her voice cut into his heart like a slicing rapier. It exposed the crevices within him, caverns that he yearned to be filled by something other than a painful hiss.

He thought of his eldest nephew. Bitter eyes, malicious tongue, heart twisted with hatred since his mother's death.

"But it is precisely because we have fallen from love, from love in its purest form, that they remain here to haunt us. True love is not to be confused with passion, with that wild emotion that can be as destructive as a curse, as threatening as an enemy arrow."

Then the storyteller's tone changed, softer now, like the gentle touch of an apologetic lover in the calm after a fight.

"When the earth was young and realms of sea and earth were mere buds upon the sapling tree of Life…"

He sighed with anticipation as the voice rose again into the winds of a great storm, like the tempest which legend told had washed a daughter of the sea upon sandy shores.

"And so it transpired that she gazed upon a Son of the Land."

The voice echoed longingly. Deep within him rose an aching for the embrace of the sea woman, a yearning to stroke her milky, translucent flesh and gaze into those emerald eyes that would tell him of underwater secrets. But just as he grasped for her, the ocean surged up again, fingers of salty sea spray snatching her away from him. He called out to her: a vow, an unwavering promise, that he would await her. They would be united again.

"In the deep sea she fitfully slept, tossing and turning with desire and the memory of him. She saw him, strolling along the shore, with starlight spilling across his features. And she danced up from the ocean, upon a melancholy moonbeam that guided her to land. But before their flesh touched, before they could unite in the physical, waves stole her again and spoke a warning word. She was not ready."

He moaned, visualising the face a mere inch from his, yet at the same time separated by eternity. The storyteller's voice rose once more to foreshadow the fate of a passionate soul, who had lost touch with themselves and forgotten their truth, caught by their lusty greed for another.

"Visions plagued her, filling her watery blood with mad desire. She saw that man, her man, with another woman. The man who she felt, deep in her bones, had been promised to her. With fury, she scratched at the sandy ocean floor, she scraped and she dug until fingers found rock. She beat her fists against it, harder and faster, louder and stronger, a desperate call for freedom from the emotions ravaging her."

Words pummelled out a hammering rhythm, over and over, in a vicious plea like an anvil upon molten steel. Then a furious bell began ringing unrelenting, insistent echoes. Elemental force responded to the unrestrained urges within her.

"And so up to land they transported her. But the sun dawned and scorched her fragile skin, turning it charred black."

A single note throbbed in the air, singing the story of her agony and grief when the son of the land did not recognise her, and when she realised that her visions were true: that he was with another woman.

"What she thought was love became a twisted thorn in her heart and she wandered, alone, her flesh tainted with the mark of betrayal. She had left her soul and her world behind, yearning for something beyond her reality that she did not quite understand, to fill a void within her that she hadn't even realised had existed. And now she was lost, in the realms above water, unable to find her way back home."

His heart sank with pity for the girl. Swept up by the storm, and her quest for another to satisfy the longing desire within her own heart.

"But she would not roam alone for long. The barrier was breached, secrets leaking. As her eyes beheld new wonders, she unknowingly sent visions to her kin beneath water, who stirred with a thirsty quest for new knowledge. To see, and to understand, another realm, thinking it would bring them answers. Help them to find themselves."

He relaxed with relief, as more of her people crossed into the lands above. As they united with her, in community, she was no longer punished by loneliness.

"They became their own race, an elemental race with powers of rock and water. A mysterious people, born from the fires of passion."

Words struck again, issuing a warning. He heard thudding, the racing of hooves across compacted earth. Rapid pounding of wings, feathers buffeted by a chaotic storm, furious winds gathering in a tormented spiral.

"But to tamper with the elements is to wrestle with the Gods, to seize control of a weapon no human should ever handle."

A pause. The crescendo of words halted.

"And so we must learn how to wield new knowledge. Above all, we must learn to love again, wholesomely and unconditionally, from the pure truth within our own, complete, hearts."

His jaw clenched, feeling the woman's fury directed at the sun, glowing orb that had spoiled her skin and made her body forever invisible to her lover's eye.

"True love is freeing. It does not bind another. It does not seek to enslave them or to take from them to satisfy an inner thirst, because that only breeds jealousy, greed, desire for conquest, and hate. We must break that cycle and return to inner wholeness. That shall guide the way to unity and oneness, as we connect with the knowing that at the highest level, there is no separation between souls. Inner and outer worlds reflect."

Hands gripped his empty mug, waiting. A tear trickled down his cheek, a tear of sorrow as he saw her sacrifice herself beneath the sun, a refracting light ray piercing her soul. Fallen from love.

"When the enemy strike our loved ones, return to the purity within you, and pray for the ascension of even those you think you despise. Know that the physical world is but one tiny facet of existence. And that we remain, forever entwined, with all souls up above."

The words sang to him like uplifting music, and he thought of Lily in the Starry Kingdoms with a golden crown upon her head, a reward for her tender, valiant spirit. Untainted.

"When the rage lashes our hearts and fuels us with vengeful urges, remember that in dealing justice we must keep our vision clear. Lest the disease of hate seize us and we turn ourselves into the enemy."

42

ORPHANED

Her face sweltered beneath the hood, the tavern heat suffocating her. But when she heard the sound of coins falling at her feet, it was as if a refreshing breeze cooled her. This was why she lived, to tell her stories: to inspire others with her words, and send ripples of change out into the world.

And of course, to inspire herself. For the words didn't come from her mind, but from somewhere else, some place beyond, and they spoke to her just as much as to the crowds who gathered to listen.

Arian collected the coins into her pouch just as in days of old. Then she bowed and shuffled to the side, giving the space to the musicians, their reedy fiddles replacing her voice.

She noticed Richard watching her, and he rose instantly from his table to follow her out of the tavern. Both knew that she could not linger. But when Arian stepped out into the cool of the night, she did not turn immediately in the direction of the main city and palace.

"There are three people I must see," she told Richard as he joined her, almost choking on her words. Her thoughts had turned to Cain's father, and the old couple who had sheltered her for so long. She would give these coins to them as a gesture for all that they had done, all that she could never repay them for.

Richard made no protest as she walked toward the smithy, and he knocked for her.

"Me son, what a surprise," the blacksmith exclaimed when he opened the door. But his features were grim, his eyes dull.

Richard motioned for Arian to step inside, and then hurriedly closed the door.

"And who be this, son?"

She lifted her hood as Richard introduced her. "She is Arian, Renala's new princess."

"Yer Highness," he said with a gasp. "Be ye too the girl I met at Midsummer? "

Arian nodded, taking in a deep breath of the heavy air, thick with the smell of the furnaces. She looked over to the hearth and the merry flames licking the logs, then realised that a boy was sitting on the floor, crouched on a threadbare rug.

The child turned to her, revealing a tanned face. Huge hazel eyes flecked with gold stared unashamedly at her.

The eyes were familiar, like Cain's eyes. But something like a glimmer of spite lingered in their depths.

"Why ye 'ere?" the boy questioned.

"Forgive him," the blacksmith murmured. That was when she realised she didn't even know his name, simply knowing him as Cain's father.

Then Richard's voice cut her thoughts. "What is it?"

"Dyane died yester-dy," the older man continued. "'Tis too much fer Estandos, after Lily and all."

Arian swallowed, her feet shuffling with uncertainty, a stranger to their conversation. While Richard and his father stared solemnly at each other, she turned and slowly approached the boy. She noticed he had a bundle of rags in his arms, and inching closer, realised it was a baby.

"Stay away," he snarled, glaring maliciously.

"I'm not going to hurt you," she said gently. "Is everything alright?"

He spat at her feet. "Course not. They comin' for me home again. Shed blood on me mother's grave, and now 'er mother too." His voice came out warped, unnatural for a child. But she could see that his bitterness was just a mask covering his pain, and she knelt to the floor beside him.

"I'm sorry, Estandos, is it?"

"Why would ye care for me name?" he whispered in return, his voice breaking.

"Because I understand."

Emotion surged through her as she cried out for this other soul. A squeezing sensation overcame her heart, and it beat rapidly, frantically, filled with compulsion to save this child.

And tears bled from his eyes as grief overtook bitterness, his sorrow replacing hate. "Are ye going to save us?" he whimpered.

Arian embraced him. "I will try. I promise you I will try."

She pulled back slightly, and reached for the pendant hanging around her neck: the one Pederos had given to her as a girl, saying it would bring aid when there was darkness. She had worn it all this time, beneath her clothes. But something told her that she didn't need it anymore.

She was not alone. She had her family, and she had her stories. Not just the ones she told, but the voices within her head, that guided and protected her, and had brought her to where she was today.

"Take it," Arian told the youth.

His eyes widened, glowing in the firelight, as he looked at the pendant. At the green stone inlaid upon silver, marked with miniscule engravings.

"Really?"

"Yes. Take care of it, and it will protect you."

"Thank ye," he replied, and she draped it around his neck. He reached for it and began to turn it over in his hands, stroking the engravings. She gulped when she realised he was missing a finger.

"I was sick, it got infected," Estandos answered her unspoken question, noticing where her eyes had fallen.

Arian closed his hand gently over the pendant. Neither said another word, they simply sat there together, watching the flames consume the logs. She was vaguely aware of Richard conversing with his father in hushed tones. But she didn't hear them, her mind in a different place. She wasn't even thinking about Estandos anymore, or who he was.

Instead, she recalled the first siege she had experienced, not long after arriving in Linuina. Remembered how the soldiers had rounded up the poor villagers who were outside the protection of the fort, and herded them like livestock to buildings within the walled city – housing reserved for the old, the young and the weak.

Arian looked down at the baby, concern for the child swelling in her chest.

"Did ye know me father?" Estandos interrupted her thoughts.

She swallowed. "Cain."

Arian saw a tear leak out from his eye, as he began sharing his own story. "After mother died, I didn't see him much. I stayed in the countryside with me grandmother, where it was peace and quiet."

Arian reached to comfort him, but Estandos pulled away, instead shoving the bundle of rags at her. "Me brother, Karl," he whispered. "Please be his mama, care for him."

She trembled at the sound of his plea, and the desperation in his voice. Somehow she knew she could not deny him, and she took the baby. Karl's lips curved into a smile, and hazel eyes stared up at her.

Cain.

"I'll look after him, I promise."

Estandos relaxed visibly, the worried creases on his brow softening. "Thank ye, Highness."

"Call me Arian," she mumbled.

They continued to sit there, until she felt a hand on her shoulder. "Highness, we should return before it gets too late."

She rose, noting Richard's frown and the way his glance flickered between her and the baby.

"I'll take him to the palace, and care for him there. For Cain."

He didn't reply, looking instead to Estandos. "Be strong young man."

Estandos jumped to his feet and bent his malnourished body into an awkward bow, before running over to the door to open it for them.

"Thank ye," Cain's father said gruffly as she passed.

Arian noticed some of the weariness had eased from his features, and she managed a smile, before pulling the hood over her face in preparation for the streets. "Goodbye," she said to Estandos.

He raised his hand to salute her. It was the last thing she saw before the door closed and she found herself alone with Richard and the baby. She looked up to the scattered stars in the sky and smiled, feeling stronger.

And with the baby in her arms and her head bowed low, the princess looked just like a common mother.

43
SHADOWLAND

In the darkness
of the new moon rising
I sit, I wait
as the emptiness stirs
deep within
longing for release
into the night
shadow
dispelling shadow
and rebirth
after Death

* * *

Fredrik returned to his father's study, head reeling after all the discussions. He slumped down into his father's cushioned chair, its frame much too large for him and reminding him that it was too soon to be taking over this role.

Then, just as his weary body began to relax, a scrap of parchment on the desk jolted him back to attention.

The panic rose in him as he read Arian's note. The thought of her outside the fortress walls, roaming the streets of the outer town, filled him with anxiety, as he recalled the night that she had first arrived in the palace.

He tried to dismiss the memory, and scrunched the note in frustration. There was nothing he could do now, except wait for her to return. Besides, there was nothing really to fear – was there?

He tossed the parchment into a corner of the room and rested his head down on the smooth wood, noticing how exhausted he was.

Wind brushed against the glass panels, a soft music lulling him into a fitful slumber. Boys shouted, warriors roared and civilians screamed. Frightening images of war sullied the peace of night. A premonition.

Yelling.

Where?

Suddenly he was being shaken awake. Groaning, his eyes flickered open and he saw Marcus.

"There is a fire in the outer town."

Fredrik gasped as the full implications hit him, and he realised the sounds he had been hearing were in this reality. Not a dream.

"Arian's out there."

His cousin recoiled in shock. "Why?"

"She went to tell a story at a tavern," Fredrik answered, jumping to his feet.

Marcus shook his head in disbelief. "I'll lead a search party to find her."

Before Fredrik could respond, his cousin had run from the room. The prince raced after him, fear replacing his fatigue.

* * *

Hungry red flames licked their way down the street, while civilians scurried out from the burning buildings. Soldiers hurried in the opposite direction, buckets of water in hand.

A combination of screams had replaced the previous stillness of the night. Desperate cries of those trapped sounded against the orderly shouts of the brave men trying to bring an end to the chaos.

Arian ran after Richard, clutching the baby in her arms. Holding his little body helped her to feel stronger, as though by holding him, she was in reality holding the child within herself.

They dodged into a side street away from the commotion. She paused for a moment to catch her breath, and as she did, it struck her that the old couple she had lived with were in that burning building.

Here she was, running again like she had on Midsummer, when she had run away from Cain without even saying goodbye…

"Fleeing from something, miss?" A grinning rogue had appeared, illuminated by the demonic combination of pale starlight and the orange of nearby flames.

Arian's instincts hurled her body into motion after Richard. Though not far from her, he had continued down the street without realising she had stopped.

"There's no need to run," the rogue laughed as he covered the short distance between them and caught hold of her wrist.

"Get away." Arian struggled for breath, unable to even utter a scream. She tried to twist herself free, but there was nothing she could do without putting the baby Karl in danger.

"There's nowhere to run now, nowhere to hide." The rogue smirked, his free hand reaching for the dagger at his belt.

"Halt!"

Arian sighed with relief as Richard appeared nearby, sword drawn and body in a crouch, ready to fight. The rogue turned to confront him, letting go of her as his attention focussed on the new threat.

"Run," Richard called.

But she remained frozen as the rogue leapt forward, his dagger aimed at the young warrior.

Cain's brother.

It should have been an easy fight for Richard, the rogue's dagger no match for a sword. But this was no ordinary villain: he ducked and weaved, making stealthy thrusts and swift reprises. Moving so fast, his blade seemed to exist in multiple places at once.

This time Arian knew she couldn't run. She placed Karl in the safety of the gutter, and drew her own dagger. Occupied with Richard, the rogue didn't notice her sneak up behind him, and she pounced at his unprotected back.

He toppled to the dirty cobbles, the impact catching him off balance. She rolled him over immediately and placed her point at his neck, while Richard pinned down his flailing arms.

"Who are you?" she snarled.

The rogue stared up at her, eyes defiant though she was the one in control now.

"Your Highness, kill him and be done with it."

Arian pressed the dagger harder against the rogue's flesh, drawing a spot of blood. His lip twitched, but he did not whimper, so she threatened him again with the dagger point. The metal blade glinted in the fire, dripping red.

"Speak!"

He opened his mouth, as if to respond. But instead, a piercing scream tore from his lungs, and Arian looked down in horror to find a black-feathered arrow protruding from his chest.

"We are rising," the rogue whispered. Blood and spittle frothed from his mouth, before death froze his eyes over.

A strange word in some foreign language she couldn't understand, started echoing over in Arian's mind. As she stumbled to her feet, her eyes came to rest on the window of the opposite house. Curtains swished, recently disturbed.

"Your Highness," Richard called. "Come, we must be gone."

She ran to retrieve Karl from the gutter and hushed his cries with a kiss upon his forehead, hugging him close to her breast.

"Let's go."

* * *

"Arian!"

Her brother was in the courtyard when they arrived, surrounded by a group of knights. He ran over to her with relief evident all over his face, though he stopped short at the sight of the infant in her arms.

"Cain's son," she murmured. "Please, I need to lie down…" She gripped Fredrik's hand, her fingers clutching his.

"You had us sick with worry," her brother said sharply, wrapping a steadying arm around her shoulders.

The sound of the concern in his voice stung her. She had been stupid. *Foolish girl.*

"I'm sorry," she whispered. "The fire…"

"I've sent more men."

She nodded, and glanced over at Richard. Tried to tell him with her face that she was sorry for involving him in her escapade.

She closed her eyes. She felt so weak, like she would collapse.

Everything blurred. She tried to combat the fog in her mind, but the struggle to remain in the present drained away all her energy.

44

REDEMPTION

The hour was well past midnight when Richard finally returned from his tasks. After speaking with the prince, he slipped through the palace halls to the nursery, where his nephew had been taken.

He pushed open the door, and stopped short at the sight of Sarah holding Karl in her arms. She looked up, her slender face illuminated by a ray of moonlight.

"Sir!" she exclaimed, eyes flashing with surprise. "What are you doing here?"

He shrugged. "I just thought I would see how he was." A lie, and he could tell she knew it. Other duties occupied soldiers, leaving no time to care for orphaned babies. "His name is Karl. My nephew," he explained.

Sarah opened her mouth as if to speak, then closed it, and offered him the bundled babe instead. He tentatively reached out an arm, but stopped. In fact, he had never held a child before.

"It's easy," she said with a smile.

But he shook his head, and backed away.

"Is something the matter, sir?" Sarah asked, confusion covering her delicate face. But Richard had already turned, and he simply left the room without a backward glance.

* * *

He walked slowly down the palace hall, then exited and crossed the courtyard, making for the guard's quarters. All the while, thoughts of his brother swam in his mind: murky thoughts, clouded by the permeating guilt that infiltrated his soul.

It's your fault.

He had only wanted to prove himself as a soldier. But good soldiers are not reckless fools, caught up in their ego. They do not seek out trouble to show off their bravery.

And drag others into the path of harm.

Lily's face swam before him, a shimmering blur. He recalled how she had looked that day, dressed in the characteristic cream tunic worn by nurses. He remembered how she had run out from shelter, as if believing she could save all the soldiers who lay massacred on the ground.

A black shaft arched in the sky, a piercing needle, plummeting through the air like a foul curse.

Richard quickened his pace. He was almost running, as though he was back in that valley and could somehow change the way events had unfolded.

A scream.

Too late, and the story repeated, played over in his mind.

But at least he could fight for Princess Arian. Fate had brought her to adopt his nephew, and he would not let the baby lose a mother twice.

He could continue serving, as loyal as Cain had been for Lily.

He had a chance to redeem his soul.

45
ELEMENTAL WHISPERER

Silent waters of this mirror,
oh they collapse
the conflicting, revolving
chambers of a heart
that's torn between
reality and a dream
this life and the next
the glassy skies
that melt into
that ocean deep,
cleansing source –
Down and down
to fiery realms
where we found union,
hidden in
the ghosts of ancient
ancestral truths
where night meets day
and light meets dark
erupting in
the angelic kiss
of spiralling
eternal flight

* * *

Sunlight was only just bleeding over the moist earth of dawn, when Jerim arrived with the Northern Kings at the gates of Linuina. Guards were waiting to greet them as they crossed the marble bridge, an arc of pure white swallowed by the granite barbican.

Stable boys took their weary horses, while they were led into the palace and allocated rooms. But though he had travelled all night, Jerim knew he would not be able to rest. Not now.

He asked for directions to the palace temple, and when he arrived, felt the familiar calm wash over him. The presence of the stone, its elemental force, supplied him with strength for battle.

But his people did not worship the Gods in the same way as other Meridisians did. They were outcasts: a race that had rejected the authority of anything external and sought to make their independent way by returning inward and honouring the authority within every sovereign being.

It remained to be seen who would do a better job taking care of the earth. For many Meridisians, their worship of the Gods was superficial. People didn't truly live by the values that they preached and supposedly believed. Besides, by labelling external entities as having some kind of higher authority and influence, the people had an excuse to abdicate responsibility for their own actions and for their power to influence happenings in the world around them.

His race had their imperfections too. Few had truly mastered their practices – and those that did kept to themselves, living in a completely different reality to those trapped in the present cycle of war and peace, battling against the Henalas. As for the others, mortal human egos often tainted the purity of intentions. Many had sought to impose their own limited beliefs upon a realm which already existed and functioned perfectly fine without them, or sought to fix others when they still had their own work to do on themselves.

They were just as bad, if not worse, than those who abdicated responsibility and deferred to the higher authority of the Gods. There is great danger in the mortal who believes he is superior to his fellow man, that he has attained a higher level of thinking and being, and thinks he is here to instruct and impose his views onto others. So too is there great danger in the one who comes with answers and not questions.

If you know everything, you wouldn't be here. You would have already transcended the physical.

Too often, creation wished to become creator, when it wasn't truly ready.

And he knew that was what was responsible for *this*.

* * *

She lay on the seabed, the rubbery touch of waterweeds tickling her silky, translucent flesh. The ocean breeze whistled its salty breath through her hair, teasing her lips with a watery kiss.

Stirring, she rolled over onto her belly, and rubbed against the sand. Fine grains gently massaged her body, and she sighed with pleasure. She pressed down eagerly, firmly, as though aching for the granules to enter her skin.

She needed to know.

The realisation made her eyes snap open and her head jerk upright, her body snapping into a feline crouch. She glared straight ahead through the inky deeps, her emerald irises lit by amaranthine flares.

A craving consumed her, and she gasped. Her body arched up and then descended back to the seabed. She began to writhe, her salty blood coursing harder and faster through her veins, her heart beating in a frenzied, rhythmic pulse, lacking all sense and reason.

She would know.

She panted, drinking up the seawater, desire wetting her tongue yet at the same time draining away all moisture. She needed more.

But the fluid turned to corrosive acid, as her body rejected the very substance it needed. Scorching water seared her lungs, and tears flowed from iridescent eyes that shone with magenta pain.

She let loose a screeching howl. Tried to stop. But she had gone too far. She scooped desperately at the sand, flicking it to either side, the grit gathering under her nails as she dug and dug.

Hard. Fingers encountered something hard.

Her hands curled into claws and she tried to scratch the foreign surface away. But it would not move. It only ripped her delicate flesh to shreds, droplets of blood soiling the water.

Rock, it was rock.

Her body pushed against it with the power of distilled passion. Limbs ached and agony speared her mind, but she could not stop, could not control herself.

Then it was over, and she felt herself drifting.

She lay on something soft.

Leafy.

A breeze stirred her hair, and trickled into her mouth.

She licked her lips, savouring the taste of this new substance.

46
THE OTHER RACE

In the expansive fall
of these opening doors
gateways, true
melting between time
as we shift and play
through heaven's arms
and the endless horizon
stretches far, beyond
this world's spiral
around the sun
in cosmic trance
in hidden dance
the butterfly knows
the eagle calls
and the gentle rock
of waves afar
sings for the dawn
of this age
this kingdom come

* * *

Knocking on her door woke Arian the next morning, and before she had time to reply, her brother had already hurried into her room.

"Fredrik?" she mumbled, rubbing the sleep from her eyes.

He crossed over to the bed and sank down beside her. "The enemy are approaching fast. A huge dust cloud on the horizon."

"Father?" she gasped. He could already be fighting...

"Dearest sister, do not fear for him." Fredrik ran a hand through her hair to calm her. "He has fought many battles, and survived them all."

She closed her eyes briefly, exhaling. "So what must we do now?"

"The two Northern Kings and Lord Jerim arrived this morning, and we will meet soon to confer. Our knights are overseeing the arrival of the Nardan and Laminan soldiers as we speak."

"That was fast."

"They marched all night to reach us. There was no time to waste, with the Henalas so near."

Arian nodded. Then her thoughts turned from the upcoming battle, to the events of the previous night. Her mind replayed the scene and recalled the rogue, the black-feathered arrow caught in his chest like the thorn of a vicious weed.

"How is Karl, the baby?"

"He is fine, your maid is caring for him."

Her brother continued, as if sensing that there was much more to her thoughts than concern over an infant. "Arian, I spoke with Richard after I left you last night. He told me what happened, so I sent him with several soldiers to find the rogue's body. It was gone, but where it should have been, they found this."

Fredrik reached inside his doublet and pulled out a small leather pouch. Opening it, he showed Arian a silver pendant smeared with blood.

Her immediate thought was of Estandos, and panic seized her. But as she scraped off the blood, she saw that this stone was slightly different to hers. It had more of an amethyst hue.

"Fredrik... Pederos gave me a pendant like that."

His eyes widened as recognition dawned on him, and he recalled the necklace she'd been wearing since they met. "That pendant?"

"Yes."

He shook his head. "It is strange that a common rogue would have something like this on him."

"But that was no common rogue," Arian protested. "The way he fought! And I believe he was hiding something, which was why he was killed. As he lay dying he said something was rising. It was so strange Fredrik. When he said that, I started to hear some words in my head, but I don't know what they mean."

Fredrik looked at her long and hard. He clearly didn't know how to respond, and when he finally did, he didn't engage with Arian's deeper worries. "We must not let this distract us from siege preparations. Readying for war needs to be our priority right now."

Arian nodded. But the memory of the hungry fire shone painfully in her eyes, and she forced herself to ask the question. "Did they survive?"

Fredrik lowered his head. "I'm sorry."

And her heart clenched, her body wracked by great, shuddering sobs for the old couple she had thought to be her grandparents.

Strangers, she now would never know.

* * *

The last of the siege preparations had been completed, with the residents of the outer town brought to safety inside the walled city. There was nothing left for Arian to do, and she still had several hours until the war council at midday.

Which meant she was alone, isolated with her thoughts.

She contemplated going to the sparring chamber to practice before the battle, and let the focus consume all her attention. But they expected the Henalas to arrive at nightfall and she knew she should conserve her strength.

Instead, she sought the temple yet again, drawn to it like an addiction. Perhaps she was just yearning to meet that woman once more, who she had met on her first visit. The strange woman with the soothing touch, who had said she studied the mind.

Harness your emotion. Feel it, acknowledge it, but never let it rule you.

Arian mouthed the words again, advice that sounded more like a command. Or perhaps even a warning. It was true, but not so easy to do in practice.

She pushed open the temple door, and inhaled deeply as if trying to absorb the power held within its magnificent architecture. Yet by day the room didn't hold the same energy. The flames of the central fire needed the contrasting black of night to bring their force to life. Light needed shadow: they would dance together for eternity.

Arian walked over to the granite tree sculpture, and up to the three great boughs in search of guidance. She recalled what she had preached last night in the tavern: cautioning words against the destructive potential of passion.

Love in its hollow, distorted form. When it became an envious or hateful motivation and twisted around to snarl in your face, spitting the curse of an infectious disease, that would eat you up and tear you apart.

All too often these days, love's antithesis reigned supreme: the loathing to take revenge upon the enemy.

She gulped, and instinctively her hand jumped to her chest, reaching for the comfort of Pederos' pendant. But it was gone. She had given it to the boy who had spoken to her so spitefully at first, the dagger of grief cutting his heart wide open.

Estandos. He had lost so much – even more than her. At least she had her father and brother now, though Jasmine, Mathieu and Pederos were up above in the Starry Kingdoms. At least she had never known her mother, the queen, had no comprehension of what she had lost. And she had been distant from her foster-grandparents here in Linuina, strangers in life as in death.

Arian knelt and looked into the fire, the binding element that joined earth, water and air.

And the flames of emotion that make humans who they are.

Those were the words of an old man she had known in Vulesa, a master cloth dyer.

She did not have many memories from her time in the Soonadan capital, though she had spent half a dozen years there. After the turmoil of losing everyone in Tarvesi, she had arrived blank, like an empty journal, soon to be filled by the stories of other people, other experiences and memories. She had longed for anything and everything, to distract her from her own story.

Life in Vulesa had been a period of study, of rigorous sparring lessons, of endless reading. Always searching through the legends of Meridisia, looking for something, though she could not say what. Her identity had faded, merging with words on the scrolls of ancient parchment.

But she did remember the artisan dyer and her visits to his workshop. She had enjoyed going there despite the suffocating smells and heat. He had a huge stove that dominated the space, keeping the concoction in the dye bath at a smouldering temperature. It had to be because of the mineral composition of the dyes. Too low and the mixture would separate, the salt grains clump and solidify.

She recalled gazing into the depths of the thick, bubbling liquid, and stirring it for him while he unrolled the sheets of blank silk to be dyed.

The real colour of the mixture never showed in its hot form. Only upon the silk did the lively hues shine forth, true in their glory.

A footstep sounded behind her, bringing Arian back to the present.

She turned to find a tall warrior with intense green eyes staring at her. For a moment they both remained silent, then he smiled and extended a hand.

"I am Jerim, commander of the combined Northern forces."

Arian took his hand and they shook, his grip firm.

She couldn't prevent the gasp escaping her lips as she felt the sensation of something spread from his fingertips and into her own body. Like a ripple of pure energy, carrying with it the potency of his warrior's spirit.

And also carrying with it a feeling of warm calm, like when the woman had touched her the other night.

"I am Arian," she said simply.

He nodded and released her hand, then gestured to the blue prayer carpet. "I am sorry, was I interrupting?"

She shook her head. "I was just... thinking."

He sat down on the carpet and she descended to his side. She could not keep her eyes from him and a strange feeling of desire overcame her. The urge to run her fingers down the line of his jaw and then tangle them in his hair...

He had been looking at the flames, but now his attention returned to her as if he could sense her acute gaze. Almost as if he knew what she had been thinking.

Green eyes. Poisonous tinge.

When the realisation sparked in her mind, she could not contain the words. "Is it true?"

He lowered his eyes. Though she had uttered an incomprehensible question, the spasmodic twitch of his thick eyebrows told her he understood.

"Not many people would ask. Not many people see these legends as what they are: history, not myth. Many would never draw conclusions."

"I am not like many," Arian whispered, tentatively reaching out to touch his hand again, craving another taste of the sensation. But his flesh was flaming hot now, and she recoiled.

"I know." That was his only response, and the way he said it suggested he knew much more about her than she might even know about herself.

She tried to ignore the feeling that her thoughts were being watched, and voiced her curiosity. "What are they like, the equatorial lands?"

He raised one of those thick brows. "You speak of Nariga, and I do not know. My father was exiled. I was born on the continent, a Melekan child, in Hajeara. Normal, you could say. I did not embrace the other culture."

Arian swallowed. "But... but why do they not join in the fight for Meridisia? With their aid, surely we could defeat the Henalas and cast them from our world."

His gaze bore into her, eyes tinged by sorrow. "The people of Nariga are different. They follow their own rules, and the Henalas neither know of their existence, nor threaten their lives."

She turned away to look back into the flames. Within her heart, she simultaneously felt a sinking sensation, along with a thirsty burn for knowledge. Frustration, confusion, but nonetheless an element of hope: for these people existed.

Jerim's words turned over and over in her head. *The Henelas neither know of their existence, nor threaten their lives.* What was it that protected those people? That kept them in an alternative reality, untouched by the troubles faced by the rest of the world?

"Arian," he was speaking to her again. "Arian," he repeated her name.

Finally she returned to meet his stare.

"Arian," he said once more. "Please, do not speak of this. And do not concern yourself in these affairs. This is not the time or place."

Then he rose, leaving her on her knees before him. He looked down, his eyes penetrating. Not cruel, but commanding.

She wanted to ask, wanted to understand. But something in those knowing eyes told her that for now she should keep her lips firmly sealed, and stop seeking knowledge. Perhaps she wasn't ready for it. Not yet.

Jerim turned. She watched him walk away, listening to the echo of his footsteps. The temple door eased open, then shut, obscuring him from sight.

Still she could not move, could not speak. It was as though some force was paralysing her.

Then came the image of that woman from the other night.

The force lifted to be replaced by a veil that erased all memory of meeting Jerim: the encounter blurred, and faded from her consciousness. Arian left the temple with a subtle feeling of confusion, and turned her mind to the practical matter of readying for the war council.

47
BEAT OF STEEL

Christophe gathered with the other soldiers in the inner ward of the fortress. Around him, men jostled for a better view of King Melchior who stood on the parapet near the portcullis. Armour clanged together, singing its discordant tune beneath the gruff shouts of soldiers.

Drums sounded now, a harsh thumping, dictating the rhythm of his heartbeat. Men in the courtyard raised their fists to the air, while those looking on from the battlements drew their swords and beat them furiously against their shields. Senseless hammering, the heinous peal of metal shredded the air.

A trumpet blared and the din hushed. Then Melchior's voice cried out, filling the silence with its authority.

"Once again the Henalas come, seeking to lay waste to our land."

Angry roars bellowed in response, whipping into a vortex that ruptured the stormy sky with an arrow of hate. Christophe howled with the other men, letting loose his fears in a ripping shriek that engulfed his soul.

"Once again we must fight. Fight to defend our homes, our women and our children."

Three stomps in quick succession, three thuds of sword on shield, three cries.

"Fight, and never give up!"

Fists shook, drums beat, men shouted, consumed by their hunger to claim enemy lives. Blinded by passion they yelled in hideous, clashing harmony.

"We stand in unity, empowered by the Gods!"

The trumpet returned, screeching its notes, stirring the crowd with the promise of an almighty presence.

"We join together and remember Faith, Justice and Love."

Christophe squeezed his eyes shut, the words falling on wounded ears, deafened by desperate prayers that had all remained unanswered. And the men around him cheered and stamped, energised for the battle.

"We fight!"

Men rushed forth in a vicious wave, like the surging of a deformed ocean, sweeping Christophe along in the inexorable will of its current.

* * *

Arian joined Fredrik for lunch in the large communal dining hall, where Renala's military leaders had gathered. Her brother indicated who the Northern Kings were, though from their demeanour their identity was obvious anyway. These were men who lived on the Henalas border, and a lifetime of war gave them a characteristic look.

A squat and muscular warrior, King Farrow was clothed in a thick leather tunic. He had two blue-grey eyes, nestled inside hollowed sockets, and orange stubble clung to a weathered face.

The other, King Oras, was a younger warlord with a tall build and slim shoulders. He had dark brown eyes and a tanned face, with a thin slit for a mouth that made his appearance even harsher.

Between the kings sat the northern commander, like a faithful bodyguard. Her brother had described Lord Jerim to her, but the sight of him only intrigued Arian more. Something about his appearance nudged her mind, as if trying to alert her to a forgotten memory.

Like they had already met.

But before she could focus on the feeling, the sound of scraping chairs filled the air as the assembled men stood to acknowledge the royal siblings.

Fredrik saluted in response, then they all took their seats together. On Fredrik's other side was Duke Numelov of Jalas, who sent her a fatherly smile as though to offer comfort and encouragement. But it only made Arian wish that Melchior were present instead.

Her brother raised his hands, and servants came running with platters of meat, bread and vegetables. "Let us drink to the health of Linuina, and let us eat to sustain her in the siege ahead!"

At the prince's words, the men cheered and raised their goblets in a toast. Arian took a cautious sip from hers, to find that someone had been gracious enough to fill it with apple cider instead of the wine that the men were drinking.

Her brother conversed with Numelov throughout lunch, while she remained withdrawn. She ate in silence, ignoring Marcus on her other side, the food tasteless in her mouth.

Then servants arrived again, replacing the savoury platters with sweets. Fredrik called for silence: the time had come for serious council to begin.

"Commander Berdov, please give our strategic summary for the benefit of the Northern Kings."

The warrior he had addressed nodded. "We have responded well to the emergency. King Melchior and Duke Nerilek have gone with a dispatch of troops to the Karama fortress. They will lead offensives in an attempt to split up the Henalas forces and divert attention from Linuina."

The commander continued to explain the defensive strategies for Linuina itself. They had troops stationed in the marina, which served as a secondary point of attack. The Henalas always approached from the northwest due to favourable terrain, as opposed to the dense tangle of the Kayamara Wood stretching east of Linuina.

But in order to conquer the valley and lay siege to the main city, they had to traverse the east-west trade bridge. The narrow crossing constricted the enemy's movements, and harassing them at this junction always helped reduce their numbers.

At that moment a knocking came from the door and a scout rushed in. Fredrik motioned for him to speak, and he delivered his tidings.

"As they have done in the past, the Henalas seem to be preparing for a preliminary attack. We have seen a small group of knights riding ahead of the hordes. They will arrive at nightfall without a doubt."

King Oras smiled, his lips stretching even thinner. "We should ambush them from the western banks with a cavalry charge."

Berdov shook his head. "No, I advise not. We launched such attacks in the past, but it has proven more effective to simply fire on their ranks from the safety of the marina walls."

Jerim spoke next, addressing the scout. "Do the Henalas knights number the same as in the past?" After the nod, he continued. "And the Linuinan cavalry?"

"Our ranks have increased," Berdov answered.

"Good," Jerim said with a grim smile of satisfaction. "Reinforced by my Nardan and Laminan knights, we surely have a superior force. We must fight an offensive battle at all opportunities: attack, to defend. If we restrain ourselves, the Henalas will simply smother the city."

Murmurs of agreement sounded, and the plan to launch a cavalry attack was confirmed.

"And in that case, what of other reinforcements for Linuina?" Farrow asked, fingers stroking his stubble.

"We have sent messengers around Renala," Fredrik explained. "Able men from the south, Kamina and Illarn, have been instructed to join us. The other cities in northern Renala will keep their own troops, in case the Henalas commence new fronts."

"Indeed," Numelov said, a fierce glimmer in his eye. "And Jalas will be another rallying point. The Hevedh Suhil provides a natural barrier against the Henalas, but with the loss of Regofala, we must stand strong." Then he turned to the Northern Kings. "What of Soonada and Hajeara?"

"We sent them word when Regofala collapsed," Jerim answered. "Many Nardans left for Hajeara, civilians and soldiers alike. Some warriors are remaining to guard the east, and others are circling back via boats along the River of Rena, to gather in central Renala. But I told Soonada to keep their troops to themselves. The kingdom must remain strong to counter the Henalas from the west."

"But surely they should aid us," began a Linuinan knight. "For if we fall, they will not stand a chance anyway." His argument sent ripples of unrest around the room.

Jerim shook his head. "Trust me. With Regofala fallen, we must keep the west fortified. Only the Gods know how many reserves the Henalas have, and their ships dock too close to Soonada's northern border."

Silence fell, as all men hushed. Regofala's downfall and the collapse of the northern realms left them exposed, and their vulnerability was not something anyone liked to admit.

"Numbers?" the Linuinan veteran spoke again. "What is the total estimate? And I still do not understand how Regofala was overcome so fast."

Arian looked across at Jerim.

Irises of piercing green.

She gulped, struggling to remember whatever it was that she was supposed to. Still, there was nothing, though he gazed across at her with a misty stare. She shut her ears off to his voice. She did not want to know the estimate…

"… I said before, they are fighting a new war now. Perhaps they have new weaponry, perhaps their success goes beyond their endless troops this time."

Arian shivered, returning to reality and Jerim's words. But she summoned her courage, and called out to the council in an attempt to infuse the room with a shred of positivity. "We have done all we can to prepare. Our strategies are well coordinated and our plans sound. We can fight, knowing we have done our best to be ready for this battle. We will stand together, united for Meridisia. With Faith, we can bring Justice. And if that is not enough, then our death is the will of the Gods."

The men roared in response, knuckles beating the table in agreement.

"Then we have nothing more to discuss," Fredrik called above the din. "Council is over, and as for now, enjoy the last few hours before the attack begins."

He brought his hand down in dismissal and the men began leaving the room, with the exception of Marcus and Roman. Duke Numelov passed Arian and he leant over, smiling. "Be careful, young princess. I know you have decided to fight, but do not undo all your father's efforts to keep you safe."

Her mouth twitched, but she did not respond, and he left without another glance.

"Roman," her brother called, slumping back into his seat. "Is it certain that nothing is left to be done?"

Their cousin confirmed. "For us, there is nothing to do but wait until nightfall."

Wait, wait for the Henalas.

"A game, anyone?" Roman asked as he went to fetch a chessboard from a nearby cabinet. He tipped the box upside down, and wooden pieces with gold inlay tumbled out.

Arian jumped immediately at the opportunity – anything to distract her. She had often played chess with Pederos, and she liked the game because it involved strategy as opposed to chance. The players had control, success depending on skill.

"Arian," Fredrik began. "Maybe you should rest?"

She ignored her brother, and simply continued to help Roman set up the board.

Before they could begin, two young ladies entered the room. Arian recognised her cousin Thera, with her long blonde hair and large brown eyes, and Roman's wife Juliana.

"Who's playing chess?" Thera asked curiously, taking a seat beside Marcus.

"I am," Arian answered, and without further word they started. Roman moved his knight, skipping over his line of pawns.

"I don't see how you can play games when there's a battle on the horizon," Juliana purred in her husband's ear. Her eyes begged for him to finish so they could spend some time alone.

"This is life, now," he replied, keeping his attention fixed on the board.

But he carelessly moved a bishop into the path of Arian's knight, and she took it as soon as he removed his hand.

Juliana laughed and kissed him on the cheek. "Looks like you need some practice. Though I suppose there are no good players back home, so no one challenges you."

Roman ignored his wife, intent on recovering from his error. "There!" He smiled as he moved in a position to take Arian's knight on the next move. She pretended not to notice, moving another piece instead.

He did as she had predicted, taking her knight with his queen. Now she could strike.

"Congratulations." Arian beamed, moving in for the checkmate.

Her opponent froze.

48
PRIESTS OF THE ABYSS

It is hard to pinpoint when it began.

He was referring to *the madness*, although he didn't think that was the correct word for it.

When he had been a little boy, it had been okay. Of course it had. His mother had been there to guide him, to make sure he would grow into a human and not a monster.

Then Alexander remembered pain, incredible pain.

A child, severed from his mother.

Every child needs a mother. To be connected to that birthing portal from the cosmos, the gateway that brings spirit into flesh. The mother provides an anchor point to all that is beyond this world, and a guiding light within the vast expansive womb of the universe. And the mother holds her child within the fortress walls of her unconditional love, a guardian against all evil and corruption, which cannot dwell within her pure realms.

What happens when that is taken away?

The child is plunged alone into an abyss with no grounding tether to the earth. Floating, without an energetical umbilical cord, overwhelmed by the infinite extent of existence. Suddenly the physical world becomes colder, *bleaker*. Enemies are everywhere, no one to trust. Confusion and uncertainty dominates. Above all, there is an emptiness craving to be filled.

His mother had been a sanctuary. And she had given him strength.

But when she had left, *they* had abducted his fragile and hungry soul.

And children are vulnerable to influence.

He clenched his fists together. He remembered that night. He felt that pain.

* * *

The shadows returned. The shadows cast by *their* long black cloaks, and the entities they conjured. There was nothing but swirling shadows, in different shades of black.

You ask me, how can black have more than one shade?

I do not know.

I just know that the evil is so thick, so real and multidimensional, it seeps through your body and penetrates every pore of your skin.

But it doesn't just stop there.

It seeps into your mind, in the space between memories and thoughts.

It coats your senses, and it changes your perception.

* * *

Alexander trembled, remembering the way it felt to be in their presence.

Tonight *they* were going to come again.

Coming to play with his mind…

Coming to prepare him for battle.

49
SMOKE ARROWS

Richard spurred his charger on, riding in close formation with the knights of the Linuinan cavalry brigade on either side. They headed across the east-west bridge, away from the shelter of the main fortress and towards the western riverbank where they would ambush the Henalas knights.

Over on the west, the boatsheds of the small Linuinan marina were but silhouettes against the darkening sky. The sun had already sunk below the horizon, and only a faint golden residue remained to combat the incoming night.

Richard gripped the reins of his horse, recalling with heaviness the last time he had fought. But at least he was a knight now, riding upon a sturdy warhorse. Strong muscles flexed beneath him as his stallion galloped, reassuring him. Better to be mounted, than a soldier on the ground.

The group gathered along the northern wall of the marina, preparing for the enemy front to arrive. Richard glanced across at the other knights, then at the fortifications behind him. Though lower than the main city ones, they had been developed further over the three-year period since the last siege. A double wall with a moat in between, formed by diverted river water, offered reasonable protection to the division of troops fighting from this secondary outpost.

* * *

Jerim frowned, staring straight ahead into pitch black. Every now and then his eyes flickered to the watchtower of the main city on the opposite riverbank, awaiting the signal to begin the ambush.

On his left spread the Laminan and Nardan knights. To his right, the Linuinan men, shifting anxiously in their saddles.

Tension strung the air, greater than that in a crossbow string just before the release of an arrow. His stiff muscles begged for the wait to end, yearning for the physicality of battle and the action of a fight.

The seconds drew on, and he sensed something different. He of all men was not one to be nervous, but something uneasy stirred inside him.

His stallion pawed the soft, loamy earth, twitching every now and then, and flicking his long chestnut mane. Jerim tightened his clutch on the reins, and bent to whisper a word of comfort to his horse. Well trained, the beast refrained from whinnying, despite its clear apprehension that mirrored Jerim's own.

Time eased on. Slowly, like moisture oozing through the miniscule holes of mortar, which bound together fortress walls. Eroding even the strongest of structures.

As he waited, it felt like Jerim was hovering in another dimension. Everything seemed so surreal, as if he was not quite bound to the present.

Then flames. Pulling him back to earth.

Light erupted up in the city watchtower, signalling for them to charge, and a cry from the Linuinan cavalry commander spurred the knights into action. Jerim bared his teeth as the group rode forth, lances pointed straight ahead. His helm captured the heat of his breath, creating a hazy film before his eyes.

Peering through the slits in the metal shielding his face, Jerim saw only darkness speckled by orange and red firelight dancing in contorted waves. Then a narrow line of mounted Henalas appeared, galloping forward. Easily overrun.

But the Henalas pulled their horses to a halt, and Jerim almost jerked his own reins in surprise.

A scream pierced his ears, and to his right a Linuinan toppled to the ground. Jerim frowned, for there was not a single arrow in the sky.

Another howl. And another.

Something small whistled over his head. He couldn't make it out against the night sky. The only trace it left was an unnatural corrosive smell.

A twisted cry battered against Jerim's ears, coming from directly behind him. But he had no time to look as he rushed forth in the momentum of his charge, onwards to meet the enemy.

Squinting, he tried to make out what they were doing. They appeared only to be standing there: proud spectres against a backdrop of the looming hordes behind. They each held something small, indiscernible. Not a crossbow, nor a sword.

Jerim squeezed his knees together to steady himself, gripping his shield and the reins in his left hand, while his right directed his lance at a Henalas knight.

Wind rushed as he charged, making a whistling noise against his armour. He clenched his teeth, blindly continuing on his trajectory, preparing himself for the force of impact.

And then shockwaves were reverberating up his arm and through his body, while squeals sounded all around. The lance tore out of Jerim's hand and for a split second he teetered atop his horse, before recovering and drawing his sabre from the sheath on his back.

Increasing pressure with his left knee, Jerim steered his stallion around to confront the Henalas knight. The man had his arm extended straight toward him, and Jerim found himself looking into a hollow tube.

A puff of smoke, somehow darker than the night itself, billowed into his face. Then a rotten smell besieged him and he bounced backwards in his saddle, the scene titling in his vision and his sabre slipping from his hands.

Jerim struggled to hold on as he dangled from his bucking mount. A neigh shredded through the night air.

He blinked.

Still alive.

Heaving himself upright, Jerim came face to face with his opponent once more. With the last vestiges of his strength, he brought his shield crashing down.

The man teetered on his horse, stunned by the blow, and Jerim managed to grab a hold of the strange weapon. Then his attention turned to his own men, and the remains of their cavalry.

Another front of Henalas knights were galloping forward to meet them, weapons in hands. Jerim stared at the puffs of smoke appearing before his eyes, stinging fumes that sent men tumbling to their deaths. He spotted a small wound on the neck of his own horse. The flesh was seared, as if by flames.

"Retreat!" Jerim shrieked above the din of whinnying horses and howling knights. His mount responded to the pressure of his knees, careening away from the battle at full pelt despite its wound.

The Linuinan commander led the knights assigned to the marina defensives, whilst Jerim made for the main city with the remainder.

* * *

The call to flee echoed in Richard's ears, and he wheeled away from the battle, needing no encouragement. Ducking his head, he bent his body as close to his mount as his armour would enable, all his muscles convulsing with fear.

Hoof beats pounded in his ears, helping to drown out the sound of his hammering heart and the booms of the Henalas who had begun their onslaught against the marina. Then finally he heard the clatter of stone beneath hooves. They had reached the marble bridge.

Fortress walls called them home, beckoning, eager to provide sanctuary.

50
YOUNG SACRIFICE

It would take for you to turn
to leave me broken
on the floor
a death and rebirth
in a parallel reality
'till I would see,
truly, deeply
into the shadows
of my own soul
that somewhere,
on another timeline
I had done this to you
I had brought this upon me –

And now, I breathe
slowly, gently
to let go of
that Story

* * *

The alarm sounded and Arian rushed outside, the image of Roman's defeated white king etched in her mind. The enemy were black, evil creatures. She had won the game of chess with that colour: did that mean that Linuina would fall? That it would be the end of her father's great empire, after so many years standing strong against the Henalas?

She sought reassurance that the game had no impact on reality. In any case, each opponent considered the other to be the enemy. Maybe the Henalas thought of the Renalans as evil.

But what had Meridisia ever done wrong?

They left the palace, heading for the stairs that would lead up to the inner battlements. Then with Fredrik on one side and Marcus on the other, Arian ran towards the watchtower. They climbed up the steps, taking several at a time, until they reached the top and could observe the battle unfolding on the western riverbank.

Arian caught her breath, spotting the Linuinan cavalry as they ambushed the advance group of Henalas knights. The scene shimmered red from the fires in the watchtowers and she tried to calm her ragged breathing. She took a moment to look up to the shining stars, and pray to the Gods for aid. Then she drew her sword and raised it to the night, her bronze hair and green cape billowing around her in the wind.

"To Renala!" Arian cried.

A roar of war calls joined with hers. She glanced below, and over to the soldiers on the outer battlements of the northern face. A secondary wall surrounded the parts of the city that weren't protected by the half-mote of the river bend. Deep trenches separated the two battlements, with drawbridges in between to provide an extra barrier.

"Arian, when the Henalas cross into the valley, promise you'll stay on the riverside walls." In the firelight Fredrik's eyes glinted red, giving him a fierce look that did not match the sound of his unsteady voice.

She turned back to watch the cavalry charge, knowing Richard was down there. Wave after wave of knights were tumbling off their horses before the Henalas, as though an invisible force plucked them from their saddles. Screams echoed across the water.

"What is happening?" she asked but no one answered her question, all likewise caught in disbelief.

Their knights had barely been fighting when they commenced their retreat, decimated by invisible Henalas weapons. The clattering of hooves on the marble bridge rang up to her ears in a depressing, defeated whine.

When the last of their own forces had made the traverse across the bridge, Linuinan archers on the lower battlements launched their fire arrows. The wooden logs positioned on the bridge began to burn, forming a protective barricade of flames against the enemy, while the defeated knights scrambled through the gates. Then the heavy iron bars closed with a squeal that made

Arian's ears throb.

She heard Fredrik curse. The small group of Henalas had crippled their huge cavalry ambush. It should not have happened. It did not make sense.

Arian fought her fear as she gazed across the river at the approaching hordes. At least the flaming east-west bridge separated them, and they still had troops at the marina to harass the Henalas at that junction.

Then a shout from up in the watchtower caught their attention, followed by the thud of footsteps. Moments later a young soldier appeared, his face grave.

"Highness," he said sharply to Fredrik. "The Henalas are coming down the river in small boats."

Arian looked through the arrow slit of the fortress walls, searching the waters. She squinted through the smoke haze that obscured her view, until she spotted them: rowboats overflowing with Henalas soldiers, partially concealed by mist. ,

Linuinan archers leapt to attention at the new threat. But the angle was too steep for the tiered crossbows, which were designed for shooting across at oncoming forces and not downwards, and they had to make do with their regular longbows.

"Why isn't the central bridge flaming?" Fredrik growled.

The realisation came crashing down on Arian. The logs on the bridge leading directly to the palace had still not been lit, and Henalas marched freely along it. Though the drawbridge was up, the close proximity of the enemy loomed ominously.

Arian was the first to start moving, and she sprinted down the stairs of the watchtower to the lower level, then along the battlements, until she was directly opposite the threat. Henalas archers on the central bridge were firing to cover for the rowboats in the river. The nearest boats were already at the fortress wall and Henalas soldiers were launching ropes up to the closed grille of the small drawbridge.

"Fredrik… If they get that down they'll have direct access…"

"I know," he spat through clenched teeth.

A Linuinan commander arrived on the scene, followed by a group of youths clothed in simple linen tunics. Knees trembling, they dove into the water, while Linuinan archers sent flame arrows over to pierce the logs on the marble bridge. Small puffs of smoke appeared, the wood failing to light.

"Why are the logs wet?" Arian hissed, turning to find her brother's eyes wide and panicky. Below them, the Henalas in the boats had begun climbing ropes, swinging like acrobats as they pulled and prised at the latches on the drawbridge gate.

"Tar, we'll use hot tar," Fredrik yelled, passing on commands through barely moving lips while he watched the horror scene unfold. The youths had reappeared after their dive, little mouths sucking in air, before they returned beneath the boats to drive daggers into the wooden hulls. Their attempts to pierce the planks apart appeared fruitless, and blood bubbled up as the Henalas slashed at them.

Finally, just when it seemed all had been in vain, the overcrowded boats began to sink, forcing the enemy into the water. The Henelas thrashed about, drawn down by their heavy armour, the river shining crimson in the moonlight.

"We have to get the kids out of there now!" Arian hissed desperately. In the mayhem, she spotted some of the Linuinan divers struggling amidst the enemy. The heavy soldiers were pushing the youths under, using them as flotation devices to try to save themselves.

She didn't wait for Fredrik's response, and instead grabbed a coil of rope that was secured at the top of the drawbridge. Flinging it into the water near a youth, she watched with bated breath as he grabbed hold of it.

Marcus helped her pull. But they had only managed to haul the diver a foot above the water before a Henalas soldier reached up and grabbed hold of his ankle.

One of their archers spotted the predicament, and successfully directed an arrow at the assailant. Released from the added weight, Arian and Marcus managed to haul the boy up to safety. He had been clinging onto the rope with one hand, but the other hung uselessly at his side.

"Ilos?" Arian gasped as a flash of light revealed his face.

He smiled weakly, but then his face screwed up with pain, and he vomited a mouthful of blood and water. Arian tore off his tunic to find a great gash in his stomach, and she hurriedly tried to staunch the flow with her hands while Fredrik shouted for a physician.

"What are you doing out here?" Arian whispered and cradled the boy in her arms. It was useless to try and stop the blood. It just poured out of him... so much blood from such a tiny body.

"I wanted to fight too. I wanted to be a hero." He spluttered up another mouthful of bloody water. "And I was always a good swimmer."

Arian wiped a wet lock of his hair out from his eyes. "It's alright. You're going to be alright." She hugged the boy to her chest, tears streaming down her cheeks and into his soaked hair.

"I will?" Ilos asked, eyes widening. But he went limp in her arms, his one useful hand still grasping her shoulder.

Arian stood, holding the boy, and began walking slowly along the parapet with Fredrik behind her.

"He was just a child," she said softly, looking blankly across at her brother while the grief bubbled up inside her. She sank down to rest on the stone, clutching the body.

"I know," Fredrik replied gently. Then he cursed, and slammed one gloved fist into the palm of his other hand.

But Ilos had not died for nothing. The youths had weakened the fleet of boats, buying them the time needed to bring supplies of hot tar. They'd managed to eliminate the river threat. For now.

Yet…

Another sacrifice.

The young had paid the price.

51
THE NEW WEAPONS

After rushing through the gates, Jerim wasted no time and went directly to the palace. Sufficient Linuinan soldiers had already arrived to assist his knights, along with physicians and nurses to tend to the wounded.

He abandoned his horse, still standing strong despite the neck wound, and stripped off his armour. All that he held onto was the enemy weapon he had seized.

He had to speak to an earth-scientist. Jerim's mixed heritage meant he *felt* the unnatural energy, unlike other men. Humming in his veins, throbbing in his blood.

He denied participating in this kind of sorcery, of course. He was a warrior. He wielded a sword, and fought the honourable way.

But he knew that if Meridisia did not respond to the Henalas using the enemy's own tactics, there was no hope. Physical weapons were now a thing of the past, however much he tried to prevent it taking over.

Inside the palace, Jerim ignored the soldiers and commanders rushing to speak with him. There were enough warriors handling the siege, and they could do without him for the moment.

Instead, he made for the rooms of learning, and tapped on the first door he arrived at. A tall young woman answered, and Jerim faltered momentarily at the sight of her grey-green eyes staring at him. Dark curly hair framed a tanned face, and smooth red lips softened her intense gaze.

"Sir?" she asked questioningly, her voice sharp as a military instructor.

Jerim hesitated, but the urgency of his mission pulled him away from further thoughts about her heritage. Anyway, of course there would be others like him.

"Sorry to bother you, my lady. Do you know Reaveno? I heard he resides in Linuina these days."

The woman nodded, and pointed down the hall to another room. Then she brusquely shut the door, presumably returning to whatever experiment he had interrupted her from.

Jerim strode to the room she had indicated. If anyone could help him, Reaveno could. He had met him briefly once in Hajeara, where the scientist formerly lived. Thanks to his engineering skills, new weaponry to combat the Henalas was being developed.

Jerim knocked and waited impatiently for the reply. Finally, the man he was after appeared in the doorway. If Jerim had not known of Reaveno's accomplishments, his hopes would have dissipated at the sight of the man, so different to how Jerim had recalled him many years ago. Wavy, un-kept brown hair reached to his shoulders, and emerald eyes sparkled with an almost deranged look above a pronounced nose and thin lips. In a plain white shirt and brown breeches, he could pass for a mad, wandering artist.

"Reaveno?"

The man nodded, and extended a hand in greeting. "Lord Jerim, we meet again."

Jerim did not say another word. He simply thrust the metallic tube he had taken from the Henalas knight into the scientist's hands, ridding himself of the device's foul touch. There was no skill involved with this.

Reaveno raised his brows in curiosity, examining the weapon. "From the Henalas?"

"Yes," Jerim muttered, holding his composure despite the frustration inside him. It didn't help that the scientist looked more intrigued by the object, than fearful of its dangerous ability.

"What does it do?"

Jerim coughed, disguising his discomfort. Yes, he had seen many men die in battle. He had experienced destruction. But the *unnatural* was something else entirely. The smell of it on the air, and the way it sucked manipulatively at the soul. It was the reason he had turned away from these arts.

"I don't know exactly. I need you to find out for me, see what we can do to counteract it."

"Can you describe what happens?"

Though nodding with apparent confidence, Jerim struggled to find the words to explain. "That trigger there on the side of the tube, it seems to launch something that sears a hole in whatever it encounters. All my knights were clothed in heavy armour, yet it penetrated straight through. I think I was only saved by my horse, his neck absorbing the force. And after they launch these… invisible arrows… black smoke appears."

"I'll see what I can do, and let you know when I have answers," Reaveno replied. One eye glinted, perhaps with the excitement of having a new project. "But tell me – is your horse alive?"

Jerim paused as he realised the strange discrepancy in the way the weapon appeared to affect humans, as opposed to the horses. Then he nodded, to confirm to Reaveno that his horse was indeed alive.

"Interesting," Reaveno murmured. He turned without further word, letting go of the door that began to ease shut behind him.

Hovering in the hallway for a moment, Jerim spotted Reaveno point the weapon at something in the room. The smoke appeared. The stench. The suction. The tug at something deep inside his mind, like a hook dragging him against his will and into a vortex.

He had no power against this. He had denied it.

He was a warrior.

But his body snatched him into flight, and he ran down the corridor with all the fear of a frightened child.

52
CAT'S EYE

It's like through time
I've dissolved
myriad vortex
of the old
has spiralled away
as peeling back
the translucent remnants
of former lives
I've sunken deep
through the endless sea
back into golden
memory
to that day
when your eyes met mine
and I faded sweetly
into the sublime

* * *

"Arian, you cannot stop here," Fredrik said gently, shaking her into the present. "The takeover of the valley has begun. The Henalas have ladders and siege towers, and are mounting the northern walls."

She returned to reality, loosening her grip on the dead child and summoning her strength to fight. She climbed to her feet, and with a roar of fury, flung the tiny body of Ilos over the battlement and into the River of Rena. War allowed no time for proper burial. At least the waters would embrace him like they did the ash of the midsummer bonfires, and carry him away to the pristine ocean.

"Arian, I'm going to the main gates, but I'll return soon. Promise me you'll stay on the western walls. You can supervise here and make sure the Henalas don't return with another assault from the river," Fredrik instructed, before hurrying off.

But as soon as he disappeared from sight, Arian began for the northern walls. Marcus shouted in protest, but she ignored him. There were plenty of soldiers here on the western side, and if the enemy had siege towers, every able body was needed in the north to combat them.

Smaller and faster, Arian darted ahead of Marcus, and crossed the nearest drawbridge to the outer battlements. The sight of the enemy bombarded her vision: they flooded the valley, stampeding it beneath their feet. They were making for the castle in solid column formations, with shields above their heads to protect them from the Linuinan arrows.

And the sheer number…

Endless expanse of black.

She tightened her grip on her sword, for already the Henalas had entered the beautiful Linuinan valley. Now all that separated the civilians from the enemy were the thick columns of granite and slate blocks that formed the fortress walls.

She had no time to ponder their fate any further, as at that moment a Henalas soldier rushed over the wall and lunged for her. She swivelled just in time to make a parry, and clenched her jaw as she felt a throbbing up her arm.

This soldier had none of Marcus' mercy, but she remembered her training session in the palace. She quickly twisted her body so that she could break the engagement without risking an injury to herself, and then ducked when he swung again, beginning a lithe dance away from the blows. He growled in frustration, and worked himself up into a fury as he smashed his sword from side to side in an effort to reach her skull.

"Arian!"

The manic slashing of the soldier separated Marcus from coming to her aid. But she had worked out the pattern and timing, and in the next moment her metal blade sliced cleanly through her opponent's neck.

Blood spurted over her, coating her chainmail, and she groaned. It brought such a stench of evil that it made her gag, and she held her breath as she wiped her sword across the corpse.

Marcus arrived and slapped her back in bravado, relief shining visibly in his eyes. She didn't feel victorious though. Suddenly, it felt as though there was a blade within her own body, carving her in two.

"I've... I've never killed before," she confessed.

Marcus grimaced and reached out to give her hand a reassuring squeeze. "You'll get used to it."

Screams rose in the night air, the sound drowning out the pain that Arian felt within her. Or perhaps it was an external manifestation of that inner turmoil. She gulped, watching as their troops pushed back another Henalas siege ladder, and the cycle repeated: shrill cries in the night, followed by the haunting thud of bodies splattering on the earth.

How many men, dying senselessly, and for what?

A tear escaped Arian's eye: a tear for all those who would lose their lives, for the blood-soaked earth of the Linuinan valley, and the folly of whatever motivated the Henalas to pursue their endless attempts at world conquest. For the first time, she felt a deep grief beyond simply grief for the tragedies that had befallen her people. An emotion that transcended the bipolar division between friend and enemy, good and evil, stirred from out of her spirit's depths.

The pain within her intensified, as though her soul was split into two halves, and her heart was desperately trying to unite them. Emotions rose in violent crescendo, while all around her cacophonous sounds from battle echoed back over and into her head. Beside her, an archer pulled on the lever of his crossbow. The noise of the recoiling string launched an arrow that whistled through the unexplored corridors of her subconscious memory.

They were dancing, twirling, spinning. Round and round in blissful escape, to the minstrel song that wove through time and space. They were bound to this reality only by a piercing crystal thread, connecting the ocean blue of their irises.

Another clamour came from below, bringing her back to the stark scene of battle. Arian looked down to see the Henalas had arrived with a battering ram for the gates, and the dull thudding of wood on metal added to the din.

"Arian, I told you to stay away!"

She turned, to find Fredrik running along the battlement with Roman at his side. She dropped into the shelter of a watchtower to meet them, sweating despite the cool night air. Her armour stuck to her and she was coated with the rancid reek of the man she had slain.

Ignoring her brother's appeal, Arian gestured to the gates, under constant assault by the battering ram. "Will they hold?" she asked, her voice high pitched in concern.

Fredrik nodded. "They'll be fine. Father and I had them reinforced after the last attack, and in any case, the hot tar is coming."

His eyes told another story: one of fear and insecurity. But Arian's thoughts were soon diverted as she looked over her brother's shoulder and saw five Henalas soldiers surrounding Roman.

Time slowed for Arian as her concentration centred on her cousin, besieged by blades, all poised to strike. He was going to be butchered.

She managed to overcome the fear that was clogging up her throat, and release a shout into the night. It pierced through all the other sounds of battle. Nothing remained but the sound of her cry, as if her voice was a sabre, silencing an opponent.

Then Arian charged the soldiers, bronze hair streaming behind her as she ran, catching the glimmer of the fires. It shone a brilliant red and her sword shimmered like liquid argent, creating the illusion that an ethereal shield of power surrounded her.

The Henalas stopped in their tracks at the sight of the beautiful princess, the tips of their swords faltering at Roman's neck, as if they were under hypnosis. Seconds ticked by, as though time had been fractured, a moment splitting into eternity, imprisoned by the spell of Arian's soul.

One of them managed to break free from her captivating presence. "Boy, the master will love this beauty, she can even fight."

But the distraction that Arian had caused was enough. Fredrik used the opportunity to creep up behind one of the soldiers and hack him down, while Roman sidestepped a blade. Then Arian was alongside them, and the three of them managed to eliminate the remaining four Henalas.

Sighing with relief, Arian took a moment to rest against the wall. The battle was devouring her, draining her energy. Since she'd slain her first opponent, it was as though she'd cut her own womb open and her life force was bleeding out into an endless abyss.

Sucking her, into a dance of cat and mouse, embroiled in a chase of kindred spirits, grappling to find their way home. He was smiling, laughing, blue eyes twinkling as she drew closer, almost as though he wanted to be caught. Left then right, a playful child, then suddenly...

"Are you alright, dear sister?"

She nodded slowly in reply, brushing a hand over her sweaty brow. Her fingers lingered, as if making sure that her body was really real.

"Do you want a break?" Fredrik continued. "I see you're a fast learner in the ways of battle, but sister, you're exhausted."

"I'll be fine," Arian muttered, and turned to check on Roman who was kneeling on the ground.

"Marcus," was all he whispered, looking at her with pleading eyes.

"What? Where is he?"

Roman shrugged despairingly. "I don't know. I saw him with you, but then..."

"What?" Fredrik frowned nervously, but Arian had already leapt to her feet and was running along the wall, dodging arrows as she went.

The music stopped, and he sank down to his knees. Their hands remained connected, and through that touch, energy rippled out from him and into her. As though struck by an electrical charge, her skin began to tingle and pulse.

Then his hand went cold.

His eyes turned red.

And she faded from the present, holding his spirit in her palm.

53
BIRDS OF THE SOUTH

Soaring away from the destruction, yet with the grounding feeling of hooves on earth, air ruffled through feathered wings. Beneath, the landscape blurred into a whirlpool of colour, a blend of pastel shades and lucid tones like mineral dyes on a pallet.

Faster, faster, the wind sweeps me along.

Pulling in one direction only, like a powerful ocean current, sweeping out to sea.

Alone.

Gulping breaths, air and water rushed through lungs, all the while wheeling the spirit further away.

Your place is with the wind.

Fuelling wind, potent force, filling the body. Nourishing, feeding the hungry mouth of a starving child with its rushing particles.

All I need.

All I know.

* * *

It took the men a moment to leap into action after Arian.

"What does she know?" Roman asked, his voice betraying a combination of anxiety and bafflement.

Fredrik did not respond, he just picked up the pace until they were running after his sister. But a group of enemy soldiers emerging from a ladder soon separated them. In the time it took the pair to cut the Henalas down, she had already disappeared beyond the next tower.

"Gods, spare us," Fredrik muttered, then cursed. "She cannot fight those Henalas warriors alone."

Roman nodded grimly and they sidestepped another invader, leaving a nearby Linuinan to deal with him. They continued the chase, each man driven by worry for his sibling.

Then Roman dropped to the ground, as he came to a body laying face down on the battlements, features concealed from view, an arrow protruding from its back.

"Arian, no!" Fredrik cried, a surge of terror overcoming him as he joined Roman on the stony floor.

But the armour did not belong to his sister.

Beside him, Roman broke into hopeless sobbing, as he rolled the body over and caught sight of Marcus' glazed eyes. Meanwhile Fredrik spotted his sister, who sat slumped against the wall opposite, a hand firmly clasping Marcus' pale one. She stared blankly ahead as if she were the corpse, her face frozen.

Fredrik's attention was totally diverted from his fallen cousin now, and he found Arian's side. Her eyes were unmoving, as if she didn't recognise him. She sat as if in a trance, and though he started to shake her, he could not bring her back from her dreamlike state.

"Arian, please speak to me," he begged.

Still she would not respond, and Fredrik felt her pulse. The only thing that indicated life was the faint thudding of her heart. Even her breathing seemed to have paused.

"What does it mean?" Roman turned his tear stained face toward him, and Fredrik could see his cousin's warrior courage crumbling away.

Fredrik's jaw moved up and down uselessly, unable to reply. Only when a soldier stumbled past them and saluted did he finally regain his voice to issue a command. He steered them into movement away from the deathly scene.

"Take the body to the palace, and… My sister…"

At that moment Arian opened her mouth as if to scream, but before any sound escaped her lips, her head collapsed onto her chest. Suddenly she fainted down onto the brickwork.

The sight of Arian on the ground jolted Fredrik fully into action. He sprang to his feet and gathered up her body into his arms, then began urgently in the direction of the palace. Oblivious to the shouts of battle around him, to the thud of catapulted stones on the walls, the clash of steel and the roaring fires, the prince continued on.

"Will she be okay?" A youth helping in a medical team tugged on the edge of Fredrik's cloak, but he ignored them all. He wouldn't entrust her into the arms of anyone else. He wouldn't let anyone take her from him.

And he walked blindly on, for his eyes were fixed only on the girl.

The girl, who was his sister.

54
Winds of Darkness

She had no sense of time or direction, yet instinctually *felt* the knowledge arrive. A message spun from a golden thread, connecting her deep to the molten core of the planet.

Send the people south.

Go away from the rotting earth, crumbling solid rock. Go before a haematic sea floods the land once more, seething crimson instead of calm, pristine blue.

For fortress walls tear apart, and youthful love twists into a spiteful snigger.

* * *

Arian felt someone pressing something cool to her forehead. Faces swam in and out of her vision but she could not focus on any of them, they were nothing but shimmering colours.

She tried to make sense of them, and patch them into a recognisable image. But whenever she tried, the colours became white-hot daggers of pain that thrust at her mind.

So she closed her eyes off from the world in front of her, and the faces faded away.

But oh, the sounds!

There was a hideous cacophony around her, a mixture of orderly cries and despairing wails. The sounds stabbed at her like the colours had, like knives in her ears.

She recoiled from the pain of her senses being assaulted, and nestled herself into the comforting arms of night. A dark night, where there was no stabbing colour. A silent night, where there was no piercing sound.

But as she sank into this delirium, slipping away from her reality, she found herself in a place that was far more frightening.

And she could not utter a word. She was unable to warn them.

Visions of death danced through her dreams, and her brother kept materialising. His face appeared on every soldier, moaning at the pain of a fatal wound, and in every anguished spirit, unable to break free from its tortured body.

Sweat dripped from Arian's brow, and her fists became clenched balls at her sides as the images came and went. But there was nothing she could do to save her brother. She was helpless, tied back and restrained by higher forces.

She knew, deep down, that he was next.

* * *

She became conscious of someone speaking to her. She kept her eyes closed for some time, listening. Her brain failed to register the words, but just the sound of something other than her own screams relaxed each of her tensed muscles until she was breathing regularly again.

Her eyelashes flickered open and she saw a man sitting beside her. As he noticed her waking, he smiled and shifted his hand from where it had been resting on her arm. She looked up into his clear, blue eyes, shining gently in the light from a nearby candle. They stared back down at her.

She just lay there, as time drew on. Then she managed to pull herself into a sitting position, although the world immediately began to swim again. She leant back against the cushions of her bed as her senses readjusted. The only light in the room came from the candle, and the reflection in the man's eyes.

She became aware of the man stroking her face, softly and gently. She attempted a weak smile to thank him for his comforting presence, a presence that soothed her spirit.

But she didn't know why...

She should try and remember. She should break away from this current state of oblivion. It did not help to deny the truth.

Truth was important.

"Arian, my dear." The man bent to kiss her forehead. Then he tightened his fingers around her hand, providing an anchor in reality.

Her eyebrows creased into a frown. "Who are you?" she murmured. Squinting, she tried to see the man's features and gain some insight into his identity.

"Arian, whatever is the matter? It's Fredrik."

His grip lessened, and he unclenched her hand so that one of his fingers could stroke her palm. Perhaps he was trying to read her fate in the map of its lines and creases. Perhaps her destiny was engraved there.

But she needed a compass. A map was no use without a sense of direction.

Then the man shifted slightly, and his eyes picked up more light from the candle. She stared into their depths which were blue like the ocean, tinged with green. Swirling layers, merging into one another, uncertainty and confusion... But who knew the answers anyway.

Half his face was in the shadow, while the other half was tinged with mellow orange. Two halves.

She kept staring at him, hypnotised, until realisation made her body spring rigid. It was as if the Gods had spoken to her from out of the depths of those eyes, instructed her. Commanded.

Her mouth opened as if to scream.

But no scream came from her throat.

Then she leapt from the bed and groped her way through the dim room, until her hands encountered the door handle.

"Fredrik... Marcus..." Her voice rose to a panicked wail, and she whimpered as the memories came flooding back.

Her brother was at her side in an instant, fear and sorrow etched over his features.

"I am here dearest. We are safe." He reached out to her and held her for a moment, while she slowly exhaled and tried to calm herself.

"Are we really?" Her voice sounded forlorn in the huge room, and although it was a mere whisper, the haunted sound reverberated back at her, harsh to her ears. Her senses were still recovering. She was like a newborn babe just emerging from the sanctuary of her mother's womb. Reality was still taking shape, and she was rebirthing into a nightmare.

"Please," Fredrik murmured softly. "Be calm, you are just tired."

Arian pulled away so she could see his face, and mumbled words escaped her lips. "That villain... killed the night of the fire. And Marcus, shot by one of our own..."

"What!" Fredrik yelled in surprise, the sharp noise making her jump.

Arian bit her lip, in some ways just as startled by the words she had uttered, as he was. It was like this knowledge came from somewhere else. Random thoughts and ideas were erupting in her conscience, without her having any comprehension of what thought process had led her to her conclusions.

That came later. The knowledge first, the reasoning second...

She paused as she waited for the explanation to come to her.

"Marcus..." Arian's voice broke as she tried to stifle the tears. But grief was human, an inescapable experience.

Her hands clawed at her eyes as if trying to stop the salty water from leaking out, and she grappled to return to her logic. "It was one of our own," she hissed, lips barely moving.

"That's not possible," he protested.

She shook her head. She knew, instinctively. "He fell the wrong way to have been hit by an enemy archer. And the arrowhead entered..."

Fredrik waved his hands dismissively. "That doesn't mean anything. He could have been facing inwards at the time."

Arian glared sharply at him, then turned to leave the room.

"Where are you going?"

She opened the door and light from the hallway flooded in, catching them both off-guard. Surprisingly, Arian found she was first to recover. Despite her current sensitivity, there was a task at hand. And when there was a task, her sense of duty and determination took over, allowing her to transcend all her physical barriers.

"I want to see him," she replied, striding out.

Fredrik nodded and took the lead, guiding her down the corridor towards another room. When they entered she spotted her dead cousin on a bench, a black sheet draped over his body from neck to feet. Covered except for the head, revealing those blank, wide eyes staring blindly at the ceiling.

No one had closed them yet, as though they were all trying to cling onto him, by staring through those empty windows into his soul.

Arian reached for Fredrik's embrace. Several weeks ago, she could have handled death much more easily. But since meeting her true family, her heart had begun to open up again, making her feel so acutely.

Such joy before the battle had begun. She had felt as though she was running through meadows, fresh air cleaning out her lungs, soft grass bouncing beneath her feet. There had been bright yellow daffodils and a sparkling blue sky, shining just for her.

But now life showed its ugly side, a sneering face that opposed joy, a plummeting feeling of sorrow. Made her remember their human fragility.

Letting go of her brother, Arian dragged her reluctant feet toward Marcus so that she could see him clearer, attempting to confront her grief. She approached until she stood just inches from her cousin's pallid face. She felt the hot tears in her eyes, remembering the young knight who had competed for the title of champion. Those rosy cheeks were hollow now, all joyous life sucked from them. Smiling lips were nothing but cracked, phantom blue lines, never to joke again.

"Arian, come away," Fredrik pleaded.

But she shook her head defiantly. This is what it meant to be a leader in a time of war. It meant staring death in the face, and overcoming its monstrosities. She breathed in deep and imagined light flooding the room, chasing her fears away.

As she did, a short wail came from one of the room's corners, threatening to shatter her own mental resolve. Seconds later Thera appeared, staring bitterly at Arian. It was as though the death of her brother had made her cease loving the living.

"He died for you," Thera hissed. In the dim lighting of the room, she looked like a creature from the spirit realms, more ghostly than her brother.

Arian struggled to control her own grief, and prevent herself reacting to Thera. She looked back at Marcus. It was easier to face him than her glaring cousin.

Fredrik stepped between them. "Thera, please."

"I had nothing to do with his death," Arian replied. Her words came out in a convoluted sneer from the confused mix of emotion that whirled within her.

Thera recoiled at her remark, and retreated into the arms of her mother who had joined her. The two began sobbing shamelessly, and Arian could not watch.

Instead, she brushed a hand over Marcus' staring eyes, closing them forever. Then she turned back to Thera, her expression gentler now.

"I'm sorry," Arian whispered.

"He... he didn't deserve... to die," Thera moaned between her sobs.

"No one deserves to die," Arian replied.

The room hushed, save for Thera's crying. The death of Marcus had swept a veil over them all, bringing with it a heavy darkness. The kind that troubled the soul, made you question who you were. Wonder what was right and wrong.

It was lucky that the door opened at that moment, bringing another beam of light into the room. Roman entered, followed closely by his wife. He was still in his amour and coated with blood.

"We need to be strong," he called to them. "We cannot help our beloved

Marcus by letting our sorrows overtake our own will to live on. So let us transform our grief into a reason to fight bravely for our land. Let us use our emotions as fuel in the battle to defeat the Henalas!" He pulled the sheet up to cover his dead brother's face, then left the room without further word.

"I'm going too," Arian insisted. The other women took no notice of her, but Fredrik followed her outside.

"Arian please, you shouldn't. It's too dangerous," he begged.

"No." She would not sit around with the other women while there was a battle to be won. "We've lost so much time already. How long was I...?"

"You have slept for an entire day, and it is the eve of the second night since the Henalas attacked," Fredrik explained. "They have taken the valley."

Her fists clenched as he spoke, and she knew more deeply than ever that she needed to fight. Perhaps fighting would occupy her mind to distract her from her grief, as she thought only about how to stay alive.

Ignoring Fredrik's protests, her ears became deaf to her physical reality. She changed her clothes, and in her battle attire she became a fearsome warrior once more. When she strode atop the battlements she saw only the vast Henalas army, enemy men she must conquer.

She refused to see the suffering.

Refused to see the death.

55

VENGEFUL LAND

Blood spattered upon the ground as Taalin coughed, the air rushing from her lungs in wheezes. She collapsed onto her knees, trying to control the brutal, jarring gasps that viciously forced her body to expand and contract.

Squeezing her eyes shut, she tried to block out the sight. If she could not see it, it was not there. If she did not accept it, it was not real.

But the image remained seared in her mind. Devastated trees. Logs piled high like corpses, heaped on the ground, spoiled by scorch marks. Ash, there was grey ash everywhere.

A world without colour, a world of black and white, and a world of enemy soldiers who she could not escape.

They were already running towards her, and she could hear their shouts. They had seen her when she stumbled out of the forest and into this wasteland of slaughtered trees. Charred branches twisted and warped, curling desperately to the sky, like souls begging for mercy. Pleading to enter the Starry Kingdoms, freed from the entrapments of this earthly reality.

Freedom.

No more, no more, she would be free no more.

A rough hand grabbed her shoulder and hauled her to her feet. She snarled, thrashing her body from side to side, trying to escape.

But she was weak, too weak. A young girl, a warrior with no sword or strength, a princess with no home or land.

An abandoned child, left to struggle, alone on the earth with no aid from the Gods.

Tears rolled down her cheeks and onto the ground. The burnt ground, sprinkled with ash, impure and forever tainted.

Why!

She cried, she screamed, she called to the Gods for mercy and struggled to find an answer. There had to be an explanation why this was happening to her, why the Gods were allowing her to suffer.

But no answers came. Her screams echoed in a hollow vortex, her world a blur of dull shades.

More shouting sounded. Different shouting.

The man was dragging her away, while the sound of fighting followed them: clashing steel, blades whistling through the air and hammering with metallic force upon shields.

Taalin looked back through the film of her tears. She saw savage looking men, spattered with dirt and blood, fighting with all their strength against the Henalas group. They must be survivors from another Regofalan city.

A glimmer of hope ignited in her heart. Hope that her people were here to save her.

But she saw the Henalas cut them down, one after the other. The dishevelled company were no match for the enemy troops who came fresh and energised from whatever godforsaken place they originated.

Taalin wailed as she watched the last Regofalan fall, his scream curdling the air. Her last hope, reduced to nothing but a sound, congealing in air thick with death.

The Henalas had done this.

The Henalas must pay.

And if the Gods did not respond, then they were no Gods of hers.

* * *

She saw whitewashed terrace houses crumble to dust, atop pink granite cliffs that turned smoky grey. She watched the city burn, sitting helpless while a glimmering azure sea became a dark, empty abyss.

She remembered. She was there.

She recalled a journey. A girl, with a young woman named Jasmine. They left the ash shores and blackened ruins. They walked, following a star that guided them to the great city of Vulesa, capital of the Western Kingdom. It was a realm of culture and learning, away from the Henalas reaches.

Except for that one night when the Henalas had attacked Tarvesi.

They walked, but Jasmine was frail and weary. So gaunt and thin that the child could see the outline of bones beneath her flesh, while only scraggly clumps of hair clung to her scalp.

They took it slowly. Step by step.

They were lucky to have water from the many little streams winding down from the Fhea Karadid. Yet they had no food. Sometimes they managed to catch small animals, but hunting was hard. Jasmine was too weak, and the child had no experience.

Rains came. Autumn wore on into winter.

I'll remember that day forever.

It was morning, and the two were in a little outcrop of trees where they had sheltered during the night. The girl was ready to walk again, but Jasmine just lay down on the soft moss.

I cannot go on.

The girl pressed her ear to Jasmine's lips to hear, for the woman's voice was only a faint whisper.

I cried and I begged to the Gods, praying for Jasmine to stay with me. She had to fight. She had to be strong and join me in Vulesa.

But no matter how I cried and begged, I knew it was not so simple. My tears fell over Jasmine's face as I watched her sigh and close her eyes forever. I had never had my own mother, but at least I had had her.

Jasmine lay there upon the ground, a corpse. The journey had destroyed the beauty of her spirit and her body, taking the sparkle out of her emerald eyes. Now she was ravaged and broken, and she just slipped away. The little girl's prayers to the Gods went unanswered. The earth hadn't cared. Life was fragile, and there was no justice.

I couldn't bury Jasmine, for I didn't have the tools and I was too small to move her body. So instead, I picked the pretty purple flowers off a small prickly bush. They were the only flowers that I could find, but I managed to gather enough to scatter over Jasmine's body.

Then the girl turned her back upon that glade of trees, and continued alone. That night she ate leaves and beetles, but it didn't bother her. She couldn't taste anything anyway.

She made a fire, but it didn't warm her. She hugged her young body, and rocked back and forth in prayer.

* * *

The girl was strong.
The girl lived on.

56
THE EDGE

You'll find me, dancing
through the cycle of the seasons,
between the salt-laced fold of oceans
at the edge of Reason's grip

Where in the gentle darkness
beside the flames licking the firewood
a whisper grows, a yearning turns
the blood to honeyed-wine

Then I'll seek the giddy silence
that spikes the music, with its notes
of melting snow, begging
for the burnt touch of the stars

* * *

The day dawned to greet Arian with her first true glimpse of the battle carnage. Yet she remained oblivious to it all. She just fought, pushing beyond the bounds of what should have been physically possible, just to claim more enemy lives.

Fredrik watched her, fearful for her sanity and safety, helpless to do anything. He recalled her reaction at the sight of their cousin's corpse, before she had fallen into her unconscious stupor.

The same demonic look was back again now. Her eyes gleamed red, whilst her face was pale from exhaustion. A ferocious spirit filled her with such bloodlust that it took all his composure not to flee himself.

He couldn't help but fear, for her and for them all. He had thought it would be easy to command Linuina in Melchior's absence. After all, he had many of the king's advisors and army officials to aid him, men who already knew how to lead a city during siege.

But the moral responsibility burdened him in more ways than physical duty ever could.

It was easy to hate the Henalas. After all, they were the ones trying to take over his city, his land, and his world. They were the cruel ones, bringing ruin wherever they marched.

Yet, as leader of this battle, their deaths were his responsibility. And death was a verdict that only the Gods should ever give.

* * *

It was noon when Arian finally broke, after fighting relentlessly for more than twelve hours. She had just thrust the point of her sword into an assailant's stomach, and then her knees gave way beneath her.

Fredrik carried her away from the open battlement and to the safety of a nearby tower. He propped her head against the granite, and she sighed deeply as he descended to her side.

"Arian, come back to the palace, I beg you! You've been fighting all night, you are going to kill yourself if you continue."

Hunger cramps tore through her stomach, bringing her out of her possessive trance, back to reality and human form. She allowed Fredrik to wrap an arm around her.

"Please, my dearest sister. I know it's been hard for you." He held her trembling shoulders, steadied her. "Just please, will you at least eat something?"

Arian opened her mouth to protest. But she didn't have the energy, and the ferocious feeling within was abating. She felt calmer now. Here, in the safety of the tower, with her brother at her side.

"Eat."

Fredrik was breaking bread. He must have already signalled for someone to come by with rations, and he had some sticks of dried sausage and cheese. She swallowed hungrily as he pushed some into her mouth, before she regained enough of her wits to start eating of her own accord.

When she had devoured all there was, Arian gulped down water from a flask. Then when she could drink no more, she splashed what remained over her face. The cool of the liquid was good. Soothing.

"That's better," Fredrik said, munching on some bread himself. He leaned back against the tower wall and closed his eyes.

Arian watched him, realising he was exhausted too. "Thank you, Fredrik."

"Just promise me you shall never be so foolish again," came his response.

She didn't reply, instead standing to go to the tower window and gaze out over the wreckage.

"Deep down, I'm afraid, and I don't know what else to do but distract myself. By fighting," she said eventually.

Fredrik rose to join her. "Fear is only natural in a time like this. I feared for you, I didn't want you to fight. But now I see that you were born for battle, to stand by my side and lead Renala."

Arian smiled as his words of encouragement echoed around the tower. Yet her smile was only a superficial one. It faded quickly as a voice lurking deep within her gut whispered sinister words.

The battle cannot be won with weapons.

The feeling that rose in response to the message was something far stronger than ordinary fear. But she had no time to reflect further, because at that instant Fredrik started spluttering and clutched at his side, his face turning a ghastly white.

"Fredrik!"

An image returned to her. Her brother's face: *on every soldier, moaning at the pain of a fatal wound, and in every anguished spirit, unable to break free from its tortured body.*

She began to shake, as the horror scene from her dream began to unfold. Her brother collapsed onto the floor of the watchtower, writhing uncontrollably. Groans escaped his lips, and sweat ran in rivers down his face.

"Help!" Arian cried as her brother began to lose consciousness in her arms. She pressed her palms to his face, feeling his fever, and the pain became her own: amplified into her mind, until she was screaming herself.

Then she became aware of a soldier shouting in her ear. Unable to move, she clung to Fredrik until her hands were forcibly removed, left to claw emptily in the air.

"Your Highness, we must find out what ails him!"

Thoughts deserted Arian as she succumbed to blank emptiness. She watched silently as the soldier peeled her brother's breastplate away, his movements gentle despite the urgency.

Then she beheld it. A bloody gash ran from beneath Fredrik's armpit to near his waist. It was not deep, but it oozed with the yellow puss of infection. The edges of the wound were blackened, in heinous contrast to the pale skin of his torso, and she could see green veins, like vines, spreading their plague from the wound and into the rest of his body.

Arian could not even scream anymore. She just watched as a group of men with a stretcher appeared in the winding stairwell of the tower, and lifted Fredrik onto it.

Then she walked behind them, a living carcass, as it happened all over again.

* * *

As the group descended from the barbican's battlements down into the city, men looked up from their positions and cried out to one another. Despairing voices confirmed their fears: their leader, Prince Fredrik, lay prostrate upon the stretcher.

The group entered the palace courtyard, and someone called out to Arian. She didn't turn around, but in her peripheral vision she saw Roman approach.

"By the Gods, it is true." He looked at the body of her brother, and wrapped an arm around her shoulders. "Don't worry cousin, he was always a tough one when it came to injuries." But still his voice quavered.

A deathly hush descended as they walked toward the palace infirmary, where the soldiers laid Fredrik upon a bed. The fever had consumed him, and his eyes rolled crazily beneath half-open lids.

Nurses flooded into the room, along with a man who Arian assumed was the royal physician. She pushed her way closer to him, eyes fixated on this one hope, the man who must heal her brother.

Then Thera's familiar voice sounded from behind, filled with sympathy. "Why do I have to lose every man I love?"

Arian turned to see her cousin enter the room, skirts billowing gracefully. But the pastel blue fabric did nothing to soften Thera's harsh appearance, and accusing eyes that stared vehemently at no one in particular, filled with anger and blame towards the Henalas.

"I cannot lose him," Arian hissed. She hurried after the group as Fredrik was carried away into an adjoining room, but the physician stopped her.

"Please remain out here while we bathe him."

Arian paused, lacking the strength to argue. But Thera was not so easily stopped, and she pushed forward roughly.

"What are you going to do?" she demanded, her cheeks flushed. Steam from the bath was spreading into the room, making them all sweat from the humidity.

When the physician didn't answer, Thera turned to Arian. "What does he think he's doing, killing him with all that steam? It's bad enough that Fredrik has a fever, he doesn't need any more heat. Any goddamn fool can see that."

Arian sighed. Knowing nothing about medicine, she wasn't going to intervene. The energy was leaving her again and she had no will to fight – not in any way. Helpless, she could only pray now.

But did prayer even do anything? Did the Gods listen? Or did they not care that all the people she loved were disappearing from her life?

She was beginning to doubt even the Gods. Those mighty beings had gone from inspiring her to taking everything away. Why, if they had the power, did they not intervene?

Arian sank into a chair, remembering how Fredrik had stayed awake for her all night while she recovered from the shock of Marcus' death. Now it was her turn to stay and watch over him – only this time, her brother's ailment was serious.

Silent screams reverberated in her mind, and in that clamour she remembered her father for the first time in days. He was out there somewhere, fighting. Or perhaps he too had already left the world?

A cloud of steam fogged up the room, and Arian looked up as the nurses carried Fredrik back to the bed. She rushed over to his limp body. His skin shone a sickly yellow colour in the heat, and sweat that was tinged with fresh blood dripped from his wound. It made him look as if he had just emerged from a festering swamp, half-devoured by leeches.

Arian moaned, brushing a lock of damp hair away from her brother's eyes. His forehead was hot, too hot.

Then the physician nudged her aside, checking Fredrik's pulse and temperature. She was vaguely aware of instructions being issued to the nurses, and movement around the room.

"Find me salicin for the fever. We will have to risk the consequences. And I will need plenty of the Nemurshan Fungi."

The nurse returned moments later, holding a jar of green syrup. "The juice of willow bark we have in plenty, but I fear we have nothing to aid the infection. The demands have been too heavy and many needed the fungus." Her voice shook as she spoke.

"No!" Thera squealed, but her courtly upbringing deprived her of the necessary, vulgar curses that Arian responded with.

"What do you mean there is none? This is the prince…"

"The fungus is rare," the nurse replied, mumbling her words. "It can only be found deep in the domain of the Henalas Emperor, in the northern mountains of Hevedh Nemash. We have already used the little supplies we had. There should've been a private store for the royal family. I can't see how we don't have any for his Highness. Before the battle we made sure of our supplies..."

Her eyes brimming with tears, Arian turned to the physician. "What now?"

"The fever will pass. But for the infection..."

Arian wiped the moisture away so that her vision was clearer. She could spot the same deep concern etched into the physician's face. He was afraid. Just like her. It was like he was already grieving for the probable outcome.

She let him move aside, and watched as he went to prepare a mixture from the green syrup. Then she turned, and slowly made for the door instead. There was nothing for her to do here.

The supplies were gone.

She was unable to believe it. Then again, what was there to disbelieve? Her mother, Queen Kristina, had died of a fever: suspected poisoning by Henalas spies. A mere disappearance of royal medicinal supplies should not surprise her.

Anger surged within Arian, but she fought it down and tried to focus. She could not let him go: she would try everything to prevent it.

She opened the infirmary door.

"Where are you going?" Thera asked, placing a hand upon her arm.

Arian had no reply. She did not know. A few lonely tears trickled from her eyes, but instead of seeking comfort from Thera, she simply pulled herself away and hurried off down the corridor.

57
BLEEDING COLOURS

I cannot explain where it comes from. When the rage takes hold of me. It's as though a lump grows from my heart. A clump of diseased tissue, a deformity that leaches all good feeling from me. Takes it away, and leaves me alone with this wild rage.

The tears are hot when they roll down my face. They burn me, my flesh. Dye my cheeks with their mark, like the hot solution of the master dyer in Vulesa. Only these tears don't leave beautiful colours behind. They leave acidic etchings of pain.

I stare at my reflection in the rippled water of a river. I can see myself, so clearly, despite the distortion of the streaming fluid. My eyes are what hold me. My eyes are what take me. I see my pupils swollen, their inky blackness consuming my irises. Wiry red lines stain the whites of my eyes, crimson blotches, blood upon snow.

The horrific mirror into my soul makes me cry more, more and more. Fuels me with insane desires of no origin and no purpose. Unexplainable. Inexplicable.

Hold me.

I do not know where the call comes from. I do not know who the speaker is, or what they want. I do not realise the mouth that utters that desperate plea is my own.

Take me away!

I want to go into the river, into the cleansing waters. I seek soothing calm to escape from stabbing pain.

Stabbing pain.

The words are familiar, but as are all words to me. For the words are my identity, my hope and my sanity.

All I need, all I know.

I need to rewrite the story.

* * *

My world bleeds.

The wounds stretch deep beneath the sea and the rock, threatening to rip her apart. Molten rivers gouge their way through her bowels, and I feel her writhing in agony.

The rifts widen in the depths, separating us from help. The Gods can no longer intervene to spare their creation, because the disease has become a part of it. Like an infection that has spread completely around the body, it is impossible to cut it out.

Oh Meridisia!

I wish I knew what I could do for you. But I am still trying to understand how all this could have happened. What has become of the land of magnificent culture and talent, with the turrets of beautiful cities rising fair and proud to the ever-blue sky?

How I hate them, for what they have done. Bringing this disease, they have corrupted the soils so nothing pure grows anymore. Their hearts no longer balanced, the people have lost touch with who they are.

And I am diseased too. I have the disease of hate.

Because I watch it all happen. I see… *I see…*

It makes me burn.

And it makes me destroy what I love.

58
CALL OF THE DIVINE

Don't hold back
as the knowing rises:
it has come
to guide you on
through the jungle deep
the shadows of
a forest, ancient
with its wisdom true
speaking of new pathways
beyond all that we can
even, ever
begin to comprehend

* * *

Arian found her feet taking her once more in the direction of the temple: towards the sanctuary of its pillars, and the hope of its flame.

Part of her felt faith deserting her: what use was a prayer, when Fredrik lay caught in the throes of his fever? When the medicine needed to cure him was unavailable? When fortress walls could do nothing to protect him from the disease in his body?

Yet another voice was guiding her. Commanding her to trust.

Arian pushed open the temple door and made straight for the prayer mat. She knelt down, closing her eyes and pressing her forehead to the ground. She took some deep breaths, inhaling and then releasing slowly, to bring herself gently into the present moment.

After a few minutes she adjusted herself into a seated cross-legged position, with eyes still closed. When she finally blinked them open, she nearly jumped, finding grey-green eyes staring across at her. They were coming from across the altar, on the other side of the fire: seeming to pierce right through it.

"It's you," Arian whispered, realising she was finally crossing paths again with the woman she had met on her first visit here. "Who are you?" The woman had never given her name.

"Does it matter?" came the quiet response.

"Yes. You know me, I want to know you."

A pause. Silence, save for the crackling vibrancy of the flames, as though they were chuckling at Arian's girlish lust for knowledge.

"You already know me," the woman returned finally. "But people call me Ileana."

Arian nodded, then realised that knowing the woman's name brought her no further satisfaction or comfort. As if, indeed, she already knew all there was to know. Or all the knowledge that was *available*.

"My brother is dying," Arian found herself saying next, in a mechanical, detached voice.

"No," Ileana whispered softly. But though soft, it had all the power of a commanding war call. "Only if you will it so."

"What?" Arian begged, barely daring to allow those words to light the flame of hope inside her. The possibility that she might have some control…

"Leave these fortress walls. They constrain you."

And with that, Ileana rose and left the temple, leaving Arian to her thoughts. She remained spellbound, as the minutes passed and she tried to make sense of what it was that she needed to do to alter fate.

59
WHISPER ON THE WIND

The sound of a flute greeted her ears. Pure, beautiful notes, soothing and calming music. It drove away the last vestiges of anger and filled her with motivation, replacing her bitter urges.

Beyond anything imaginable, she could not exactly describe it. Perhaps because the Earth herself was singing to her, both the harmony and melody, depicting the beauty of Life itself.

There should be no attempt made to describe this beauty. Humans cannot. When we try, we just ruin it. Casting labels, black and white, good and bad.

Fracturing the rainbow, and giving light a shadow.

* * *

I will listen to the music. Feeling the rhythm in my blood, I will strive to be motivated by Life, with both its faces of pain and happiness. So that even when the rain is pouring, even when I have to hold myself because I feel like mentally and physically I am falling to pieces, part of me can detach from my situation and smile.

Smile.

Knowing that I am alive and experiencing something, for one reason or another. And knowing that I have a greater purpose.

60
GUILTY ONES

"Your Highness?"

Arian stopped, brought to an abrupt halt by the voice of the young knight. She turned slowly, cautiously.

"Where are you going?" Richard asked.

"Nowhere, please. I want to be alone."

"Your Highness, your safety is my priority. And with the unfortunate passing of your champion, I am now sworn to protect you."

Her eyes narrowed. She did not want his vow. She did not need more deaths to feel responsible for.

"Please, leave me alone."

Richard's eyes softened. "Your Highness, I am truly sorry. I understand how it is to lose loved ones."

"Then please, let me mourn in peace." She turned, ripping her eyes from the sight of Cain's younger brother. And she ran down the hall without looking back.

* * *

Richard watched her go, cloak swishing at her heels as she fled. Her words had sounded harsh, commanding. But he knew how she was feeling, and he had to protect her.

Loyalty overrode all else. Because of his stupidity, Lily had been injured on the battlefield, leaving her too weak to survive Karl's birth. He had never told his brother that it had been his fault. He had just avoided Cain, and distracted himself. But physical strain, pushing his body and working to become a better warrior, ultimately did not cure the mental scars.

The princess had disappeared around the corner now, and Richard willed his body into motion. He would follow her, and keep her from harm.

61

A DOOMED MISSION

Arian crept towards the room with the trapdoor that Fredrik had shown her before her coronation. Slipping past a group of guards in the hall, Arian hurried inside. Moments later, moving with a reckless urgency, she was kneeling on the floor.

Her hands ran over the complex lines of parquetry in search of the edges of the promised trapdoor. The secret underground passage would lead her out beyond the barbican to a dingy alley between some of the poor houses on the southern side.

She breathed deeply as her fingers tested each suggestive crack. The minutes ticked by, but still nothing opened.

Arian stood, her eyes sweeping desperately over the floor as a myriad of feelings swirled inside her.

She tried a different spot, only to find nothing.

And another spot.

She was moving erratically, frantic from the anxiety sweeping over her. A voice within hustled her, telling her that perhaps it was a sign not to go: that she should stay in the palace.

But giving up wasn't an option. Fredrik needed more from her.

She breathed in deeply in an effort to calm herself, and dispel the rising frustration. Almost instantly once she relaxed, her fingers found the crack. She summoned her strength to slide the floor in the required circular motion to open the trapdoor: but strength was unnecessary. The secret opening rotated easily without much effort, as though her shift in attitude had oiled the mechanism, or as if someone else had used it not long ago.

Arian looked down into the gaping hole that had appeared in the floor. She slipped her foot over the edge, resting it upon the rung of a ladder, and slowly began the descent.

As the hungry blackness of the passage swelled around her, a surge of fear made her lungs contract. It was squeezing her chest, and she gasped for air, her breathing rattling out from her mouth.

Below the level of the floor now, Arian paused and braced herself on the ladder while one hand reached up to slide the trapdoor back into place. Total darkness enclosed her and the rungs of the ladder seemed slippery now, as she lost all sense of direction in the disorienting abyss of the cavern. But she had to keep going. Keep moving.

Finally her feet touched the tunnel floor, and she took a moment to regain her balance. She touched the walls around her, blindly searching her surroundings until her fingers encountered a lamp and tinderbox resting upon a stone ledge.

She managed to light the lantern and when it sprung to life she had to shield her eyes. Her pupils had already dilated significantly since leaving the palace room, and the sudden luminosity made her head spin. It was too bright.

Slowly her eyes readjusted, and she began to move cautiously down the passageway, lantern held in front. The light was far from comforting: it made her see the walls pressing in on either side, cold stone surfaces glaring at her as she passed, while the smell of dank earth filled her nostrils.

Arian shivered despite her woollen cloak, as an image of the walls collapsing in on her sprang into her mind. She countered it with thoughts of Fredrik, and how important it was that she continue on this mission to save him.

But thinking of her brother only led to other feelings rising within her: the maddening feeling in some corner of her soul, a craving to shed the blood of the enemy, of those men who mercilessly slaughtered her people.

The light of the lantern brought no comfort. It was not a nice light. Not like the light of hope, but a cruel light, vengeful flames.

The darkness provided no sanctuary either. The night was no longer a safe, warm womb. Not a place of sleep and innocence.

She moved, one step and another, with her attention on her breathing. Around her, thoughts and feelings danced dizzyingly, trying to distract her and drag her into their drama. Slowly but surely, she navigated the maze.

So deep in her focus, Arian barely realised she had come to the end of the tunnel until she was standing right beneath the grille of the exit. Light from the silvery moon seeped down, making a lattice pattern on the stone floor.

She extinguished the lantern and hooked it on a crooked nail protruding from one of the walls, then climbed the ladder to the grille. When Arian pushed, it slid smoothly away like the first opening, and she crept stealthily out onto the street.

She immediately shoved the grille back into place and ducked into the safety of the shadows. Her caution was not without reason. An enemy guard was pacing nearby, and if she hadn't been more alert she could have walked right into his view.

She crouched behind a low wall and waited until he passed, then swung out and slammed her dagger into his skull. He uttered a short scream before she silenced him, but only a flock of birds bore witness to his end.

Without wasting another moment, she pushed the body into a house and stripped off the uniform, which she changed into as a disguise. Then she walked with confidence down the lane between the clustered cottages, to emerge on the rise near the eastern gates without further encounter.

Arian paused behind a little thatched cottage, looking to the northeast at the enemy tents dotting the valley. From her vantage point, she sighted a large tent on the edge of the camp, which she reasoned must be for the wounded. Her best guess at where she could find the fungus.

She descended the slope without stopping, her rational mind abandoned. And taking a meandering course through the camp, she blended in with the other soldiers who moved around on their various errands.

It took all her efforts to suppress the nausea, as she walked between sweaty men coated in Renalan blood. Her breathing came in ragged gasps now as she concentrated on trying to prevent vile curses from escaping her lips.

But the thought of Fredrik kept her going, her focus narrowed on the tent ahead.

Finally she arrived, and peeked through the rear entrance to find that her guess had been correct. Groaning men filled the tent, and others hurried about administering doses of medicines.

Her eyes searched for a store of medicinal ingredients, and she panicked, realising she had not asked the royal physician what the fungus looked like. But she didn't have time for further thought, because at that moment a shout met her ears and a hand caught hold of her arm. It was like the surge of panic within her had illuminated her true identity, revealing her to the enemy.

She found herself spun around and came face to face with a stocky warrior who grunted some words in the Henalas language, and jabbed a finger in her chest. Unable to reply, she tried to dart away but to no avail, as he tightened his grip upon her.

Then another man arrived, although this one had gold embroidered on the sleeves of his uniform, suggesting a higher-ranking official. An air of authority surrounded him, and he barked something to the soldier who was still holding Arian.

They exchanged a few words, and the soldier let go. But the commander laughed savagely and took her arm, pulling her to another part of the camp. No use struggling, she just submitted to his crushing grip. At least her helmet covered her hair and face, so the secret of her femininity was safe for the moment.

They arrived at a guarded cluster of wagons, and Arian was pushed inside to find other Renalan prisoners shackled to the walls.

No escape now.

Her chance was gone. Hope was gone. With each second, each breath she took...

Her brother was closer to death.

She bit her lip fiercely to stop herself from crying out. One of the guards shoved her arms behind her back, clamping them into a shackle bound to the wall. He left without further remark, and she struggled to fight the tears squeezing out of her eyes.

A snarl sounded to her left, and she looked to see a Renalan soldier spit at her feet. But of course, she was clothed in Henalas garb, her face still masked by the helmet. Her captors hadn't even bothered to remove it.

"I'm one of you," she said breathlessly. "Please, what are they doing with us?" She couldn't stop the sob of terror from escaping her mouth. It did not make sense. The Henalas never took male prisoners. They always just killed.

"Only the Gods know. They bring new men here and take old ones away. No one returns," came a forlorn voice in reply.

Arian looked across at the Renalan knight who had spoken. Curly hair hung in knotted clumps around his ears, and his pale blue eyes were the only part of his face not smeared with grime. Even the whites of his eyes were tainted.

Bloodshot.

She swept her eyes over the other men, all in similar form. Honest men, captives now. Nausea gripped her stomach, and a few spluttering noises slipped from her lips.

"Scared, lad?" came the voice of another knight, staring across at her in sympathy. His own face was blank, resigned to his fate.

She didn't reply. She strained against the chains, trying to break free, thrashing pointlessly from side to side.

After a long minute she stopped. It was no use.

No one spoke again and she simply closed her eyes, her whole body weary. It hurt to see. The world was dim and blurry and the only light came from the moon, slipping in between cracks in the boards of the wagon roof.

62
ENSLAVEMENT

Going back became an impossibility:
because I saw,
I knew,
that to go back only lead to Death
an attachment to a shadow spiral
from which there was no hope
for Light

* * *

She stared back at the charcoal eyes, boring into hers.

Focus on them. Nothing else.

Shut out everything. Emotion. Thought. Family, city, nation, world…

"How nice of you to join me, pretty girlie."

The voice seemed to slither through the air, reaching its slimy fingers to tickle her cheek.

"My name is Taalin," she spat, straining against the chains. Fingers curled into claws, nails longing to bite into the Emperor's neck and strangle him for all he had done…

Shut it out. You'll go mad.

Focus.

The thin slit of his mouth curved into a smile. "Taalin, my pretty. Let me tell you something."

Metal-capped boots clicked across the marble floor as he walked. Closer. A pasty face leered at her. Eyes glinted lustily above that hooked nose, pointed at her neck like a dagger.

"I took a girlie like you once, a pretty northerner. She failed to give me the son I was destined."

The muscles in her stomach contracted in revulsion, and she felt her resolve faltering.

Hold on. Control. Stop.

Help.

"The Gods promised me a girl. It is written in the lore of the land that I shall have her, and that she shall bring me victory."

Taalin tried to be brave. Strong. Recall the bitterness and anger and fury and hate, emotions that steeled and empowered her.

But only fear remained. Trembling, squirming, begging, *mercy, please!*

"You will not do as a replacement."

Taalin gulped and tried to make her face a mask. Hopefully he would kill her. Get rid of her. Free her through death.

"But you will do in the meantime."

He was closer now. The eyes, the eyes, the…

Oh!

"We will dance to celebrate, as my wait is nearly over."

His hot breath rustled down her neck. Stinking. Vile. Evil.

He touched her with hot hands that formed shackles around her wrists, firm and tight, squeezing.

Pressure.

Pain. Burning. Heat.

Let me go!

A fire licked at her hungrily, consuming her.

Enslaving her.

* * *

Alexander swallowed as he saw the commander lead another man past his tent, heading for the prison wagons. This one wore Henalas garb, so either he was an imposter, or a traitor to the Emperor. Not that it mattered. Their fates were all the same.

Repulsion filled him, as he thought of the experiments being conducted in the nearby forest. There was power in those trees, energy that *they* sought to use for their own manipulations. Sucking it from the earth, draining away the beauty.

At least the progress was slow. The new weapons had only been used on the first night, tested to combat the cavalry ambush. As far as he was aware, it would still be some time before they could manufacture more and do significant damage.

Then again, he was not privy to those plans. He had no real control, though these were his forces. Not that he wanted command anyway: if he were in charge, it would make him even guiltier, more responsible for failing his mother.

Alexander lay down on his bed, clamping his eyes shut and trying to find some peace. But when he closed his eyes he just saw her face.

Then another face appeared, foreign yet strangely familiar, as if he had met her once in another life.

He snapped his body upright.

Now, tonight!

A strange sensation whipped through him. In that moment he felt stronger, like a surge of energy had enhanced his senses and fortified the purer desires within his heart, the ones that too often were suppressed by fear.

He could break free.

The feeling had only rushed through him for a brief instant, but it was enough. He hurriedly donned his robe and grabbed the tinderbox from his oak chest.

He slipped out into the night, out of the suffocating tent and into the cool, making for the prison wagons. When he wasn't far off, he knelt at the edge of a tent and struck the flint, lighting a fire.

He scurried away as the flames began to spread behind him. It wasn't long before soldiers noticed and shouts for water filled the air. But he didn't look back. Only forward.

The soldiers guarding the wagons had left their posts: the prisoners were chained to the walls anyway, and the fire demanded more attention. So it was unhindered that Alexander flung open the door of the nearest one, to the surprise of the men within.

Some glared at him, while others looked up with pleading, hopeful eyes.

Alexander didn't pause. He just rushed from soldier to soldier, unlocking the chains with his key. Then he went into the next wagon, oblivious to the storm of chaos that was swelling behind him. The escaped soldiers were running into the camp, shrieking triumphantly and channelling their energy into wreaking havoc.

Men rushed by him, his mother's people.

Then a knight called out, grabbing his attention.

And he stopped short at the sight of the latest prisoner. The one he had seen dragged by his tent earlier, in oversized Henalas garb.

He saw the lock of bronze hair peeking out from beneath the helm. He just stood there, riveted, unable to move.

63
UNDERWORLD

Richard struggled down the tunnel, squinting in the dark. He should have gone back to get a lantern, but he could not risk leaving the princess. She was ahead of him somewhere, and if he stopped following her now, he could lose her forever.

Then from nowhere some unseen force blew into his chest. He collapsed onto the floor, the hard stone biting him with its chill. He squirmed as ropes wrapped around his body, trapping him in a web from which there was no escape.

A tug. Something pulled. He was moving, being dragged across the tunnel floor.

Down. Away.

The princess!

Gasping, eyes watering as the twisted strands chafed his arms, Richard prayed to the Gods that she was safe. That she was alive. But his prayers were drowned by the ugly voice of despair echoing in his mind: a voice that made him doubt whether the Gods even existed.

Time passed.

Silence.

The shuffling noises of his body moving across the stone ceased. Cold fingers trickled across his face, his chest, examining him.

Dark, icy fingers, squeezing his throat and cutting the air brutally from his hungry lungs. He fought it. He struggled. He tried to draw his blade and cut the enemy away.

But the enemy was not there. It was invisible.

There was no flesh and blood.

A light came on. Red eyes pierced him.

Cain?

He saw his brother. They must both be dead.

But the pure spirit of his brother should have already ascended. This hellish interference could not be of the Gods' doing.

64

A Stranger's Memories

Alone
we could only ever be
one half
in the clutch of a whisper
that offers a glimpse
to the other realm
but united, we stand
one infinite chance
to cross between
to build that bridge
that heaven's song
is calling us, for
that wisdom's voice
beckons true
in the mind's eye
in the soul's sweet nest

* * *

Arian snapped out from her nightmarish stupor as guttural barking sounded outside. There was some sort of a commotion in the camp, and amidst the din she heard Renalan.

The knights around her were likewise stirring, blinking the sleep from their fatigued eyes. Then the door banged open and a strange man appeared, probably around Roman's age. He wore simple garb, knee-length breeches and a black robe embroidered with gold symbols. It was open at the front, revealing a tanned chest latticed by scars.

He moved to the first captive, unlocking the shackles. The Renalan soldier jumped up and darted out of the wagon, the lure of freedom pulling him into a mad run.

"Over here!" called the knight who had first spoken to her.

The strange man turned. It looked like he understood the words, as opposed to just reacting to a noise.

His eyes met hers. At first they had a crazed look to them, but then their fiery light faded until they were just soft brown.

Warm brown.

He stood there, unmoving. The knight called again desperately, inclining his head towards her.

"He's just a young boy. Get him out of here," he begged.

The stranger hovered one moment longer, then ran over to free her. She stumbled, trying to gain her balance, her shoulders stiff, her arms aching from the contorted way that she had been bound to the wall.

Though she'd been freed, Arian just stood there trembling. The shouts outside were getting louder, and she screwed her eyes shut to bring an image of Fredrik to mind.

Remember, he needs you.

Strong. Be strong.

The other Renalans in her wagon were also freed now, and one reached for her hand. "Quick, come on."

More men rushed by in their eagerness to find freedom, though running into the camp was similarly a death sentence. Yet at least they could die as free men, instead of Henalas captives.

Something kept her rooted firmly in place. The Linuinan knight was swept away in the surge of escaping prisoners, and she found herself alone in the wagon with the stranger. He consumed all her attention. Captured her with his gaze.

Stunned, he was stunned.

"You're a woman."

She swallowed, noticing the sensation of her hair draping down her neck, which had slipped out from the leather tie that she used to bind it atop her head.

"So?" Her terror made the word come out as a shaking hiss.

"What are you doing here?" His Renalan was perfect.

Fredrik.

"My brother is dying," she whispered, struggling to breathe, for the heavy armour was constricting the movement of her lungs. Something about this stranger held her. Despair and sorrow was engraved visibly on his features, enchanting brown eyes were etched with pain.

Her gaze wandered lower over the scars riddling his torso, orderly patterns like symbols in the language of torture.

A white-hot stamp, a coil of iron descending.

She screamed as she felt it on her own chest, felt it as though it was real. The vision had come from nowhere. Conjured by her mind, yet so true.

And a girl, there was a girl. There was fire, and shadows along the walls. Screams echoed around the cavern, tremors, agonising noises in the ears.

The stranger crossed the space between them and ripped the helm from her head. His hand clamped shut over her mouth, preventing her wails. She squirmed, trying to free herself, and to banish the images.

But they came again.

She remembered. She was there.

She recalled her capture. She was at the top of a tower, her fortress tower. Within the walls the city was nothing but a crumpled ruin, and outside a black blanket smothered fields of flowers. Their colour gone, their brightness dimmed.

Radiance subdued.

She felt the chain pulling her forward again, chafing her wrists. Blood dripped down to the earth from her wounds.

She had to be strong.

She saw him smile, a warm smile. She looked into his eyes, murky irises. Brown again, warm brown. Kind brown.

The colour of the furry squirrels that scurried around in the autumn, gathering nuts to last the winter.

Then they turned harsh, sharp. His voice hissed, sibilant. Mean.

Rasping her ears.

She ran and she ran. There was a star up above, guiding her in the direction of the Fhea Kharadid.

She was alone on her journey.

She ran between trees, flitting about like a spirit. But she emerged from the forest to find ruined fields once more. There was nowhere to go, she was trapped in the cycle of destruction.

They captured her again.

And then she was in a cell, a cavern beneath the ground. Chained to the walls, arms wide in a sacrificial gesture of forced submission. There was a man, a man with charcoal eyes that bored into hers.

Shut it out.

He laughed, a harsh laugh bursting from thin lips. The shadows slithered. Flames rose up on either side of the cavern, dancing flames, morphing into human form. A woman wrapped in white robes, her figure slender and graceful as a young birch, her silver hair streaming in the breeze.

You'll go mad.

She was trapped. She was caged. She was caught between shadows that held her there, stronger than iron chains, despite being mere insubstantial energy.

She had to save herself. She had to escape.

I want me!
Give me myself back.

65
FIRES OF FEVER

I was burning.

So hot, so unbearably hot, like nothing I have ever felt before. Like everything I knew and comprehended was being ripped apart, and rearranged into new patterns, new understandings, new knowledge.

I burned, in the middle of it all. I tried to fight it, hold on to myself: my dignity, identity and sanity.

But control slips away.

It was like someone else entered my body then, and I became aware of a new texture and depth to my reality. At the same time, it was all still robed in a blur, as though I was still not ready to truly see it all. To see the details beyond the matrix.

But one thing will remain etched on my mind, no matter what happens.

I will remember the faces of darkness.

* * *

Their impossible shadows flickered in places where there was no light. They were shifting shadows, conjured by the pain of their emotions.

They were caught within a distorted array of feelings and images, sweeping them along. There was bliss and happiness from a time when the world was young and fertile. A time before they sought to comprehend secrets that no mortals should discover.

In their folly, they had destroyed beauty. And now, they grieved for the past.

The agony for what they had lost made them burn. As if they were caught in the fiery wrath of a flame god, despite being in a lush valley with a cool wind sweeping past them.

They were swimming through an icy sea and they could not see the opposite shore.

"Help us," they cried repeatedly, their voices forlorn and hopeless.

They were lost, with no way home. The path was just a jumble of scenes and events with no recognisable meaning, yet crucial to their survival.

The knowledge was too much, and they sank into the depths of despair, though a haunted part of their souls was filled with glee at what was happening. They were Light, but born from the pits of the Underworld. They were Dark, yet born from the shining glory of the Realm of the Gods. They could not be both. *No, they did not exist!* They could not exist, but here they were in existence.

There was no more balance, only this chaos that reigned in the fabric of time and space itself: a jumbled collection of opposites, contradicting each other and causing conflict. For the beautiful balance of the brief but eternal garden of the Star Children had been destroyed. Unified light, loving peace of a divinely intertwining rainbow, had separated into a cluster of harsh, fragmented, polarities.

Only they could save themselves, but the opposition within them did not want to. Only they could save their world, but was it even possible to alter her fate?

* * *

I get these strange images. Feel something growing inside me, a cancerous growth, unnatural yet nonetheless part of me.

And through it all, I keep on burning.

66

THE KAYAMARA WOOD

Alexander's heart beat wildly in his chest as the girl squirmed in his arms. Her blue eyes were wide and filled with agony, such pain manifested upon them that they almost shone red. Then she fell limp before him.

In panic, the prince stripped off her armour so that she would be easier to carry. Then he pulled the hood of his cloak down to cover his face, and ran from the wagon.

There was still a commotion as a group of freed Renalans struggled to claim as many Henalas lives as possible. Others ran away from the camp, and a few had even stolen horses.

Unnoticed in the mayhem, the prince found his own stallion and leapt atop it, dragging the girl up after him. She didn't resist, and she slumped against his body as he kicked his heels into the beast and steered it towards the trees of the Kayamara Wood.

His mother had told him about this ancient forest, which had bordered the inland sea. Perhaps it would respond to the girl's needs. Perhaps it would save her.

Thick trunks loomed ahead, and he gulped nervously. Somewhere beneath the same canopy, the priests performed their experiments. Somewhere in there dwelled a danger, far greater than hordes of armed men.

But he had no other option, nowhere else to run. The army camp separated him from the sanctuary of the Linuinan fortress walls. Not that he could get inside, or would be welcomed there. Not that he was safe anywhere, his own captors ready to pounce from out of the shadows.

He looked down at the girl in his arms, and summoned the courage to spur his horse onwards. He avoided the path, which he knew would lead to *their* camp. Instead, he wove his way through the tangled branches, mind numb to the pain of sticks thrashing at him as he rode, scratching his limbs.

He pressed his body forwards, sheltering the girl with his own form. He had no plan and he knew not where he rode, but still he urged his mount to continue. And the stallion rode as if he knew the forest, and knew where to take his passengers.

Voices whispered in his ears.

He tried to find the source of the noise, but he could not. Something prevented him from focussing, and the words escaped his ears like the remnants of a dream, fading in the light of dawn. He closed his eyes. He could not keep them open: weariness overcame him however hard he fought to hold on, and stay awake. The girl needed him with his senses intact.

But he could not resist the fatigue.

His body sagged, his fingers losing their grip on the reins. But somehow his knees remained firm against the flanks of his mount, and the girl was beneath him, locked between the saddle and his body.

The horse cantered on. Muscles flexed beneath him, powerful legs carrying them through the forest. Neighs joined the song of the wind through the leaves, and hot breath from the stallion's flaring nostrils curled up into the air.

Then, silence. Motion ceased.

He opened his eyes, and gasped as he found they had arrived at a clearing. His mount had stopped right before an old man with black eyes and long metallic hair.

"Alexander, I have waited for you," said the man in Nemanipelian.

He stared back, stunned. "How do you know my name?" he finally whispered in Renalan. He did not want to speak *that* tongue. Yet here was a man who spoke the language of his world.

He could not deny that that was half of his identity.

"I was there at your birth."

The words hit him hard. He didn't know how to react.

"Come, boy. You may call me Erik."

Alexander almost toppled off his horse, his body unsteady from the confusion rippling through him. But he managed to make it to the ground safely, with the girl in his arms.

The man turned and began making his way to the other side of the clearing, towards a rundown hut that was covered with vines. Alexander stumbled after him, with nowhere else to go. For a second he wondered if it was a trap, if this man was another of the emperor's sorcerers experimenting in the forest.

But something deeper told him that this man wasn't one of *them*: although who he was and what he wanted was a mystery, his energy was not sinister.

They entered the hut, which was filled with smoke. The vapours made Alexander's throat burn and his hands shake, but still he held onto the girl. His hands would not drop her, as though they were permanently fastened to her flesh.

"Lay her here," said the man who called himself Erik.

Alexander did so, placing the girl down on a wooden bed covered with straw. The old man draped her with a blanket, and then led the prince over to the table.

There was a bowl resting upon it, and steam spluttered up from the hot liquid contained within. Instinct led Alexander to cover his nose and mouth, trying to prevent the vapours from entering his body.

"They will not harm you," Erik said. "They enhance the senses of my race, and though your blood is mixed, you have no reason to fear."

Alexander slowly removed his hand and inhaled some of the steam. The old man was right. A feeling of calm spread through him, lifting the fog of confusion and fear, and he began to see with more clarity. To smell more acutely.

To hear.

He noticed the whispering again, the quiet murmuring he had heard in the forest on the journey to the hut. Only now it was stronger, like a surging whoosh of air. He imagined flying through the sky, the noise of the wind rushing by.

Calming. Gentle.

"Who are you?"

"I am Erik."

Alexander gulped. "But who really are you? Why am I here? How do you know me? And the girl?"

The old man chuckled, waving his arm to dismiss all of Alexander's questions. He walked away, and began rummaging through his cupboards. The prince eyed him for long minutes.

Then Erik pulled out a jar of some yellowish ointment and went to sit beside the girl. He began rubbing it over her forehead, in the central space between her brows, and then at her temples. When he was finished, he returned to join Alexander again at the table.

"You will have heard of her, the Renalan Princess. That is she, Arian. Her brother is dying from an infected wound, and you will go back to the palace with her to save him. You will take this ointment, and use it in a poultice as you would have with the Nemurshan Fungi."

Alexander nodded unquestioningly. It was like the smoke was hypnotising him, and taking away the ability for him to think for himself. But he could still follow the man's words, and he understood the instructions. His mother had trained him in the ways of a physician: she had done all she could to steer him on a righteous path.

That was before the Emperor had discovered, and taken her away from him, and away from this earth, in the cruellest possible way…

Heal. That was all he had ever wanted to do. Yet instead he had found himself trapped, forced to cause the destruction.

"The wind and the trees will protect you on your journey back," the man continued. "She will be asleep, until you reach the outer houses on the southern side of the fortress. You must never mention me. And she will trust you for who you are."

No! She could not know who he was. She would hate him if she knew.

"She must learn to love," came the voice.

No, it was impossible for anyone to love him.

"Show her the way to love, by loving her. By loving yourself."

More of the steaming vapour wound through his nose, calming Alexander.

"And you will cure her brother."

The man rose, having uttered the last of his instructions. Alexander staggered up after him, his senses returning to normality as he distanced himself from the smoking fluid that spurted from the bowl.

"Won't you tell me anything else?" he pleaded.

"You will heal each other." At that, the man held out his hand and whistled. A dove flew to greet him, perching atop a finger.

Alexander looked closely at the bird, noticing how half of it was deformed, as if it had been caught in a fire. He swallowed, the sight of this creature reminding him of the hot iron stamps thrust onto his flesh, searing it with symbols of the Dark Gods.

"His name is Filpai, son of peace. He will guide you back through the forest."

Alexander reached forward tentatively to take the bird. It gave a soft coo, nibbling his finger, and looked up at him with one black eye, flecked with gold. The other was smaller, beady red.

Then it flew over to the bowl and dipped its beak into the liquid, before spinning around in the air and landing back on his shoulder. Startled, Alexander blinked, as if trying to be certain he had seen correctly.

"Go now," Erik commanded.

Alexander nodded and pocketed the jar of ointment that the old man passed to him. Then he went to lift Arian off the bed, and made for the door.

They exited, leaving the strange old man at the threshold. Alexander found his horse, and mounted hurriedly with Arian in front of him just as before. The dove wheeled in a circle around his head, then flapped toward the trees at the edge of the clearing.

Alexander looked back over his shoulder at the outline of the man against the hut, lit by the moon and the soft orange lamplight coming from within. But he turned away quickly, the sight stinging him, so many unanswered questions in his mind.

* * *

Arian's body ached, her joints stiff and her back sore. She opened her eyes, to find she was sprawled on the cobbles behind a low slate wall in the outer town. It was dark, though not the pitch black of night. More like the wee hours of morning, a hint of light suggesting that dawn was not too far away.

Arian let out a deep breath, and lifted a hand to her forehead. It ached, more than her body. As though she had been caught in a raging fever all night long.

Fredrik!

The panic rose in her, as she began remembering her wounded brother and her mission to find a cure for him. Then she recalled her capture. There was no memory beyond that.

"Princess, stay calm," someone whispered to her.

She turned to find a man sitting on the wall above her, and she jumped to her feet in surprise.

"Who are you?" she hissed, reaching for her belt, only to find there was no dagger there.

"I am Alexander. A healer, I can cure your brother."

Her lip trembled as she tried to make sense of it all and to remember what had happened since her capture. Then her eyes met his, staring into them deeply.

Soft brown, warm brown.

They were familiar, and she relaxed at the sight.

"You have the fungus?" she said desperately. There was a tingling in the back of her mind, a drifting memory. Doubt and suspicion rose to the forefront: but this man said he could cure her brother.

She would do anything for Fredrik to live. It didn't matter who the stranger was, if he could help.

"I have something else that can be used instead. An ointment, which works in a similar way." He took something out from the folds of his cloak, and showed her a small jar filled with a yellow gel.

Arian nodded. It seemed reasonable, true enough.

"We must hurry, before the Gods claim his body and his soul ascends."

Ascension.

He spoke of ascension, so he must be a believer. His tongue was perfect Renalan, so he could only be a Meridisian.

She could trust him. She would take him back to the palace through the trapdoor, and he would save her brother.

67
RELIEF

One frozen moment
upon the breeze
unravelling spiral
as my unease
fades gently with
the melting glow
of an eternal sun
whispering through
unfurling time
that today
your day
has come

* * *

Arian sat biting her fingernails as the man called Alexander examined her brother. She watched him carefully, dubiously, but without wanting to speak and distract him from his work. Despite her doubts, she could see he acted like a competent physician.

"Will he be alright?" she asked softly, when he finally stepped away from Fredrik's limp body. "You can heal him?" The question was more of an insistent statement.

Alexander nodded and placed a hand on her shoulder. "The wound and the infection I can handle easily. But the potion that your physician gave…"

"What of it?" she hissed, the worried creases on her forehead deepening.

"He used salicin, which is a substance extracted from willow bark. It helps to relieve the symptoms of fever, but can cause hallucinations and nausea later."

Arian frowned. "It won't harm him will it? Fredrik will still recover, won't he?"

He nodded. "I will begin operating now so we don't waste more time. Do not fear: I have dealt with ailments like this before. And I have every confidence in your brother's survival."

Arian breathed deeply, feeling calmer with each passing moment, though she could not explain why she trusted this man.

Alexander turned to a nurse and gave her a list of tools he needed, as well as several other ingredients including garlic and liquor for the poultice. Meanwhile he lit a burner, sterilising a knife in the white-hot flame. After cooling it in water, he used it to scrape away the puss that had congealed around Fredrik's wound.

Arian held her breath as the stranger worked. He was making a lattice of small cuts on her brother's skin, from which blood and sickly puss oozed out.

Then Fredrik began to pant, beads of sweat appearing on his brow.

"Don't let him move," Alexander commanded sternly, immersed in his work.

Nodding, Arian assisted the nurses to hold her brother in position. She was handed a cloth to press to Fredrik's brow, to help cool him down.

Arian forced herself to watch as Alexander operated, despite the gruesome sight. He was carefully cutting away the scabs and diseased skin, and little by little Fredrik's blood ran ever purer shades of red.

A nurse handed Alexander another rag that had been soaked in boiling water, and he used it to wipe away the blood and gangrene, to leave raw pink flesh behind. Fredrik screamed again as the hot rag came into contact with his wound, and the nurses increased the pressure on his arms to prevent him thrashing wildly. His teeth were gritting together, his head rolling from side to side. Arian tightened her own grip on him, feeling a surge of pain rush through her body, as though she was feeling everything her brother was.

Then Alexander left Fredrik's side, instructing a nurse to continue wiping the wound with the sterilising liquor. Meanwhile, he began making a poultice with the ointment, and returned soon after with a thick grey mixture that smelt of moss.

Alexander applied it gently over the wound and the surrounding skin. Arian watched his hands move, in a tender circular motion.

A movement so…

Loving.

When he was finished with the ointment, the nurses assisted him to wrap bandages tightly around Fredrik's torso, until her brother was bound like a mummified corpse.

"What happens next?" she asked curiously. Fredrik was laying on the bed calmly now, in a peaceful slumber. His convulsions had ceased, his breathing returned to normality.

"I'll need to change the bandages every day to monitor the infection," Alexander replied. He paused, scrubbing his hands. "What remains of the fever should go naturally now. You can rest, and trust that your brother is in a stable condition. I assure you."

Arian nodded, a weary smile of gratitude inching across her face. She closed her eyes, taking a moment to pause and savour the sound of Alexander's comforting words.

She thanked the Gods, hopeful now that her brother would live.

* * *

Arian left Alexander in the company of a guard, with orders for him to be escorted to the guest chambers. She needed some time alone now. Physical fatigue from the last few days was catching up with her, as well as a deeper fatigue of the soul. Satisfied that her brother was in safe hands, at last she could afford to relax and process the muddy mess swirling in her mind.

She went to her own rooms, and called for Sarah to bring her hot water so that she could wash. Then she carefully began to unpeel the sweaty layers of clothing from her body. When she finally lifted off her filthy chemise, it felt like a dead weight had been removed.

Arian rolled down her breeches, and when their hugging tightness was gone from her legs, she moved to the tub and began scrubbing herself clean. Scrubbing not only to remove the dirt from her flesh, but the impurities of her soul. Through the fog of her weariness, flashes were coming back. Flashes of battle, of her mania to kill and destroy the enemy, of the whirlwind of hate she had been caught up in.

Layers of filth flaked off, tainting the water. Arian finally stopped scrubbing, for she reached the point where to use the water would just make her dirty again. Not to mention that she felt so weak, she barely managed to towel herself dry before she went and collapsed into her huge bed. The sheets had never felt so silky, the cushions never so fluffy. She closed her eyes, relaxing into the comfort of night, as mellow darkness embraced her. She was safe here, she could soften…

Show her the way to love, by loving her. By loving yourself.

Arian gasped as she heard a strange voice echo in her mind. She gulped and brought her hands to her head, rubbing them across her forehead and trying to remember what had happened after she entered the camp.

She had been captured, and taken to a wagon with other war prisoners.

Soft eyes, warm brown.

A few detached scenes flashed through her mind. There had been a man who freed them, and a fire in the camp. Renalans, some fleeing and others fighting, while she had stayed behind.

She rose from her bed and went back to the bathing room again, to splash some cold water on her face. At least the terrible ache was gone. She remembered that her head had felt like it was splitting apart, hot and feverish.

Returning to her bedchamber, she went to the window and pulled back the drape to find that the sun was just rising. She had been out the whole night, and there was nothing left but a few shards of memory. As if her mind was a glass vase, and it had been dropped, broken.

Sleep was no use. It would not come to her now, especially with the daylight breaking through the gauzy fabric of the curtains. She should check how Linuina was faring under siege.

But a deeper, intuitive voice, told her to seek out the library instead of battle.

68

DARK ARTS

Jerim stared across the table, eyes fixed on Reaveno.

"You're telling me… they attack with *energy?*"

The earth-scientist nodded, his expression grave. The gravity of the situation outweighed any initial excitement he may have had of making a new discovery.

Jerim slowly let the breath out of his lungs. His gaze darted to the right, to look at the woman he had first met. She was twirling a lock of her hair pensively in between slender fingers. Her name was Ileana.

"Please explain," he asked sharply, returning his attention to Reaveno.

The scientist nodded. "Now every molecule in the air, in the atmosphere that we breathe, has stored vibrational energy in the bonds between atoms. This weapon sucks in air when the trigger is pulled. I have yet to determine exactly how it works, but my experiments and calculations lead me to believe that the device removes the energy from these said molecular bonds. It then propels the concentrated energy forward. A tiny weapon, but powerful."

As Jerim absorbed the information, he tried to keep his face a mask, devoid of emotion. Tried to hide the fear that was crawling through his insides: he was supposed to be a warrior.

"Surely… surely this has consequences, beyond just…?" his voice trailed away. He wasn't sure what he was referring to. But if something *took energy* away from the atmosphere, it most certainly did not sound good for the planet.

Reaveno dipped his head. His eyes flickered to look at Ileana, as if inviting her to speak, but she remained silent.

"Yes, Jerim," Reaveno finally answered. "They do not seem to possess many of these weapons, or at least have not utilised them since the incident on the first night. But to use weaponry like this on a large scale, the earth would be destroyed."

Jerim swallowed. "What do we do?"

Reaveno cast another look at Ileana, and she finally stopped twirling that strand of hair. She placed her hands atop the table and looked across at Jerim, long and hard.

"Now Reaveno simply speaks about the mechanics. There is more to the story, at least, more that I believe is happening here. Energy itself is not good or bad. Our bodies are energy. They should be able to absorb more energy, to integrate it. I do not believe that what these weapons release is in itself responsible for death."

Jerim frowned, following Ileana's reasoning. Her sharp, intelligent eyes penetrated deep into him.

"You said your horse lived?"

"Yes," Jerim replied. "In fact, as far as I'm aware, none of the horses were killed in that way. What does that mean?"

Ileana nodded slowly. "It supports my theory. Horses are powerful, noble creatures, pure of heart and with much stronger auric fields. And they are symbols of freedom." She paused, for what seemed like an eternity. Jerim waited, struggling to see where she was going with her reasoning.

"So…" he finally prompted her to continue.

"The *energy* itself isn't responsible for the deaths of your men. I believe that it is their own inner turmoil that is. A heart that is loving, awakened, and free, would feel the purity of any injection of energy. The energy would do no harm: in fact, it could elevate the soul yet further, through higher planes of consciousness. But an injection of energy into a heart that is distorted with negative thoughts and emotions, will simply amplify those feelings. And I believe this is what is consuming your men."

Jerim didn't know how to react to that. At a fundamental level it made sense, and in some ways Ileana's reasoning brought hope. Because it suggested that each individual had the power over how they reacted and responded to the weaponry, and that there was a way to combat the Henalas simply by reclaiming one's sovereignty and resolving the darkness within.

Yet at a practical, physical level, Jerim felt lost. This was entirely unchartered territory. He also knew that personal healing to resolve one's traumas and transmute negative energy, was no easy task.

"But it has to happen," Ileana murmured, responding as though she'd read Jerim's mind. She blinked, and for a moment her long lashes flickered down to veil the intensity of her jade eyes, flecked with sooty grey.

Then they returned to stare at him. "Now," she said firmly, "Prince Fredrik has talent too."

Jerim stiffened. "You mean like…?"

She nodded. "I do not know how he could have inherited it. Besides, it must have been dormant all this time, or else I would have sensed it given how close I live. I think his recent ailment, the fever, has triggered something. He is powerful. Very powerful. We may have a weapon of our own to retaliate with."

Jerim gripped the table fiercely. In his mind he saw the young prince, prostrate in his bed, as no more than an innocent boy. The thought of him being used in this way made his insides squirm.

But sacrifices had to be made, for the greater good.

69
NO ONE'S CHILD

I rise, with the mystic call
of a lonely dream
that binds me to
new life
and love
that with the birthing
of the moon
is ready, to guide me
on…

* * *

I am no one's child.

The empty absence of the void need not be a frightening place. It may be seen as an empty absence that carries with it freedom from the past, and the blank canvas potential of infinity's dream, the possibility of endlessness…

I am not defined by my heritage, though I may learn from my ancestors. I will take my own road. Following my own path, I will let no one dictate my destiny. I will not be driven by the pains and trauma of generations.

I will not be told what to do or prevented from responding to the tug on my heart, the tug that guides me to rise beyond fear and walk into a new, clear day.

I will be my own person. Creating my own memories, I will fill my spirit with substance.

You are mine.

The voice lunged at me again. Trying to trap me, the sound solidifying into a stone cage.

You will not escape.

I screamed, as I heard the words inside my head as my own words, trying to corrupt my mind.

I prayed then, I prayed to the Gods, but they weren't listening.

Not because they don't care, but because only I can help myself.

And so I am searching, to find out how.

* * *

Arian sat with her head resting against a shelf, a book open on the floor beside. Her eyes were closed, for she had long ago abandoned reading. The story gave no answers. Not that she knew what she was searching for anyway.

Morning slipped on into afternoon by the time she woke, her stomach growling. She rubbed her eyes and climbed to her feet, replacing the book and looking around as though she had no recollection of what she had been doing.

Then she left the library and walked down the long corridor past the rooms of learning. Past so many doors that were closed to her, hiding secrets of sciences she had neither studied nor ever sought to comprehend.

A door opened ahead of her, and she saw the northern commander leaving a room. Lord Jerim, that was his name. She remembered him from the strategic meeting the day before the siege had commenced. Not to mention that it was impossible to forget the colour of those emerald irises.

"Your Highness," Jerim said in greeting as she approached. "I hear your brother is recovering well."

She nodded. "And how are our troops faring?"

Jerim avoided her gaze and looked straight ahead in the direction of the staircase. "There was a skirmish in the enemy ranks last night, and they halted their attack on the walls. Some Renalan prisoners escaped and returned to the city, and we are holding them for questioning. We must be wary, lest there be Henalas spies among them."

Arian took a deep breath. She knew about the incident, she had been there. But still she struggled to remember clearly what had happened.

"You will also be pleased to hear that we received word from your father," Jerim continued.

"Good news?"

He nodded. "Their attacks from the north are proving effective in splitting the attention of the Henalas. The enemy have made no surprise moves, yet."

"Yet?" She had noticed a muscle in Jerim's jaw twitch, although his expression was otherwise assured.

"Your Highness, there is nothing for you to worry about." He looked away again, so she could not see his face. His voice was strong and unwavering, nothing to betray even a hint of unease. Yet Arian could feel a subtle undercurrent of tension in the air, as though something was wrong.

"Forgive me, but what business do you have down here?" she asked softly.

This time when he returned to meet her inquisitive stare, his eyes were troubled. "Is a warrior allowed no respite either? I came to seek relief in learning, just as you sought relief in your stories."

He bowed respectfully and moved away from her, walking quickly up the staircase. She followed at a slower pace, allowing her mind to relax and think of her father. At least he was still alive, and his strategy was working. Not that she had ever doubted his competence.

But she did fear the unknown, and something about Jerim set her on guard. She did not feel threatened by him, but she sensed deeper understanding beneath those strange eyes.

Do not concern yourself in these affairs. This is not your place.

She jumped, recalling a fragment of lost conversation, hidden away in her mind. A spark of recognition flared up, a feeling that she had met Jerim before that war council.

It faded, and she turned her thoughts away, to instead focus on the stranger she had brought home to cure her brother.

Brown eyes, soft and warm, troubled by an inner turmoil.

70

THE ENEMY PRINCE

Though shown to a spacious bedchamber, Alexander could not rest. He simply sat there for long hours as the night faded and the sun rose. His mind was on the princess. She would most likely be sleeping now, after the ordeals of the night.

Part of him wanted to go and speak with her. But there was nothing for him to say. He could not confess who he was. He could not answer her questions with the truth. And if the truth escaped, what would happen anyway? Would he be taken prisoner, executed?

He realised that he would prefer death, over returning to his reality. If he ever did return, he knew he would be punished severely for his betrayal.

No matter what he did, he was a betrayer. A traitor.

At least he was helping the righteous people now, his mother's people. But he could only do this for so long. Soon they would find out, he could not hide forever.

He thought of the strange old man in the woods, and the instruction.

Show her the way to love, by loving her. By loving yourself.

The promise.

You will heal each other.

Alexander closed his eyes and recalled holding her young body in his arms, the touch of her limp form against his chest as he rode through the night. So comforting. He craved for a loving touch, and it felt like she needed him.

But he could never have her.

Do you want her?

He clenched his hands into fists. The mocking voice that came into his mind was his father's, teasing him. He had always rejected the women the Emperor offered. Women stolen from raids in the north, captives like his mother had been.

Frightened girls, they were no older than the princess. Spared temporarily because of their beauty, then cast aside once they had served their purpose.

You can have her.

Droplets of sweat dripped down Alexander's back, as the voice of a hissing priest resounded in his mind. It forced the memory back, of that horrible day almost six years ago when his father had sent a woman upon him in the hope of producing a grandson.

The Emperor had been unsuccessful in his own attempts to yield another heir. Alexander was his only son, his failed son. A boy who had grown into a cowardly man, not the merciless warrior needed to complete the conquest of Meridisia.

You will heal each other.

The old man Erik, from the forest, had claimed to have been present at his birth. He had spoken firmly yet kindly to Alexander, like a loving father. *So unlike his own.*

And so the sequence repeated again in his mind. Alexander thought of his heritage, yearned for acceptance among his mother's people, and begged for answers. He felt the memory of the young princess in his arms, vulnerable and weak. Shook his fists with rage at the cruelty of his father and the actions of his people, then softened as he heard the wise man's promise.

Over and over again.

The prince stayed trapped in his thoughts until late afternoon, when a knock on the door interrupted him. He rose and went to answer, finding the princess before him. Faltering, his insides quaking, he hovered there for a moment. He was so startled he could offer neither a respectful bow, nor a word in greeting.

She stood there, fresh after a bath, the sweat and grime of battle erased from her honey flesh. Luscious bronze ringlets framed her face, and two clear eyes gazed at him, a piercing bright blue.

While he remained entranced, she spoke. "I must thank you, for healing my brother. I just saw him, he sleeps peacefully and the fever seems to be gone."

Alexander finally managed a bow. "It is a pleasure to serve, Highness. But he is not cured yet. Each day I must change the bandages, and cover the wound with a fresh moss poultice to assist the body in clearing the infection." Those words strengthened him. He was a true physician now. He was practicing the art his mother had introduced to him as a boy. The art he had secretly studied, his one and only act of defiance against the Emperor.

And right now the princess needed him. She could not cast him away without risking her brother's life.

"Of course," she said, averting her eyes. "I will have food brought for you. You must be hungry."

"Thank you," he returned. Yes, he was hungry. But the physical hunger was nothing compared to his starving need for love.

He realised he was holding his breath, and exhaled slowly. Sweat trickled down his spine, his blood rising with a foreign heat that he could not control. For here was the princess, a free woman, unlike the captive northern girls.

"I'll… leave you now then," the princess said hesitantly, breaking him from his fantasies. She left the room abruptly, leaving him alone.

The food came but he ate mechanically without really tasting it, his mind totally consumed with thoughts of the princess.

71

GREATER POWERS

"My lord!"

A knight entered his tent, and Melchior looked up expectantly. They had pitched camp to rest for the day, before the planned attack at twilight. He would be leading a cavalry charge on the Henalas reserves that were stationed north of Linuina. The plan was to drive them in the direction of Karama, where more Renalans were positioned with Nerilek to ambush them in the gorges.

"Yes?"

"Please, come quickly. A wounded scout has arrived. Our healers are tending to him, but they do not expect him to live much longer."

The urgency in the guard's voice startled Melchior. It was common for scouts to arrive wounded after crossing land riddled with enemy troops, but something told him that this was different.

Melchior followed the guard through the camp towards the healer's tent. He thrust open the canvas flaps and entered to find the scout laid out on a canvas sheet.

A boy. His pale torso was exposed, and speckled by burn marks.

"Majesty," the scout spluttered.

Melchior rushed over and knelt beside him, grimacing when he saw the boy's face. The burns were mere tiny pricks upon the flesh, yet so deep that in places even bone was visible. A nurse was on his other side, gently dabbing some green ointment over the wounds. But there were too many of them.

Melchior took hold of the boy's trembling hand, giving it a squeeze in an attempt to offer strength and support. The pain in the boy's eyes was enough to sear holes in the king's own heart.

Despite the child's suffering, he managed to form words for the king. "The Henalas have been taking war prisoners into the Kayamara Wood." His voice came out squeaky, forced. "I followed. They have some sort of base there, conducting experiments on our men with these new weapons."

The boy was shaking now, his mouth twitching uncontrollably. Melchior looked across at the nurse, who averted her gaze, her features grim. They both knew what the boy's fate would be.

"Majesty..." the unsteady voice trailed away and Melchior could not control the tear that rolled out of his eye to splash on the ruined child. "Majesty," the boy tried again. "I don't think the Emperor is there, someone else is in charge."

Then his little chest began to rise and fall in ragged gasps, while his hand tightened its clutch on Melchior's own. For tense moments spasms wracked his body, before he went limp, pale blue eyes frozen in death's stare.

Melchior stayed by his side for long moments, allowing himself some time to pray for the courageous boy. Then, when he finally detached himself, he walked out without a backward glance. There was much to be done.

Melchior returned to his own tent to reflect over their possible options. In the end, the conclusion he kept coming back to was that he needed to return to Linuina. Events had turned, and Arian was no longer safe in the city. Not that she was safe anywhere.

Of course, there were others at Linuina who could help them. Perhaps Ileana and Reaveno had insight to offer. Or Erik, though his old advisor had cautioned him against returning. He remembered the sage's words.

It is no longer safe.

If the Henalas were occupying the Kayamara Wood, that made sense. But Melchior shuddered to think of the implications. The forest was alive with natural energy, a powerful land, untouched and untainted. For so long the Henalas had steered away from it, always forced to approach Linuina from the northwest. It was the very reason Karama had been built in its current location, in order to launch offensives and trap the enemy from the northern side.

Melchior called to the soldier on guard outside his tent, having made up his mind. He issued instructions for the other commanders involved in the cavalry charge to meet him as soon as possible. If the attack tonight proved successful, sufficient attention would be diverted away from Linuina to allow him to return with a small group of knights. He could use the underground passage to enter the palace.

His commanders could easily lead the cavalry. They knew the plan as well as him, and were competent enough. Besides, Nerilek still held his position at Karama. Adequate authority remained for Melchior's absence to cause no trouble.

Certain with his decision now, his mind turned away from strategy and back to his daughter, though he tried to restrain it. Part of him wished she had never been born, for then it would have been so much simpler. Yet that was beyond his control. In the end he was just another person, another servant of the Gods. If it was their will, he could only do his duty.

His sturdy shoulders began to shake as he thought of the fragility of life, and his daughter at the mercy of greater forces.

Arian.

Never would she be able to live normally. Chained to other powers, she was more helpless than a slave. And at the same time, she was the only thing he had left of his beloved queen.

Before he could stop them, buried memories of dear Kristina resurfaced. He recalled their wedding night, he a prince at Fredrik's age and she a young maiden full of virtue. Images swam before his eyes, as he battled his tears.

Such long nights he had stayed awake, watching over his wife during her illness. Then that final night had come, the night not many years ago when he and Fredrik had awaited the horrid announcement.

It had come in the early hours of dawn. In agreement with him, the healer had not given Kristina the dose of her drug, the only thing keeping her alive but which kept her in a numbed state blank of any thought, feeling, or memory. She had been awake just long enough to say farewell, before leaving the planet forever.

Seek justice. But do not hate.

Those had been her last words. She had been a woman with firm beliefs, determined to stay true to her values: stern but kind, and above all, emphasising the need to love others. Even upon her deathbed, she had not been one to condemn her enemies.

As he recalled the moment that the breath had faded from her lungs, Melchior relaxed, tension fading from his body. It was over now. Her torment had passed. But he wondered why these memories were coming to him now, of all times, when he had kept them locked away for so long.

Perhaps if Kristina were still here, she could help. Somehow know what to do, have an answer. Be the mother his daughter needed.

Yet she was not, and he could only hope that he had done enough to steer Arian on the right path. It was out of his hands now, and into those of the Gods.

72
DECEPTION

Only when
you hold me with
the unconditional love
of a father for
his dying child
without fear for the future
or entrapping expectation
just pouring into this
present moment
the light of your being
the light of your soul —

Then I shall flower,
petals blooming on the wind
a new spirit rising
from the ashes of the past
as the winds shift
to cool my pulsing body
my passions softening
to reveal within
a golden thread
of Love

* * *

A beam of gold from the lanterns in the hallway outside streaked into the room, piercing the shroud of darkness enclosing Alexander. He looked up from where he was seated on the bed, his brows creasing into a frown.

The princess was here. Slender frame silhouetted against the light.

Her hand fumbled with the knob, then she closed the door behind her and the night consumed the glowing river once more. Natural moonlight spilling through the uncovered windows illuminated her form, radiating with an unearthly beauty.

Alexander swallowed. Rising to his feet, he managed to cross the room without tripping on the fur rug, although when he arrived he could not say a word. He was too consumed by the sight of her. Rich bronze hair curled past her shoulders, shimmering in the backdrop of the twinkling stars. She wore a white silk gown over a lilac nightdress, black frills contrasting against her slender, honey-coloured legs. The aroma of fresh herbs emanated from her, sensual scents wavering delicately over her crown, like the halo of an angel.

"Your Highness, what may I do for you?" he finally asked.

"Please, call me Arian," she murmured.

He did not respond, simply waiting for her to continue. Part of him trembled, thinking of the answers he owed. Answers he could never give.

Yet he was in her domain, and he knew the questions would come.

"Will you tell me who you are, really?" she whispered. "I have no recollection of last night, I do not understand."

He gulped and looked away, then felt the soft touch of her finger on his clenched hand. "Please talk to me," she said, even softer. "I sense you are pained. I can see it, written all over your face. And your body…" her voice trailed away, and he knew her attention had fixed on the scars covering his chest.

He stood there, and forced himself to look back at her, so young and innocent. He fought for control, breathing slow and deliberate.

"You were the one who freed the prisoners in the Henalas camp, were you not? You are one of us, a Renalan? You speak perfectly. You must be."

Trembling, he nodded.

"Sir, you are so brave. And I would've died without you, no doubt. My brother and I both owe you."

He saw her clutch her robe around her. She was shivering slightly, probably from the cool breeze drifting in through the window he had left ajar.

"You owe me nothing," he returned, a little sharply. Part of him wanted to tell her the truth, and he searched his mind for a way in which he could explain. Justify who he was.

But there was no way. No simple way.

Nor could he describe the pain that ripped him apart, yet formed an integral part of his identity.

She reached out and touched his chest, one finger tracing the line of a scar. "These are not battle wounds."

He cringed. "No."

"Who did this to you?"

She would not stop questioning, but of course she had every right to ask. He was in her territory. She ruled this city, the city his father had instructed him to attack.

The words just slipped out of him. "The Emperor."

She winced, her eyes wide. "He captured you? You were tortured?"

He only nodded. It was the truth, in part, and his eyes watered at the memory of the pain, though it was only physical pain.

Not the worst kind.

A vicious urge shook him, and he grabbed a bunch of Arian's curls in his hand. Pulled her closer, until they were only centimetres apart, and her crystal-blue eyes shone right into his own. Hers were the colour of his mother's eyes, before flames had tainted them in her dying moments. But no amount of red could make her look evil, like the shedder of blood the Emperor was.

The princess did not move. Did not struggle.

He relaxed and drew back. "Forgive me, Your Highness."

"Please, call me Arian," she repeated again, ignoring his apology.

The blood began to boil in Alexander as passion coursed through his veins like a gushing torrent, echoing to the far reaches of his body.

You can have her.

The haunting voice of the priest sounded again in his mind, and he could not contain his gasp as the painful truth of his past simmered to the surface. But the princess didn't seem to notice his attention had flickered to other places.

Instead, she wrapped her arms around him, and he did not resist. He needed physical contact, loving physical contact, after so long without.

He tried to clear the fog that was clouding his rational mind. But he realised he didn't want to. The fog obscured those painful memories, thoughts, and feelings. He was a human again. Not a tool, not an agent of destruction. He had control of himself.

And Arian wove her hands upward to clutch around his neck like a frightened child.

Yes, she needed him too.

This was justified. The old man had promised.

You will heal each other.

This was his cure. Finally the Gods had answered his pleas and given him this gift, the gift of a pure princess to cleanse his soul.

He looked down his nose at the top of her head, that was pressed against his scar-laced chest. But he felt a drop of moisture on his skin, and pulled back to find her with tears caught upon her delicate lashes, like morning dew.

"Why do you cry?" he asked softly, wiping away the moisture from her eyes and holding her head tenderly, stroking her hair.

"The war... I..." Arian looked up. Her warm breath tickled his neck, like a dancing wraith, sending tingling sensations all over him.

He brushed a finger over her lips to silence her. "I promise to protect you."

And he watched her eyes grow large, shining with an innocent gleam of hope. Unable to contain his desire, he descended the gap between them and pressed his lips to hers.

She moaned, and as they kissed, he slipped away and down a path of bliss where nothing mattered but that moment. Parts of him began to awaken, that before had only experienced suffering and pain. Ever so slowly, through their contact, history began to rewrite itself.

Gently, they broke apart, his lips lingering on hers. But then he flinched, recoiling as his rational mind returned. He should not have done this. She was a princess, and a snarling voice within told him that he was that which he most hated.

"Your Highness, I forget my place."

He saw her lip tremble, her lashes lower. "It's okay... I..."

"Will you stay?" he asked quietly, as the fears once again subsided. The echo of the old man's promise sounded one last time.

Show her the way to love, by loving her. By loving yourself...

You will heal each other.

Arian looked up at him, at his soft eyes pulling her closer, and making it impossible for her to resist. The light from the last flickering candle near the bed was ample enough for her to see those brown irises. Murky secrets dwelled in their fathomless depths. So much pain, she could tell that much. But the detail of it, she did not know, though she felt in some way deeply connected to this strange man she had only just met. There were some things that she could simply just *understand.*

She could not help it. She wanted him. She wanted his arms and the strength within them. She wanted to join with him, share whatever pain he had experienced, lighten the burden, press against his torso and rub away the scars. The touch of his lips had taken away all memory of the last few days, the terrible sights of battle and then her brother on the verge of death. She only wondered what else he could do.

"Yes," she whispered. Reason had gone. She could trust this man. He had cured her brother, and his noble actions had saved her life. She wanted to touch him. She yearned for him to touch her. Her fingers loosened their hold on the gown, and she allowed it to slip from her shoulders.

He reached out, running a hand down behind her neck and across the line of her shoulder blades. She shifted closer, tangling her fingers in his hair and begging him to tempt her lips once more.

Alexander's hand wandered lower, caressing the rise of her hip and dipping down over her thighs, into the valley between her legs. Then he wrapped one arm firmly about her waist, to pick her up and carry her to the bed. Sliding a hand beneath her nightdress, he drew it away and she quivered with a combination of excitement and nervous modesty.

He guided her hands up to slip off his own shirt. As he did, her fingers hovered for a moment over one of his scars. Then he was across her, straddling her trembling body. Her lips parted, and the hesitant voice of a maiden spilled out.

"Alexander? Alex…" she sighed as he silenced her with another adoring kiss. His fingers trickled across the tender skin of her belly, enchanting her within a web of sensuality.

"Yes?" he said softly.

"Please, don't go. Don't ever leave me." She looked at him intensely, her eyes glimmering despite the waning candlelight, as if lit from within.

"I never want to be alone again," he whispered.

Her heartbeat quickened as their bodies collided. She arched her back towards him, driven to heights where there was everything. Energy hummed through her body, at every frequency, every wavelength of light, refracted into a rainbow of a thousand colours. It pierced her with such pleasurable pain that she thought she would rip in two at the paradox.

A squeal escaped her lips, and Alexander shivered at the sound of her delighted moans.

The Emperor loved listening to the screams of women, as his torturers cut the limbs from their bodies and shaved off their scalps.

He gasped in pain, his body convulsing and pressing harder against the princess.

She was responding to the pressure, aching to drink the nectar of this strange, addictive substance. Filled with longing to inhale the ethereal vapours, so that they would enter into her mind and send her spinning with the new knowledge and understanding.

While he stood, in the deepest and blackest of the Emperor's torture chambers. Listened to his mother scream as they flayed her naked body, tied to a stake. Held by the men, forcing him to watch.

He roared, pushing down upon the princess again, crushing her body in his descent. He thrust fiercely as if to prove he was a man, that he was not weak.

Yes, he had escaped the Emperor at last.

A free man, he was free.

"Stop!" Arian screamed.

Through a veil of fire, she saw a young boy. He stared across at her, his eyes wide and fearful, pain flaring in those muddy eyes. Men were holding him, and she struggled against her own bonds, wanting only to take him from their clutch and hold him in her own arms forever.

Flames restrained her, agony hit, as she began to burn.

I clenched my teeth together as fire smothered my body, its hot flaming fingers caressing the swollen welts of my flesh. Still, more welcome than the Emperor's touch.

The boy was crying. Her boy was crying.

I choked away the sob. I was strong, and my son would be too. I had planted my seed in the Emperor's evil line. This child would not be a tyrant. He would save Meridisia.

She raised her face proudly, though her body was crumbling to ash. She would not break. She would give him a strong image to hold to, to remember. He would not see his mother weak.

You will not fail, my son. I will always live within you.

73
THE TRUTH UNVEILED

The madness left. The vision faded and he was empty. It was over. And the sound of a flute greeted his ears, tinkling notes that drove away the last vestiges of torment. With a sated sigh, he collapsed onto the bed.

But a sob split the hush, and Alexander jolted upright to find the princess shaking before him. Eyes wide with fright, mouth sucking for air, slender body bruised and battered.

He returned to the present with horror, and scrambled away from her. Left the bed, where she lay trembling. Left the sheets, streaked by blood.

He could not speak. He was that which he most hated. He shuddered to think of the horror that he had transmitted…

"Alexander."

The sound of her plea hovered in the air behind him. She needed him.

And he turned. He had to go to her. He approached slowly, his feet shuffling. Anxiety blended with terror, over what he had done: deceived her true spirit and destroyed her pure body.

"What happened?" she moaned, her fingers at her temples.

"I'm so sorry. So sorry," Alexander whispered, taking her body into his arms and rocking her tenderly.

"I was burning," she began, her voice so soft. "I saw myself in a chamber, tied to a stake, flames all around me."

He froze. It was impossible. He wanted her to stop talking but he couldn't open his own mouth.

"I saw a boy in the distance, through a curtain of fire and smoke. I could not go to him to stop his screams, because I was dying. But I had faith in him, that he would be strong and that he would take the right road."

Alexander began to cry uncontrollably, his tears showering the princess.

"My mother," he groaned. "You saw her."

Her body tensed. He refrained from looking down, could not bear the thought of seeing her face and her reaction.

"Who are you?" she said, her voice quiet but sharp. Jolting him. He had to tell the truth. He could not deny it. He had to accept who he was.

"I am Alexander," he began, his tone blank and hollow. "I am the Emperor's son."

Then she screamed, louder than before. An anguished wail, it filled the room and spilled out of the window into the night. Around the city it spiraled, as though in search of an answer, in search of a path leading up to the gates of the Starry Kingdom.

The dying gold flame of the candle flickered out, and the room plunged into total darkness.

"No!" she cried again. She ripped away from his arms, only to thrust back in rage, scratching him with clawed fingers.

He did not move. He did not try to escape.

When she was done, she rushed to her abandoned gown and pulled it over her soiled body. Ran from the room and left him alone.

Alone.

He sat there, unable to move, unable to forgive himself.

Yet still he yearned for her. For her to return and accept him, and putting the past behind, see him for the man he wished to become.

74

AWAKENING

A sharp pain shot through his chest. A strange pain, unrelated to his wound. And with a gasp, Fredrik opened his eyes.

He looked down his nose and saw the bandages wrapped around his torso, holding him rigid. He could not move. Trapped in the bed, he was helpless as he felt the stabbing pang once more.

Arian.

He gulped.

A hand descended onto his forehead, and he looked up to see a woman standing over him. Sharp green eyes returned his stare, though softened by a hint of pastel blue, spotted with grey.

He began to relax.

"You must rest, my prince," came the woman's voice.

"Who are you?" he mumbled, her touch making him drowsy.

"People know me as Ileana. I work for your father. I am a mind specialist."

She spoke confidently, assuring him that she was someone he could trust.

But when her hand left his forehead, he felt the strange, stabbing sensation inside him again.

"Arian!" he cried. He did not know what was happening, but he felt that something was wrong.

The woman hushed him, brushing her hand over his eyes. With his lids closed, it felt better.

"I will see to her. Do not fear."

* * *

In a storm of angry confusion and frustrated fear, Arian stumbled down the corridor and back to her own chambers. She did not understand, could not comprehend, what had happened.

She opened the door, and jumped at the sight of the woman sitting on her bed. Then she remembered who the intruder was: Ileana, the woman from the temple. The one who could calm her with a touch, whose whispered commands of advice kept resonating over and over in her ears.

You have control… harness your emotion… never let it rule you.

Arian ran over to the woman in desperation, diving down onto her bed and letting the tears run down her cheeks. She did not know what to think, or what she should feel. Everything swam in her mind, in a dizzying blend of no meaning.

"My child," Ileana said softly. "Hush."

"No!" Arian cried, fearing that this time nothing could help her. She couldn't find the words to describe her rising emotion.

No words, empty of words.

"What have I done?" she murmured finally.

She should never have gone to the stranger. But something had urged her to seek him, to take his hand. The memory of his tortured eyes had called her, and she had followed in search of their secrets.

Now she wished she had never learnt the truth.

"You have done nothing wrong."

"But…"

He is different.

Though he had deceived her, he was not cruel.

You should never have gone.

Arian squeezed her eyes shut, trying to erase what she had done. How could she have betrayed herself to the enemy? Given her body so willingly?

She could only tremor with fear for the future, and the implications of her actions.

"Dear child," Ileana said firmly. "There is nothing to be ashamed of."

For a long time, Arian did not respond. When she finally did, it was to speak of other thoughts troubling her mind.

"I don't understand," she groaned. She didn't know why, but she hoped that this strange woman Ileana could help. "Sometimes there are other voices in my head. Visions…"

"I know. I can see them too."

"What are they?" Arian begged.

"I do not understand."

Arian shook her fists. "But you… you must." Ileana had claimed to study the mind. Surely she could explain.

"I have not seen the likes of this before." The voice was grave.

Arian lay there for long moments, breathing in and out in an effort to steady the beating of her heart. "It is like there are two spirits inside of me," she began, hesitantly. She sounded mad. Perhaps she was mad.

But Ileana nodded. Her eyes were not judgemental.

"It is like someone else is calling me from within my own mind," Arian continued. "I do not know who or what it is."

"Sometimes you must turn away from your mind."

"What do you mean?"

Ileana sighed heavily. "When your mind is at war, you know not the right questions to ask. So you will never find the answers you crave. The search is fruitless."

Arian nodded, greedily absorbing each word.

"In those times, you must turn from your mind and seek within your heart. Hold to your values, stay true to who you are."

"And when you do not know who you are?" Arian whispered.

"Then you must create yourself. You can be whoever you want to become."

75
YOUNG KING

Strength –
is allowing yourself,
sometimes
to break down in tears
let those rivers roll
down to the sea
without fighting the current
of emotional release
just holding yourself
in your arms
like a child
accepting,
without judgment
noticing
and, with love
permitting the armour
to dissolve
till your soul
is free

* * *

After a morning of strategic planning, Nerilek rose from his seat at the council table in Karama. Around him, warriors rushed to fulfil their duties, and messengers hurried away to deliver their tidings.

Nerilek watched them leave, then turned his attention to the young prince who had walked gingerly over to the window of the fortress. Soon they were the only ones to remain, and Nerilek joined him there.

"The ceremony has not yet made it official. But you are a king now," he said, placing a hand on the boy's shoulder. Christophe turned to stare at him, his hazel eyes wide.

Nerilek breathed in deeply, thinking of what the poor child had experienced. How it would feel to be the only one left of your family, and among the last of your nation. A leader of no one, save the tattered remains of a once-glorious people.

Some Regofalans had arrived at dawn earlier that very day, survivors who had fought their way through occupied territory to join the allied forces at Karama. A small group of brave men and women, warrior people who had been fending off the Henalas their entire lives.

"I have confidence that you will grow to become a mighty king," Nerilek said softly. He watched the boy tremble, eyes darting to look out through the window slit.

"I remember the day they came," Christophe murmured. "I remember standing at the top of the Halisaan fortress, with my sister. And she told me…"

We'll defeat them. We'll fend them off like always. And survive.

"You survived, my young king. You survived."

Christophe shook his head, and kept his gaze averted. "We did not defeat them. We were crushed."

"No," Nerilek said, his voice firm. "No, you were not crushed, though your city and your home was. But so long as one soul remains hopeful, our world is not defeated."

"How?"

Nerilek gripped the boy's shoulder. "It is what lies within that matters, in the heart and spirit. Our mortal bodies are mere physical vessels that encase a greater, deeper force. You have power, young king. Power of soul, a power no enemy emperor can take away from you."

For a long time Christophe remained silent.

"I am expected to lead," he said finally. "I am a king now, you said it yourself. But I don't have courage. I am not a warrior. I do not understand, whose blood did I inherit? All my people are strong, and I am not."

"My boy, even kings are allowed to be afraid. And you are no coward. You simply desire this bloodshed to end. I can see that you are angry that your family were slaughtered like they were."

Yes, yes he could see the flame in the child's eyes. A dim flame, but a flame nonetheless.

"Yet you have not allowed this rage to consume you. You do not seek vengeance."

Despite his suffering, the boy was pure of heart and spirit.

"It is more people like you who are needed in our world, a world that is infested by disease. Too many allow the purity of their love for their women, children and land, to twist into a storm of hatred. That will not be you."

Christophe raised his head, revealing to Nerilek the tears that ran from his eyes. "That will not be me?"

"No. A good leader is not one who charges blindly into battle, thirsting to claim enemy lives. A good leader is one who is faithful, standing true to the Gods and all that he values. A good leader must deal justice, but allow his verdict to be led by reason and righteousness. And a good leader will love both his family and their slayers, seeing that which is noble in even the most haunted souls."

Nerilek loosened his grip upon the boy's shoulder, having said all he could. He hoped it would be enough.

"What is my role tonight, in the battle? Must I stay here in the fortress with you?"

Nerilek took in a sharp breath. "Young king, you tell me what it is that you wish to do."

"I… I am a good rider. I have practiced since I could walk, training in the regions south of Halisaan. The terrain is similar on either side of the Hevedh Suhil, and I know the strategies of gorge fighting well."

"My king, I did not intend to convince you to lead this battle," Nerilek replied, his tone sharper now. He felt a stab of anxiety, concern for the youngster. "You are still young and training is never the same as a real battle."

Christophe met his stare. Nerilek could see there was fear in the boy's eyes. But it was mixed in with something else too now: a newfound strength.

"Please, let me ride with the cavalry front. I know the plan. I have been listening."

"Explain to me the plan, then," Nerilek suggested. He resolved that, if the boy explained correctly, he would let him go, no matter how foolish he thought the idea. If this was the boy's choice, and he understood the strategy, then he should allow it.

Christophe nodded and walked back to the table, where some blank sheets of parchment still lay. "Here. This is the junction where we will be fighting."

Nerilek watched him sketch the landmark, two great valleys crossing each other.

"Our forces are split, half waiting in the northern gorge and half in the south." Christophe drew several smudges to mark the troops. "The Renalan forces are driving the enemy across from the east. When the Henalas arrive, we ambush them from both sides, while the Renalans close off their escape."

Nerilek nodded. The boy knew the details well. "And then?" he prompted.

Christophe added several arrows pointing towards Karama. "The enemy have only one direction in which they can retreat. West, we will push them. Where you await to finish them off." He looked back at Nerilek now, waiting for an answer as to whether he'd passed the test.

"You will join the cavalry division in the northern gorge." It was the safer of the two, narrower and more sheltered, harder for the Henalas to manoeuvre. "You will be in the rear ranks, your main task as a rider is to drive the enemy west. Are you sure you want to do this?"

Christophe smiled. "Yes." Then the young king dipped his head. "Thank you, sir. Your words have been inspiring."

Nerilek grimaced, quickly praying that the night ambush would not be the death of the young king.

"Go now, get some rest before the battle," he said.

Christophe turned, and Nerilek watched him leave the conference chamber. Just a boy, he had probably not seen many more than a dozen summers. But there was a time when boys must grow into men.

* * *

The sun was retiring from the sky, casting a golden glow through the mist that descended from the mountains. Spiralling shadows were swept up within the fog, announcing the imminent approach of night.

Christophe stood in the courtyard of the keep, beside the horse he had saddled for war. Riding was something he had experience in. He had not lied about that, though he had put on a brave mask before Nerilek, while inside he had been quaking with fear.

Yet this was something he felt he had to do. He placed one hand on the flank of his horse, closing his eyes as he allowed the beast's warmth to comfort him.

"My lord!"

It was a woman's voice, followed by a bright tinkling laugh. His eyes snapped open and he turned.

"Saachi?"

She had been a friend of his sister. She was another survivor from the capital, and here she stood, ready to fight too. Fine chainmail hugged her slender body, and a green velvet cape hung from her shoulders, clasped by a silver brooch around her neck.

"Yes, my king," Saachelle replied with a bow.

"Please. Call me Chris," he mumbled back, unaccustomed to hearing the title that he felt should still belong to his father. He had not earned his right as leader yet.

"I'm sorry." She tentatively reached out to take a hold of his gloved hand, and he met her eyes. Though they were grey, they were far from dim. Lit by her fierce spirit, they shone like the metallic gleam of a polished sword.

And the truth hammered home. She was more of a warrior than he was.

Christophe felt the squeeze of her hand and gulped, summoning his strength in an attempt to match hers.

"How did you survive?"

She lowered her eyes. "I wasn't in Halisaan when they struck. Father sent me to join a cavalry front in the south. If I had known... I would have stayed. I would have died with my family."

Christophe swallowed. She was exactly the opposite of him. He had fled death, while she embraced it.

"Part of me feels guilty, though it is not my fault," Saachelle confessed, lifting her face to the sky. "But then I remember them. I know they are in the Starry Kingdoms watching down over me."

Her gaze returned to him, her jaw a firm line. "My king, Christophe, we lived for a reason. And our families can see us and all that we do, so let us fight for them."

A trumpet call sounded as if emphasising her words, and Saachelle turned to her chestnut mount. She thrust one boot eagerly into the stirrup, and skilfully pulled herself up.

Christophe followed her example, and they led their horses at a walk to where the others were gathering at the gates. They would be taking a different path into the valley to the one which he had first arrived at Karama along: a wider one, though still treacherous.

"Saachi?" he murmured, and she looked over at him.

"Yes, my lord?"

He took a deep breath. "Do you ever feel afraid?"

Her grey eyes were not judgemental of his fear.

"All the time," she whispered, before inclining her head to the stars again. "But they give me strength. And if the Gods decide that it is my turn to pass, then I will die." With that, she flicked her long braid of ebony hair over her shoulder. Then she lifted her helm atop her head, masking her delicate features.

Cold steel returned to stare at him. Not the soft visage of a girl, but the hard face of a warrior.

76
HEAT OF DARKNESS

Find a peace
within the storm,
calm
within the wild
grip of insanity's
clutch —
as you walk at the edge
gathering the pieces
polarities, colliding
surrender into paradox
so deep, we move beyond
there is a beauty in the mayhem
of an other-worldly song
and there is purpose in the emptiness
where our hearts
once belonged

* * *

Warm breath touched my neck and I turned hurriedly, desperately, needing to find its source.

It came again, fierce and passionate, stirring my hair and making my body ache, sighing hungrily.

Faster, harder, the hot breeze pushed against my flesh, forcing through the pores of my skin and entering my blood.

I opened my arms in a beckoning gesture of submission.

Take me now, I whispered through parted lips, then rubbed my tongue over my teeth, like some wild creature.

The burning came from nowhere and everywhere at the same time. The darkness shifted and ethereal shapes began to form, and I drifted between them in search of something solid. Searching for my tether, my anchor... like an umbilical cord, between a child and mother.

A touch.

I felt something. Physical, real, I gasped with expectation. Yearning for the warmth of a loving embrace.

Then it intensified, heat rising. It became hot, too hot, wrapping me in the arms of lava.

An instinct surfaced in me, to turn and run. But then suddenly I did not want to escape. I succumbed to the heat, as it filled me with its crazed, powerful fluid, up from the molten core of the earth. Blood coursed through widened veins, thrust apart forcefully by the quaking movements of the earth's crust.

I saw creation, and I saw destruction.

And elemental union through the flames, balance in the chaos.

Alchemical essence of the Earth's gracious heart.

77
BEFORE THE STORM

The crescent moon above gave little light to the riders. They moved almost intuitively, taking their places at either side of the valley intersection, warriors jostling against each other as they kept their horses in check.

Christophe turned his mount to the north, following the commander of his division. His heart pounded in his chest as the hour of attack approached, though it calmed him somewhat to know he was not fighting in the front lines.

Wind hummed along the gorge, teasing the rock. A ghostly sound, it drilled a foreboding cold into the very marrow of the young king's bones.

There was one light ahead: a flaming branch held by the commander. It sent shadows, like scars, across the granite walls, and gave an orange glow for them to see by. Thick mist above concealed all smoke, committing them to secrecy.

The murmuring of low voices whispered amongst the ranks, then came the words. "A messenger has arrived, he departed just before the Renalans commenced their attack. About another hour, and they should be here."

Christophe gulped. Another hour of waiting, waiting for the enemy to come. He let go of the reins to massage his hands, stiff from gripping tightly. Ahead, some of the warriors had dismounted to stretch their backs. There was time, too much time.

He raised his visor, freeing his face from the stiff metal cage. The breeze upon his flesh flushed away the stifling heat of his helm, and with it, dismissed some fear.

Looking behind, he saw Saachelle jump to the ground. She had removed her helm, and it sat hooked on the horn of her saddle.

Her silvery eyes turned to him.

Christophe swallowed and removed his own helm, to feel the breeze ruffle his hair. He joined Saachelle where she stood, leaning under a nearby ledge. They were close to the rear of the group, where it was less crowded. Pressed against the rock, they waited together.

Christophe listened to the sound of her breathing, and watched the gentle rise and fall of her chest. A regular motion, rhythmic and disciplined, confident.

"Chris?"

Hesitation softened her voice, as though she feared speaking his nickname now that he was a king. But he sighed with delight, for the sound of his name dispelled the burdens of leadership and his status. Made him feel as though he was just an ordinary kid.

She must have mistaken the reason for his silence, and hurried to speak again with formal words. "Forgive me, my king."

"No, please. Call me Chris."

He was staring at his feet, at the leather boots latticed by steel strips, a metal grid to give protection from slashing swords. But the boots were not too heavy, enabling the wearer to fight on foot too.

He hoped he would not have to do that, as he would be no match against a heavy warrior. Like most of the northern youths, with their small and nimble bodies, their skill was in riding, charging down a gorge to drive the enemy towards foot soldiers waiting in ambush. Or towards a fortress, like they would be doing tonight.

Christophe became conscious of the breath on his cheek, and glanced up hesitantly though his head remained bowed. Saachelle was close to him, her eyes picking up the glint of torch glow, a bright grey reflector in the surrounding gloom.

"Chris," she said again, surer now. There was no intonation at the end, no raised pitch. It didn't sound like a question, but a statement.

Warmth spread through his chest, as the name grounded him further, making him feel stronger and more real. He was more than just a flimsy question, he was not just a cowardly youth.

She took his hand. At the contact his heart beat faster, her touch making his skin tingle, even though leather gloves separated their flesh. She was so lovely in the moonlight. Her young features were soft and womanly, but at the same time, she bore herself with the pride and valour of a veteran soldier.

He cleared his throat and nodded to the stars. "You have faith in them, don't you? The Gods?"

One corner of her lip curved upward in a sad smile. "They are all we have, in the end. They are the only ones to live on, while our cities crumble and fall."

"Doesn't that make you bitter, though? Because sometimes it feels like they have forsaken this planet. That they do not care about what goes on here, how much we struggle."

Saachelle nodded, her left eye glistening with the moisture of a tear.

"I know. But in the end, does it matter? If we stay true to them, we will ascend. I believe in striving for that. To live up there…" She was staring at the sky in awe now, though the mist in the gorge obscured the stars from sight. "It must be wondrous. Life with rock beneath our feet is just a test, before we go up there. That is where true life begins. Nay?"

"You speak like a wise man," was all Christophe managed, caught in the beauty of her speech. Embraced by the thought of eternal life in a land away from war.

A giggle broke the surreal ambiance. "I hope I don't look like one."

Now Christophe smiled with her, her joke masking all anxiety about the looming battle. He turned to look at her directly, but quickly averted his eyes. His cheeks felt hot, as if he'd been riding at a thundering pace.

"Chris?" Her voice sounded questioning again.

"Yes… Saachi?"

"Sometimes I wonder what it means to be a woman."

When he didn't respond she hurried to fill the silence, her voice now awkward and flat. "They say that it is rare for southern girls to fight. The men protect the women, the women are weaker."

Christophe returned to study his feet. "I suppose it is different for them. In the north, we need everyone to fight. Otherwise there wouldn't be enough people."

He heard her sigh, as though he hadn't given her the response she was hoping for. Then he heard her breathing break from its disciplined rhythm. Warm air on his cheek tickled him.

"Chris? What I really mean is… I wonder what it is like to be with a man."

Christophe finally met her gaze, and saw that her eyes were wide with innocent wonder. She was more girl than warrior now, though her daring spirit showed plainly upon her face. Suddenly the young king found her lips descend to his, pressing with urgent need.

She took him by surprise, but he did not resist.

78
SPIRIT OF THE EARTH

I walk the drying riverbed
of your dying wish
to plant the seed
of a sunken prayer
transporting you up
through and between
to the ether beyond
to gardens lush
that hold the answers
in their flowering jewels
of magic music
and sweet sage song

* * *

Taalin lay in her crude bed, in a cell in the uppermost tower of the Henalas fortress. She lay there, cold and alone. Away from the world, distanced from reality.

Her senses had detached themselves, her body numb to pain. Her eyes had become blind to the monstrosities, her ears deafened to the tortured wails, and her flesh deadened to the vile touch.

Her heart was closed off to morality. Otherwise it would hurt too much.

* * *

It is hard to describe what I am, for I am so many things.

I am the plants and the animals, soil and rock, water and sand. I live in the air that every entity breathes, and I feel the resonance of all those souls.

I have the knowledge that no mortal should ever have come across. I did not ask for it, I was just born. And for some reason, I discovered something I was not meant to.

But that was aeons ago now, and since then I have changed.

I am trying to ascertain what motivates me.

I was born a human, and humans need something special to motivate them and keep their hearts beating. To wake them in the morning, ready to face the day.

I thought that Life itself motivated me, in all its forms and with all its wonders. I thought that my amazement with Life brought the sparkle to my eyes. Because whether the rains fell or the sun shone, I felt like I was soaring with the birds. I was in touch with the spirit of Life, this powerful essence that encompasses us all.

But then I realised that there was more to Life, or else more just came into being.

Now I feel the earth shuddering, bleeding... weeping.

I want to restore balance, order, and harmony. I can. I have the power. All I have to do is wake up.

But to wake up I must have a motivation.

And to be motivated by Life, I must also be motivated by Death. Two great opposing forces, coming together as two dancers.

One day they'll twirl together, harmoniously hand in hand.

79

LAST KISS

Saachelle gently pulled away, her need fading, passion sated.

"Thank you, my king," she whispered. Her voice sounded serious now.

Christophe stared into her pearly eyes. His heart rate slowed once more, back to normality, though his cheeks remained hot despite the breeze.

He took a deep breath then slowly exhaled, savouring the memory of their tranquil moment. Peace before the storm of battle, sunshine before the rains of war.

"Saachi... thank you."

She smiled. "I just wanted... you know. Before we fight, perhaps for the last time."

Christophe nodded. Earlier that day, hearing those words would have made him tremble with fear at the thought of death. But now Saachelle's strength flowed into him, the words of her empowering speech fresh on his mind.

Life with rock beneath our feet is just a test.

He returned her smile, before pointing towards their horses. "We should mount. Be prepared."

Saachelle reached for his hand and squeezed it, and they leapt back atop their steeds. Knights ahead of them had likewise done so, and a few shreds of hushed conversation filtered down between the gorge walls.

Then up ahead, the commander pressed one end of his flaming torch into a crevice to deaden the light. Nods were exchanged, confirming the proximity of the Henalas, and all warriors fell silent.

Soon after, Christophe caught faint sounds in the distance. A few cries, and the high-pitched clash of swords. Then came hooves, growing from a dim pulse to a thundering beat.

He exhaled sharply, and his helm trapped his breath, heating his face. The night started to grow brighter again, as torch glow wrestled through the mist.

A call sounded from the cliff tops where their archers were stationed, and flames erupted above as men lit signal torches. Arrows pounced down into the valley from overhead, and a shower of screams followed.

The first wave of cavalry kicked into motion, the knights ahead of Christophe riding out into the fight. He nudged his mount a few steps forward, waiting for the next signal, his turn yet to come. As the seconds ticked by, his stallion tossed his mane and flared his nostrils, smelling blood.

Horses whinnied as their riders jerked the reins, catapulting them forth into the fray. The sounds wove together, louder now, as the granite cliffs picked up the noises of battle and concentrated them down the channel of the gorge. In the deafening roar, Christophe could no longer hear himself think, or feel. He knew nothing but a fiery whir of blinding smoke, stifling armour, and the bloodlust of warriors as they allowed their hatred for the enemy to consume them.

Then came another command, and a neigh sounded behind him. Saachelle was urging her charger into motion, and she scraped by the rock to cram in beside Christophe.

"Soon it's us," she cried, drawing her sabre from its sheath across her back. He followed her example, first winding both reins together in a loop so that he could hold on to them with one hand.

They were near the narrow opening that led into the wider east-west valley. The Henalas ranks should have been pushed further along by now, and they would ride to bring up the rear, combatting the stragglers and driving the troops forward.

"Charge!"

In pairs, the remainder of their group shot between the cliff walls. Christophe leant forward, his head against his mount's neck, his legs pressing firmly against warm flanks. Booms sounded in his ears, like the thudding of great trees falling to earth.

Peering through the thin slits of his visor, the world was a dim blur, flecked with red from the signal torches lining the cliffs. Then figures solidified before him: the dark outlines of Henalas foot soldiers.

The scene became a chaotic whirlwind of charging horses sweeping between the enemy men on the ground. Swords slashed through the air that was alive with crazed screams and dying moans.

A pause, and Christophe gasped, realising he had been holding his breath, overwhelmed by all the sights and sounds. Saachelle swiftly overtook him, riding hard to plunge right into the midst of the enemy.

"Saachi!"

The sight of her urged him on and Christophe rammed his knees harder, sending his mount bolting forwards. A head appeared before him, and without even thinking, he brought his sabre down with a slash. A gurgling scream tore from the man's lungs as blood gushed down his chest.

Christophe screamed with the man, but his physical body carried on, as if separated from the spirit that cried in anguish. Another head was looming before him, and he whipped with his sabre, making another clean slice through flesh.

These soldiers were not properly armoured, as Nerilek had explained. They were from the enemy's reserve camp, which had been ambushed by the Renalans.

Men who had been forced to flee. They were fleeing now.

And Christophe was the aggressor.

There was no time to grieve the tragedy. There were simply more men to kill, more men to butcher... and men surrounding Saachelle.

Christophe roared with a voice that wasn't his own: the voice of a man, not that of a frightened boy. The sound of the noise fuelled him, toughening his heart.

Saachelle was just ahead, her mount prancing in circles while she cut away at the men surrounding her on the ground. She was like the centre of a powerful storm, her body spinning around and around.

And he felt the urge to join her.

He navigated the confusion as knights galloped on either side of him: the rear of the Renalan cavalry division that had begun the charge. Hooves. Pounding faster. Preparing for the final gallop to push the enemy to Karama. They were trampling the Henalas with ease, like a surging, raging tide.

Horses crushed men. It was the reverse of the battle where his home city had fallen, when enemy troops had smothered the flower fields...

Saachelle.

Something told him he needed to be by her side.

He finally reached her, tearing a seam through the Henalas soldiers without another thought for the destruction he was wreaking. Then pain erupted from his left thigh. Christophe faltered and looked down, spotting the slash that had broken through the leather of his light riding gear and marked his flesh: a ghastly welt, a mark from his first true battle.

More shouting, men squealing, and then his aggressor fell beneath the sword of a Renalan knight.

He looked across to Saachelle to see that her head was exposed: her helm must have been knocked off. Ebony hair shone its lustrous black sheen, in stark contrast to the milky fog and firelight. She grinned at him fiercely, then turned with a yank of her reins, steering her mount towards another cluster of Henalas who were fighting with the protective cliff at their backs.

The main charge raced by Christophe, with only several Renalans remaining to eliminate the stragglers. The roar dimmed, just as Saachelle cut down the last of the enemy men in that group.

Christophe breathed in relief, calling to her. It was time to ride fast now, towards Karama.

She raised her sabre in a triumphant salute, and he smiled. They had done it. *Done* it.

But Christophe watched with horror as suddenly the rear leg of her horse crumpled. She slid backwards, her sword flying from her hands as she grappled to hold on to the horn of her saddle.

A Henalas soldier was tottering to his feet, his great broadsword dripping with the blood of her horse. The squeal that left Christophe's lips was like that of a mother, watching the butchering of her babe.

He jolted his horse towards her, his eyes fixed on the enemy man who had the tip of his broadsword raised to Saachelle's back, like the accusing knife of an executioner.

It all happened too fast. Christophe sliced at the soldier but the man was already stabbing upwards, while Saachelle slid off her mount. She attempted to swing away, but all her strength had clearly been drained trying to hold onto her horse, and her movements were feeble and weak.

Then the three collided in a snarling embrace, a deathly union of steel, flesh and blood.

Christophe toppled from his horse, his wounded leg folding beneath him. One hand still held his reins, performing a balancing act that saved him further injury, while the other plunged his sabre into the enemy's chest.

The man rolled to the side, and Christophe dragged himself to Saachelle where she lay motionless, face down upon the ground with the broadsword in her back. She moved, the tiniest movement, and he gasped, a glimmer of hope flowering.

"Saachi?"

He nudged her gently onto her side so he could see her face, features contorted in pain. His own wound forgotten, Christophe ripped his helm away so he could look at her properly. See her.

She gave a grim smile. "The Gods will it so."

He blinked back his tears, shaking his head.

"You will be a good king," she whispered. "I know it. Keep loving." And she shut those grey eyes of her own accord, before death turned them frosty and deprived her of the choice.

Christophe just sat there with her, the ride to Karama forgotten. The fight was a faded thought, a battle that did not matter.

80
FORCED CHOICES

Illusion cracks
this false veneer
I see right through
and right between
as the fluttering veils
shrouding the way
dissolve away:
distortions fractured
while I watch myself
with all my shades
melt together
light and dark
finally, finding
an answer
a sweet blessed answer
within

* * *

Arian stirred as morning light wafted like a gentle breeze into her room. For some time she remained perfectly still, perfectly calm. The past was a distant memory, and the future a hazy blur that for once she did not worry about. She had no need to search for the answers, neither backwards nor forwards in time.

Her eyes half closed, she rolled over. A rustle sounded on her right, then a shadow fell over her and she let her lashes lift gently.

"Father?" her voice came out slurred. His features clarified before her, as though she had first seen his reflection in the rippled waters of a river, and now in the clear mirror of a glassy pond.

"Yes, I'm here."

She saw him smile. He took a seat on the bed, and brushed her hair to either side of her face.

She smiled back. Breathing in and out calmly, she remained in a state of peaceful rest.

"It is so good to see you again," Melchior said, planting a kiss upon her forehead.

"Father…" More words wouldn't come. She held a hand to her head, as if trying to extract some information from it. "What news?"

"I decided to return, but our forces still stand strong in the north. Do not worry. Your uncle fares well at Karama."

Arian nodded. So her father's strategy had been effective. They were safe. He would keep all of them safe.

"How did you return?"

"Arian dearest, trouble yourself not."

She frowned. The tranquillity of her dreamless sleep waned, while her present reality solidified in a confusing mess of different snapshots from the past few days.

"Father…" Her voice rose with a hint of hysteria. She became conscious of her aching body.

You were fighting, remember.

She should not be alarmed. It was normal for her muscles to be sore, her flesh tender.

Melchior placed a hand upon her shoulder. He was back, here to look after them all.

"Fredrik?" she whispered, remembering her brother.

"I saw him before I came to you," Melchior responded. "He sleeps well. The fever has eased."

She breathed in relief at her brother's miraculous recovery. With her family about her, there was no reason for concern. No reason to be angry.

They crushed your home.

"Who?"

Her father frowned. "Whom are you talking about, dear?"

"The Henalas." Words escaped her lips, but she wasn't even aware of what she was saying.

"Arian, do not worry about them. The fighting has halted this morning. There is no need for you to fear."

"Halted?"

Melchior nodded.

"Why?"

He chuckled softly. "Arian, even they are human and must rest at times. Besides, last night my men ambushed another camp of their troops in the north. They are probably recovering."

Well, that made sense. "I… Can I go to Fredrik?"

"Of course, I will leave you to get dressed, and see you there."

Arian waited until he left, then she quickly rose from her bed and rushed in the direction of the bathing room. But as she passed by the mirror, the sight of her reflection brought her to an abrupt halt. She had bruises around her forearms, and a red mark on her neck.

Charcoal eyes bored into hers.

Slowly, fearfully, she lifted up her nightdress. Marks like hot brands covered her thighs, her belly, her chest.

The feeling of panic returned, and she ran away from the glass and into the bathing room. She dipped her hands into the ewer of water and started desperately scrubbing at her skin, trying to remove the tainted symbols.

They were not hers.

Back in her chamber she found a chemise with long sleeves, and pulled a tunic over it. It covered the stains on her flesh, hiding that reminder of a haunted reality that her subconscious mind knew existed, but that she had no real recollection of.

Then she left her room, walking briskly and mechanically down the corridor.

A guard opened the door when she arrived at the infirmary. She hurried inside, making straight for the bed where Fredrik lay. He was sleeping, but she could tell his condition had stabilised, just like her father had promised. There was no longer sweat upon his brow, and he no longer thrashed about.

"See, there was nothing to fear," Melchior said from where he sat in a corner.

Arian nodded, feeling the tension in her body ease. But then a tall man entered from the adjoining room and she froze.

"Your Highness," he said with a bow. His voice sounded unsteady, and he avoided her eyes.

Alexander. His name came back to her now, along with the feeling that her flesh was on fire.

"Arian?" That was her father now, questioning.

"Him," she said accusingly, glaring at the tall man.

"Arian, he is a healer," Melchior explained. "I was told if it weren't for him…" He left the phrase hanging.

She breathed in deeply to try and calm down.

You must turn from your mind and seek within your heart.

Her heart told her that the man was not cruel, and looking into his troubled brown eyes, anyone could see that. He had not meant to hurt her. No, he had saved her life and the life of her brother.

Justice. Be strong. Be true.

She fought to ignore the aching bruises on her body, and the snarling voice in her mind that spoke of betrayal. Deception.

He is different. Another voice told her, and her mouth remained closed. She could not speak, could not reveal the truth.

Perhaps if she ignored the truth, then it would cease to be. He could not be. He could not be that which she most hated.

He was different.

"Arian?"

"Sorry," she mumbled to her father. "I… My head hurts."

Melchior rose and took her into his arms, though he clearly had no idea what was troubling her. She kept bringing herself back to her breathing, attempting to steady herself. It was becoming easier to focus on just that.

Then a knock sounded, breaking them apart, and Jerim entered. He was frowning, his lustrous green eyes dimmed by anxiety.

"My lord, lady," he dipped his head in greeting. "A small group of Henalas knights have gathered at the main gates. They have raised the flag of truce and are requesting an audience."

Arian glanced at Alexander, whose grim expression betrayed his own worry. She quickly turned her attention away and back to her father, who had begun to pace around the room.

"Have they given any indication as to what they want?"

"Only that they desire an audience with you, to discuss your captive."

"What?" Melchior growled. "What captive?"

"I know not," Jerim responded. But he looked over at Arian, with eyes that seemed to know her secret. She noticed that Alexander had backed into the adjacent room, occupying himself with cleaning some of his tools.

"Prepare an envoy," Melchior instructed. "We will meet them outside the city. I will not have them enter, but we need to hear what they have to say."

Jerim nodded and left without another word, and Arian was alone with her father once more. She felt his attention focus on her, his jaw twitching.

"Do you have any idea what this is about?"

She trembled at the question, and the silence that followed weighed heavily down upon her. Her father didn't speak again. He just waited for her to answer, and she knew she had to say something. There was no other way. She was trapped. He was trapped.

"Father…"

But before she could say anything else, Alexander rushed back from the adjoining room and dropped to his knees. "Please, please Your Majesty. I am not like my father. Spare me."

Melchior looked from her to the man grovelling at his feet. "What are you speaking of?"

"Father," Arian murmured. "Forgive me. I was foolish. I could not bear the thought of Fredrik dying, so I went to the Henalas camp using a trapdoor Fredrik had shown before my coronation. I intended to steal the fungus that he needed for his recovery, but I was taken captive. This man… he freed me. He claimed to be a healer. I trusted him… and now Fredrik lives." She gulped for air, her heart beating wildly in her chest.

"Who are you?" Melchior whispered.

As Alexander raised his voice to identify himself, Arian's words rushed over his, coming out as a distorted plea in the kaleidoscope of her twisting emotions. She found herself defending the man who moments before, she had felt such a storm of anger against. "Please, he is not what you think. He is not like his father."

"Arian…" Melchior groped for words. When he couldn't find any, he strode to the window where he spent long minutes looking out silently over the city.

"How could you bring him to the palace?" he asked eventually.

"It is my fault," Alexander interrupted. "I did not tell her who I was. Please, forgive me."

Melchior ignored him. "So this is why the Henalas are requesting an audience?"

Arian nodded slowly. "It must be."

"And when will Fredrik recover?"

"Alexander said he should be well within the week," Arian replied. She bit her lip, almost choking as she said the name of the Henalas prince.

"You leave me in an impossible situation," Melchior said softly. Then his tone sharpened, as he barked a command. "Arian, leave."

She clenched her fists together and hurried from the room.

* * *

Melchior remained silent for a long time after Arian left, while the Henalas prince stayed on the ground, kneeling before him. Something within Melchior sensed it.

His dear daughter, so unknowing and innocent in the deceptive ways men played their games. He thought of her unblemished soul yet to learn the harsh lessons of the world. Although she could survive in a brittle environment, this was different. He begged to the Gods that she would not be seduced to a terrible death.

"You leave me with no clear choice," Melchior began. "You have proven yourself loyal by healing my son. But what is your intention? And what am I to do now?"

The Henalas prince did not respond. In the silence, Melchior's thoughts returned to Arian with her soft heart, that he feared would lead her far away to a place of no return. He thought of her being used. Corrupted and destroyed, ruining Meridisia as foretold.

No!

An image of Erik's face came into his mind, as though the sage were right here in the room speaking to him.

No, he could not afford to think such treacherous thoughts. She was his daughter, and he knew she was strong. He had to believe in her, because if he did not, then there was no hope at all.

He breathed in deeply, wondering what he was doing, and how he could trust this man.

"My son needs you," Melchior said eventually, straightforward and firm.

The prince looked up at him with wide eyes that seemed to tell a story of deep suffering. Melchior shuddered to think what those eyes had seen.

"Your Majesty, in healing him I hoped to atone for some of my sins," Alexander murmured. "But he has reached a stable condition, and the truth is that I am no longer needed to cure him. What is my future now?"

Melchior hesitated, caught off guard by the man's honesty. "Perhaps you can tell me?"

Alexander shook his head.

"Rise," Melchior instructed. "Come, look at my city." He gestured for the prince to join him at the window, looking out over the walls of the inner citadel to the tall buildings and the cobbled streets. "Your people came to ruin my world," he began. "Why did you invade?"

"Greed is a terrible thing," the prince finally said.

Melchior just waited, staring at Alexander sharply until he continued. "There is another world, I have heard. The powerful ones have almost destroyed it, so they have come here."

Melchior gasped, and his fingers gripped the windowsill tightly. Again, he didn't speak for a long time.

"How?" he murmured.

Alexander lowered his head. "It is not common knowledge, and I am not privy to many of my father's secrets. But I have heard whisperings. There is something in the ice of the Northern Ocean that enables them to travel between worlds, and that is where our endless supply of troops originates from."

"A universal war," Melchior growled. It seemed believable enough. The Henalas had first arrived at the northwest shores of the continent of Meleka, and had established their empire in the north. The geographical establishment fitted. And since the Meridisians had their own sciences, it was not impossible that the Henalas had similar arts, enabling them to harness natural energetic power.

It all started to make sense in Melchior's mind, and he shuddered as he thought of the knowledge that the Henalas must have acquired in order to accomplish such a feat. His worst fears were confirmed: greater action was needed now.

"I do not know why I should trust you," Melchior began. "But I think that it does not matter anymore. There are greater forces out there shaping events, forces beyond my control."

Alexander nodded.

Then a tap on the window broke Melchior's thoughts. He turned, and jumped at the sight of Erik's dove. Another tap, and Melchior frantically pushed open the glass to rip the parchment from the bird's claw.

He swallowed, his hands shaking as he read the message. Then his eyes returned to the prince.

"Go back to the guest chambers assigned to you, and do not leave. I must speak with the envoy at the gates."

81
VOICE OF HOPE

Alexander.

The Henalas Prince.

Her father knew him now. She was not the only one to bear the burden of his identity.

Her father would deal with him, handle the situation, and the demands of the Henalas knights at the gates.

Her father was back in Linuina, in command, and in control.

But the tone of his voice was branded upon her mind, and those last words telling her to *leave*. Was it disappointment? Anger? Or simply, confusion?

Arian did not know, just as she did not know how to feel.

But he was different, spoke the voice inside her heart.

That much felt true, and the woman from the temple had told her not to be ashamed. It felt right to trust that strange woman, with her soothing touch and calm, all-knowing eyes. She seemed to understand some part of Arian's soul, that Arian herself did not understand. She also seemed to want to help.

Arian's own words came to her ears now. The words of the story she had told on Midsummer Eve. The night it had all changed, when Cain had approached her at the door of the tavern, inviting her to join him for the next day's festivities.

Then she had chosen to be a woman again. Forsake disguise for a day, to honour the Gods with her true face. To feel the fresh air on her skin, rejoice in the sunlight, and dance in a dress around rejuvenating bonfire flames.

Go to the girl. Stay by her side as she walks the beach, bare feet treading the pale sand.

She thought of the girl, lonely on her journey.

Be the sun that is missing from the dismal sky, covered with clouds to protect a wounded heart of blue.

She tried to smile, tried to shed some light upon the bleak coast, the sea stretching on one side. An incarnation of tormented grief, the waves surged like a reflection of her inner turmoil.

Blow life into her hollow, sunken features, and wipe away the sooty smudges on the flesh beneath her eyes.

She saw brown eyes, Alexander's eyes.

Remember happiness in its pure, glimmering form. Drink the salty waters, banish the pain from mind, the agony from spirit, and the darkness from heart.

She had the power to relieve his burden. If she would only embrace his true self, for it was a good self. He was not evil. Not like his father, the manipulative Emperor, who used his son as a pawn to do his own dirty work.

She wondered if she should go back… to her father and to Alexander, and plea for his case.

But she could not bring herself to do so. Her allegiance must first remain to her family, and then to her nation and people. Her father, the king, must be the one to determine Alexander's fate.

Alexander. The healer.

A memory seized her: of the smells in the hospitals, where she had volunteered in the last siege. The reeking stench of distilled fear, of so many hopeless, helpless dying men sprawled across makeshift beds.

She recalled helping the physicians tend to the injured. No words could describe it. Nothing can capture what it is like to be surrounded by so many bodies, so many mouths crying out to be saved, and so many who could never be cured.

Arian swallowed, realising where she wanted to pass the time now. She would go to those in need of healing.

She wrapped herself in plain garb once more, inhaling the comforting smell of the old travelling cloak. A musty scent, like old books, that carried the richness of stories sprawled across disintegrating parchment.

She left her rooms, making her way out of the palace, and across the courtyard. A route that was starting to become pretty familiar to her. There was a hospital just outside the inner citadel, on the avenue beside the palace gates. She called for one young knight to accompany her, and he did so unquestioningly.

They reached the hospital just as a girl came rushing out of the doors.

She was clothed in a little blue frock, spattered by blood, wet from the tears dripping down her cheeks. She didn't notice Arian, blinded by whatever horrible operation she had just borne witness to.

"Highness, are you sure you want to continue inside?" came the reluctant words of Arian's companion.

She nodded, and made her way ahead of him, leading by example. She covered her nose with the sleeve of her coat to protect her senses from the nauseating stench that assaulted her as she entered.

So many bodies.

Arian lowered her eyes. She could not look at the room as a whole, but had to break it down bed by bed. One at a time, otherwise the sheer magnitude of the injured and dying became too overwhelming.

There was a young man on her left, his breeches rolled up past a knee which was nothing but a mangled mess. Bony splinters pointed at impossible angles out from a bloody ball of clumped flesh.

It appeared to be his only ailment. He would most likely live without a leg, provided that the wound did not fester.

She approached slowly, and he turned a frightened face to hers.

"Highness?"

"Hush," she murmured.

"They gonna cut it off, gonna cut it off…"

She took his hand, gripping it firmly. This was probably his first fight, for he looked younger than her by several years.

"You're going to live." She tried to smile.

"I don't wanna live. Live for what?"

She tightened her clasp, as her own sweat mingled with his clammy palm. She spoke, not just for him, but for her, holding on to each word.

"I know the future is a scary and unstable place. But clear your mind and reconnect with the heart. Believe. Linuina can emerge from this stronger than before."

No longer aware of what she was saying, the world and all her senses blurred. She simply heard the sound of her disembodied voice, in a thousand different ways.

Arian moved between the beds, between the injured and the dying, saying what she could. She held hands, felt pain that was not her own, breathed with these wounded men, and helped them to find a moment of calm and light.

"… And having endured, you will appreciate the light all the more. You will see a greater spectrum, as your understanding of yourselves and the world is

enhanced and enriched…"

Notes folded, bending in crisp, orderly patterns amidst so many frantic moans. Clean and nurturing, bringing discipline to chaos. A harmonious echo, it soothed the fires of so many minds.

Men looked at her, hope in their eyes. Men looked to her with faith. Trusting she who brought a light to them, a light that she too clutched, rising through darkness.

For their faith renewed her too, their revived spirits restored her own belief and spurred her forth in the fight to create a better world.

A world with no war, no hideous wounds for either side.

I cannot blame them all.

Not all of them burnt her home, and blackened her sea.

Not all of them trampled her flower fields.

Not all of them shadowed her rainbow.

82
BLOOD LEAVES

I saw the end
I journeyed there
and back again
and it gave me strength
even in the darkest hours
and it gave me the heart
to love even the shadows
for I saw it all
each facet of every soul
in its unified perfection
in a dimension beyond
the stories of this time
all faded away
the echo of their pain,
pale beneath the light
of a thousand suns shining
and a thousand nymphs dancing
to the sacred drumbeat
of the eternal lasting breath
of forces entwined
that shine in purity
and with their spell
awaken deep
to reveal a path
beyond this Death

* * *

The forest stretches ahead. Trees wrestle with each other in their search for the sun, yearning to be gilded by light. But their growth is warped, bodies twisted, locked together in a vicious embrace.

She thrust apart the branches, struggling between sentient trunks. Twigs recoiled, and thorns clawed her face until tears flowered upon her cheeks.

The blisters on her soles split open once more and the moist earth drank her blood, muddy soil hiding all trace of her tormented pilgrimage.

Onward she walked, until a branch whirred by and struck her chest. Falling, she uttered a scream that died off into the abyss of a savage land. Her captor.

Come.

The silky voice was like a physical presence, rubbing over her body to soothe her wounds.

Rise.

A command.

She staggered to her feet and looked back in the direction she had come from. No longer a narrow trail through the wilderness, but a wide path that disappeared into silvery fog.

A paved road, leading to civilisation.

Help.

The desperate plea tugged at her heart, filling her with need to respond.

* * *

I walk in search of the speaker. Hard stone rejects the sores on my feet, scattering blood droplets to either side of the road. They solidify, sanguine globules morphing into autumn leaves, my pain banished in these glorious remnants of life.

They are rusty remains, soon to dry and shrivel, pierced by icy splinters of winter.

I must make it before then.

Gazing ahead, I see a luminous cloud beckoning. Cobbles shine in reflection of its lustre, dark stone accepting a gracious gift of pearly light.

I long to reach the vapour: touch it, feel mist on my cheeks and inhale its cooling air. Escape the cage of forest limbs, thick with decaying leaves, and suffocating closure.

I can see a figure, waiting for me. Body slender as an aspen, a shadowy contour against the nebulous orb.

I know I must reach her.

I know I will reach her.

For a blackness flourishes at the planet's core, and rotten fruit hangs from scarred boughs.

But the time has come for awakening.

The time has come for healing.

And the day will come, where we transition from healing to healed. When we truly acknowledge and celebrate, the interdependence of all things.

83
Pilgrimage

Later that day Melchior found himself at the head of his conference table, massaging his temples. Their conversation was looping around and around through topics he had never even imagined discussing a mere day ago.

To his right was Numelov, his trusted advisor for so long, the only one still alive who had known of Arian's secret since birth. Besides Erik of course, though he could no longer go to see the old sage.

Ileana and Reaveno sat side by side on his left, while Jerim paced impatiently up and down the length of the otherwise empty chamber.

"Do you know anything else?" he asked wearily, looking at Ileana again.

She shook her head. "I am sorry. I only know that they must be separated. This… talent that has been triggered within Fredrik connects the two more strongly than ever. Through the mind, that is. Until I know what your son is capable of, and until we can teach him to harness that power for good, he is a danger to Arian. The Henalas can reach her through him, through the corruption of mind that manifests these diseased realities."

Melchior clenched his fists together.

"And what of these new weapons?" he asked Reaveno.

"I am working on it. As yet I am still only able to explain how they work, not replicate them. It would help if we had more information on these supposed experiments in the Kayamara Wood."

Melchior nodded. The consequences could be too great if they took no action. He would have to send more scouts there, no matter how risky it was, and how much he despised the idea of sending men into the potential path of these evil arts.

He instructed Jerim to prepare such a mission, which would leave at nightfall, and the commander left with Reaveno who was organising testing equipment for the scouts to use.

Then Melchior turned the topic back to Arian once more.

"Sire," Numelov began. "Forgive me but I see no other option. She must be sent south. Your daughter will be safe there."

Melchior nodded. "But the question is how to ensure her safety during transit? I can think of no way. It could all be a trap, we cannot say with the Henalas."

He had still not told anyone about Alexander. Or Erik's message. He could think of no rational reason why he should not share his knowledge, but still he remained quiet.

"She should leave soon, while the Henalas are yet to recuperate," Numelov continued. "Our soldiers in the marina can lead a diversion attack, while a small group of knights ride south with Arian. Too many and they will attract attention. But your scouts have already proven that the territory south of Linuina is relatively safe. There have been no reports of Henalas venturing into the region. Their attention is focussed here for the moment, and at Karama."

"Indeed." It was a good plan. Numelov was right about that, and if Arian was truly in danger by remaining so close to his son, there was no other option. "I want you to begin preparations for her journey," Melchior instructed. "Thank you, my old friend. And please send for Arian to join me here."

Numelov smiled and, after a quick salute, left the room.

But when Melchior turned back to Ileana, the only other person left at the table, he saw her frown had deepened.

"You do not like the plan?" he asked.

She shook her head. "I think Arian should be deciding where she goes. I think she may have her own ideas, ideas that you must listen to. She is not a child to be sent away across the continent, forever fleeing. If she does not choose her own path towards the light, she will remain forever haunted. She needs to find herself, as a sovereign being. You can support her of course, but by simply acknowledging her sovereignty."

Melchior gripped the edge of the table. "Of course I will speak with her. But does she really have the knowledge to decide?"

Ileana inclined her head. "I think you underestimate her. And what will you do about the prince, about Alexander?"

He recoiled. "How do you know about him?"

"You forget what I do. My lord, I can feel her projections. His too."

Melchior nodded and hurriedly opened his mouth, desperate to glean any insight that he could. "What do they tell you?"

"They tell me that which is impossible to explain. But I can conclude that you must trust, you must let go of this battle for control."

Erik's words: she was saying the same thing.

"So what do we do?"

Ileana glanced down at her fingers, and started tapping them on the wood. "I would suggest following Numelov's plan, only with a decoy. If Arian indeed were to travel south with a group of knights, she would no doubt be wearing plain clothes. Robes, a hood… It would be easy to send another girl in place of her. But I would suggest keeping this private. Speak to no one else. You should only trust your daughter and the prince."

"And you?"

She laughed softly. "You don't have a choice, do you? I already know now. But take or leave my advice, whatever you wish. I will go for the moment, your daughter is at the door."

Ileana rose gracefully from her seat, heading for the rear of the chamber where a back entrance led straight down to the rooms of learning. She disappeared just as Arian entered from the opposite, main entrance.

Melchior turned to look at his daughter, and all he could see was the baby he had held long ago in his arms. Perhaps the Gods were in their favour after all, if she had survived all this time on her own, enduring so much since the fall of Tarvesi. Surely she would survive for longer, and choose the right path.

"Father!" she exclaimed. "What happened this morning, with the Henalas knights? What did they say?"

Melchior sighed. "Fear not. They simply wanted to know what our intentions were with the prince, and if we would be making demands. They seemed certain that we had him, so I confirmed that he is our captive. But I made no deals with them."

"Perhaps request for them to retreat from Linuina?"

Melchior shook his head. "No. I do not want to give them time to regroup. With our attacks in the north and strong fortifications here, we have the upper hand. But only for the moment, as we do not know what further plans they may have. I will not risk our current advantage."

Arian nodded. "So… what will you do about him?"

He looked at her, uncertain of how to begin. There was no right way to explain, but he knew he could not mention Fredrik as the reason. It was an unnecessary burden.

"Arian, Linuina is no longer a safe place for you."

The words hovered in the air, and Arian began to shake uncontrollably.

She felt herself trapped by the rough hands of fate, grabbing her without care or mercy.

"Father, what do you mean?" She gazed into his troubled eyes, searching for a clue. Anything.

"I am sorry, my child. We think that you must… leave."

She stood perfectly still and waited for him to continue. As he spoke, the terror in her heart grew.

Finally he stopped talking, awaiting her response.

"Soonada," she stated, without realising. "I want to go to Soonada."

The words formed now of their own accord. Someone else spoke through her mouth, dictating her path.

"I must go back to Tarvesi. And then I will go north, to meet the Emperor."

Remember the girl, trapped in the flames.

Melchior sat there in horror, eyes fixed on her. "What do you mean you will go to meet the Emperor?"

Heed the cry of the tortured boy.

Arian stared blankly back at him, as if possessed.

"Arian, I said you should leave Linuina. But there is no reason for you to go north into enemy territory."

"Father, I must do something. The world has a horrid disease, and I must stop it from spreading. I feel it, I know it deep within me. To stop it spreading, we must confront it at its core. I am not here to hide in the shadows."

Her words rang passionately in the air, and Melchior sank down into his seat. The seconds drew out, creating a thick and impenetrable silence.

"My daughter," he whispered, "is this a personal quest?"

She waved her arms with frustration. "What is any quest?"

"And your Henalas Prince," Melchior continued. "What does he have to do with this?"

Tears stung her eyes as she thought of him. She did not want to think of him. But the image of his face thrust itself into her mind.

Touch the one who has known only pain.

"He knows nothing of this," she said bitterly. It was true. She had not seen him since that morning when they had all been together in the infirmary. In fact she had not spoken to him, alone, since their night together.

But she had spent the entire day in her room, with his screams echoing in her mind.

Over and over: calling, pleading.

"Father, I will go now." She turned and left him, where he sat unresponsive at the table.

* * *

Struggling to hide the tremor in his voice, Melchior called for a guard to bring Alexander to him. The enemy prince entered his conference chamber, standing hesitantly in the corner while the door closed behind him.

"What do you know about my daughter?"

Alexander met his eyes with a deep and sombre stare. "Your Majesty, the Emperor keeps things from me. But I have heard things about her, and that she is desired. For one reason or another, I know not. Perhaps he just wants another Meridisian to warm his bed." His voice cracked. "Like my mother."

At those words, the fear within Melchior deepened. The reason why he had hidden Arian at birth bubbled to the surface of his mind.

"My daughter will be leaving the city, to make a journey south."

Alexander gulped. "Your Majesty, why are you telling me this? And what about her safety?"

"Why should you care?" Melchior whispered, his tone bitter.

"Your Majesty," Alexander returned, with his voice a fierce plea. "I am not like my father. But believe me, I know the Emperor. I know there are men spying on her, and they will report her absence from the palace. She will be tracked across the continent: she will never be safe."

"And is she safe here, at Linuina?"

Alexander shook his head. "I cannot say, Your Majesty. I do not have the information. I am not trusted with any of these matters. But I wouldn't think so. Nowhere, really…"

The king rose abruptly to his feet. "Alexander. You have betrayed your people by coming here. What is to prevent you turning sides again?"

Abandoning all his pride and dignity, the prince sank to his knees. "Your Majesty. My blood is only half Henalas. They are not my people!" As Alexander looked up with his pleading eyes, Melchior noticed the tears spilling from them.

He was homeless. Motherless.

And he was torn, with conflicting blood raging around within him.

The seconds passed. Time stood still.

Melchior looked down at this broken man, a man with no home, a man who belonged with no people. He tried to put himself into those shoes, and imagine how he would feel if his father was a tyrant. Leaving him, lost and alone, to wander and drift in a merciless universe.

"Rise," he commanded, through stiff lips. The prince struggled to his feet while Melchior cleared his throat, dreading the words he was about to utter.

"Prove yourself to me, son. Protect my daughter. You will go with her."

And Melchior found himself praying that tomorrow would never come, that his daughter would never leave.

Unless the Gods willed it so...

84
THE CORRUPTION

The image clarifies before me now. I see her. I see my sister. I see her with swollen eyes, puffy from crying. Salty stains on her cheeks, remnants of ancient sorrow, dried liquid proof of turmoil.

She is looking at me. She is searching for an answer. An answer I cannot give, I do not know. No one knows but her. She is alone and I cannot help her.

The image changes now. I see another girl. I do not know who she is, but her pain burns into me. She is different. Yet she is the same.

Prickly bumps on her flesh betray the repulsion of her body to the man who is her captor. He stands over her, a tyrant and a conqueror, depriving her of dignity, hope and love.

I feel deep anger at the injustice of it all. I yearn to hold her and restore her faith in existence. Tell her that someone in the world cares.

The man turns and I see charcoal eyes. The colour of the ash left over after the Midsummer bonfire. Grey, coating the slopes of the Fhea Karadid after an eruption.

Yet I have never been there. I should not know.

Anger is gone from my heart now. I do not understand. I do not really know where it came from in the first place, and then to where it ran away. Retiring from my body, it leaves me alone.

I see a forest. Something unnatural lurks between the tall trees. I try to find a way between them, but there is only a maze.

Then stumbling into a clearing, I see it. I see them.

No, I don't see them.

I feel their presence.

I do not know what they are. I do not want to know. I turn and I run, away and away.

But they have touched me with their mark. They have branded me. They know where to find me. With a chilly whisper they hiss at my mind, and leave lingering trails of spite that caress my trembling heart.

They are taking my memories. Replacing them with others. I shake my fists and tell them to go, then I draw my sword and fight for freedom. But physical weapons are useless.

And I have no hands to hold them with.

I realise that I cannot fight, and I cannot run.

Those are not the answers.

The path to freedom is a different path.

* * *

He stood in a dim chamber, squinting in an attempt to make out his surroundings. There were pairs of figures processing along at either end, chained together by black ropes.

Other figures now, hooded figures. They carried candles, and as they neared, he began to realise where he was.

He opened his mouth to scream, but no sound escaped.

And silently I call upon a soft breeze, a warm breeze, to come and banish the frigid kiss upon my cheek.

85
STAIRWAY TO HEAVEN

Love is when
there is no separation:
where fear vanishes
with the blink of an eye
melting all suffering
back to the beating heart
of glimmering
stardust

* * *

After leaving the conference chamber, Arian went straight to the infirmary, hoping that she would find Alexander there. She needed to speak with him.

But he wasn't, and at a loss of what to do, she went to the palace nursery to see Cain's baby son. Sarah was there when she entered, and immediately handed the child over.

"What shall you do with him, Your Highness? If you don't mind me asking, that is…"

Arian sighed. "I do not know. I cannot look after this child properly."

Sarah lowered her head, as if she had a thought in her mind but was too ashamed to speak it.

"You have cared for Karl more than I shall ever be able to, thank you." Arian's attention flickered between her maid and the child. His little eyelashes blinked open and his mouth broke into an adorable smile. "If you wish to adopt him in my place…"

"Oh, Your Highness," Sarah exclaimed with joy, her unasked question clearly answered. "Thank you, so much."

Arian smiled and took a seat beside the cot, with Karl on her lap. It was comforting to sit here in the nursery, in this little corner of the palace reserved for infants. Blissful innocence, sheltered from the outside world.

She was lost in her own thoughts when Alexander walked in, and only realised he had entered when he cleared his throat awkwardly. She saw him staring at the child in her arms.

He's not mine, I adopted him," she murmured in explanation. Then she returned Karl to Sarah, and gestured for Alexander to leave the nursery with her.

"You looked so natural," he said softly as they emerged into the empty corridor. She quickly glanced away from him without responding.

"Highness," the prince began, his voice uncertain. "Shall we go somewhere private?"

She nodded and led him to her chambers, both of them walking in silence. When they entered, it was Alexander who found the courage to break their awkward spell first. "I spoke with your father, just now."

"Why? What is happening?"

"He... set me a task. He wants me to accompany you on your mission."

"What does this mean?" Arian asked, avoiding Alexander's stare. She could not even look him in the eye for more than a few moments. It was too painful, too many feelings surfaced.

And now it seems she was destined to be with him on a journey across the continent: the winds of change snatching her, tossing her like autumn leaves before the snow. Before winter came.

Cold, bleak, winter.

"Alexander, I don't understand..."

Suddenly she was in his arms, as he gently drew her close. However her mind had been racing, her body did not resist. She allowed her face to relax against him, feeling the comfort of his chest.

"Do you want me with you?" he said into her ear.

"I..." She hesitated. The truth was she did, and slowly she nodded. "You saved my life, and my brother's. I must thank you once again."

"Princess, you need not thank me. You heal me."

She closed her eyes, breathing in deeply. In his arms she was calm, in his arms the anger was gone. He reminded her: she need not hate all the Henalas. They were not all bad.

He was different.

She clung to that. She had to. She had to trust and believe, and if her father had instructed him to accompany her, then it must be fine. She had nothing to fear.

Still…

"Alex," she mumbled. "I don't understand who I am." She looked up at him as though pleading for an answer, but his eyes were like muddy water. Impossible to see anything, she would get no clues in their reflection: a reflection of the muddiness within her own soul.

"I know how you feel. I have had no one since my mother died. And over and over I've failed her, and her people. I'm no one. I belong nowhere."

She closed her eyes, because it hurt to look at him and see that sorrow there, plain and obvious, an open wound.

Maybe she could close it up.

"Princess," he continued. "Be strong for me. So that I can be strong too."

"I'll try," she whispered. "And one day, one day…"

Alexander took both of her hands in his. "One day the war will end."

* * *

I look down from the gates, down below to the realm of rock, waiting to welcome another ascending soul.

The body of Saachelle rests atop a pyre, wrapped in silken white sheets, anointed with oils. Soon to be lit, flames will consume her and unite us.

Christophe is by her side, the young king of Regofala, king of a fallen realm but still alive, destined to grow and become a leader of men. Though only a boy, he is a boy with strength of heart. Making me believe that purity will reign above vengeful urge.

She comes now, and I reach forth my hand in a gesture of guidance. Moonlight filters down in a bridge across the ether, a pathway for a gliding spirit.

She moves beyond me, above me, while I remain at the gates. I ask for her to let me through too, but she does not hear. She has moved beyond the physical while still I hover in-between.

The moonbeam breaks, split apart by shadows. The path is a ladder of broken rungs, with each step more treacherous than the previous. Reality is a dream of crumbling thought and lost wishes.

A pond forms around my feet, water rising up to my waist. Swallowing the remains of my body, my flesh turning to fluid.

Here I wait, and I watch my reflection morph before my eyes.
I see my yearning for a mother to guide me home.
The divine mother within my soul.

86
PREPARATIONS

Arian listened as her father explained the details of the plan. She was leaving the following night, while a decoy headed south to divert the attention of the Henalas.

She spent the evening resting, alone in her chambers, catching up on the sleep she so needed before the long journey. Now that decisions had been made with finality, she was beginning to relax into the realisation that this was indeed her task, her calling.

When she woke the next day, she found relief in preparing for the mission and taking those simple practical steps that served to order her mind.

She went to the kitchens to gather rations for her and Alexander, including cheese, cured meat, dried fruit and nuts. They didn't need much, because they could hunt rabbits on the plains, and would restock once they reached Jalas.

She also took a tinderbox and a set of copper mugs and bowls, along with two water skins. That would suffice, for the many rivulets coursing down from the Hevedh Suhil offered opportunity to refill.

She packed all this into two sacks, along with a quiver of arrows and a number of short knives and daggers. Not a sword, which would draw unnecessary attention and prove cumbersome for long distance travelling.

Finally, she added her thick woollen coat into one of the bags, which would also serve as a blanket at night. It would take them at least three months to reach Tarvesi, and as winter approached, only the Gods knew what weather would befall them.

Satisfied with her preparation, she went to her brother. She had to see him before she left. She could not go without a goodbye, perhaps farewell forever.

* * *

Deep below the city of Linuina, in the network of cellars and caverns that criss-crossed beneath all other secret paths, a lone figure garbed in black fell to his knees. Another man towered above him, and he silently waited for instructions.

"The princess is departing," came the master's cold voice. "You must prevent her from leaving the palace. And if I hear you have failed…" The voice trailed off and the grovelling figure pressed his body closer to the floor.

"I shall not fail, master."

"Good," the other snickered. "But remember she is wanted alive."

"Yes of course, my prize when I complete…"

The master laughed, the sound chilling the air like the winds of the northern mountains. "No, not your prize anymore."

"But…" the traitor protested, the agreement worsening.

"Oh don't you worry," came the reply. "You shall get your good pay of women if you don't question and stick to your task."

"I wanted the girl. That was the deal!" he shouted as his master turned and began retreating down the tunnel.

The other paused to fix him with a menacing stare from beneath the hooded fold of his cloak.

"You can have all the other damn women of this palace when Linuina falls, just not the princess. Don't fail now."

The lesser man nodded, his teeth chattering more from fear than from the cold of the cellars. There was nothing else he could do. So he rose to his feet and began to make for the passage that he knew the princess would use.

Yes, the king might know his palace. But he did not know about the new developments of secret passages, designed to intercept.

Thoughts of victory calmed the betrayer, and he forgot the mishap regarding the princess. He had been promised other things anyway. Once this was over he would become a royal servant of the New Order, with plenty of beautiful women at his disposal.

87
UNTIMELY SEPARATION

I wake, though it feels as if I'm still dreaming
transported through time,
back to when our souls met,
right in the beginning —
seed pods in the expansive, tree of eternal life,
growing from source light
weaving mystically
from roots to leaves
fabric of love and
collective conscious memory

In that golden light
of the awakening dawn,
a single bright shooting star
plummets opposite the sun,
and oh I wonder,
if it's truly real —
but indeed, one delicate
omen of prosperity
is surely here —
to bless us on this road

* * *

Arian entered the infirmary to find Alexander at her brother's side.

"Can I speak with him?" she asked hopefully.

Alexander nodded. "I have given him a drug so that he will wake up. You should be cautious though. He will be weary."

"I understand." Arian smiled, her heart filled with gratitude. Then he left the room to give her some time alone with her brother.

She waited nervously, watching every movement as Fredrik began to stir. His eyes flickered open, and he gazed up at her.

"Arian?" he managed with a cough.

Relief flooded her and she embraced him, arms gently wrapping around his body. He felt frail to her touch, like the fever had eaten away layers of his flesh. Yet here he was, emerged from the quicksand of disease that had been sucking him closer to death.

The boy was strong.

The boy lived on.

Arian pulled away as Fredrik stretched his stiff limbs, and then struggled to prop himself into an upright position. As his eyes searched for hers she bowed her head, her curls falling to cover her face. She was not sure if she was ready to reveal the truth, and she knew that if she met his gaze, he would be able to see right through and read all her secrets.

But Fredrik moved the veil of her hair, and soon enough discovered that tears moistened her cheeks. He brushed them tenderly away with a finger.

"I'm sorry sister dear. I promise I won't leave you again."

"Just promise me not to be so foolish again, not to keep fighting if you're wounded," Arian muttered back.

Fredrik grimaced and looked down to examine his torso, wrapped in bandages. "But it's not like you can talk, either..."

Arian swallowed. It was true. She could see her brother as the mirror he was, the reflection of herself. He had pushed on when he was wounded, ignoring his physical condition. So too, she had pushed on in battle instead of pausing to process the emotions that had surged within her when Marcus had died. That had led her into a senseless quest to draw enemy blood, ripping yet deeper wounds in the fabric of her world.

Arian noticed a ball of anger directed at herself, stuck deep inside her heart. In a way, she had done this to Fredrik.

But he was back now, truly back. She saw that a roguish glint had returned to his eyes, and knew that signalled he was amongst the living for good. He had that spark of life.

"Tell me, what has happened?" Fredrik murmured, interrupting her thoughts.

Arian shrugged, unsure exactly what he was asking for, or what to tell him. How to say goodbye to her dear brother? She knew that the news would shock him, and he was still weary.

So she decided to remain silent on those matters for now, and instead informed him of their father's return, and then the general happenings since he had fallen ill. Except that she omitted all detail of her venture outside the city walls, Alexander's involvement, and identity.

"You were only saved by a miracle," she whispered finally.

Fredrik looked down again, to the bandages covering his wound. "I thought I was going to die. Have you ever felt that way, dear sister? I don't know how to describe it. And my head... Why, I felt mad!" A pause. "Burning..."

She bit her lip. She had not had that feeling, like she was going to die. She had never been on the verge of death, with fevers gripping her. But she had felt the burning of insanity's edge, and she thought she understood.

Fredrik sighed. "Well, I was lucky wasn't I. Can you send for my physician? I'll have to thank him."

Arian grimaced, and despite her attempt to lighten the mood with a smile, she knew that her brother had noticed that something lay beneath the surface.

"Is everything alright?"

She nodded, but turned away quickly so that he would not read the truth in her eyes.

"Arian, please tell me." Fredrik tried to reach out and touch her. But she pulled back further from him, and he couldn't follow because the bandages held him rigid.

"I do not want to burden you now."

"Tell me," he repeated, his voice a firm instruction this time.

Arian paused, and her response finally came in hushed tones. She couldn't stop the truth.

"Fredrik, the man who healed you is the son of the Emperor. I went to the Henalas camp."

"No, you can't possibly mean?" he gasped.

"He is a good man. His name is Alexander," she whispered again, eyes glowing with her emotion. She reached for her brother's hand, and felt a painful sting inside her when he recoiled from her touch. "Please Fredrik, don't fear. You are alive, thanks to him. And he is going to help us save Meridisia."

Fredrik just lay there watching her, his features darkening further with each passing second. "Don't tell me you've fallen in love with him or something."

Standing, Arian went over to the window. "I'm sorry I had to tell you that, Fredrik, after what you've been through."

She opened the window to let in some of the cooling air. She could feel her brother's stare upon her back, and she hardened herself to resist his judgment. Whatever he thought didn't matter anyway. He was healed, and she was leaving. She was in charge of her decisions, and this was her choice to make.

"What else, Arian," Fredrik asked desperately. "What else is going on?"

She returned slowly, away from the icy fingers of the night air.

"I am leaving tonight, Fredrik. I am making a pilgrimage back to Tarvesi to face the ghosts from my childhood. I feel that the ruins hold answers for me, a key for how to end these wars."

For tense minutes, all was silent. In that time, both prince and princess seemed to age and drift further apart.

"Is the prince going with you?" Fredrik asked eventually.

Arian nodded. "He is a good man," she repeated. "Besides, it was father who decided. It would be unsafe for me to travel alone, and two swords are better than one. As a physician he can look after my health... and his ability to speak Henalas may prove useful. I couldn't ask for a better companion, especially now, when it is so hard to trust anyone."

When Arian finally met her brother's gaze again, she saw him staring at her in despair.

"And you trust... you trust..." Fredrik couldn't finish his sentence. "Why are you even doing this?"

"Something must be done."

"Oh Arian. But... the son of the Henalas Emperor, whom I thought was your greatest enemy?" He fell silent again, and Arian said nothing.

For another stretch of agonizing time, they looked across at each other. Arian could see hatred growing in her brother's eyes, while in contrast she softened more and more into the idea of having Alexander as her companion. The more time ticked on, the better it felt. Like the truest decision she had ever made in her life.

She just wanted it all to end: the war and the destruction. She just wanted to heal, herself and her planet, and she knew that Alexander could help her with that.

She knew the burning that her brother spoke of, perhaps not the same facet of the burning, but she knew the flames nonetheless. She recalled how she felt when possessed by the bloodlust, and how destructive those emotions had been.

She had to stop hating, for it didn't serve anyone. She had to learn to practice what she preached. Just as she knew Fredrik had to learn, to take his own journey too.

"I'm sorry, Fredrik. I am going to miss you so much," Arian mumbled, tears upon her cheeks. In the glow of the lamp, they shone orange like autumn leaves. The seasons were changing, the summer over. Winter was coming.

Fredrik bowed his head, avoiding her eyes. "I know you are leaving for the best. You have my thoughts with you, wherever you go." His words were clearly forced, but Arian held onto them as a blessing.

Arian returned to his side and they embraced again. She held him as tightly as she could, without squeezing and hurting his wound. She felt his breathing calm somewhat as they connected.

Then she thought of the boy.

"Fredrik, will you do one thing for me?"

"Yes?" he replied, his voice shaky.

"Just keep an eye on the baby Karl for me. My maid should care for him. But just see to it that he does not come to any harm. I made a promise."

Fredrik smiled, clearly relieved at the simplicity of her request after the intensity of their previous conversation. "Rest assured, dearest. I will protect that child with my life, and he will remind me of you. I won't lose you then, no matter what."

"You won't lose me at all, Fredrik," Arian vowed. But inside she felt like she balanced atop a precipice, a sheer drop on all sides. The only way not to fall was to stay strong, by trusting deeply.

"That is the thing I fear for most."

"Don't fear, please," Arian whispered. "I am so glad I found you, and my true family. I will never let anything break us apart again. You will always be here, with me."

She let herself teeter on that precipice. She let down the gates barring her emotions, allowed herself to cry into the linen sheet covering her brother, which hungrily drank her falling tears. Allowed herself to feel and to release, to let go and to heal.

"I'm not good at goodbyes, Fredrik. Normally I would not have anyone to say goodbye to, but now I do." She tightened her clutch on him. "I think you know everything I could say anyway."

Sniffling, Arian kissed his cheek, and slowly regained her composure. Then she pulled back, lifting her head confidently.

"I love you Fredrik. I'm going to heal our land for us."

Her brother smiled, and she caught the ghost of his roguish grin. It wasn't quite back to how it was before the topic of their discussion had turned, but she knew he would adjust to the news. He would understand in time.

Then he motioned towards the door. "Don't waste more time here. Get ready, and go with speed so that you don't leave me alone too long. Goodbye sister dearest, until we meet again."

88
MOTHERHOOD

Oh, despite the destructive potential if it becomes distorted, love is the most wondrous of all things. It can manifest miracles, an unstoppable force for good.

When love is true, when love is pure, you know it deep within you. A soothing feeling, you are comfortable and peaceful. Joyous for no apparent reason, you feel you could run unbelievably fast, climb the highest mountain peaks...

You smile, and people wonder why. You stand tall and strong, though a war may rage around you. Encased by the protective embrace of love, you navigate sorrow, pain, and hardship, with the freedom of a dancing song.

Not many people will experience this, because sometimes to love truly means to let go. And to brave pain on your own, so that others do not hurt. So you don't launch upon your clan, the arrows of your own wounds and judgments.

But in the end, if you persist with your practices, your righteous soul will break free. And then never will you hurt again.

* * *

When he looked at her, he saw a mother.

Not a mother of one child, or a mother of one family, but a mother of the world.

He believed that she would save them, because her determination to seek truth and bring justice would be balanced by her love and compassion. She would not be swept up by the corruption of power. She would not be caught up in bloody vendettas fuelled by hate.

Instead, she would reach out to the rich and poor alike. She would embrace the healthy and the diseased, and cure all with her touch. She would even forgive her enemies, because she would understand that they are wounded people, with souls that crave saving.

That is the way he saw her, and he knew that was why she had been born a woman.

To serve her people: as a mother.

* * *

True love dissolves the ego, and when the ego is dissolved, there remains only the heart. The heart does not distinguish between the good and the bad, does not create such separation. Division is the realm of the mind, with its judgments and its mental constructions, and yearning for an ideal perfection that can never be attained. For the ego is never satisfied.

True love embraces the perfection of the present, just as things are. At once, desiring the best for the other, being there to help them become the highest version of themselves: but trusting them to live their process, surrendering into their flow and allowing them to make their own choices in their own rhythm. Believing in the other's own relationship with the divine.

True love is presence: with the way things are, just as they are. Presence in mind, body and spirit. For it is through the deepest possible presence, that we find release. Connection with all that is beyond, and all that is infinite. Anchoring, through the heart, the magic of the universe.

I am learning and I am growing.
And I finally feel like I have begun to live again.

89

DEPARTURE

Later that night Arian followed her father down to the lower levels of the palace where she would depart from. He led her along a hallway where the rooms of learning were situated, with the great Linuinan library at one end.

Melchior unlocked one hidden door with a great bronze key. They stepped into a strange room that she had never visited before, had not even known existed. Glass cabinets lined the walls, displaying scrolls and ancient stone tablets, tapestries and paintings. In the centre of the room was a beautiful carved pedestal, holding a globe that depicted the known world of Meridisia.

She realised she had entered one of the few remaining places that preserved the ancient history of her land. There was another such room in Soonada, where she had been once as a little girl.

"Why did you never tell me of this place before, father?" Arian asked in awe as she gazed at a suit of armour pinned to a marble column. Then her gaze fell to the fragments of a shattered sword, which had belonged to one of the heroes of old...

Oh, the rich history of her world.

But there were not many accurate records of the ancient realms: most of the history books had been written centuries or even millennia after the events had happened. And so history had become nothing but story and myth.

"I only wanted to bring you here when I thought the time was right to see such treasure and absorb such knowledge. But now you must come anyway, for the passage entrance is here."

Arian nodded, still looking around the room that was overflowing with information. She knew she could easily spend months here, and that that would still only be scratching the surface.

Melchior approached an old mirror with a great crack running through its centre, like a warrior's scar. He ran a hand along the wall behind it and pushed gently along what must have been a fault line, causing the wall to slide apart and reveal another room.

This one was dimmer, probably to aid in the preservation of the engraved stone tablets it contained. Arian took a moment to look at the writing. Staring at those foreign symbols, she felt herself slip back to another time and place, when the Sea People still interacted with those on the land.

"Arian," Melchior called her back to reality and out of her musings. "Come, quickly now. Knowledge is not what we seek tonight."

She pulled her eyes away from the mesmerising letters, and followed her father through the room. They turned a corner to find Alexander where he was waiting, leaning against a wall. He gave her a reassuring smile, a smile that reminded her of why she was doing this, and of her path.

"Just know that this is the right thing to do. I can feel it," Arian whispered to her father. He stifled a sob, and drew her into his arms, rocking her back and forth like a baby. As he did, the emotions became too much for Arian to bear, and she began crying into his shoulder.

But with her tears, soon the last remnants of her fear dissolved. She stepped away from her father's hold, and raised her head to meet his eyes, chin lifted with pride.

"I promise I won't be gone for long. I'm not even really going." Her voice didn't waver, as a newfound sense of purpose rushed through her body.

She could see that Melchior felt the rising energy within her, as he smiled back confidently. "Oh, you shall be our heroine, with your name praised for generations into the future."

"We are all heroes, we all do our part."

"Wisely spoken. Now just promise me you will take care of yourself."

Arian nodded. "I will. And take care of Fredrik. He needs more looking after than me, in any case."

Her father chuckled wearily, and then gestured to the wall ahead.

That was when she noticed it: a magnificent tapestry, like the one in the palace throne room. But the White Woman was not depicted with the blue-green stone of Knowledge. There was no paradise, only a bloody battle surrounding her. She stood, not as the world's saviour, but as the world's murderer, a blood-red stone in her palm.

Just like in the other tapestry, the White Woman's face was concealed, but the skill of the weaver had left her eyes faintly visible beneath the gauzy fabric of the hood. They had a scarlet gleam emanating from between narrow slits, as if she was possessed. A polluted vapour radiated from her heart, instead of light and goodwill.

Arian swallowed, caught by the eyes of the White Woman and this image of destruction. This was the other half of the duel prophecy, declaring that if the White Woman's knowledge was not used rightly, it would destroy Meridisia.

She recalled the prophetic words clearly, and the parting farewells between the Underwater Empires and the Rock Kingdoms. *'Until war unites us, let us go our own ways.'*

When the Henalas had begun their invasion of Meridisia, many had believed that this was the war to bring the ancient peoples together. But so far, no help had arrived.

"My dear daughter, do not fear over a legend."

Melchior brushed the tapestry aside, revealing a hidden opening and stairs that spiralled down, down into the dark.

"This ancient passageway goes under the river, and there is one intersection. You must take the left turn. You will emerge in the plains south of here, where reinforcements have arrived from Illarn."

He gave Arian a thick envelope. "In here you will find false papers to disguise your identity, and money to make any purchases on your journey. You can pick horses up from our reinforcement camp, and any extra provisions you may need."

Arian nodded. "Thank you father, for all you have done for me. I hope you will realise with time that this was the right choice. I am sure it is."

"Of course. May the Gods be with you."

She stepped away from him before emotion over their parting took control again. She kept her eyes averted, but her ears picked up Alexander's voice.

"I'll look after her. I'll bring her back."

"I know you will, I know you will care for her. Good luck my son."

Then Arian felt a hand on her shoulder, and turned to find Alexander ready to help her travel pack onto her shoulders. "You have disguised yourself well. I did not recognise you for a moment," he murmured.

Arian smiled faintly. "I am rather skilled at disguise, I must say." She glanced down at her leggings and tunic, and the travelling cloak swishing at her boots. Her hair was bound with a leather tie, and once they got into the open country she would pull the hood of her cloak down to hide her face from view. Just like in her storytelling days.

Arian looked back to her father one more time, noticing his eyes grim with the pain of her departure. "You will not fail, my dearest daughter."

Without a response, Arian turned for the steps. Beside her, Alexander took her hand in his, sending her love and encouragement in that simple touch. At least she would have him, though she left her family behind.

Arian took a deep breath, and one step forward into her fated future.

One step, and then another.

Suddenly there was nothing but the faint glow of their lantern to give them light: Melchior must have closed off the entrance to the tunnel with the tapestry. Arian gripped Alexander's hand tightly, and focussed on the little yellow flame that he carried in his other hand.

That little flame was enough. It gave her the courage to begin her journey.

* * *

"Master?" A panicked voice sounded in the dark cellar.

"Have you come to inform me that you have stopped the princess? That is the only thing I want to hear from you right now," the voice echoed cold and powerful, dripping with malice.

"Master, master I am so sorry," the man whimpered. "She did not use the tunnel."

"What are you telling me?" the other man demanded with a growl, sending his subject shivering with terror.

"The princess must have... have taken a different route. I... I could not find her."

"Do you mean to say you have failed?" The master spat. "Stop stuttering like a child, and tell me how you shall redeem yourself."

"Oh master!" The man fell to his knees, and his eyes looked fearfully up to the figure towering over him. "I shall... do anything master."

"Then inform the Henalas priest and tell him of what you have done. He will send real spies to track her."

"Master, please I cannot face their priest!"

"You will," the superior snarled vehemently. "Do as you are told, and do not fail or you shall pay the price. The princess must be found!"

"Yes master, she will be. I... I will not fail this time master, I promise."

Without another word, the master left his companion to his grovelling upon the stone floor, silently cursing the incompetent fool who had failed him.

He *needed* Princess Arian. Selling her to the Henalas Emperor was the only way to return peace to Meridisia, and then his righteous order would rule it.

90

PHOENIX

Ashen grey
melts to rosy dawn
in the auric field
of my shadow
that's washed away
in a symphony sweet
of falling tears
that see you
child
just as you are
that watch the hurt
fading today
at last you're free
sovereign soul
remember your truth
and live your vow

* * *

In the middle of the night, in the dark of her bitter prison cell, Taalin stirred. Through a slit in the walls she spied the crude finger of a waning crescent moon, pointing like an accusation, a silver dagger in her heart.

The blackness of her surroundings seemed to carry with it a heavy pressing weight, that sank deep into the marrow of her bones, and pinned her down like a sacrifice at an altar. She rubbed her weary eyes, eyes that were becoming accustomed to see only shadows, through the lens of a haunted ghost's nightmares.

Suddenly, she noticed the moonbeam glinting off *something* on the floor of her prison. Or rather, not so much glinting off, as shining through, as though it was piercing a hole in the stone floor, revealing something beyond the cage of this existence.

She focussed on the light, and it began to grow into a flame that twisted and spiralled around its deep violet core, a core that didn't seem to quite fit in this reality, that hummed softly, whispering secrets from a place far beyond.

Then faces started to swirl in the misty air around her, the fabric of space opening up like a window. Scenes from the lives of other women began to play. Women who had been captured in the tower before, or perhaps in some distant future too? Women tied to sacrificial stakes and surrounded by blazing fire.

Eyes stared back into Taalin's own. They were the fierce, resolute eyes of women who were determined not to utter a scream of despair. Women who armoured themselves with the truth of their dying, who found courage in their vulnerability and peace in their departure, and seemed to become one with the flames. One with the element of fire.

A streak of red.

Red.

The vivid tone of a broken prayer, blessed by the kiss of a worshipper's faith.

Red.

Bright colour restored, to a world of black and white.

And through the flames, Taalin *saw* her.

The women were all her, and the women were all aspects of One, different facets, mirrors for different truths, and they merged together until there was but one face. The face was split into two: shadow and light, two halves of a single soul. It was smiling, one half joyfully, the other half twisted, each side beckoning and calling to Taalin in a different way. Reminding her that she had the choice: she could shape her destiny, shape how her life would unfurl.

The lips of the woman opened. Her mouth was a gaping hole that grew and grew until it consumed the entire cell around Taalin. It revealed two portals, two gateways, two stairways out of the prison tower. Taalin could not see where they led. One wound its way left, and the other right, each disappearing into infinity.

The image was hazy, but growing stronger, clarifying. Then Taalin felt the weight of a key drop into her hands.

It was real. It was here.

A key, materialised out of nowhere. A key, offering her an escape.

She stared into the abyss of the woman's mouth, at those pathways leading out of the tower. Light began to whirl around her like a tornado, light that was split into all its different components. She felt her spirit dancing on those beams, jumping between colours, between planes, between dimensions, and seeing the world with so much clarity.

And Taalin found herself smiling, through the rainbow of her refracting tears, as she fell into the emerging light of her Soul's dying shadow.

* * *

So I start to trust again
as I dissolve these broken walls
and rebuild a fortress
of pure loving truth
with the dancing flames
of my united heart
that's rising
infinitely
Alive

ABOUT THE AUTHOR

Cara Goldthorpe is a writer, mystic, holistic health practitioner, and lawyer. Her storytelling is inspired by her diverse life experiences, and aims to provoke deep reflection on human nature and our connection to the universe.

Born in Melbourne, Australia, Cara moved to London when she was 18 years old. She studied Law with French Law at University College London, graduating with a first class degree and going on to complete her Bar exams. She obtained her tenancy at Wilberforce Chambers, one of England's top commercial chancery sets.

Cara was then locked down in Costa Rica when borders closed in response to the Covid-19 pandemic. She took a sabbatical leave to focus on health, having suffered chronic health issues in her twenties, which led her down a path of spiritual exploration and towards holistic healing methods. It was during her time in Costa Rica that Cara also reconnected with her heart's true passions: writing, poetry, and music, and met her now-husband Alex Flett, who shares many of her interests.

Besides her creative work, Cara's main focus these days is on developing a community centre and healing sanctuary in southern Costa Rica. She also offers private healing sessions, group ceremonies, and mentoring. You can read more about her and her work at: https://songsofgaia.com

Acknowledgments

As I have shared, birthing this book has been quite the process, extending over most of my life. In some ways every person I have encountered and every experience I have had has somehow shaped this story or shaped me as the portal: bringing me to where I am today in order to finally release it into the world.

I'd first like to thank my mum and dad: for lighting the spark within me as a child, and supporting me to reconnect with that essence when I chose to take a sudden turn off the traditional track in which my life was headed. Dad, you opened my eyes to the wonders of the universe and debated with my little child self "what came before the Big Bang – there couldn't just be nothing." Mum, you were the first to read this story in its infancy, and you watched it grow over the years, offering your encouragement and critical analysis as I fine-tuned the drafts, sculpting into what it is today.

Thank you to my brother Austin, for the cover and map designs of the earlier version of this book. You were the one to first give colour to the story in a tangible way, and made me dream that one day I would see it on the shelves. The story has evolved beyond those earlier artworks, but they gave it the boost it needed on its evolution towards a published book.

Thank you to Fay Thompson, Editor-In-Chief of Big Moose Publishing, for your work to finally get this book published. You've made the process a breeze and your enthusiasm has kept the momentum going: an energy I so needed, given how long I've sat on this work. I'm so grateful that we connected, and for your expertise and professionalism – this book wouldn't have made it to the shelves if it wasn't for you.

Thank you to Antonio Cesar, my cover designer, for the beautiful artwork capturing the soul of this book. I am grateful for all the adjustments up to the last minute to get this image right, and for a final omen before releasing this book to the world.

Thank you to my mentor Alejandro, for all the guidance, support and teachings, aiding me in my own personal healing journey and broader explorations of spirit and shamanic work. This past year of working with you has been truly transformative and necessary, in order for me to be ready to release this book to the public.

Thank you to the Authonomy community, who knew this book as *The Awakening: Dawn of Destruction*. I received so much during my time there, including having my book ranked in the monthly top 5, as well as critical feedback, editorial support, and encouragement for my writing journey. In particular, I'd like to thank Scott Toney for being one of my first readers who perhaps believed in this story more than I did. Your words of support over the years – not just with this book, but all my writings, have kept me going and given me the courage to share my voice with the world.

And last but not least, thank you to my husband Alex, for giving me the last push and connecting the dots, in order for this book to be published. Thank you for finding me in the Costa Rican jungle, bringing me to the wild Canadian prairies, and introducing me to Tammy and Aimée at Aware House Books – who led me to Fay. Thank you for being by my side in these final stages, through the huge energetic shift of releasing this book into the world, for drawing my map and taking my photos. And for everything else that you do for me every single day, lifting me up and inspiring me to keep pursuing my dreams, and creating heaven on earth.

Printed in Great Britain
by Amazon

20114992R00194